D1506317

INDISCRETIONS

Carol Doumani is also the author of

UNTITLED, Nude
CHINESE CHECKERS

INDISCRETIONS

a novel by

CAROL DOUMANI

Wave Publishing
Venice

HICKSVILLE PUBLIC LIBRARY
169 JERUSALEM AVE.
HICKSVILLE, N Y

Copyright © 1999 by Carol Doumani

All rights reserved under
International and Pan-American Copyright Conventions

Manufactured in the United States of America

First Edition

Published by WAVE PUBLISHING
Post Office Box 688
Venice, California
tsunami@primenet.com

This is a work of fiction.
The names, characters, places, story, and
situations are purely the product
of the author's imagination
or are used ficticiously.
Don't take it seriously.

Doumani, Carol.
    Indiscretions : a novel / by Carol Doumani, -- 1st ed.
        p.   cm.
    ISBN 0-9642359-9-4
    I. Title
PS3554.086I53   1999
813'.54--dc21

                                                        98-42992
                                                            CIP

Printed and Bound by Haddon Craftsmen Inc.
Dust Jacket Printed by Gardner Lithograph
Book Design by John Deep

10 9 8 7 6 5 4 3 2 1

All that we do is done
with an eye to something else.

Aristotle
4th century, B.C.

1

Patrick

There she was. In the window. Watching him. Again!

Although Patrick had been leasing the house in the Palisades for nearly a year, he had not met his neighbor face to face. But recently he'd noticed her peering out, staring straight into his study. Did she think the tinted glass made her invisible? Or did she want him to see her? *Please don't let her be a stalker*, he prayed, although it did occur to him that having an obsessed fan would give him a golden moment in the media spotlight. And at this point in his career, the publicity wouldn't do him any harm.

But deep down he knew this neighbor wasn't a threat. She was just worshiping him from afar. The problem was she wasn't *that* far away. Land on the bluffs overlooking the California coastline was so precious that most homes were built with mere five-foot setbacks on either side of their conjoining property lines, much too close for comfort. Thank God the workmen he'd hired had finally begun erecting the wall which would restore his privacy.

Patrick sighed and turned his attention back to the work at hand, a stack of scripts to wade through, more fan letters to answer, bills, invitations, requests for endorsements, and just plain junk mail, which had been accumulating for weeks on his prized Biedermeier desk. He had paid dearly to restore this treasure to its present splendor, and he loved it, even though most of the time it was a cluttered mess. He caressed the burnished wood, its understated refinement pleasantly tactile, and it occurred to him that the next time Barbara Walters or *Entertainment Tonight* called for an interview, he should hold court from behind the desk, to show the world his sophistication and style, to prove that he wasn't just a clown whose tastes ran to grown-up toys, like the often-photographed model train set in his bedroom.

Then again, a glimpse of *Patrick Drake, man of culture*, might distort the image that Peter and his retinue of public relations people at Reagan & Coward had so carefully cultivated and fertilized. Peter was adamant about limiting what was told to the media. God forbid they learn some of his secrets.

Such as the fact that a few years back he was detained by Customs at LAX after a vacation in Cabo San Lucas. The officer had insisted on opening his black bag of love toys — nothing illegal, but embarrassing nonetheless. Thank God Peter had been able to keep that out of *The Inquirer*. It was bad enough having everybody standing in line (and every person each of them blabbed to) know that he enjoyed using a little hardware with his software.

No, he'd be wiser to forget the Biedermeier and stick to the train set. It made him appear cute and accessible, just a kid at heart. The less the public knew about the *real* Patrick Drake, the better.

Patrick opened the desk drawer and idly pulled out a hand mirror. He turned on the desk lamp and adjusted the warm glow so that it flattered his features. Was vanity an occupational hazard for a film star, or did people become actors because they *were* vain already?

He studied his image in the glass. His gray-green eyes were a little bloodshot, but nonetheless expressive and piercing, framed as they were by long, blond lashes. They were his best feature, he thought, conveying his feelings far more accurately than the dialogue in most scripts he read. Too bad his rapidly worsening vision forced him to hide behind prescription sunglasses on those maddeningly frequent occasions when what one saw was more important than how one looked.

The rest of his face was appealing, but not overly handsome — his nose was straight, if a bit too long, his chin firm and manly, with just a hint of a cleft, and his ears, once a little large, were now tucked neatly to his head, thanks to the deft hands and scalpel of Dr. Timothy Mueller, professor of plastic surgery at UCLA.

If his forty-seven years showed at all, it was in his hair, still thick and lush to the touch, thank God, but streaked with silver. This sign of age by itself was insignificant, for directors over the years had colored him reddish brown, raven, and even totally blond, depending on the roles he played. But those damn roots.

He sighed and tried to look deeper into the mirror, past the visual image it presented. Who was the person behind the facade? Was he Patrick Drake, movie star extraordinaire, renowned comedian and international celebrity, or was he Patrick Drake, the aging, graying, overweight son of Muriel and Harold Drake of Kewasha, Indiana, who had repeated seventh grade twice and never made it to college? He knew who he saw, but he prayed the public saw the other.

His eyes were drawn back to the window and he wondered which image she saw. Was she just another curious fan, ravenous for an intimate detail about him that she might use to buy status among her friends, or did she see, was she looking for, something more?

The phone rang him back to reality. He listened as his machine kicked in, relishing the twisted thrill of eavesdropping on himself. "You've reached the machine of Patrick Drake. I'm not taking this call because I may not want to talk to you. So leave your name after the beep and I'll either get back to you or I won't, depending on how I feel."

"Paddy, if you're there pick up."

Sara's voice. Patrick pounced on the phone, glad for the distraction. "Yeah, what's your problem?" he growled. It was his standard greeting, but it always threw Sara. Poor thing, she took everything he said literally, and knowing this, he delighted in confusing her.

"Me? Nothing." She was instantly defensive. "I'm just returning your call from yesterday. It was on my machine."

"Sara, we were together last night and we've spoken already this morning. I think you can safely assume I've said everything I had to say to you when I called yesterday."

"Okay, Sweetie, just wanted to be sure. You know how p.o.'d you get when I forget to check in." Sara had an incredibly resonant voice that presaged her voluptuousness; it never ceased to amaze him that even her vocal chords were well developed.

"Besides, I probably just called to hear the sound of your voice," he said. "A little *aural* sex," he added, even though he knew his bright play on words would be lost in the murky shallows of Sara's mind.

"It sounds better in person," she purred, missing the pun entirely. "I've got some pizza left over from Spago's last night."

Patrick remembered his embarrassment the previous evening when Sara had asked Wolfgang himself to provide a doggie bag for the remains of dinner for six. Fortunately, Wolf was a sport, and he even acted pleased that none of his high-profile cuisine would be going to waste. But Patrick didn't miss the expression of distaste on Barbara's face, and the smirks of the others at the table, who knew bad form when they saw it and put up with Sara only because she was with Patrick.

"Honestly, Sara, people will think I don't feed my girlfriends. It was bad enough that you wanted your leftovers, but to ask for LeMar's. . . . " Still, he was beginning to salivate thinking of the doggie bag full of duck sausage pizza, and fettucini with gorgonzola, which the perennially dieting LeMar, his agent, hardly tasted.

"Is that what I am?"

"What?"

"Your *friend?*"

His hunger formed a hard lump that fell to the pit of his stomach, as it always did when a woman tried to corner him. "Sara, it's just a convenient term."

"Oh, so now I'm a convenience. Kind of like a microwave oven?"

"Well, come to think of it, you are a pretty hot number, and you have been known to nuke men who don't treat you right." Patrick chuckled, not so much because what he said was funny, but because he knew his laughter was an aphrodisiac to Sara. It was, in fact, what most of his women liked best about him.

Sure enough, he could sense Sara melting on the other end.

"Then why don't you come over and I'll zap you?" she countered.

Patrick looked around him at the chaos on the Biedermeier. "I'd love to leap into your microwave, truly I would, but LeMar's going to kill me if I don't wade through these scripts. I haven't even opened the one from Dominion." He picked up a screenplay with a light blue cover and fondled the note on the cover, which was discretely engraved with the initials "J.K." and bore the typed message, *Paddy, this is you. Read it tonight and I'll speak with you tomorrow.*

"But save me a piece of pizza," he said to Sara, "I'll eat it when I pick you up tonight."

"Speaking of tonight, what should I wear? I mean, how do you want me to look?" In typical Sara fashion, she began cataloging every item in her extensive, expensive wardrobe, as though she were reciting Shakespeare. "If this thing is really dressy, I could wear the Armani with the cowl neck, or the backless black Versace. Or if it's not that formal, I could wear the Valentino pants with the bolero. The pants are a little tight, but if I take a thirty-minute sauna . . ."

The second line began to ring. Patrick eyed it nervously. He hated to deal with more than one call at a time, and the machine didn't pick up off the rotary. Plus there was every chance the caller could be Kesselman's secretary.

"Sara, I've got to get the other line."

"Can't Jeremy get it?"

"He's gone to the market."

"Oh, well, call me back later because I need to — "

"I will. 'Bye." He cut her off by pushing the urgently flashing button. "Hello? hello?"

There was a pause. "Yes, may I speak with Patrick Drake, please?"

The voice wasn't exactly familiar, but it wasn't altogether foreign either. And it certainly wasn't Kesselman's secretary Marion, who spoke with a nasal New England twang that was as phony as her hennaed hair.

How annoying to have to deal with a fan. Patrick wrestled with the idea of pretending he wasn't himself, but on an empty stomach it seemed like too much trouble. "You've got him."

"Oh, Mr. Drake!" Whoever it was sounded surprised. "This is Enid Carrouthers."

Patrick thought about it. "Do I know you?"

"I'm your next-door neighbor."

The mysterious voyeur, or should he say voyeuse! Without changing position, he glanced out the window. The facing window was vacant. "Yes, of course," he said slowly. He hoped his voice didn't betray his bemused curiosity. "I'm sorry, I didn't — I don't believe I ever knew your name."

"We saw you on the Fourth of July, at the Will Rogers State Park picnic. But everyone wanted to talk to you; I don't blame you for not remembering," the voice said.

"No, no, it's just that, over the phone . . . if I'd seen you, surely I would have remembered." Yeah, right, as though anyone famous ever remembered anyone who wasn't. "So then, Mrs. Carrouthers, how may I be of service?"

"Oh, please, call me Enid."

"Enid." His mind wandered back to Sara and the pizza. If this Enid would just come to the point, maybe it wouldn't be too late to call Sara back and take her up on her offer.

"Well, I don't mean to bother you, but I was wondering, you see there's something I want to talk to you about and I know you must be terribly busy. But I was thinking, hoping, that maybe you'd be able to join me for lunch one day this week."

With a prick of male ego, Patrick noted that her voice rose an octave when she blurted out this last sentence. If he was any judge of women, she was at that moment blushing at her audacity to have blurted out this proposition, flagrantly offering much more than just an invitation to lunch.

He considered the possibilities. He had never paid much attention to his neighbors, but this one couldn't be all that bad, married to a man as wealthy and powerful as Sam Carrouthers. And her voice on the phone sounded pleasantly refined, yet appropriately reverent.

On the other hand, things were going so well with Sara. And she did have that leftover duck sausage pizza on her side. Perhaps it was unwise to rock the boat.

Then again, he could find out why she'd been spying on him. And if he remembered correctly, there was only one small piece of pizza left.

"Well, I am swamped, but I do have to eat. How about today?"

"Today?" Her voice sounded worried.

Damn, he thought, *I must have sounded too eager.* "I'm swamped the rest of the week, the rest of the month, it seems. So if it's critical . . ."

"Oh, today would be wonderful! It's just, I hadn't expected you to say yes at all, let alone for today."

Oh, God, wait until he told his shrink Ellen about this conversation. She was always chastising him for begging affection from his fans. The "puppy from the pound" syndrome, she called it.

"Then let's make it one o'clock. Giorgio's?"

"That would be wonderful. Shall I drive? I can come by for you."

"That's right, we are both leaving from the same general vicinity, aren't we? No, why don't I come by for you? The Rolls needs an airing anyway." As he spoke, he remembered the Beast's faulty water pump and wondered if Jeremy had gotten around to fixing it.

"About one then? I'll be waiting outside."

"Splendid. See you then."

He hung up the phone with a sigh. What had he gotten himself into?

Enid

Enid slowly lowered the receiver, her hand lingering on it as though hesitant to break the fragile connection. How many days had she agonized over making this call, beginning to dial and stopping after three digits? Or, after summoning the courage to punch all seven numbers, how many times had she listened to his voice on the answering machine and then lost her nerve? At last, she had taken the plunge! Her body tingled with delight. She had called Patrick Drake and he had accepted her invitation to lunch!

She looked at the clock. 11:15. Should she call Shelley and tell her the news? No, better to wait until after the lunch, if and when she had accomplished her mission. Besides, she didn't want to use the phone again just yet, while it was still resonating from his famous voice.

As she stepped into the shower, Enid wondered for the ten-thousandth time what her famous neighbor was really like. Since he had moved in next door, she'd spied on him shamelessly, trying to catch glimpses of him as he came and went in his Rolls Royce, even going so far as to peek through the window of her den into the facing window of his house. To her disappointment she couldn't see much, just a distorted view of him sitting at his desk.

She'd tried to find all of his movies on video, but few of the old ones had been released on tape. And although she had read every article she could find about him, they only told her the facts. She was still curious about the person. Very curious.

It wasn't a physical attraction. When Enid thought about what attracted her, she envisioned strong, solid, masculine men like Sam, her husband. Patrick Drake, though tall, was slightly effeminate and sadly out of shape. Oh, he was cute, but cute the way a teddy bear is, in a little-boyish, silly way.

Anyway, she'd never been attracted to another man. Sam was a model husband, kind, generous, even-tempered and loving. And their marriage was one of the few happy ones in her Los Angeles social set. For twelve years they had lived the kind of life most people only dreamed of, filled with travel, beautiful possessions, interesting experiences, and, most important, joy in each other's company. If she had any complaint at all, it was that Sam worked too hard. But what successful man didn't?

So no, her fascination with Patrick had nothing to do with a physical attraction or a need to escape her marriage. Quite simply, she admitted to herself, she was dazzled by the fact that he was a movie star. And he'd moved in right next door! She'd lived in Los Angeles all her life, and she had not one famous friend, had never before had lunch with a celebrity, unless you counted Sam's business partner Harry Ingersol. And Harry wasn't really a star, he was just famous for his $2.5 billion net worth, and that only counted in the business world. It was entirely different, and not nearly as alluring.

A thrill of pride shot through her when she or Sam casually mentioned that Patrick Drake was leasing the house next door. *The* Patrick Drake, people always asked with envy, *the movie star?* It was as though the coincidence of their geographical proximity was some special accomplishment, like setting the world's record for the broad jump, or giving birth to quintuplets. Amazing, the universality of the movies. Even Sam's business associates in Japan could name most of Patrick's films — she smiled to herself — and at least half of his girl-friends.

That was another thing. Patrick Drake was as famous for his romantic flings as he was for his movies. And there was a certain titillation to being in the company of a ladies' man — the flirtatious attention, the sexual subtext that underlay every utterance, the flattering image of herself as the object of a desirable man's desires. God, she sounded like a love-starved housewife from New Jersey reading *The Bridges of Madison County.*

Get a grip, Enid, she told herself. *This is business, not pleasure.*

But still, he had such a reputation as a Casanova. . . .

She turned the water temperature up to a steamy 102 degrees and let the spray drench her imagination. Then, distantly, she heard the phone ring. A pang of anxiety shot through her. *He's canceling,* she thought, *I knew it. I knew this was too easy. Damn!*

She turned off the water and wiped away the steam on the glass door so she could see the phone on the bathroom counter. Its little red light blinked, then held firm, which meant the Carrouther's Chinese houseman, Wallase Ting, had answered it downstairs. Was it Patrick, saying he had something more interesting to do than have lunch with her? She concentrated on wrapping a towel around herself and stepped out of the shower, waiting for the intercom to buzz with the bad news. When she allowed herself to look at the phone again, the little red light was off. She breathed a sigh of relief.

Enid turned on the light of her magnifying mirror and saw the result of thirty-six years of L.A. living. An honest appraisal revealed wide brown eyes (which would need the obligatory eyelid lift in the not so distant future) and hair the color of butterscotch (which she dutifully highlighted with vanilla streaks once a month), a fair bone structure, lightly freckled skin that betrayed her age only when she ate the wrong foods (dairy products) or neglected to get enough sleep (seven hours a night), and straight white teeth, (thanks to two years of orthodontia). Enid thought of herself as looking like someone's older sister, the one who was too short and too shy to make the cheerleading squad, and who dated the president of the French club.

The trick now was to put on enough makeup to look good, without seeming to have gone to too much effort. She opened her dressing table drawer and studied her arsenal of cosmetics. If Sam had his way, she would never wear any makeup at all. Well, that had been fine when they had met and married twelve years earlier, but no facial in the world could restore the smooth, fresh face of that twenty-four-year-old. God, it had been easy then.

The sudden buzz of the intercom made her heart leap again. "Yes, Wallase?" She tried to sound calm, but it wasn't easy the way her heart was pounding.

"Sorry to bother, Missy Carrouthers. Mister Patrick Drake call. I tell you take the shower," the houseman said.

Despite her disappointment at hearing just the words she dreaded, Enid imagined Patrick listening to Wallase's message. Had he been aroused at the image of her, wet and naked?

"Yes, and what did he say?"

"He say, please he can pick you up for lunch at 1:15 instead of 1:00, since late he is running."

"Then he didn't cancel?"

"No, Missy, only he say that he can come late."

Wallase's broken English was music to Enid's ears. "Thank you then, Wallase. I'll be down shortly." Again, Enid studied her face in the makeup mirror. She smiled. At the rate her heart was pumping, she wouldn't have to worry about what color blush to use; her cheeks were as rosy as a bride's. She went to the closet to dress.

The dressing room had been designed by the former owner of her house, a socialite whose personal vanity was exceeded only by the size of her decorating budget. Mirrors covered every available surface and gave the room a disconcerting "fun house" aspect that Enid had learned to live with. But with all of the reflective surfaces, there was no way she could hide from her body and its imperfections.

Early on, she had realized that she would never be voluptuous, and this made life difficult in a city where breast size was a kind of currency. After turning thirty, she had contemplated artificial augmentation, had even visited a plastic surgeon who had successfully resurrected the small or sagging fortunes of many of her friends. It was still an option. But with silicone a questionable solution, she had decided to wait until the medical world came up with something better.

For the time being, she fought the good fight, exercising to keep the rest of her figure slim, keeping her hips, waist, and bosom in proportion. So although she wasn't curvy, at least she had the compensation of being able to wear a French size four with comfort.

Enid tried on five outfits before arriving at an acceptable combination — a light pink Jill Sanders jacket from two seasons ago over beige Armani slacks. Where had she read you could never be mad at a person wearing pink? Probably in one of those magazines targeted at desperate single woman who were willing to try anything to snare a man, hardly her personal profile.

Anyway, why should Patrick Drake be mad at her?

Sam

Sam Carrouthers was having a bad day. It had begun when he wrenched his back getting into the black Porsche Turbo Cabriolet that was his pride and joy. The physical pain was brief, but the realization that at forty-eight he was getting too old and stiff to squeeze behind the driver's seat of the sports car really hurt. Then when he'd reached into his briefcase to get his sunglasses, the titanium pair he'd had handcrafted in Germany, he'd found that somehow their right stem had gotten bent, and they were unwearable. It wasn't so much the expense of having the glasses fixed — although it would surely be costly — as it was the inconvenience. The little old optician in Munich was an artist, but it always took him months to get around to repairs.

Without sunglasses, by the time Sam had arrived at the public tennis court where he played each morning, he had developed a raging headache. To make matters worse, his partner Blair had failed to show up, and it was almost impossible to find a pickup game at 6:45 in the morning. So instead, he had had to be satisfied with an hour's jog in the hills which, though grueling exercise, did not give him the mental satisfaction of a competitive game of singles.

And when he had stepped on the scale after the workout — a cheat he knew, to weigh in after sweating for an hour — his weight had been 204, two pounds higher than it had been the week before, and four pounds more than he thought his 6'1" frame should carry.

But these had all been minor annoyances compared to what had awaited him at work. Usually he considered his law firm ICCM (Ingersol, Choate, Carrouthers, and Morris) a haven. When designing his office, he had gone to great pains to create an environment that reflected his status and made a statement about his style — clean, strong lines, simple furniture crafted of elegant materials, and just a few of the right contemporary black and white photographs.

His working space contrasted distinctly from the offices of his three partners, Leo, Jim, and Harry, who were so devoid of style that they'd hired a decorator to recreate the staid and stately look of a traditional law firm — the generic leather couches, dark paneled bookshelves, reproduction empire desks, and botanical prints framed in faux gold leaf frames.

But rather than establish them as members of the Old Guard, these accoutrements only advertised their lack of vision. How could they expect a client to put his or her faith in their foresight, when all around was evidence that they were living in the past, and trying to be something they weren't?

If you had old money and came from an established banking family, fine, Sam thought. Use the family antiques. Wear your grandfather's cuff links bearing the family crest. But no amount of new money could be a substitute for the old stuff. And the guys who bought the real antiques at ridiculous auction prices, rather than discovered them in a dusty back room of the family manse, were even worse than the ones who bought the reproductions. Those poor schmucks thought money could buy class. It couldn't.

Sam prided himself on his individuality. He had never conformed to the stuffed-shirt traditions of his trade, but was respected for having forged his own image and career. In a world where everyone was scouting for new deals, Sam was the man out front with the machete, clearing the path for the others. And he had been very successful at it, a fact that was well known among the cognoscenti — and to a much lesser extent, the public. He normally avoided the press, leaving publicity to his partners, who loved to bask in the spotlight.

So when he got to his office, he was surprised when his secretary Margie informed him that the pain-in-the-ass financial reporter from the *L.A. Times*, Carmen Leventhal, was waiting to see him.

Carmen Leventhal. Although they had met only once before, he'd seen her at numerous functions, and he remembered her well. She was by far the most strident and aggressive woman he had ever known. True, she was a knockout, Pamela Anderson Lee in a business suit, but what gave attractive women the right to assume they could manipulate men simply by virtue of their looks?

He had no idea what she wanted today, but he was wise enough to realize that to dismiss her without an audience, however brief, would be asking for trouble. He buzzed Margie back and told her to send Carmen in, then took another phone call so she would see he didn't have time to waste.

His back was to her when she entered, but he could feel her eyes boring into him. Even though he wasn't interested in this piranha, he was glad his daily tennis kept him solid and strong beneath his bespoke suits, and that she had noticed. He found that for many women, the twin aphrodisiacs of money and power were enough to inspire attraction. Only a few realized that a shorter route to his ego was recognition of his steely physique.

He hung up the phone and turned to face Carmen, his smile polite, but carefully calculated to project indifference to whatever it was she was selling. "Hello, Carmen," he said. "If I'd known you were coming, I would have blocked out a little time, but as it is . . . "

She was perched on the edge of his desk, not even trying to hide her interest in the papers that littered it. "Hello, Sam," she replied. Her voice was low and smoky. "I would have called first, but," she leaned closer as though to impart a secret, "I don't think your secretary likes me. She always tells me you're out of town."

"I frequently am. In fact, if it weren't for this benefit tonight for the mayor, I'd be in Tokyo right now."

"Ah, yes, the Major Donor's Dinner. I would love to be there myself, but the price of a ticket is more than my annual salary."

"Maybe you should try another line of work."

"Such as?"

He was tempted to say *hooking*, but settled for something less suggestive. "Writing movie scripts?"

She laughed. "I was hoping you could come up with something a little more provocative than that."

Time to cut this off at the knees, Sam thought. "Look, Carmen, this is a hell of a day for me, and if you don't mind, you're sitting on my briefs."

She handed him the papers. "I can't help it. I'm fascinated by the thought of what's in your briefs, and you know it, Sam."

Her meaning was as sheer as a silk stocking, and was it his imagination or were her eyes really focused on his crotch?

"But actually, I've got a busy day today as well." She flashed what he had to admit was a dazzling smile. "What I had in mind was lunch at Jimmy's. I've got some information I guarantee you will find enlightening, but I'm not willing to trade it for anything less than an expensive salad, your treat."

"In the first place I don't eat lunch," Sam replied. "And in the second, I can't imagine what kind of information you might have that I would be remotely interested in hearing."

"Do the names Leo Choate and Paul Whitney-Smith mean anything to you?"

"I know you know that Leo's one of my partners." Sam looked at his watch. He had better things to do, and he wanted to do them.

"And Paul Whitney-Smith is the CEO of World Investment Trust."

"Gosh," Sam said, "you must read the business section."

"Well, what I have to tell you wasn't in today's paper, but it may be in tomorrow's. And I'll bet my byline you'd rather hear it from me first."

Sam was hooked. He knew Leo had been snooping around Paul Whitney-Smith and WIT for weeks, and it had crossed his mind that Leo might be trying something underhanded, such as making a deal that excluded the other partners. Leo had pulled this stunt before, and Sam had been furious, not only because of the lost financial participation, but for the insulting way Leo had used Sam's contacts to screw him. It wasn't going to happen again.

Sam looked at his calendar. "It will have to be early. I've got a full afternoon. 12:00?"

Carmen's eyes shone with victory. "I'll be there," she said as she went out the door.

One thing he had to say for her: she was smart enough to know that when you got yes for an answer, there was no point hanging around.

Margie's buzz reminded him that the staff meeting had already begun in the conference room, so Sam didn't waste any more time thinking about Carmen Leventhal and their lunch date. As he breezed by Margie's desk, he asked casually, "Leo in today?"

Margie shook her head. "I believe he left word that he'd be out of the office all day. I can check with Karen."

"Just make sure he's coming to the dinner tonight. There's nothing worse than two empty seats at a table of ten. And be sure the driver knows to pick us up at 7:15. I want to get there before everyone is seated so I can chat with the mayor."

"Will do." Margie was already picking up the phone to carry out his wishes.

CARMEN

On her way out of the building, Carmen stopped in the ladies room to sneak a celebratory cigarette. She never lit up in public, but allowed herself three or four private smokes a day, to punctuate important moments, or to calm her nerves if things were going badly. The modest amount of nicotine they pumped into her system also helped control her weight, a form of dieting that was far less of a health risk than the fad diets her friend Mary was constantly trying, or the strenuous Iron Woman exercising Sharon was addicted to, or so she convinced herself.

As she inhaled the silver vapor of her Marlboro Light, Carmen indulged in a moment of self-congratulation. She was very pleased with the way she had handled Sam Carrouthers. And she was glad she waited for this situation with Leo Choate to rear its head, although waiting had been difficult — because Carmen was ready to settle down, and she had set her sights on Sam Carrouthers as the perfect man to settle down with.

Carmen wasn't embarrassed about her calculated effort to snare a man. She knew other women considered her a predator. But she'd lived in Los Angeles long enough to know that only predators survived, and she was nothing if not a survivor.

Of course, it would have been a lot easier if he were a single man with no encumbrances, but Carmen had never been one to let a little thing like a twelve-year marriage stand in her way. All men were fair game; in fact, men weren't even the players. It was a competition between women. And it was up to the wife or girlfriend to keep her man satisfied so he wasn't vulnerable to another woman's attentions. Although Carmen had never met Sam's wife, she knew this Enid was ignorant about the rules of the game. How many times had Carmen observed Sam at business dinners without his wife? There were no pictures of her in his office. Why, he didn't even wear a wedding ring. And she had learned through her sources that there were no kids, therefore, no unbreakable bonds.

Carmen stubbed out her cigarette and took the elevator to the parking garage. On the way down, a young executive tried to flirt with her, and although she was flattered, she rebuffed him by putting on her sunglasses and pointedly staring straight ahead at the elevator doors. Carmen never allowed strange men to approach her. She was *always* the instigator in her relationships, and had never understood how otherwise savvy women waited patiently at home for Mr. Right to call. If you wanted something, you had to go out and get it. And Carmen always did.

In the subterranean garage, she bypassed the line waiting for the attendant and slipped into her car, a 1959 Mercedes 190 SL. It was her pride and joy, its smooth, rounded lines and sleek simplicity a perfect complement to her own curves and svelteness. She was always happy to tip the attendant an extra five dollars to let her park it herself, and most times the attendants were just as happy to comply, since people who drove classic cars were notoriously nasty about screeching tires and grinding gears.

As she waited to merge into the traffic on Avenue of the Stars, she considered whether to turn left and head back to her office for a few hours, or right, in the direction of Neiman Marcus. In the future, she'd have to be appropriately dressed when she was with Sam Carrouthers, and it had been months since she'd indulged in a shopping binge.

No contest, the little Mercedes seemed to turn right of its own accord.

Ten minutes later Carmen was riding up the escalator at Neiman's to the second floor designer section. She spotted her favorite saleswoman, Nadine, near the Valentinos and made a beeline for her. But before she could flag her down, Nadine disappeared into a fitting room.

"May I help you find something, Madame?" Another saleswoman tried to intercept Carmen.

"Thank you. I usually work with Nadine."

"I believe Nadine is with a customer right now. Perhaps I can show you something while she's occupied."

Carmen resented aggressiveness in other women. But she had done her time in retail sales and had learned quickly that it was part of the job to convince customers to buy, preferably something expensive, and the best way to accomplish that was through intimidation.

Carmen ignored the girl and began to flip through the dresses in the Escada section. "I'll wait for Nadine. I'm sure she won't be long."

"Oh, but she's with a very important customer right now. The wardrobe lady for *Eye on L.A.* They could be tied up all morning." The saleswoman positioned herself so Carmen could not move down the rack without barging into her. "Perhaps if you tell me what you're looking for . . ."

How dare you imply some other customer is more important than I am? Carmen gave the girl one of her haughty looks, and said nothing for an uncomfortable minute, to make the girl squirm. *You'd think in a store the caliber of Neiman's that more care would be taken in the selection of salespeople,* Carmen's expression said more clearly than words. *Look at your slouch. Even in an Armani uniform you look like a slob, and my God, look at your skin. You could pose for the "before" picture in a Clearasil ad.*

The girl got the message. She stood a little straighter and tried to dig her way out. "We've got some Anne Klein dresses on sale," she said, in a voice as flimsy as her polyester blouse.

"I'm not interested in your sale items," Carmen sneered. "I want something current, a cocktail dress or suit, preferably silk."

The girl seemed relieved to have some input from Carmen. "Will you come with me?" she pleaded. "You look like a perfect size six. Let me show you the Ferre collection. With your figure and coloring I think one of his new white silk suits would be stunning."

Carmen looked over to the Valentino section. Nadine had not reappeared and Carmen had no more time to waste. She followed the girl to the far end of the floor where the Ferres were displayed.

The girl held up two versions of the same suit. One was tailored and traditional; the other had a hand-embroidered silk chiffon scarf attached to its lapels, which made the jacket seem to float.

"These are the suits I was thinking of. I would especially like to see you in this one, with the scarf. Not too many women can carry it off. You have to be strong, yet feminine. It would be striking with your hair and skin, don't you think?"

Carmen hated to think she was a sucker for compliments, but she could see herself wearing this suit to dinner at L'Orangerie with Sam Carrouthers. She could tell without trying it on that the fit would be perfect, and she could tell without looking at the price tag that it would cost her next month's salary to buy it. But if she was going to play in the big leagues, she was going to have to dress for it. And just maybe, by the time the bill came, somebody else would be picking up the tab.

"It's very nice. Bring them both. And I'd like to see some blouses as well, no prints, just intense colors."

"I've got a gorgeous St. Laurent silk, it's just the color of cafe au lait. I'll put you in a dressing room and get it."

Carmen followed the girl into the back, past two women of Carmen's age, who were fingering a magnificent Zandra Rhodes cocktail dress.

"The good thing about her clothes is that they are completely unbody conscious. You could be pregnant and wear this," said one.

"Who wants to spend two hours a day in the gym to wear something that hides every inch of muscle tone? Besides, Joe hates it when I wear this kind of stuff. He likes me in Alaia, skin tight and slit up to here," replied the other.

"If you're going to wear Alaia, I suppose you aren't interested in lunch," said the first.

"I can't anyway. I've got a tennis lesson at twelve and then my herbal wrap at Aida Thibiant. Oh, say, do you have time to swing by

Tiffany's with me? There is the most gorgeous pair of ruby earrings in the window. They'd be perfect with my ruby necklace for the SHARE benefit."

It's not that Carmen envied these women, but she knew she could play their roles with so much more panache. Soon, she thought, soon.

2

Enid and Patrick

nid was keenly aware of Wallase watching her as she checked her purse to make sure she had her favorite sunglasses. In the eight years he had worked for them, she had learned to read the nuances of his moods, and she knew he had developed a sixth sense about her own. So she could tell by his heavy-lidded glance and the intensity with which he was rubbing the silver picture frame he was polishing, which was already shinier than it was new, that he was worried about something.

"If anyone calls, say I you be home, Missy?" Wallase asked, keeping his eyes averted.

"It's only lunch, so I should be back by two-thirty."

Ah, so that was it. He was curious about her lunch date. Well, he had good reason. Since Patrick Drake moved in next door, the only real contact they'd had with him was last week, when Patrick had invited Sam over to discuss the building of the wall. Sam had returned totally charmed by Patrick and eager to cooperate in the creation of this barrier between the two houses, which Patrick had called a "friendly fence."

"He needs it to keep his dog from running around the neighborhood," Sam had explained.

"You mean that little Yorkie? I don't think that animal's feet have ever touched the ground," she had answered. "Every time I see it someone is carrying it."

"Well, obviously he wants to let it outside, but can't until he builds the wall. I think it's a good idea anyway, to separate our properties. Good fences make good neighbors. I agreed to pay half." And he'd gone back to his Lakers' game.

Dear, generous Sam, she thought.

Sam! What if he called while she was out? If she left it to Wallase to tell him where she was, he'd wonder why — having lunch with a famous neighbor wasn't exactly part of Enid's daily routine.

She picked up the phone and dialed. "Margie, is Sam in?"

"Oh, hi, Enid. He's not here. He's at lunch."

Enid was stunned. "Since when does Sam eat lunch?"

Margie laughed. "I know. I couldn't believe it either. But that's what he told me. He's at Jimmy's if you want to call him there."

"No, no, it's nothing important. Just tell him I've gone out to lunch myself, and I'll talk to him this evening. Thanks."

She stole a glance at Wallase who was still bent over the frame, but was now rinsing it at last, apparently relieved he wouldn't have to explain Enid's whereabouts to the master of the house.

She headed for the door. "I'll be with Mr. Drake at Giorgio's. If anything important comes up, the number's in my red book."

"Yes, Missy. Have a good time."

Patrick chuckled to himself as he turned another page of the Dominion script. There were possibilities there. It needed work, of course, but he could see himself in the role, and that was the first step.

He ran his fingers through his short, graying hair. There were more barriers to a movie deal than there were to the 400-meter high hurdles. First, he had to like the idea and feel comfortable with the players, both in front of and behind the camera. In the past ten years, he'd made a total of fourteen movies — seven of them had been forgettable and unprofitable, three had broken even, three had been modest successes, and one, *Just You and Me,* had been a home run. These days, unless you had a home run to your credit, you couldn't even get into the game.

But it had been years since he'd sent that one over the fence, and he needed to get back onto the playing field again. People assumed that just because he was a celebrity, he was automatically rich as well. But it was very costly to maintain the appearance of a superstar lifestyle, and the $2 million price tag LeMar insisted on attaching to his acting services made the offers few and far between. Of course, two expensive ex-wives and a penchant for making disastrous investments didn't help matters. He hated people like Sam Carrouthers who seemed to have all the money they could ever want or need, and had no problem making more.

He picked up the script again. *For Love or Money.* Could he really see himself as a fabulously wealthy playboy who falls in love with a mentally retarded girl? A lot depended on the girl. Probably they'd want to go with an unknown, a girl-next-door type, so he would have to carry the project.

Carrouthers . . . girl-next-door! The clock on the wall behind him scolded 1:20 P.M. He was already late. He put down the script, stood and stretched, and the instant he was out of the chair the little Yorkshire Terrier who had been waiting patiently at his feet leapt into it.

"YoYo, down!"

Patrick tried to be forceful, but the dog knew him too well. They had a running battle over the chair, and they both knew the only way Patrick could keep the dog off it was to lock him in the kitchen, which he was loathe to do. Too bad for the burgundy suede, $175 a yard; it even smelled like the dog now. But Patrick decided he'd enjoy his lunch a lot more if he allowed the dog to stay on the chair, just this once, again.

As he eased the big blue Rolls Royce out of the garage he could see

Enid waiting in front of her house. He squinted through the wind-shield, having opted to forgo his glasses in favor of a positive first im-pression. She didn't have Sara's figure, but then who did? She looked well proportioned at least, and, thank God, she wasn't one of those middle-aged women who insisted on wearing jogging clothes every-where. Her outfit was subdued — tailored, but not mannish. She was not his type, at least not yet, but acceptable to be seen with.

Patrick's own outfit was his usual mix of corduroy trousers, muted blue and green plaid shirt, and shabby tweed jacket. He was comfort-able with the fact that women weren't attracted to him for the way he dressed, or even the way he looked. His appeal came from his warmth and his wit. Several years ago, when he was named one of the five sexiest men in America, he was asked in countless interviews why women swooned over him, even though he was not the classic example of tall, dark, and handsome.

After pondering the point to show the interviewer his modesty, he would explain that when women looked into his eyes they could see he loved them unconditionally, and it made them want to love him back. He purposely neglected to mention how many hours he had spent in front of the mirror, working on just the right expression to invoke this response.

He also didn't talk about phase two in his seduction approach, a technique he called "the stroke." It worked like this: While still look-ing into the woman's eyes, he would grasp her elbow ever so lightly, applying just enough pressure to get her attention, but keeping his touch gentle enough to send an erotic signal. When he saw in her ex-pression that she was aware of his hand and his touch, very slowly and expectantly he would let his fingers trickle up the inside of her arm, toward that secret spot where it would be wedged between the sup-pleness of her inner arm and the softness of her fluttering breast.

If this did not make her swoon, he would just continue the motion, brushing his hand slowly up and down the vulnerable inner arm, un-til her eyes glazed over and she succumbed to his charms. And they always did. It was pathetic in a way, how women were such easy prey to the slightest sexual innuendo. It almost (but not quite) took the fun out of it.

He pulled the Rolls to a stop in front of Enid and was quietly pleased that she did not wait for him to get out to open her door. Rather, she ran around to the passenger side and slipped into the luxurious seat beside him.

So far, so good. He would time "the stroke" carefully today, probably somewhere between the entree and the espresso.

$\equiv$nid sensed something was wrong the minute she got into Patrick's car. It wasn't the way he greeted her. His casual, "Of course, now I recognize you. You're the one who jogs by the house at the crack of dawn, half naked," was so like something he'd say in a film that she felt instantly at ease with him.

But there was a peculiar look in his eyes, a fleeting cloud that darkened their vast gray greenness before he put on his sunglasses and turned to the road ahead. Did she have lipstick on her teeth? Was her part crooked? Had she buttoned her shirt wrong? She put on her own dark glasses to hide her anxiety.

"Three days a week, I do yoga at Shelley's down the block. She has a teacher who comes at 6:15." Enid discretely checked the buttons on her shirt and turned her head to the window so she could check her smile in the reflection. Everything seemed okay. "You must be an early riser then," she continued. It was just something to say.

Patrick looked over his shoulder to make sure no cars were coming and eased the Rolls into the street. "Only when I have an early call at the studio. If I had my way, I'd never leave my bed." He meant this to sound sexy, but worried she might interpret it as lazy. "I can survey the block from there," he amended, "and you see some pretty interesting things." The car chugged slightly as he brought it up to speed.

"For example, I remember one morning I was still pretty groggy, and there you were, jogging by as usual. All of a sudden I realized, 'my God, she's finally done it! She's forgotten to put on her pants.' "

He turned his eyes to meet hers, to see how she was reacting to his teasing. "When you got closer I realized that what I thought was bare skin was just flesh-colored stockings, or whatever you call them." He chuckled. "I was disappointed, but it definitely woke me up."

"I'll have to remember not to wear those tights again, at least not so early in the morning," was Enid's feeble reply. She turned again to the window, just in time to see the expression on Suzanne Cole's face as the Rolls pulled past her. *Oh, God,* she thought, *the whole neighborhood will know about this by the time we get back.* She began to chuckle.

"Usually I have to work a lot harder for a laugh. What's so funny?" Patrick asked.

"Do you know Suzanne Cole? She lives across the street."

"The lady with the twins?"

"Right. Well, we just drove by her, and I was thinking that by the time we finish lunch, the whole neighborhood will know we were together today."

"Is that a problem for you?"

"That she saw us together? No, not at all. In fact, it'll be fun being the most popular girl on the block this afternoon. I'm sure my phone will be ringing off the hook."

"Good, because if we see anyone *I* know, chances are you're going to be in *The Inquirer* tomorrow."

"You're kidding."

He shrugged and gave her that familiar smile, the one that made his eyes twinkle. "For some odd reason, the press is ravenously curious about my private life."

"Sam would die. He's not very fond of publicity or the press."

"Sam?"

"My husband. You talked to him about the wall you're building."

"Oh, of course, *Sam.*" He drew the name out into two syllables. "I think of him as Mr. Carrouthers."

Why?"

Patrick shrugged again. "Well, for one thing, he's very rich. And I always call rich men Mister."

"And what about their wives?"

"Mist-ress?"

She blushed at the implication.

☞

The Rolls pulled to a stop in front of the restaurant. The valet opened the door for Enid, and as she stepped out she realized to her horror that the fly of her slacks was unzipped. *Oh God,* she thought, *what a klutz!* No wonder Patrick had looked at her so strangely!

Instinctively, her hand moved to her crotch, to shield this gaping gaff, but there was no way she could secretly execute a zip as she walked around the car to where Patrick was waiting. She pulled her jacket around her, but it was buttonless, and the best she could do was to hug it close, which she knew looked stupid and unnatural.

Patrick steered her toward the restaurant. "Bit of a chill today, eh?" he asked, misreading, she hoped, the reason for the clenched jacket. "It'll be warmer inside." He held the door open for her.

Having grown up in L.A., Enid was used to seeing celebrities in restaurants, at the beauty salon, and occasionally at galas and private parties. And she knew the public was not always kind in its scrutiny. She herself had snickered at starlets in skirts that were too short and tight, or wearing accessories obviously meant to attract attention.

Today, she was the butt of the joke. Was it her imagination or did a hush fall over the room when they entered? Could everybody see her open fly? How ironic — this moment, which she had imagined being one of her proudest, was instead one of her most humiliating. As Patrick propelled her further into the room, nodding to fans at the tables they passed, she was certain she saw smirks and pointed fingers directed at her crotch. Why hadn't she worn her cashmere bodysuit, which had no zippers, snaps, or buttons to cause trouble?

Although their own table waited in plain sight, Patrick made a detour to stop by a table of four, three men in business suits and a petite woman in an enormous hat. Enid was in such a daze of embarrassment that she didn't catch their names, but she was keenly aware that her open fly was nearly level with the woman's face.

When the woman leaned forward to receive Patrick's proffered kiss, her hat grazed Enid's side and it was knocked askew. Enid leapt backward, as though the hat brim were razor sharp. She was, in fact, surprised not to see a streak of blood soiling her gabardine slacks where the hat had touched them.

"I'm terribly sorry." The woman adjusted her hat. "I don't know why I wear this gargantuan thing."

"You wear it so people will see you, Elaine." Patrick was so smooth that he sounded charming, even when he was insulting someone.

"Lucky you. You don't even have to wear a hat to be observed," she countered. Her expression was not kind.

"If Elaine wants to be noticed, she should do lunch with you, Patrick," one of the men commented. "You could have heard a pin drop when you came in. I thought it was Madonna, or at the very least Liz Taylor."

Patrick leaned close to the man as though sharing a private joke. "I only had to pay these people a dollar each," he whispered, motioning to the diners at the surrounding tables. "Except for the two in the corner who insisted on SAG minimum."

Patrick nudged Enid away while the others were still chuckling, their laughter sitting like oil atop the pool of silence in the restaurant. "Whew," he sighed as they took their seats, "it's like running the gauntlet, isn't it?"

Enid could only nod.

"I've just got to take a quick run to the men's room. That kind of an entrance always makes me feel like my fly's unzipped. Back in a flash," Patrick said, and he was up and moving away before Enid could respond.

Her face burning, she furtively zipped the errant zipper and locked it shut.

"Excuse me, Miss, are you somebody famous?"

Enid looked up to see a woman in her sixties standing next to the table. She was poured into a floral print dacron dress and was wearing plaid tennis shoes with bobby socks. Clearly this woman was not from L.A.

"No, I don't think so," Enid replied.

"You sure?" The woman looked skeptical. "I told my husband Ray you looked like *someone*. We came in from Des Moines two days ago, and since we been here we've seen Goldie Hawn, Tom Arnold, that one who used to be on Cheers, what's his name? Ted Danson! And then there was . . ."

She turned to her husband, hovering a few feet behind, his bald head gleaming in the sunlight that poured through the domed skylight, like an ad for Jiffy Wax. "What was that other one, from that night show?" she asked.

"Conan O'Brien," he replied.

"Conan O'Brien," the woman reported to Enid. "Ray says he's got a show on T.V. I never seen him myself." She smiled at Enid. "D'you know him?"

"Not personally, no," said Enid apologetically, feeling as though she was letting the woman down.

Indeed, the woman slumped in disappointment. "Oh, well, seeing you here with Patrick Drake, I thought you must know all the stars."

"He's the only one, actually."

"How'd you meet him, if you don't mind my asking?"

Either the woman had nothing else to do or she was desperate for conversation. But then, Enid would prefer to be talking to someone when Patrick returned, rather than have him find her waiting alone, like an obedient German Shepherd. "He's my next-door neighbor, actually."

"Go on! Ray, did you hear that? This lady lives next door to Patrick Drake!"

Shit, shit, shit. Patrick splashed cold water across his face, stalling for time as he decided what to do. In a city of eight million people only he could manage to run into Elaine Marx. Even that enormous hat couldn't hide her gigantic mouth, which would soon be wrapped around the nearest telephone, blabbing to her client, Sara Benton, that she had seen Patrick having lunch with another woman.

Elaine was an agent, the kind of agent who represented the girlfriend of or the cousin of somebody famous, using their relationship to the celebrity as her calling card to find them work. She was actually quite devoted to her clients, wooing wanna-bes by becoming their best friend and confidante, and giving them the kind of emotional massage that was usually only lavished on actors who had proven their box office ability. But she was no dummy. She knew you could call a Brian Grazer and rave about Patrick Drake's gorgeous new girlfriend whom you'd met at dinner at Tom's and Rita's the night before, and in seconds you'd have an appointment for an interview, or even a screen test, because you knew Grazer wouldn't want to offend either Patrick or Tom Hanks. Besides, few men said no to a beautiful girl.

Elaine had leapt on Sara the first time Patrick had brought her to a screening, effusing about her hair, her eyes, her legs, and practically every other visible body part, interrupting the rapturous flow of compliments only to introduce Sara to all of her dearest personal friends, practically every celebrity in the room.

Patrick couldn't blame Sara for getting hooked. Even he was not immune to the narcotic of flattery. Once you got some, you had to have more, and you only felt comfortable with people who provided it. Eight months after meeting Elaine, Sara was like a junkie, moping about until the agent called to supply her with her daily fix. It was pathetic, but hey, it was a lot better than being hooked on cocaine the way everybody was in the old days.

There was a knock on the bathroom door. Patrick pulled himself together and unlocked it. Two fresh-faced young things slipped in as he stepped out.

"God, Patrick Drake. Isn't he cute?" one breathed to the other as Patrick walked away. He slowed his step so he could overhear their conversation.

"I get to use the toilet he just used, can you believe it?" the other one replied.

"He probably didn't sit down, Marie," the first countered, closing the door.

"Well, maybe he blew his nose or something. Check the wastebasket."

Patrick winced. Were everybody's fans getting weird, or did just his seem to be vying for a nod in the Guinness Book of Records under "Strangest Celebrity Memento Ever Acquired"?

As Patrick passed the phone booth on his way back to the table a thought struck him. He could solve the whole Sara problem by calling her right now, beating Elaine to the punch line, so to speak. He threw a quarter into the phone and dialed Sara's number. She answered after half of one ring.

"Hello?"

"Yeah, what's your problem?"

"Patrick? Elaine's on the other line. She just told me she saw you at Giorgio's having lunch with some woman." Sara's voice was shrill with indignation.

How in hell could Elaine be talking to Sara? There was only one phone and he was on it.

"Well, actually, that's why I'm calling. After I talked to you this morning, YoYo got out and I was running around the whole neighborhood looking for him. Then the lady next door, Enid Carrouthers is her name, called me and said she'd found him. He was swimming in her birdbath, if you can believe it." He was winging it, hoping that the wilder the story, the more believable it would sound to someone like Sara, whose I.Q. was on a par with her bra size. "The poor pup almost drowned. You should have seen him."

There was dead silence on the other end. Then, "How can a dog drown in a birdbath?" Her wariness surprised him. Usually Sara was a sucker for wounded animal stories.

"It's a very deep birdbath, like for seagulls, and . . ."

"So what does this have to do with your having lunch with her?" Sara was a little slow, but she compensated by being suspicious.

"Well, I had to thank her for saving his life, didn't I? I couldn't let such a humanitarian act go unrewarded, could I?"

"I guess not."

Patrick breathed a sigh of relief.

"So why are you calling me?"

Why *was* he calling her? "Well, she invited us to have dinner with her and her *husband* tonight, and I wanted to call and ask you what you thought." Not bad for a spontaneous fib.

"We can't. We have that fund-raising thing for the mayor."

"Oh, right, right, I completely forgot. Well, I'll tell her we'll have to take a rain check." This was easier than he'd thought. "I'll call you when I get home, okay?"

"I'm going out at two-thirty to have my hair done."

"I'll call you after that."

He hung up, relieved, but sweating. That had been close.

As he reentered the dining room, he made a point of passing Elaine's table. Sure enough, she was talking into one of those tiny Motorola cellulars that looked like a mousetrap. He would have liked to have snapped it shut on her oversized ear.

"Tell her to wear the green dress tonight," he said as he breezed by, not even stopping to savor the surprised look on Elaine's face.

"Sorry. I ran into some fans who *had* to have a memento," Patrick reported as he slid into the chair across from Enid with a sigh.

The waiter materialized instantly. "What would you like to drink?" Both Patrick and the waiter looked at Enid expectantly.

"Mineral water, please."

"That's all?" Patrick was incredulous. "If I order a bottle of claret, do you think I could convince you to have a sip or two, just to keep me company?"

"Well, the problem is, I'm allergic to red wine." Patrick frowned, so she quickly added, "But I'd have some white, I guess, if you want."

Patrick brightened. "The Cakebread Chardonnay, Scott. The '92, if I didn't already finish it off."

"I'll check, Mr. Drake. In the meantime, would you and the lady like to start with Mario's fried oysters, as usual?"

Patrick raised his eyebrows at Enid. "I hope you're not allergic to oysters too. The chef makes them especially for me."

How could she tell him she never touched fried foods, let alone oysters, which she had despised ever since she contracted food poisoning from one at a New Year's Eve party so dismal that her nausea had been the high point.

"Great," she replied, hoping her tone had conviction.

Patrick sent the waiter off with a nod, then leaned close to Enid to whisper, "I don't know how Mario got the idea that I love oysters. Frankly, I detest them. But I hate to hurt his feelings when he's trying to be so nice."

"To tell you the truth, I really don't care much for oysters either, but I didn't want to disappoint you," Enid confided.

They smiled at each other, pleased to have found that they had something in common, bonded by the false front they had erected to preserve the chef's feelings.

The sommelier arrived to uncork the wine, and Patrick bantered with him, giving Enid a chance to observe him in action. How relaxed he was, and how charming, not only to the waiter and the sommelier, but even to the busboy who brought the bread. Everyone seemed to know and like Patrick. She wasn't surprised. She, too, was falling under his spell.

He handed her a glass of wine and raised his own glass, swirling the tawny liquid with the ease of someone who drank a great deal. "What shall we toast to?"

"Oysters."

He laughed and touched his glass to hers, pleased to see the warm glow spreading across her face. As usual, his magic was spinning its web.

Patrick let the Chardonnay trickle down his throat, savoring its tart crispness. He was glad Enid had talked him into the white; it would be delicious with the crab cakes, and he could always order a glass of Merlot later with his lamb. It pleased him just to think about it.

For the first time, he concentrated his attention on Enid. She was busy cutting her bread with a knife, a difficult proposition since the hard-crusted roll had been sitting too long in a warming oven. He noticed a wrinkle of concentration form between her eyebrows, and thought to himself that in a few years it would be a permanent part of her face. Ah, the inevitability of the aging process.

But otherwise, her complexion was smooth and fresh, unlike Sara's skin, which had pores the size of mine craters, requiring her to plaster her face with pancake makeup. By contrast, Enid was the picture of health and purity. Her hair was straight and shiny. Yes, he could see a few streaks of gray mixed in with the predictable light brown, but not so much as to dull the overall sheen. Her eyes, partially hidden behind long bangs, were the color of chocolate milk, nothing exciting, but nice nevertheless.

His first wife, Sandy, had brown eyes. Like a cow, he had teased her. And it was true, she was a placid, bovine kind of creature. In a way, it had been a relief to be with someone so undemanding and complacent. He had been casually unfaithful to her in their first month of marriage, and he had continued to fool around with greater frequency, until it simply became easier to keep an apartment in town rather than go home to her in the suburbs every night. By the end of the second year, he was only coming home for birthdays and holidays, so what was the point?

"What are you looking at?" Enid interrupted his daydream.

"Actually, I was thinking that your eyes are the same color as my first wife's."

"Sandra Lester?" Patrick showed his surprise. "*People*," Enid explained. "According to what I've read, you've had two marriages, three live-in girlfriends, and an engagement that lasted only a weekend."

Patrick ducked his head, feigning remorse. He was secretly proud of his resumé of relationships. "Ah, yes, Leslie Lavingston," he said. "We met in Bora Bora. It was so damn romantic it would have been a shame to waste it by *not* falling in love, even if it was temporary. How about you?"

"How many times have I been married?" Patrick nodded. "Only once. To Sam. We had our twelfth anniversary last month."

"Congratulations. I must say I envy anyone who can stay married. My normal pattern is two years in and two years out. Knowing that gives me a sense of stability, being able to gauge where I am at a given time in a given relationship."

"And where are you now, with Sara Benton?"

Patrick nearly choked on his crab cake. "Do you know Sara?"

"Only what I've read."

Better to get her off the subject of Sara, Patrick thought. "So what's the most interesting thing you've read about me?"

Enid was delighted. Unwittingly, Patrick had given her the perfect lead-in to the subject she wanted to broach, the purpose for her lunch invitation. "That as a teenager you were misdiagnosed as having spinal meningitis, and that you spent a year living in a hospital getting treated for it, when what you really had was a bone disease that was curable. And you were the one who studied the medical books and finally convinced the doctors to give you the right treatment." She sat back, proud of herself.

"Yeah, and what's so interesting about that?"

Patrick always feigned flippancy when someone referred to his traumatic medical history. If the truth be known, the whole story was a lie, fabricated by a press agent early in his career. But somehow it had caught the fancy of the public and it became valuable to his image — having triumphed over personal tragedy had lent him an unimpeachable integrity: if a reviewer proclaimed him a talentless schmuck, someone else was sure to say "Give him a break, think what he went through as a kid. It's a miracle he's even alive!"

"I can safely say that those were the worst years of my life," Patrick said soberly, thinking not of his health but of his anonymous youth in Kewasha, Indiana. "But they did teach me to suck the marrow out of life, and that if I wanted something, really, really felt it, I should follow my instincts and go all the way."

He moved his hand to Enid's elbow and grasped it firmly as he looked into her eyes. "My instincts tell me you and I could be a great team. Don't you agree?"

She nodded, her expression fervent, her face flushed scarlet. He wondered if he was rushing her, but after all, they had finished their entrees and were halfway through the espresso.

Apparently she was waiting for him to make a move. Women of the nineties paid lip service to liberation, but it was still rare to find one who would take the first step. "I can't believe you've been living next door all this time and I haven't found you until now," he crooned, the words fondling her verbally as he began to inch his hand up the inside of her arm. He was pleasantly surprised to feel the firmness of her triceps. Muscle tone here boded well for the rest of her body. Patrick looked into Enid's eyes, which now had a glazed cast to them. *She's ready*, he thought.

"Is this the first time you've done this?" he whispered, using a tone that was both seductive and sincere, to give her the encouragement she needed. It was always so much easier if the woman thought it was her idea.

"Done what?" She sounded genuinely confused.

Oops, wrong tactic, but now he had no choice but to pursue it. "Well, inviting a man to lunch. You must have more on your mind than food, especially since you barely touched the pasta." He continued stroking her inner arm encouragingly.

"Actually I do," Enid answered, and Patrick accelerated his stroking. "But maybe it's not what you think."

Patrick slipped his hand away and picked up his espresso. "Oh? What is it then? Do tell, I'm dying of curiosity."

Enid took a deep breath. "Well, I'm on a committee for the Westside Women's Shelter. Have you heard of it? It's a home for abused women and their children. Every year they have a fund-raising benefit, and this year I'm going to be chairman. What we're trying to do is raise enough money to hire a doctor to work full time on site. You can't believe the kinds of health problems these people have."

Patrick slid down in his seat. Boy, had he missed the boat. Here he was, wasting a good two hours nudging this woman toward an afternoon of earthly delights, and all the time she was soaring about on some spiritual plane.

"I appreciate what you said about going after things you believe in, because I really believe in this cause. I was reluctant to talk to you about it because I don't know you all that well. But when I learned about your past, I realized you obviously know the importance of good medical care. So, I thought maybe this wouldn't be asking such a big favor. Maybe it would be something you wanted to do." She looked at him expectantly.

He raised his hand to signal the waiter to bring the check. When he lowered it, he was surprised that she grasped it in both of hers and pulled it close to her bosom, leaning toward him with a look of such sincerity that he was sure she didn't realize that the knuckle of his third finger was pressed against her breast. He waggled it ever so slightly, and he could feel her nipple harden. Was she even aware of this? Her face certainly didn't show it.

She continued, "We were hoping you would let us arrange a benefit dinner for the premiere of your new movie, the one with Alison McGrath. It would be the most wonderful thing for the Shelter."

"And what's in it for me?"

He hoped he sounded sarcastic, but he really meant it. These things were a pain in the ass, and frequently they turned out to be an embarrassing waste of time. On the other hand, it would mean a lot of free publicity for the film, and A Month of Sundays certainly could use all the help it could get.

"Whatever you want."

Did she know how suggestive her tone was? He decided she didn't, that she was just another do-gooder who lived from charity event to charity event. But perversely, her breast still seemed to be forcing itself into his hand. He had an urge to grab it, to see how she would react, but contented himself to feeling its subtle weight pressing on his palm.

"I don't even know if the studio's planned anything for the film. Really, it's not my decision to make." The waiter arrived with the check, but before Patrick could take it, Enid slipped out a platinum American Express card and set it on top of the bill.

"But — " Patrick tried.

"Please, Patrick, I invited you to lunch. This is my treat." She held his hand tighter. "We've already made some inquiries. Nothing's been set yet. They're waiting to hear what you want. What do you think?"

Trapped! Patrick looked into her eyes. Were they glowing from too much wine, he wondered, or from the raptures of altruism? Maybe this really was about sex, and she just needed a little coaxing. But did he have the energy or the inclination for a long, drawn-out campaign?

It might be entertaining to orchestrate a seduction right in the neighborhood. The risk would be exhilarating, with the husband only a stone's throw away. And it would do a world of good to his ego to win the affections of the wife of the rich and self-satisfied Sam Carrouthers, a true test of his desirability. But why should he waste his time cultivating this crop when fruit was continually dropping in his lap? "I'll think about it," he said at last.

"You will!" In a burst of enthusiasm, she reached over and hugged him around the neck, kissing his cheek with a smack. "That's great, thank you! Wait until I tell them!"

"You'd better not say anything yet," Patrick warned. "I'll have to make some calls, pull a few strings."

"What matters to me is that you didn't say no. God, you can't imagine how long it took me to get up the courage to ask you this. Oh, Patrick, it will be so much fun working with you, I can hardly wait."

Patrick could hardly wait either.

3

Sam and Carmen

Much to Sam's chagrin, Carmen was waiting for him at one of Jimmy's more conspicuous tables. They exchanged greetings, and then she gave her full attention to the menu, allowing him a chance to case the room. He had hoped that because of the early hour, no one he knew or did business with would be there, but no such luck. Bill Martin of Citibank was already on his feet, heading in their direction.

"Sambo, what the hell!" Bill's booming voice would have been more appropriate on a football field. "You swore you never ate lunch, you mudsucker. What made you . . ." Carmen lowered her menu and gave Bill a dazzling smile that stopped him mid-sentence. "Well, that explains it," he finished, readjusting his glasses to give her a once-over.

Sam grimaced, seeing the look of delight on Carmen's face. "This is Carmen Leventhal, from the *Times*. Bill Martin of Citibank."

"I don't know the face, but I recognize the byline." Bill took Carmen's proffered hand and held it as though it were a Faberge Egg, obviously as impressed by her beauty as he was by her reputation. "You can believe anything he says about business, Miss Leventhal, but if he tries to tell you about his hole in one at El Dorado, it's a crock. I was there, and I saw him kick the ball the last three feet into the hole."

"I suppose the most important thing is *getting it in*," Carmen purred, "no matter how much fancy foreplay you have to do. Wouldn't you say, Mr. Martin?"

Sam could see that Bill was eating this up with such gusto he probably wouldn't have any room left for his lasagna.

"Isn't your lunch getting cold, Bill?" Sam gave him a look that said "get lost" and Bill did, with a polite good-bye to Carmen and with a wink at Sam.

"Why don't you ever eat lunch?" Carmen asked.

"It's a waste of time. And I'd rather use that ninety minutes playing tennis. I have a game every morning, which means I don't get in until nine-thirty. If I stopped for lunch too, half the day would be gone."

"No wonder."

"No wonder what?

"No wonder you have such a gorgeous body," Carmen said, as the waiter appeared to fill their water goblets.

"Look," Sam began as soon as the waiter was gone, "in all candor, I appreciate your invitation to lunch today. But I didn't come to be social. I accepted because you said you had some business information to share with me. Let's talk about that."

"The two don't have to be mutually exclusive, you know."

"What two?"

"Business and pleasure." She paused for effect. "You and me, for that matter."

Sam opened his mouth to speak, but she interrupted him by reaching across the table and touching her finger to his lips. "But all in good time. First, let me tell you what's going on with Leo Choate and WIT."

Carmen loved having Sam's undivided attention. If she'd had any qualms about telling him this confidential information, they were far outweighed by her delight in being at the center of his focus. Before

this, he'd been about as responsive as a brick wall, rebuffing her flir-
tations and ignoring her innuendoes. But he was completely capti-
vated by her knowledge of business, *his* business, to be precise.

The juicy tidbit about WIT had literally fallen into her lap. She
had been in the bullpen, sitting at her secretary's desk, because she
had trashed her own keyboard earlier in the week in a fit of rage over
a rejected story. While she'd been sitting there, the new mail boy had
tossed a manila envelope into Rhoda's "in" basket, but he'd missed,
and it had slid into Carmen's hands.

"Nice shot, Kareem," she'd called after him, but the kid hadn't
heard her. She'd looked at the envelope and had seen the name of
her nemesis, Ralph Lassiter, and "Confidential" written in red letters.

Lucky for her, Ralph had been at lunch. He was always at lunch,
or at breakfast, or having a drink with someone. *King of the
schmuesers*, he called himself. True, he got a lot of good information,
hanging around the watering holes favored by the elite of the business community. But the price he paid for it was a serious drinking
problem, and probably a drug habit to boot.

Carmen hated Ralph because he treated her like a bimbo and
never missed an opportunity to tell her that she didn't belong in the
hard-bitten world of business reporting. "They've got plenty of room
for you in the Lifestyles section," he'd tease. "How about a column on
knitting? It worked for Madame DeFarge."

Carmen had not spent four years on full scholarship at Brown and
a two-year apprenticeship with *The Plain Dealer* to write some
bullshit women's column. She was a damn good reporter, as good as
any man on the paper, and she would do what she had to do to prove
it.

Which meant she had felt it was her duty to open the envelope
with Ralph's name on it.

In it she'd found his sloppy notes for the article on WIT and Leo
Choate, along with a clean draft of the copy, typed by the editing department, and a diskette for the files. All Carmen had had to do was

slip them into her briefcase and make an appointment to have her hair done. It was as easy as that.

Now, sitting in this elegant restaurant, across from a man who represented power and privilege, substance and sexuality, Carmen felt she had reached a milestone. *Someday*, she thought, *I will look back on this moment as the true beginning of the life I was meant to live.*

She raised her wineglass. "A toast," she said.

Sam sighed and picked up his water glass. But it was not good enough for Carmen. She flagged down a passing waiter and asked him to bring her another wineglass, then poured some of her Chardonnay into it.

"I really don't want any," Sam protested.

"One sip won't hurt you," Carmen insisted.

"What if I told you I was an alcoholic and all it takes is one sip to plunge me back into the depths of addiction?"

"I would be delighted to know you are at least vulnerable to something." She thrust the second wineglass in Sam's face.

Sam shook his head. Never had he met a person, woman or man, who was this tenacious. How exhausting it would be to have to deal with her on a regular basis. He knew he should give in, it would be so much easier. But something in Sam made him want to fight back.

"What difference does it make if I toast with wine or with water?"

"It would be poor form," she answered. "And I know you have impeccable form."

"How do you know that?"

"By your office, the way it's decorated, and your clothes, the fabric and the way they fit. You're probably the only lawyer in town who doesn't wear wingtips and a three-piece suit. I'll bet you won't even put the bill for this lunch on your expense account."

"Why should I, you're not a client expense."

Carmen's smile was radiant. She had won. "I'll toast to that."

She held the second wineglass up to Sam, and although he knew if he wanted, he could win in a contest of wills, he decided that there was no point in wasting any more time over something so meaning-less as a sip of wine. Besides, he was dying to hear about this WIT business.

He took the wineglass from her. They toasted, and she waited until he took a sip before she brought her own glass to her lips.

"Now, are we going to talk about WIT, or was that just a ruse, to get me to drink with you at lunch?" Sam was back to being all busi-ness.

Buoyed by the wine and the heady sensation of having won her point, Carmen moved in for the kill.

Later, as Sam walked back to his office, he weighed the validity of Carmen's information. Was it possible that Leo had indeed made a deal with Paul Whitney-Smith of WIT to buy a controlling interest in Dominion Pictures? Where would Leo get the piece of Dominion to sell to WIT? He only knew of one block of stock that big, and it wasn't for sale. Sam had been working with Sanwa for two months on a refinancing deal for Dominion, and if what Carmen had told him were true, his efforts would prove meaningless. He wondered how long that snake Leo had been working on WIT without telling any of the partners, while Simple Sam, the naive and honest jerk that he was, had been issuing weekly status reports, outlining his slow but steady progress with Sanwa. Maybe it was time to start playing dirty. Everyone else seemed to be.

A blast of cold air hit him as he entered the 2002 building. Hot un-der the collar as he was at the thought of Leo's underhandedness, the icy blast nevertheless made him shiver.

Carmen closed her eyes and tried to relax. But how could she, ly-ing on a frigid examination table in an antiseptically clean doctor's office, naked from the waist down, with only a thin paper gown to give her privacy?

This was Carmen's third, and hopefully last, visit to Dr. Mason. Maybe hemorrhoids weren't life threatening, but going to a proctologist had to be one of life's most humbling experiences.

No, she took that back. *Being* a proctologist had to be infinitely more humbling. How in hell did you explain to your friends and family that after sweating through eight years of medical studies, you had decided to specialize in human assholes?

Fortunately, Dr. Mason was a kindly old man, and she could at least assure herself that he took no perverse thrill in sticking a syringe up her butt and telling her to bear down while he emptied the hemorrhoid medicine into her rectum.

Actually she could hardly feel the shots. What bothered her was coming and going from Dr. Mason's office, not knowing who she might run into in the building, or in the cramped waiting room.

During their first session, Dr. Mason had asked Carmen what kind of work she did, and when she told him she wrote for the business section of the *Times*, the doctor had been excited to tell her that she had just missed Stanley Gruen, an LBO specialist who had recently been implicated in an insider trading scandal. Did Carmen know him, the kindly doctor had asked.

Know him? Carmen had been the one who had uncovered the most damaging bit of evidence about Gruen, and it would be the last thing she needed to run into him here with her rear end hanging out. Wouldn't he love to tell the world that she was indeed getting what she deserved for being such a tightass?

"Good afternoon, Miss Leventhal."

The doctor already had his syringe ready and was slipping his hand into one of those ubiquitous rubber gloves. "Will you turn onto your left side please?"

Carmen obliged and closed her eyes, trying to occupy herself with thoughts about work. She was no fool. She knew that in one of two ways, her future depended on this WIT story: either she would use it merely as a lure, an excuse to work closely with Sam Carrouthers until she could entice him away from his wife, or, if by some fluke he rejected her advances, she would use the story itself to enhance her reputation at the paper, maybe even get a Pulitzer.

Of the two options, she preferred the first, the relationship with Sam. She was tired of schlepping to make ends meet, and she wanted to move up, into another phase of her life, the phase in which she was married to a wealthy and socially prominent man, living the life of the pampered socialite wife.

"All set. Now if you'll just rest until the medicine is absorbed, and then you can get dressed."

"Thank you, Doctor," was all Carmen could say before he was out the door and on to the next patient. If she didn't already know she had a great ass, she would be offended by Dr. Mason's rush to get away from it. She sighed and closed her eyes for another moment.

Growing up poor had left an indelible impression on Carmen. She'd watched her mother age twice as fast as her friends' mothers because her life was twice as hard. With no husband to help her support her family, Mrs. Leventhal had had no choice but to work nights in a cocktail lounge, bringing home what she could in the way of tips, and relying on the proverbial "generosity of strangers" to defray the costs of raising three children.

Not surprisingly, alcohol had become a problem, and Carmen and her two brothers had been forced to carry their own weight in the household even before they were in junior high school. From age six onward, all three had worked as child models, and their earnings had made it possible for the family to stay in the house their father had leased two months before he had escaped to greener pastures, divorcing their mother to marry a woman of some wealth who lived in Minnesota.

Carmen had not minded the modeling. It had taught her how to create a facade to hide behind, a talent that had served her well later

HICKSVILLE PUBLIC LIBRARY
169 JERUS   VE.
HIC

in life. If clothes didn't make the woman, at least they fooled some people into believing she could afford nice things. Carmen had learned right off that saving up for one nice dress was wiser than buying three off the discount rack. She also had learned that it was cheaper to change her hair color than it was to buy a new outfit, and that a certain kind of smile could go a long way toward helping her get what she wanted, be it a job modeling for the Sears catalog, or a spot on the cheerleading squad.

There were, of course, times that the engaging smile had gotten her into trouble. Like the day she had interviewed with Byron Kirk, the infamous owner of Kirk's Kids, the most prestigious talent agency for preteen models and actors in Los Angeles.

Little had Carmen's mother known, as she eagerly thrust her twelve-year-old-daughter's career into this man's hands, that she also was setting Carmen up for her first sexual encounter. Byron Kirk was not known to be a lecherous man, but little girls like Carmen did not come along every day. At twelve, she already had the youthful buddings of the feminine shape that would later make her the kind of woman men stopped and stared at. And Byron, whose eye was trained to read the future in young bodies, knew a winner when he saw one.

"I'll have to see her without her dress," he had said to Carmen's mother, shamelessly aware that if he arranged this striptease before signing the girl, and in the presence of the mother, it would seem more natural to her later when he asked her to disrobe.

"But why?" the pathetic Mrs. Leventhal had whined.

"Because so many of the beginning jobs are for catalogs for children's undergarments and swimwear. The way her body looks is vital to her getting work. If you'd rather she didn't, then perhaps you should look for another kind of job for her."

"No, no, Carmen, do as he says," Mrs. Leventhal had said, as he had known she would — for although Carmen was dressed expensively, the dress was so new that the Macy's tag still dangled inside the sheer sleeve, while Mrs. Leventhal's own dress was old and shabby. This was an obvious sign that the mother had poured every cent into her daughter's audition and desperately needed the income her success as a model would bring.

Even at twelve, Carmen was no dummy. She knew she was in trouble, but she did as she was told, and removed her dress. And when he pressed further, she pulled her filmy slip off over her head, removing with it the last vestige of her youthful modesty.

She never took her eyes off Byron Kirk as she undressed, already despising his smarmy smile and the short bristles of hair on his upper lip that passed for a mustache. But she didn't refuse him, for fear of losing this job. Carmen had spent too many nights waiting up until dawn for her mother to return from work, had eaten too many dinners of peanut butter and potato chips when there was no money for anything more nutritious, to let a little thing like this man's leer keep her from winning the opportunity to earn a living.

And in later months, when Carmen was well on her way to becoming a successful child model, she'd accepted the fact that Byron Kirk wanted more from her. It had begun with bear hugs and friendly kisses, but as time had passed, Carmen realized Byron was arranging for them to be alone in his office when she came in on a job. After the obligatory hug, his hands would linger on her body, the flat of his palm pressing the soft flesh of her nascent breasts, his hot, hairy breath scalding her neck, his belt buckle rhythmically prodding her bottom.

This much she was willing to endure, because the payoff was that since she had begun to work steadily, her mother had been able to cut her own work back down to two nights a week. But every once in a while, Byron would go too far, turning Carmen to face him, and with eager hands, tilting her full lips to his and tainting them with a wet, tobacco-stinking kiss. The feel of his mustache tickling her nose and mouth made her gag. And it revolted her that such kisses made his knees weak and trembly. In his pathetic, bent-legged posturing, he reminded her of her old splay-hipped German Shepherd, Woofer, urgently thrusting against the air as he attempted in vain to hump the miniature poodle next door.

She had been able to hold him off for almost a year, until shortly after her thirteenth birthday, when Byron had insisted on driving Carmen to a two-day shoot in Santa Barbara. Carmen had implored her mother to accompany them on the overnight trip, but by this time Mrs. Leventhal was a slave to the ebb and flow of alcohol in her blood, and she had begged off, telling Carmen she needed to attend her sons' soccer game. They had both known she would be settling into her faded Barcalounger with a fifth of Jack Daniels, leaving the boys to find their own way to the soccer field and home again.

When Carmen and Byron had arrived at the hotel, Carmen had not been surprised to learn that Byron had reserved a two-bedroom suite for them, rather than two separate rooms. "I promised your mother I'd look out for you," he'd told her, playfully blowing cigar smoke out of the gap between his front teeth.

She had not been amused. "I'm sure my mom would want me to have my own room," Carmen had tried hopelessly. But she'd known without being told that a line would be crossed that night, and for the first time in her young life, she hadn't known what to do. If she rebuffed Byron's advances, she would lose her job and the income her family so desperately needed. But the alternative made her sick to her stomach with disgust and fear.

After dinner in the hotel dining room, and ice cream, courtesy of room service, Carmen had gotten into her bed and waited. Sure enough, she'd heard the doorknob turn and saw Byron peer in. Feigning sleep, she'd waited as he'd crept close to the bed and slipped under the blanket with her. His naked body had sent a shiver of repulsion through her — the combination of hairy places and smooth skin, of spongy cushions of fat and protuberances hardened as bone. As he had rubbed himself against her, she'd felt the queasiness grow in her stomach, and suddenly she'd known what to do.

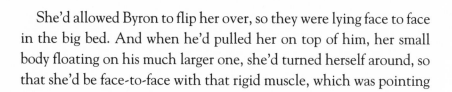

She'd allowed Byron to flip her over, so they were lying face to face in the big bed. And when he'd pulled her on top of him, her small body floating on his much larger one, she'd turned herself around, so that she'd be face-to-face with that rigid muscle, which was pointing its accusing finger at her.

That was all it took. She instantly retched, heaving up a revolting, lumpy sludge of undigested steak, French fries, and ice cream, smothering his erection with the warm bile of her hatred. Byron had leapt to his feet and run into the bathroom, vomiting all the way, in sympathy for his poor deflating member.

That had been the last time Byron or any man had taken advantage of Carmen. And although she'd never told this story to anyone, least of all her mother, she had kept it in her heart, remembering it whenever she needed an extra ounce of resolve to do what was needed to take control of a situation.

She was thinking about it as she pulled the 190 SL into a handicapped parking spot in front of the Chic Salon. Hanging the blue handicapped placard on the rearview mirror, she wondered if the Beverly Hills metermaid ever considered it odd that a handicapped person was driving a stick shift sports car. Since she'd *borrowed* the sticker from an open van two months ago, she hadn't had any problems using it.

But she only used it in emergencies. And it was an emergency — she couldn't be late for her hair appointment, or Rodney would have a fit. Besides, if she were late she'd miss Lacy Choate, and that was the reason she had scheduled the appointment on the afternoon of a night when she had no date.

It was sheer serendipity that she learned that Rodney did Lacy Choate's hair. One day when Carmen had missed her standing 8 A.M. appointment, she'd rushed in for a quick blow at 3 P.M. and found Rodney working on a glossy-haired matron, who he introduced as Lacy Choate, Mrs. Leo Choate.

Rodney loved to tell his society clients that Carmen was a famous reporter for the *Times*. It was a win-win situation: it boosted Carmen's ego to be introduced to movers and shakers, and the nouveau rich and would-be famous women he serviced loved to meet a writer who had the power to make their husbands' names household words. Often he got large tips from both parties.

When he'd introduced Carmen and Lacy Choate, the two women had not talked much, but each had stored the other's name in her memory, in case it could later be of some use. And indeed, when Carmen had read Leo Choate's name in Ralph's rough draft of his WIT story, she knew immediately where she could get the information she would need to upset his applecart.

Soothing strains of Erroll Garner greeted her ears as she entered the salon. Thank God Rodney had stopped with the rock'n'roll. She loved to dance as much as anybody, but being trapped in a small room with the chatter of ten other ladies *and* the loud music was more than Carmen could bear. Besides, it would be hard enough to carry on a conversation with Lacy Choate over the ambient noise of the salon without having to compete with the Rolling Stones.

Carmen picked up a pink robe from the receptionist and went to the dressing room to change. She could see Lacy already in Rodney's chair. He had begun the painstaking job of painting the color into her hair. Even from ten feet away, Carmen could see the abundant gray roots flowering on Lacy's scalp, and she silently thanked her mother for giving her good hair genes: her own mane was a flagrant red mass, and what gray there was provided a stunning patina rather than an indication of age.

"Carmen, darling, are you early, or am I late?" Rodney had been expecting Carmen, but he played his role with panache, figuring his tip would be commensurate with the success of the skit. "Sit, sit," he said, motioning her to a nearby chair.

"It must be me," Carmen said." I've been so busy this week, I'm wound up like a clock." Grateful for the entree, she gave Rodney a peck on the cheek and settled down in the closest chair.

"Well, unwind for a minute dear while I finish doing Lacy's color. You know Lacy Choate, don't you? Lacy, Carmen Leventhal from the *Times.*"

The two women exchanged nods. Lacy's hello was tempered by her embarrassment over having to be social while having a beauty treatment. But also evident in her face was the look of someone eager to make an impression on a representative of the press.

For her part, Carmen relished the superiority she felt, because she looked her best while Lacy Choate looked her worst. "Of course! You're Leo Choate's wife." She didn't waste any time bringing business into the conversation, because she could see that Rodney had only a few more minutes of work to do on Lacy's head before he put her under the dryer to bake.

"Do you know my husband?" Lacy fell easily into Carmen's trap.

"I like to think I know all the movers and shakers in the business community, and Leo is certainly one of them," said Carmen, knowing flattery would go a long way with someone like Lacy. "I understand he's on the brink of something enormous."

"He's got so many irons in the fire it's hard to keep track," Lacy hedged, closing off this avenue of conversation.

Carmen retreated to another tactic. "Didn't I see you at the Millhouse's party last week? You had on that gorgeous lavender Chanel suit."

Lacy jumped at the bait. "Yes, were you there too? I'm sorry, my memory for names is almost as bad as my memory for faces."

Carmen was on thin ice. All she knew about the Millhouse gathering was what she had read in the society column the day before. "I just love Bob and Jean, don't you? Their home is so conducive to entertaining. It has such a wonderful flow."

Lacy nodded, "I know, and their chef makes the best gravlax I've ever tasted."

"To die for," Carmen gushed, and decided to play her trump card. "You know, I ran into Alice Whitney-Smith at the Club."

"The Pacific Club?"

Carmen nodded. "And she told me Jean has the salmon flown in live from Seattle just so her chef can make the gravlax."

"I've heard that too," said Lacy.

Of course you have, you twit, MaryLou Lewis wrote it in her society column, Carmen thought. She waited for Lacy to pick up her clue about Alice Whitney-Smith, and sure enough, after a reasonable pause, Lacy continued, "How well do you know Alice and Paul?"

"Oh, not very. I did a story on WIT a few years ago, and we've kept in touch since then." This was not strictly a lie. She had worked as an editorial assistant on a story about WIT in October of 1987, but it had been pulled because of Black Monday and never printed. But Lacy didn't need to know this.

Carmen took the next step. "You two must be pretty close, what with your husbands' new business deal. A brilliant move on Leo's part, I must say, marrying WIT and Dominion."

Lacy stared at Carmen for a second, as though not sure she should say anything, but ultimately she couldn't resist the temptation. "You know, I was the one who got the men together."

"Really?" Carmen loved it. Lacy's ego was so monstrous that she couldn't even bear for her husband to get the credit for the deal.

"That's it, Lacy," Rodney cut in.

Carmen shot him a dirty look. Lacy was just getting to the good part! But Rodney was one step ahead of her. "Why don't we skip the dryer today, your hair will be burnt to a crisp. If you and Carmen want to just change seats, I'll do her trim while your color sets."

The two women changed seats, and Carmen said to Lacy, "I'd love to hear the story."

"Well, Alice and I are both members of the Blue Ribbon Four Hundred, at the Music Center. And one day we got to talking . . ."

With barely an outward sign, Carmen flipped on the miniature tape recorder she'd put in her pocket. She only used the tape to jog her memory, unless it was absolutely necessary to use it as evidence.

$\mathcal{S}$am hated charity dinners. It wasn't that he was stingy; in fact he liked being able to swoop in like an angel of mercy and donate a large chunk of cash to a good cause.

It was the stilted socializing he hated, the dreary no-host cocktails beforehand, with watered-down Dewars costing five dollars a pop, even though you'd paid $500 a head for the ticket. Then, on to a meal in a crowded hotel ballroom, which was totally devoid of style, where food equally lacking in taste was served. And finally, the after-dinner speeches, which often dragged on interminably, inspiring jokes such as, "I spent the weekend at the Heart Association Ball last Thursday night."

The mayor's dinner was going to be the height of bullshit, because the event couldn't even hide beneath the guise of a charitable cause. It was a political fund-raiser, all proceeds going toward the reelection of Mayor Chris Carson. Most of the tables had been bought by large corporations who either owed Carson a favor or wanted one from him. Sam fell into the latter category: the biggies at Sanwa had asked for his help in currying favor with the mayor for an entertainment complex they wanted to finance downtown. The problem was, the proposed location was near the Music Center, and some members of the City Council felt that two competing cultural centers within a few blocks of each other would dilute the attendance at both.

The mayor had yet to take a stand, and if Sam could win him over to the Sanwa point of view, which was that the two centers could uti-lize one giant parking structure and an effective shuttle service, which would cut costs and service the needs of both, it would be a major victory for Sanwa and would, needless to say, inflate his own stock with them.

Sam slowed the Porsche to a stop at the California Incline and squinted into the sun dipping into the expanse of ocean that lapped at the Santa Monica shore. He loved the last few miles of the drive home down Pacific Coast Highway — the sight of sand and sea was calming, and it was especially beautiful now, at sunset. Because most of his calls to Japan had to be placed after five in the afternoon, Sam usually missed this scene. Still, he actually enjoyed being in the office after all of the others had gone home. He simply didn't need other people around to validate him.

But this night he did not have time to enjoy the sunset. He'd barely have time to change into his tux before the limo appeared to pick them up. He decided he'd better call Enid to make sure she was getting ready. He dialed the car phone. Enid answered almost immediately.

"Hello?"

"Hi, hon, it's me."

"Oh Sam, hi, where are you?"

"Just starting up the coast. I should be home in five minutes if this light ever changes. Anything I should know?"

"Just that I love you."

"Oh, that. Nothing important?" He often tried to coax a conversation out of her on his car phone. It made the ride home pass faster, and sometimes he even felt they communicated better via telephone. But not this night.

"Sam, I'm getting dressed. You don't want me to make us late, do you?"

"What are you wearing?"

"You'll see when you get here. Bye." Her voice was not angry, just firm.

"You're no fun. See you in five." He hung up. As the light changed, he decided to call his partner Jim to tell him about Carmen Leventhal's rumor about their mutual partner Leo. Jim and Sam had met in law school and had been close friends for almost three decades, partners for eight years. He dialed Jim's number, and Jim's wife Marcie answered.

"Hi, Marcie, Jim around?"

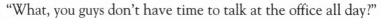

"What, you guys don't have time to talk at the office all day?"

"Gosh, I left nearly forty minutes ago. Who knows what might have happened in all that time?"

"Well, you'll have to wait until tomorrow to find out, because he's in his car on the way to Orange County and his car phone's out."

"Oh, right, he's got a dinner with the Shortfall Group. I forgot."

"Maybe you call it dinner. I call it a bacchanal. I swear I don't know how he makes it home some nights."

Sam silently agreed. Jim was one of his best pals, and the only one of his partners that Sam really trusted. But everyone had a weak link, and Jim's was his health. Sam was one of the few people who knew the truth, that Jim had a problem with bulimia, an unlikely disease for a forty-six-year-old businessman, but a potentially deadly one nevertheless, especially when coupled with Jim's nervous tendency to drink too much at business dinners.

The problem was Jim worked too hard and worried too much. Sam knew well how difficult it was to be a first-string player in the high stakes game of international law and finance and still maintain a semblance of a normal life. You tried to take time to enjoy all of the perks a successful career afforded, but you worried constantly that if you were not on the field every second, you would miss an important play. Sam always felt he had done a good job of juggling the two sides of his life, enjoying both the work and its reward. But lately, Enid had been pointing out to him with increasing regularity that he had been practically living at the office.

"Well, think of it this way, you're getting out of this damn dinner for the mayor," he said to Marcie.

"That's true. Look, I've got to run. I've got a meeting with the caterer for Tracy's wedding."

"The wedding! That's coming up pretty soon now, isn't it?"

"The invitations go out next week, if I ever get a list from the mother-in-law to be. I wish someone would write a book on etiquette for in-laws so I could tactfully give it to Margette."

"Well, tell Jim I called," said Sam, not wanting to get dragged into *that* discussion.

"I'll leave him a note, but I can't promise he'll be in any shape to read it when he comes home," Margie said.

"No big deal. This is just a nuisance call. I'll see him tomorrow."

Sam hung up, deciding it was just as well not to raise Jim's volatile blood pressure over a rumor. If the WIT story was true, he'd find out soon enough.

4

Patrick

Patrick tugged on the cummerbund of his Prada tuxedo. It was annoyingly snug — but so was everything in his closet this month. Between films he tended to gain ten or twelve pounds, and rather than alter his wardrobe or buy clothes in a larger size, he wore them tight to remind himself that he needed to watch what he ate.

But now, waiting in Sara's living room, thinking about the long, uncomfortable evening ahead, he wished he had asked wardrobe to ease the buttons just a tad so he could at least enjoy the meal.

"Sara, it's getting late."

The last time he'd checked, she was nowhere near ready. She seemed to lack a sense of time. Sometimes he wondered if she could even *tell* time. Anyway, there was no rushing her when she was getting dressed. So he contented himself to sit in her living room and watch *Entertainment Tonight*, while he savored the last of the Spago pizza.

The pizza was delicious cold, even better than it had been hot. But God, it pissed him off to see that Steven Segal was on again, this time in a spot about celebrities and their homes. He made a mental note to tell Peter to call *E.T.* to drop a few hints about the Biedermeier. To hell with maintaining his comic image — if Steven Segal could score points for his taste in flowers, which ran to pseudo phallic anthuriums — not that he could even pronounce the name — then Patrick could score a few on the side of good taste.

"Sweetie, could you give me a hand?"

Patrick flicked off the television and followed the scent of Sara's Opium into the bathroom. She was standing on the toilet.

"I know there's a good reason why you're up there, but I can't for the life of me imagine what it is."

"I wanted to see if my dress is long enough, and there isn't a full-length mirror in here."

"The dressing room is nothing but mirrors."

"Yeah, but the light's better in here."

Patrick knew better than to argue with Sara. She had her quirks, but she was a stunning girl, and thanks to years of acting classes, she really knew how to make an entrance.

Tonight she was wearing a lime-green sheath that was up to her Adam's apple in front and down to the crack of her buttocks in back. It was one of Patrick's favorites, especially when they danced, because people always turned around to stare at Sara's back, and voila, there was Patrick's face beaming at them over her shoulder.

"What can I do?" he asked.

"Could you get the buckle on my shoe? If I bend that far this'll rip."

Patrick sighed and bent over to buckle the shoe. "If only my fans could see me now, prostrate in front of a toilet seat."

"Oh, Paddy, you know you love dressing me."

"I love *undressing* you, and that's what I'm going to do if you don't stand still. It's hard enough to see without my glasses." By squinting and holding her foot at arm's length, he was finally able to locate the tiny hole and slip the buckle into it.

"Oh, God!"

"What now?"

"How am I going to get down from here? This damn dress is too tight."

The question was, how had she gotten up there in the first place? "Sara, we do have to arrive sometime before the party's over. I am the emcee, remember?"

"Okay, okay. Help me unzip."

She turned around, giving him a glimpse of his favorite perspective. Her buttocks swelled like honeydew melons under the shiny green fabric, and as she peeled off the dress, revealing the rounded flesh, bare except for sheer-to-the-waist pantyhose, Patrick began to salivate. There was only one word for Sara — ripe.

She stepped down from the toilet seat and slipped back into the dress. With some reluctance, he rezipped it, and they were off.

Carmen

Carmen sipped her vodka tonic in the staid serenity of the Pacific Club bar, and waited. The place was deserted. No wonder, she thought, the power brokers were all over at the Regent Hotel in Beverly Hills for the mayor's fund-raiser — all except a few holdouts, who didn't have the net worth or the nuts to count.

It's where she would be, if life were fair. But it wasn't. You had to make your own breaks, and Carmen was in the process of making hers. She could have wangled a ticket to the mayor's dinner, convinced her editor that it was news, but she hadn't even tried. Eager as she was to see Sam Carrouthers decked out in a tuxedo, and to get a glimpse of *the wife*, she had work to do.

So instead she waited at the tedious Pacific Club bar, wearing a ridiculous black wig and tinted glasses, knowing sooner or later Ralph would come in — at least according to his Daytimer, which she'd "borrowed" that afternoon. *Deep Throat — Pac. Club @ 9*, it read. How typically unimaginative of Ralph to call his informer Deep Throat, like the guy in Watergate way back when. But then, nobody had ever accused Ralph of being Mr. Inspiration.

It was strange just thinking about a low-class lightweight like

Ralph at this private enclave of L.A.'s wealthy. How he'd gotten a membership was beyond her. But then Carmen knew Ralph had some deep secrets in his past. She suspected there was dirty money there, probably from some ill-reputed source. When she had more time, she would definitely check it out.

But tonight she had another agenda. She presumed Deep Throat was Ralph's code name for his sources for the WIT deal, and she was expecting him to show up with one of the players in tow. She knew he was still gathering information for his feature, trying to get it into print before the community got wind of it. *The dumb shit*, she thought, *he is going to be rabid when he finds out it's been leaked to Marty Wollinsky for his column.*

Marty had been thrilled when she'd called with the scoop, and she knew he would never, ever reveal a source. Still, Carmen worried. Ralph was a vindictive son of a bitch, and he'd string her up by her pantyhose if he found out she was responsible. But to Carmen the risk was worth the reward. It was even worth making a fool of herself, wearing this ridiculous getup and paying for her own drinks at this overpriced, overdone club.

The bartender gave Carmen a smart-ass look that told her he knew she was not supposed to be there, but that she was attractive enough that he wouldn't give her a hard time, at least not on a slow night. She abhorred the service personnel in private clubs who acted like they were members themselves. Especially muscle-bound airheads like this one, who obviously valued his sperm count more than his I.Q.

"Can I buy you another?" he asked, leaning far enough over the bar to look down her dress. She could smell his arousal, it reeked like a pair of running shoes. If he came any closer, she knew she would lose it and belt him below the belt.

"No, thank you. I'll wait until my date arrives," Carmen lied, trying to maintain a modicum of restraint. He wasn't going to leave her alone, so she decided to make a quick trip to the ladies room to freshen her lipstick.

She turned in her swivel stool and put her feet on the floor. But the damn glasses she was wearing to modify her appearance distorted the distance to the floor, and she stumbled, twisting her ankle and crumpling to the floor in an unglamorous heap.

At the same moment, Ralph entered the bar in the company of two other men. *Damn, she thought, just when I wanted to be inconspicuous, here I am groveling on the floor.* She ducked her head as though she were examining her ankle, hoping Ralph would not recognize her. Luckily, he was too far into his evening's refreshment to give her more than a cursory glance.

The bartender and the assistant manager rushed to her side and helped her to her feet.

"Are you all right, Madame?"

"Yes, I'm fine, thank you. But you should do something about these stools. They're absolutely treacherous."

"Yes, Madame. Er, perhaps you'd like to make yourself comfortable in the ladies lounge until you catch your breath." The assistant manager obviously thought she was a lush and wanted her out of the pretty picture his bar made. But Carmen was not going to let him off the hook. She knew he knew how easily a lawsuit could be filed.

"What I'd really like is a cognac, Louis XIII, if you have it, and perhaps I'll just sit for a minute in the booth by the window to collect my thoughts."

"Yes, ma'am." He nodded to the bartender who poured the liqueur and brought it to Carmen. The booth was so close to Ralph's wrinkled corduroy back that she could smell the cloying odor of his Old Spice aftershave and the residue of tobacco, which branded him a chain smoker. God, she would have loved a cigarette. But this was not the time.

The cognac was in a delicately monogrammed crystal snifter befitting its $100 an ounce price. She reached for her purse, pretending she was expecting to pay for it, but knowing the bartender would say, as he did, "It's on the house."

"Thank you," Carmen said, and took a sip, eager to be rid of this unctuous man and to tune into Ralph's conversation. She wished she could turn her head to see who his two companions were, but that would be too risky. Instead, she reached into her purse and flipped on her tape recorder, setting the open bag on the tufted leather ridge of her booth back, so that not a word would be lost.

". . . no, I'm serious. She had a pair on her that made Dolly Parton look like Kate Moss," said one of the men.

"That I would have liked to see," said the other.

"You've got to wonder how they grow them like that. Someone told me it's all the hormones they've been pumping into beef the past twenty years, makes dames' tits and asses blow up like inner tubes."

"Yeah, you prick 'em and they deflate."

"Not these, they were the real bazongas."

The three men giggled like little boys ogling a *Playboy* centerfold. *You'd think their vocal chords were attached to their dicks,* Carmen sneered silently. But she was glad to think she was getting it all on tape. Even if nothing else transpired, she could use what she already had to blackmail Ralph, just for the fun of it. Rita, his wife of twenty-four years, was the jealous type, and more than once he'd come to work the morning after a binge, sporting a bruise or bandage that could only have been the product of Rita's Revenge, as they called it around the office.

"Hey, here they come," said one of the men. And Carmen could hear them all struggling to get out of the booth and to their feet. She could hardly contain herself. Would it be Leo Choate and Paul Whitney-Smith? The bigwigs from Dominion Studios? Or might it be some anonymous corporate spies who had been running a relay between the parties, allowing them to keep the deal secret? Carmen turned her head slightly to get a glimpse of the expected guests.

"God damn it," she growled under her breath, no longer caring if anyone heard her. "Deep Throat my fucking foot!"

Walking toward Ralph's table were three ladies of the night, fairly bursting out of their Spandex dresses, smiling with lip-glossed lips, ready, willing, and able to tell all and do all.

Enid and Sam

"Sam, sit still. And stop flexing your neck muscles." Finally Enid was able to hook the clasp on the bow tie. She straightened Sam's wing collar. "There, you look fabulous."

"I hate these damn straight jackets," Sam growled, looking out the window at the line of limousines waiting to disgorge passengers at the hotel. Their car was still fifty yards from the entrance.

"Thank you, Enid, I think you're looking gorgeous yourself," she teased. She wasn't angry. It was typical of Sam to neglect to compliment her looks, while fussing over his own. It had to do less with personal vanity than with anxiety about matters of fashion.

"You know I always liked that dress. I picked it out, remember?"

"I know you like the dress, but how about me in it?"

"You're perfect, as always, and you know it." He put his arm around her, careful not to wrinkle anything. "In fact, I would much rather spend a quiet evening at home with you than go to this damn thing."

"Hey, this is your event, not mine. I'm just trying to be a good wife."

"And you are. Here we go."

The driver jumped out to open the door and Enid slid out, carefully raising her sable coat so it wouldn't drag in the gutter. Sam was right behind her, still grappling with his tie, a nervous habit Enid tried not to nag him about.

The ballroom of the Regent Hotel was awash with glamour. So much for the dictum that fund-raising dinners should be low key, saving the money raised by the event for the cause in question. This party was about opulence: the lavish decor, the expensive attire of the guests, and the number of white-jacketed servers passing hors d'oeuvres through the room seemed calculated to imply that Mayor Carson's popularity elevated him above monetary concerns. Enid fingered the diamond choker around her neck as she and Sam entered. "Thirty karats, one for every year," Sam had said when he presented it to her on her thirtieth birthday. "You're lucky I'm so much younger than you," she had teased him, knowing it gave him as much pleasure to adorn her with exquisite things as it did her to wear them.

Enid and Sam looked around, getting a feel for the crowd. The guests represented the wealthy and powerful of each subculture of Los Angeles society: movie executives mingled with real estate magnates, and bankers hobnobbed with scions of families with money so old their names read like a street directory of the city — Doheny, Irvine, Burbank, or a page out of the Fortune 500 — Firestone, Ahmanson, Bren. Even a sprinkling of luminaries from the art community were scattered about the room, noticeable by their avant garde dress rather than their faces.

As Enid and Sam were swallowed up in a crush of friends and acquaintances, Enid couldn't help but think what it would be like to come to an event like this with her famous neighbor. What a stir it would cause! She shivered, remembering how seductive he had been at lunch, how he had caught her off guard by implying that she might have an ulterior motive for inviting him to lunch.

Well, he was right. She'd do whatever it took to make her benefit for the Westside Women's Shelter a success. Naturally she wanted to raise enough money to fund an on-site medical facility for the Shelter, but there was more to it than that. High society revolved around charity events; everybody had a favorite cause. And the matrons who chaired the events were granted special status in the community. Enid wanted to secure her place as one of the elite, and the Shelter benefit was her ticket. It all depended on Patrick Drake, and her ability to get him to cooperate.

Enid watched Sam plunge into the fray of black-tied guests mobbing the bar, struggling vainly to get the attention of the bartender.

Why hadn't she told him about her lunch with Patrick? There had been plenty of time on the drive to the hotel, but for some reason she hadn't brought it up. She wasn't afraid he would be jealous; jealousy wasn't Sam's style. She guessed the reason had more to do with her desire to secretly savor the experience. Sharing it with Sam would dilute it somehow, and she was not yet ready to do that. Perhaps tomorrow.

On the way home from lunch, Patrick had driven very slowly, as though he were in no hurry to end their time together. It had seemed both natural and right when he'd grasped her hand and squeezed it just before she jumped out of the car.

"Thank you for a delightful lunch," he had said.

"Thank *you*," she had replied. And then, without thinking, she had added, "I hope we can do it again soon. I'd like to get to know you better."

His smile had been friendly but noncommittal, and she had run into the house quickly, so he couldn't see how embarrassed she was to have blurted this out, as though her mind had a mind of its own.

The phone had been ringing. It was Shelley. "Suzanne called me two and a half hours ago and said she saw you in Patrick Drake's car. Have you been with him all this time? What's going on? Does Sam know?"

"Just get over here and I'll tell you all about it."

Enid had barely hung up when the intercom buzzed. *Shelley already? She must have run all the way over,* Enid had thought as she had swung open the door. But instead of 5'4" Shelley, standing on the porch was Patrick, all 6'1" of him.

"I know you didn't mean *this* soon," he had smiled, the brightness of his teeth nearly blinding her, "but you forgot this in the car." He had handed her her lipstick.

"Oh, it must have fallen out of my jacket. Thanks a lot."

"No problem." He had turned back toward the walk. "I hope I will see more of you."

And he had winked at her, a wink that Shelley, who was just coming up the walk, had not failed to see.

🕶

Enid shook herself out of this reverie and looked for Sam. The
crush of men around the bar reminded her of housewives at a two-for-
one sale at Sears. But there was Sam, fighting his way out of the
crowd, carrying her Crystal Geyser, no ice, and his virgin Bloody
Mary. There had been a time when everybody drank; these days it
was considered gauche to have anything stronger than a white wine
spritzer.

"Jesus it's crowded in here. Carson must be more popular than I
thought," Sam reported.

"Sammy, Enid, I've been looking for you for absolutely hours!" A
wall of lacquered hair brushed across Enid's face, as a woman in an
elaborate Ungaro creation offered her a halfhearted air kiss, then
swept by her to give Sam the real thing. Enid didn't need to see the
face to recognize Lacy Choate, her old college roommate, wife of
Sam's partner Leo.

Enid had to hand it to Lacy, she really knew how to turn herself
out for these social events. The brilliantly patterned gown clung seductively to the shapelier parts of Lacy's body and draped loosely over
her problem areas, so only someone who knew her as well as Enid
could tell she wasn't the svelte size six she pretended to be, but
thanks to a magician of a seamstress, whose name she refused to di-
vulge, a strategically altered size eight.

But it was more than just the dress. Even the brilliance of the emerald necklace, which hung at just the right length to draw attention
to her freckled chest, was outshone by the dazzle of Lacy's personality. Her eyes flashed and flirted, her lips parted with feigned passion,
her cheeks flushed with promised fire.

Watching Lacy perform, and that was the only word one could use to describe her demeanor at public gatherings, Enid wondered how their friendship had survived the differences in their approaches to life. Right now Lacy was breathing down Sam's neck, leaning close for a tête-à-tête, while her eyes scoured the room seeking more significant quarry. Even though he knew she was not really focused on him, Sam maintained the posture of a polite gentleman, interested in what she was saying, but keeping his distance.

The lights in the lounge dimmed and rose twice, signaling the end of the cocktail hour. "Enid, why don't you and Lacy go on to the table? I want to talk to the mayor for a minute before we sit down." Sam's voice was tight with annoyance. Enid hoped Lacy hadn't made a tactless remark. Usually these didn't surface until later in the evening, when her tongue was loosened by a few too many glasses of wine.

"If Lacy's ready to go."

"I'd love to sit down. These shoes are killing me." Lacy lifted the hem of her dress to allow Enid to admire the delicate Manolo Blahnik sandals that were strapped to her feet. "Seven hundred dollars for two ounces of leather and a foot of satin ribbon, can you believe it?" she complained, loudly enough so half the room could hear.

"They're beautiful, though."

Why did Enid always reassure Lacy with compliments, especially when she knew her comment had been uttered for the benefit of the crowd, whom she thought would be impressed either by the price of the shoes or the exclusivity of the designer. Enid was impressed by neither. In fact, she thought the shoes were as ridiculous as Lacy's dress, which seemed more costume than couture. But then, theatrical excess was Lacy's style.

"Where's Leo?" Enid asked.

"Oh, he'll try to stop by later. He had a meeting."

Obviously that's what had upset Sam; he hated hosting a table that wasn't full. "Where are we?" asked Lacy.

"Table two. It should be right next to the mayor's."

"Good. Who else is with us?" Lacy was already plotting her social strategy for the evening.

"The Gunthers, Leslie and Brian Wolfe, and Rob Rizzo and whoever he's dating now."

"Oh, God, I hope you didn't seat me next to him. All he ever wants to talk about is his hunting trips to Alaska. How can you eat when someone's describing how they murdered a poor, helpless moose and hacked it to pieces? Oh look, there's Rodney." She blew a kiss in the direction of a dapper blond in a madras dinner jacket.

"Who's Rodney?" asked Enid.

"My hairdresser. It's amazing how those guys get around. I mean, what kind of person would invite a beautician to a fund-raising dinner like this?"

"Maybe he made a big donation."

"Hardly," Lacy snorted," Haven't you ever noticed that gays aren't into city politics? They're too busy raising money for AIDS research and 'Save the Whales'."

Enid was appalled by Lacy's smug narrow-mindedness but not surprised by it. "Well, there's nothing wrong with those causes."

"I didn't say there was. Are you okay? You look like you just saw a ghost."

Enid didn't answer. Her eyes were fixed on a couple threading their way through the tables toward the front of the room. Patrick Drake and Sara Benton. What in the world were they doing here? Enid felt strangely exposed. And Lacy had a special talent for sensing such things. She followed the direction of Enid's eyes.

"Isn't that your neighbor, over there with the Amazon queen? God, he sure knows how to pick'em. Look at her dress. Talk about skin tight. It's amazing she can even walk."

Enid didn't answer, turning her attention to the other guests who were now arriving at the table. Part of her prayed Patrick hadn't seen her, but another part hoped beyond hope that he had, and that he would acknowledge her in some public way.

Patrick, not so fast." Sara gave his arm a discreet tug. "I can't walk that fast in this dress."

"Sorry." Patrick slowed his pace. Despite the countless times he had emceed events like this, they always made him anxious. It didn't help matters that Peter, whose job it was to help him maneuver through the minefield of public functions, was working the premiere of Arnold Schwartzenegger's new movie. Not only did Patrick miss Peter's capable handling of the crowds, but he felt a stab of anxiety, wondering why Peter had chosen to be with Arnold instead of him. Was Arnold paying Peter something under the table, or did Peter think Arnold was a bigger star?

At any rate, Patrick and Sara were in the hands of Peter's assistant, Clarence, who understood none of the nuances of crowd management and had disappeared ten minutes ago when Sara sent him off to get her some cigarettes, which she couldn't smoke in the ballroom anyway.

Patrick wished he had worn his glasses. Whoever made the numbers for the tables designed them for people who had 20/20 vision. So intent was he on finding the little Number 1 that he nearly ran into Enid.

"Enid!"

"Hello, Patrick."

He flashed on the image of her, only hours old, as she'd leaned over the table at Giorgio's and pressed his hand to her bosom. He couldn't help but give her his warmest smile as she said, "I didn't know you'd be here tonight."

"They've got me doing some kind of introduction before the speeches."

"Excuse me, sir." A waiter pressed between Enid and Patrick to deliver the first course to the table. Enid and Patrick both looked at the plate he had set before her and began to laugh. Oysters on the half shell.

The intimate ring of this laughter caught Sara's ear, and her instincts flared. "Paddy, aren't you going to introduce me?"

"Sorry. Sara Benton, this is Enid Carrouthers, my next-door neighbor. Enid, Sara." The two women nodded at each other with the cold formality of two athletes competing in the same race.

"I'm Lacy Choate." Enid had completely forgotten Lacy, who was leaning so close that the bow on her dress was dragging in the remoulade sauce atop Enid's oysters. Fortunately, the pattern of the fabric was so ornate that she wouldn't even notice until she studied herself in the ladies room mirror later in the evening.

"Oh, yes, I'm sorry. Lacy, Patrick Drake and Sara Benton. Lacy and I went to school together. She's my oldest friend," Enid concluded awkwardly.

"Really? She doesn't look that ancient to me."

"What I mean is . . ."

"Silly, they know what you mean." As usual, Lacy moved right in. There was no way she was going to let Enid monopolize the most famous person in the room. "You know, Patrick, I'm your biggest fan."

"No. Impossible," he shook his head. Lacy looked confused, but Enid caught the teasing gleam in his eye. "My biggest fan weighs in at 378 pounds, lives in Muncie, Indiana. You couldn't be an ounce over, what . . ." Patrick hated pushy women and knew very well how to silence them. He saw this one suck in her breath as he appraised her body. "One hundred and thirty-five?" That ought to put her in her place.

He saw Enid's friend deflate, and noted Enid's small smile, and he knew he had hit the bitch where she lived. But then again, he was Patrick Drake, and he couldn't afford to alienate his public.

"That's including, of course, the twenty pounds that necklace must weigh." He flashed his phoniest smile at the woman and winked at Enid. Both Enid and Sara caught the wink.

"Paddy, shouldn't we get to our own table?"

"Right. God forbid our oysters get cold." He prodded Sara ahead of him and turned back to add, "Very nice to meet you, Stacy."

"Lacy."

"I'm sorry, *Lacy*. Enid, thanks again for lunch today. Why don't you give me a call tomorrow and we can pursue our conversation," he added quietly, hoping Sara wouldn't hear, or see his hand linger on the silken skin of Enid's shoulder as he passed.

Patrick and Sara slipped into their chairs just as the lights were lowered. But even in the dimness, Patrick could see that Sara was seething. He tried to squeeze her hand but she pulled away from him and turned her attention to the stage, her body radiating waves of anger.

Patrick squinted back at Enid. The large, blurred shape of a man was just settling into a chair beside her.

"Yo, Mr. Drake, we need you backstage, if you don't mind."

He didn't mind at all.

2

5

Sam

Sam woke up with another headache. It was rooted at the base of his neck and stemmed up behind his right ear, flowering into a throb at his temple. What a way to start the day.

He rolled over to see if Enid was awake. Her magic fingers often worked wonders when his head got like this. But Enid's side of the bed was empty, already cold. He turned back to see the clock. Only 5:47. Strange, *he* was the alarm clock in the family, the first one up, the one nudging her out of bed in time for yoga at Shelley's.

But today, getting up and working out was going to be a chore, even for him. This awful headache.

It took him another minute to remember its source. *Leo, damn him.* He had never shown up for the benefit last night, neglecting even so much as a call of apology. It gave Carmen Leventhal's prediction about the WIT deal even more ominous credence.

And then he remembered that she'd said there would be something in today's paper.

Sam threw back the covers and swung his legs over the side of the bed, sitting there just a minute to get his bearings. He had a desperate need to pee, but an even more urgent desire to see what the morning paper's business section contained. Slipping into a pair of shorts, he rose stiffly and padded down the stairs to the front door.

Outside, the earliest rotation of joggers was trotting by. They passed in waves, beginning just after dawn and continuing on until after nine o'clock. It gave Sam a reassuring sense of continuity to see the same people running by each morning during the brief time it took him to retrieve the paper. It was maybe thirty seconds round-trip, and invariably he'd spot two or three of his regulars — the guy with the Akita, the couple in matching running tights, the mumbler with Tourette's syndrome, who seemed to be cursing the world with every step he took.

But today Sam had eyes only for the paper. He was already leafing through it to find the business section when the guy with the Akita passed and paused to let his dog mark the pole of Sam's mailbox. No wonder it was turning green.

Sam closed the door behind him and got only as far as the kitchen before he found the business section. He spread it out on the counter. Nothing on page one, or on two. Relief began to trickle into his body. She was wrong. It was all bullshit.

Then he saw it, halfway down page three, in what Sam called the "surprise column" because it functioned like a rumor mill, hinting at what was being talked about around town before the deals were in ink. It was always a toss-up whether you wanted your business to be mentioned in the surprise column. On the one hand, when two parties saw their names conjoined in print, it gave a sense of reality to an imminent deal. On the other hand, sometimes the announcement came too soon, when one or both was still bruised from conceding a sensitive point. In that case, the publicity served as the kiss of death to a floundering negotiation.

Sam had no idea which category the WIT/Dominion deal announcement fell into. He only knew that his gut clenched into a knot when he read the paragraph.

> Word around town is that Leo Choate has single-handedly engineered a powerhouse deal, selling a

controlling interest in Dominion Studios to Tokyo-based World Investment Trust. Sources say the ink is almost dry on an agreement which will put Choate at the helm of the movie studio in this surprise hostile takeover. Paul Whitney-Smith of WIT puts the buying price at US $1 billion. It is unclear whether Choate's partners at the law firm Ingersol, Choate, Carrouthers and Morris will be a part of the new management team, or if a new executive roster will be formed.

Sam ripped the page from the paper and took it with him to the bathroom. There was only one way to dignify such horseshit.

Enid

It usually took Enid all of five minutes to get out of bed and into her exercise clothes for her workout at Shelley's. Yoga class was no beauty contest, so she didn't waste time on elaborate ablutions. But that was before she found out Patrick had been observing her from his bedroom as she passed his house.

So today, since her body clock had awakened her thirty minutes earlier than usual, she spent the extra time making sure her hair, teeth, and face looked their best. Then she turned her attention to her gear.

The drawer of tights and leotards was a jumbled mess of brightly colored jersey and lycra. There was simply no way to keep it neat; she didn't even try, since everything stretched so tightly over the body that all wrinkles were removed — except, of course, those caused by contours of fat, muscle, and bone. She knew exactly what she was going to wear — the flesh-colored tights he had teased her about. She hoped Patrick would be awake and watching, and that he would get the private joke.

Over the tights she slipped on her newest leotard — neon green with a thong back, cut waist high at the legs. She chose it because she knew the style made her look thinner, and she definitely wanted to look her best today. Just in case he was looking out his window.

A glance at the clock told her it was already 6:10. She'd better get a move on it. When she passed through the bedroom on her way downstairs, she was surprised to see that Sam's side of the bed was empty. Had he left the house without saying good-bye?

She saw the newspapers spread across the counter as she passed through the kitchen, but still no Sam. "Sam?" she called.

"In here," his voice boomed, from the guest bathroom near the front door.

"What are you doing in there?"

"What do you think?" His gruff tone signaled to her that there was no point trying to find out what was bothering him.

"Well, I'm going to Shelley's. Will you be here when I get back?"

"Nope. I've got a game at 6:45."

"Okay then. We don't have any plans tonight, do we?"

"Enid, I don't exactly have my calendar in front of me."

"Okay, okay. I'll call you later on today. Bye-bye."

She didn't wait to hear his good-bye, knowing the slam of the front door would clearly communicate that she did not appreciate his rudeness at this early hour, especially when she was just trying to be nice.

Usually Enid jogged to Shelley's house, her own form of warm-up for the workout ahead. But today she walked slowly, lingering in front of Patrick's house, leaning against the partially built wall to remove an imaginary rock from her shoe. She tried to sense if he was awake, and if he was watching, but without actually looking in the window it was impossible to know. And if he were there, it would be too embarrassing. So, retying her shoe, she continued on to Shelley's and ran up the stairs.

Inside, Keri, the teacher, was just cueing up the first tape. Shelley and the others, Suzanne from across the street, and JoBeth, who lived a few blocks away, were already on their feet, ready to begin.

"Hi, everybody."

Enid squeezed into the only available space, always the last spot filled, because it was next to the window, and passersby on the street could see in, if they tried hard enough. But today Enid didn't mind being observed. She felt like the star in a movie about her own life — only she had yet to figure out the plot.

Patrick

Enid had no way of knowing that as she passed Patrick's house, he was thinking about her. He hadn't seen her stop by his wall, in fact he wasn't even in the house. He was at Sara's, where he had spent the night.

And it had been one hell of a night. Sara had seen right through his lunchtime lie about Enid and her husband inviting them to dinner. Although he thought he had been clever, explaining to Sara that she had misunderstood him, that Enid had invited them to sit at her table at the mayor's dinner, not to go out to dinner, Sara had not been convinced. And it had taken hours for her anger to turn to tears, at which point he knew he had won, because Sara always needed to be comforted when she cried. Once he had his arms around her, he had begun whispering in her ear and stroking her hair, which eventually had led to kisses and caresses, and finally, to passionate love-making. He was continually surprised that their very best sex followed their fiercest arguments. And although he hated to fight, sometimes it was worth it.

This time, their loving had been particularly intense, and he had fallen into a deep sleep soon after, only to be awakened by Sara's tossing and turning and complaints of a stomachache. It was only by sheer luck that he had gotten her out of bed and into the bathroom before she had begun to vomit. And then, for the rest of the night, once an hour or so, she'd raced to the toilet.

Just past six, as Sara was dry heaving into the pot for the umpteenth time, Patrick decided it had definitely been a bad oyster that had caused her to be so sick. Thinking of the oysters reminded him of Enid. So he tried to take his mind off Sara's retching by remembering the look on Enid's face when he'd greeted her the night before, and the secret smile he had brought to her lips when he had put down her friend.

Instinctively, he knew there was a deep rivalry between the two women, one to which neither probably admitted. They were both attractive, but in such different ways! And he could see how some men might have been torn between them. A triangle was never a comfortable shape, especially when one of its angles had a killer instinct, which Enid's friend so obviously did.

Patrick himself was not in the least attracted to Lacy. It was clear to him that she lacked the capacity for warmth and tenderness, the emotional attributes he valued most in a woman. Enid, on the other hand, seemed to have both of these qualities. Interesting.

He looked at Sara, lying in an exhausted heap over the toilet, a trickle of vomit clinging to the corner of her lip. Clearly she would be out of commission for a while. And for some reason he had all the energy in the world. Maybe he would give Enid a call later in the day. Maybe they could continue where they had left off. What was the name of her charity group?

Carmen

Carmen had been up since five o'clock. But this was nothing unusual. Looking good took time, and Carmen was willing to put in the extra hours if it helped her achieve her goals — and she was certain it would.

Her daily routine started with a bath. While she soaked in a tub scented with Eau de Vie bath oil, she applied an Ole Henriksen face mask and read *Investor's Daily*, which had arrived the night before. By the time she'd finished the paper, her legs were ready to be shaved from ankle to crotch. Then she drained the tub and turned on the shower to wash and condition her hair. On Tuesdays and Fridays the routine also included a hot condition treatment, which Rodney insisted would diminish her split ends.

With her hair wrapped in a towel, she attended to her nails and eyebrows and listened to the news on KNX. Then it was time to blow dry her hair and set it with steam rollers. She hated the steam rollers, because if she didn't pay close attention to the way she rolled them, her hair tangled and burned. But she had tried curling irons and perms and just didn't feel right about the results.

While the rollers did their job, Carmen rewarded herself with a cup of coffee, and toast or cereal. Her favorite was Grape Nuts topped with raisins and bananas. By the time the coffee was brewed, the *Times* had arrived. Carmen read the pertinent sections while she ate, the TV switched on to the early morning news. She was careful to review the world and business sections first, but she took time for the sports page as well. Not that she had any personal interest in sports, but she had yet to meet a businessman who wasn't a fanatic about the Lakers, the Ducks, or the Kings, and either UCLA or USC, depending on his family background. She knew it paid dividends to have something to talk to men about besides business, and since she doubted she could ever engage a guy in conversation about an article in the Lifestyles section, that was the only one she allowed herself to omit.

Aha!

Her review of the business section yielded pay dirt in the form of Martin Wollinsky's column on page three: the blurb about Leo Choate that she had planted. To celebrate, Carmen brewed herself a second cup of coffee, and even added the dregs of milk and Nutrisweet from her cereal bowl to sweeten it. As she drank, she planned her strategy. She would call Sam Carrouthers the minute she got to the office to make sure he had seen the article. If she called early enough and dropped enough hints about the new information she had gleaned from Lacy Choate yesterday, perhaps she could convince him to meet with her sometime during the day.

By 6:30 A.M. she was selecting her outfit. In light of her special plan for the day, Carmen opted to wear the new St. Laurent blouse from Neiman's, even though they hadn't yet sent the bill. She usually let new clothes age a bit in her closet before wearing them, but this was a special occasion, and she knew the blouse showed off her figure.

It took her a good twenty minutes to apply her makeup so it looked like she was not wearing any, and by 7 A.M. she was admiring her reflection in the mirror, as others would admire her throughout the day. Almost as an afterthought, she remade the bed, using the Frette sheet she'd been saving for a special occasion. You never knew.

Enid

"So tell us what's going on with you and Patrick Drake."

JoBeth was a real estate agent. Tact and patience were not in her vocabulary, and waiting until the hour of yoga was over had only heightened her curiosity.

"What are you talking about?" Enid asked innocently, as if she didn't know Suzanne had saturated the whole neighborhood with her sighting of Enid in Patrick's car.

"But Suzanne said . . ." JoBeth looked at Suzanne, who pretended to be busy popping Evian caps.

"I didn't think it was any secret," Suzanne said defensively. "Otherwise, you'd have met somewhere private instead of driving around out in the open like that."

"Well?" JoBeth demanded.

"Well what?" Enid was taking perverse pleasure in making her friends drag the story out of her.

"Did you or did you not spend the afternoon with Patrick Drake?

Four pairs of eyes bored into Enid as she slowly raised the glass and drank all twelve ounces of water before answering. "As a matter of

fact, we did have lunch together."

Squeals of excitement awakened Suzanne's infant twins, who immediately began to cry. Suzanne sighed and went to comfort them. "Don't say a word until I get back!"

"Look, everybody, I've got to run," Keri called on her way out the door.

"You have got to be kidding. Don't you even care about this? I leased Patrick that house fourteen months ago, and nobody's even *seen* him, let alone had a meal with him."

"Yeah, well, I've got another class to teach, and I need the sixty bucks more than I need to hear the local gossip. See you Friday."

"So tell us everything!" Suzanne was back, a baby in each arm. "Shelley, take Josh."

"God, Sue, if I'd wanted a baby, I would have had my own," Shelley complained. But she took the child with great tenderness and rocked him in her lap. "Tell them, Enid," she said.

"What do you mean, tell *them?*" Suzanne hated to be the last to know the gossip.

"She told me the whole story yesterday."

"Not the *whole* story," Enid said. The others fell silent. "I saw him again last night."

"Twice in one day?"

"Where?"

"Does Sam know about this?"

"Yes. At the dinner for the mayor. No, Sam doesn't know yet. But I'm sure he'll be pleased."

"That you're having an affair with Patrick Drake? You must have a very open marriage," snorted JoBeth.

"I wish Dennis had been that open-minded. Maybe our marriage would have lasted more than two years," Shelley put in. She was never able to speak more than five sentences without bringing Dennis into it, even though their divorce had been final three years earlier.

"Why, did you have an affair too?" Suzanne asked, greedy for the dirt.

"Not that he ever knew about," Shelley smiled. "Just kidding," she added.

"Girls, we are getting off the subject. I want to hear about Enid and Patrick, and I'm supposed to show a house on Capri at nine," JoBeth said. "Come on, sweetie, tell all."

"First, we are *not* having an affair. Obviously! I invited Patrick to have lunch so I could ask him if he would let the Shelter do a premiere screening of his next movie, for my fund-raiser."

Enid saw Suzanne bristle and flush with jealousy at the mention of the fund-raiser and her use of the possessive pronoun. Suzanne had wanted the chairmanship herself, but the board of the Shelter had chosen Enid and had asked Suzanne to be publicity chairman, a role for which she, as the neighborhood gossip, was ideally suited.

"Where did you go for lunch?"

"Don't skip any of the details."

"We went to Giorgio's, and he said he'd let me know about the premiere." Enid rose to leave. "Speaking of the Shelter, we've got a meeting this morning, so I'd better get a move on. Suzanne, do you want me to pick you up?"

"No, I can't make it this morning," Suzanne said. She sat up a little straighter. "I've got news too. I'm having coffee with Caroline Grayson, you know, the West Coast editor of *Vanity Fair*. I think I've got her interested in doing a story about the Shelter." She looked around the room triumphantly.

"God, when you tell her that Enid's got Patrick Drake to do the benefit, she'll jump on it," said JoBeth. "Those magazines love a celebrity angle."

"Oh, but you can't mention it yet," Enid warned. "He hasn't said yes."

Suzanne's lips trembled. "Don't worry. I'm sure she couldn't care less about some B actor like Patrick Drake."

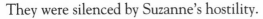

They were silenced by Suzanne's hostility.

"Well that's all he is. Name the last successful movie he made. Can you think of one?"

Enid started for the door. She didn't want to get into a catfight with Suzanne this early in the morning. "See you later," she said.

"Wait a minute. What is he like? I mean, really."

"Are you going to see him again?"

The questions were from JoBeth and Shelley, but Suzanne was listening too, even though she was busying herself with her children, pretending she could care less.

"He is exactly the way he is in his movies — funny, charming, sexy. Thanks for the class, Shelley. See you all later." Enid slipped out the door, leaving the others to speculate.

"Sam had better watch out, is all I can say," Suzanne said in an accusatory tone. "Patrick Drake is a ladies' man. Everyone knows it."

"Jesus, Sue. Enid and Sam have a great marriage. She's not going to jeopardize it, and you know it," snapped Shelley.

"Especially with her next-door neighbor. Can you imagine the logistics?" JoBeth gathered up her gear and headed for the door.

"Yeah, but did you see her face when she talked about him?" Suzanne countered. "Talk about infatuation. It was as plain as Pellegrino."

Patrick

Had it not taken Patrick ten minutes to get the Rolls started at Sara's, he would have been pulling into his driveway as Enid passed on her way home from Shelley's. As it was, she was already home and stepping into the shower when he finally pulled into his garage.

He could smell the trout sizzling even before he unlocked the door. *Good old Jeremy*, he thought. *He's worth every overpriced penny I pay him.*

"Who the hell's in there?" he shouted, absently throwing his keys and sunglasses onto the side table and dropping his jacket onto a chair, not caring that it slid onto the floor. Jeremy would pick it up later.

"Mornin', Patrick," Jeremy's Scottish brogue lilted from the kitchen. "Breakfast in five minutes."

"It had better be," growled Patrick, knowing Jeremy understood his humor and expected it. He pressed a button on his answering machine and listened to the tape rewinding.

"YoYo, whatalittlepreciouspup!"

The little ball of Yorkie fur jumped into his lap as soon as he sat down, licking his face with ecstatic abandon. "Phwew!" Patrick pushed him away. "What've you been feeding him?" he called to Jeremy.

"Kidneys."

"I liked it better when he ate chocolate chip cookies."

"The vet said that's what gave him gas. So you can have your choice — bad smells out of one end or the other."

Patrick set the dog back on the floor, remembering how cute he had been when his girlfriend-of-the-moment, Helena, had presented him to Patrick three Christmases before, a tongue attached to a ball of fluff that fit into the palm of his hand. Little did he realize that YoYo would become a one-dog destruction derby, destroying not only the carpet in his old condo ($175 a yard) but the hardwood floor beneath it (solid maple), to say nothing of one chewed sofa, four shredded pillows, and a countless number of clawed cabinets. The decimation of his condo had been the impetus for leasing this house. Anything to get away from the stench of those pee-stained carpets!

And whereas his relationship with Helena had ended two months after Christmas, he was stuck with the dog for life. Oh well, there were times when he was grateful for the unconditional love the mutt exuded.

Patrick knew that there was no way he would enjoy his favorite breakfast dressed in his tux from the night before, so he slipped into

his favorite old terry cloth robe while he listened to his messages —
two from LeMar, a hang up, and, oddly enough, a call from his ex-
wife Sandra.

The phone rang as he entered the kitchen. Jeremy picked it up.
"Hello? Oh, hi, LeMar. He just walked in. Just a minute." He ignored
the fact that Patrick was making slicing motions across his throat,
and handed his employer the phone and a cup of coffee.

"Yeah, whadda you want?" Patrick emptied three packets of
Sweet'n Low into his coffee.

"What I want is for you to finish reading that g.d. script from Dominion," chided LeMar, his Brooklyn accent thick with postnasal
drip.

Patrick envisioned LeMar, sitting at his immaculate desk at ICB,
a hands-free headphone attachment plugged into his ear and a retinue of trainee agents, assistants, and secretaries hovering around
him, hanging on his every word. LeMar thrived on the ministrations
of his staff, conveniently forgetting that it was Patrick's stature and
the agency commission on Patrick's hard-earned salaries that allowed
him to hold court in this fashion.

"Paddy, are you listening to me?" LeMar asked.

"I'm here," said Patrick.

"Kesselman's waiting for your answer. And you know what happens when you keep Kesselman waiting — he finds another actor.
Now, I know you're the greatest and the world is beating a path to
your door and all that crap, but the truth is, you need visibility. You
need a winner. And Dominion is prepared to put hefty advertising
bucks behind this picture."

Patrick closed his eyes and breathed deeply as Jeremy set the
steaming platter of fish and veggies in front of him. "LeMar, LeMar,
the sun has barely risen. I'm about to have breakfast, and quite
frankly, your tone of voice is not conducive to good digestion."

He heard LeMar sneeze and then yell to one of his minions, "Tell
her I'll be with her in a second." And then into the phone, "See what

I'm saying? That's Kesselman's office on the phone. Jeffrey wants to take a meeting with you ASAP to hear your thoughts on this thing. Now how in hell am I going to tell him you haven't read it?"

Patrick felt like saying, *you're an agent, lie to him like you always do.* But the last thing he needed right now was to alienate LeMar. Getting another agent at this point in his career might not be so easy. So instead he responded, "But I have read it. Some of it, anyway."

"And?"

"It needs tailoring, but I could be persuaded. . . ."

"Just let me set up a meeting for this afternoon. You'll have time to finish reading the script and then you can talk it over with him. Okay?" Patrick didn't answer. "Paddy, I wouldn't say this if it weren't true, but you need the money. Okay? There, I've said it."

Patrick sighed. He knew it was true. But he wished LeMar hadn't brought it up in front of the cast of thousands in his office.

Money! Although it looked like he was on top of the world, Patrick's finances were a confused jumble, and somehow there was never enough cash to cover everything. But working was such a pain. He needed to be coaxed into harness, and he knew that if LeMar didn't apply pressure, he'd never get around to doing anything.

"Yes, Master," he said finally. "Just make sure we meet over lunch. I'm not driving all the way over to Burfuckingbank to drink a Diet Coke in somebody's office."

"It wouldn't hurt you to miss a meal now and again," LeMar chided.

"Hey! Who do you work for, me or Jenny Craig?" There was an edge to Patrick's voice. He hated to be nagged about his weight, and LeMar knew it.

"Oh, come on, Paddy, don't get your ass in a sling. You're the one who comes crying when you can't fit into your wardrobe. Now let me make this call to Kesselman and set everything up. All right?" His tone was conciliatory. Like any good agent, LeMar knew when to back off.

"All right, all right," Patrick grumbled.

"Okay, pal. I'll get back."

LeMar hung up without saying good-bye, his standard exit. If you figured that he fielded two hundred calls a day, the lack of politeness was understandable.

Patrick eased the first bite of fish onto his tongue and savored its buttery flesh. Even LeMar and his diet police couldn't fault him for this meal. What could be healthier than fish and steamed vegetables? Patrick speared a Brussels sprout and popped it into his mouth. It was cooked to perfection. Jeremy might not be the best valet in Los Angeles, but he knew the way to Patrick's heart.

There was a manila envelope on the table next to his plate, and after a few bites, Patrick called out, "What's this?"

"Wallase brought it. The houseman from the Carrouthers. He didn't say what was inside."

Patrick took another bite, considering the envelope. Finally he put down his fork and knife and opened it. Inside was a wealth of printed material — brochures, fact sheets, press releases, and photographs of the Westside Women's Shelter, along with an elegant white note card with *Enid* engraved at the top.

He read the note, surprised at how childlike her handwriting was. *Dear Patrick,* it said, *I thought you might be interested in seeing some information about the Westside Women's Shelter. I hope it will inspire you to let us use your new movie for the fund-raiser. Not only would it be great for the Shelter, but I know you and I could have a wonderful time doing it together. I'll be waiting to hear from you. Enid*

He chuckled to himself at the last two lines. Just like a woman to taunt him with provocative promises of *a wonderful time* and *doing it together*, but still leave it to him to take the initiative. What the hell, maybe they could burn off a few calories together. He ate the last bite of fish and picked up the phone. "Jeremy, do you have the number for the Carrouthers?" he asked.

6

Enid and Patrick

nid was just going out the door to the garage when she heard the phone ring. She paused and waited for Wallase to answer it.

"Missy, Missy! he called. "Mister Patrick Drake is calling."

"Thank you. I'll get it down here."

That was fast. Wallase had only delivered the envelope minutes ago. Enid took a deep breath before picking up the phone, hoping her voice didn't betray either her excitement or her nervousness. "Hello?"

"Yeah, whadda you want?"

She was startled by his tone, but wasn't going to let it throw her. "I guess you got my note, so it must be obvious what I want," she said, hoping she didn't sound too flippant, too familiar, or too flat.

He chuckled, and she exhaled gratefully. "Yes, I think I have a very good idea what you want, my dear."

Enid had no way of knowing that Patrick always felt lascivious after a breakfast of fish and vegetables. That, and for some peculiar reason, airplane travel, were more stimulating to him than the pages of *Hustler*. Go figure.

"Well, now that my intentions are perfectly clear, is there any way we might . . . consummate a deal?" She had heard Sam use this phrase, and it always seemed to work for him.

"The sooner the better." Patrick's voice purred. "We could get together right now and . . . consummate it."

Enid looked at her watch. It was already 9:45, and she was supposed to be at the Shelter at 10. But clearly a meeting with Patrick Drake took precedence. "I'm supposed to be somewhere, but maybe I can be a little late. Shall I just come over, then?"

"I think that would be the best way, yes."

"Okay, I can be there in, say, five minutes?"

"I'll be waiting."

Enid hung up the phone and flopped down on the le Corbousier lounge next to it. My God, she thought, he invited me to his house! Her heart was beating so hard that for a moment she thought she might hyperventilate. But she closed her eyes and took a few deep breaths, and her heartbeat returned to a more regular pattern.

She had five minutes, what should she do? Comb her hair? Brush her teeth again? Apply new lipstick? Change her clothes?

The point was, what kind of an impression did she want to make?

Wallase was hovering at the top of the stairs, obviously curious why he hadn't heard the garage door open and her car start up. He said nothing, just gave her *That Look*, which was not at all inscrutable. It was more disapproving than any words could be.

"Wallase, I'm going over to Mr. Drake's house for a few minutes. Could you please call the Shelter and tell them I'm going to be a little late?"

Wallase was silent.

"I've asked Mr. Drake if he will let us use his new movie for the fund-raising event," she said, though why she felt compelled to explain her actions was a question she would have to ask herself later, when her brain could concentrate on something besides Patrick Drake. "So keep your fingers crossed that he says yes."

"Oh yes, Missy," Wallase said. He held up both of his hands with his fingers crossed. "I keep this way."

❦

Even though he was expecting company, Patrick had no intention of changing out of his tattered robe, but merely slipped on a pair of corduroy pants under it, so Enid wouldn't be put off by the skinny pallor of his legs. He was not the least bit concerned about his attire. He had seduced enough women to know that this unkempt, just-got-out-of-bed look was more alluring than the trendiest couture — just ask Calvin Klein, whose models always sported that befuddled post-coital look, along with their briefs.

There was just one pressing matter to attend to — getting Jeremy out of the house.

"Jeremy, d'you mind taking my tux to the cleaners? I may need it again this weekend."

Never careful with his clothes, Patrick had carelessly thrown his jacket on the foot of the bed at Sara's, and in her haste to get to the bathroom, she had grabbed it instead of her robe. She probably hadn't soiled it, but his mind was stuck on the image of her slumped over the toilet, his jacket clutched about her heaving body. Only dry cleaning would expunge the memory.

"And while you're out, maybe you could run the Rolls by the shop to check on the water pump."

Patrick was pleased with his cleverness. Not only would the car finally get some attention, but he would be able to anticipate Jeremy's return, because the throaty hum of the beast's engine when it entered the garage could be heard even in the bedroom — if by chance he and Enid ended up there.

But this subterfuge was not really necessary. Jeremy knew his boss well and understood his need for privacy when entertaining a lady. In the four years since he'd begun this job, he had seen, by his own count, eighty-seven different women drop in to be *entertained* by

Patrick. And that was during normal working hours. Who was to say how many appeared after 5:30? He had to admit, the thought of adding Mrs. Carrouthers from next door to the list was titillating, almost as good as the morning the wife of the CEO of Visual Arts appeared, dressed in transparent lounging pajamas.

By the time the doorbell rang, Jeremy had gathered up Patrick's tux and the other dirty clothes and was ready to leave. He let Enid in and himself out at the same time. "He's in the kitchen, Mrs. Carrouthers. It's just through there." Jeremy pointed through the living room to the swinging oak doors, and exited.

"Thank you, Jeremy."

Enid looked around, devouring the details of the room. The decor was just as Sam described it: comfortable and messy, with oversized, overstuffed furniture, brightly colored walls, and photographs of Patrick everywhere.

Enid wondered if Patrick really did have a model train set up in his bedroom. She'd seen photographs of it and had found it hard to believe that a grown man would decorate his most intimate space with child's toys. But now that she'd seen the house, she was more inclined to believe the story.

"Enid?" Patrick called.

Her heart turned over at the sound of his voice speaking her name. She followed the sound, replying, "Patrick, hi, Jeremy said — "

"I'm in the kitchen, come on in."

She pushed through the swinging oak doors into a room that was both kitchen and den. At one end was the full complement of appliances and cooking paraphernalia, and at the other, a cozy seating area. Patrick was on the phone, nestled on a chintz sofa near a fireplace which, even though it was mid September and already 71 degrees outside, crackled with the smell of burning manzanita wood.

He was curled up in a shabby blue bathrobe, the bristly stubble of two days' beard on his chin, contrasting the smooth, soft coat of the dog, who was curled up asleep on his lap. Enid's heart caught at the sight of this public icon in so private a pose.

How was she to know that this invitingly domestic tableau had been staged for her benefit, the fire newly lit, the dog bribed with its favorite treat, the grungy stubble on Patrick's chin doused with Zeus cologne, which the advertisements promised would *make your woman treat you like a god*. Even the phone call was fake, a computerized voice reciting the time.

But Patrick was an actor after all, and he had set this scene to enable him to play the part of "un homme chez lui" to perfection.

He made a kissing sound into the phone. "Bye, sweetie," he said, and hung up. "Sorry. Meg loves to gab."

"Meg Ryan?"

Patrick smiled enigmatically, neither a yes or a no. "We got to be great friends when we did *Wind Jammers* together in '91." He waited for her to tell him how much she'd loved the movie.

"I never saw that one," Enid admitted. "But I'm sure it was wonderful."

"Oh. Well, you should rent it some time. It was quite good. Would you like some coffee? I've finally mastered this espresso machine."

"Espresso would be great," she said. She knew she'd pay the price later for the jolt of caffeine, but she could tell he was disappointed that she hadn't seen his movie, and she had to make amends.

Patrick rose and rewrapped his bathrobe around him. "Pardon the way I'm dressed. Or rather, undressed."

"That's okay. You look . . ." she groped for the right word, ". . . comfortable."

"Like an old shoe, that's me." He turned away from her to manipulate the espresso machine.

She was afraid she'd hurt his feelings again with that careless choice of words, so she frantically wracked her brain for another subject. "I was surprised to see you at the dinner last night. Do you support the mayor?"

"Oh, no, that was a job. I stay away from politics. Peter, my public relations guru, insists that I never take a stand politically. He says that I might win a few fans by sharing their views, but I'd drive more people away if I were against their candidates. So I'm not even a registered voter. Sugar?"

"No thanks, black is fine."

He handed her a demitasse and sat again, this time only inches away. He looked at her intently, then took her chin in his hand and drew it toward him. "Open your mouth," he said, his voice so intimate he might as well have said *spread your legs.*

"Why?" Enid whispered.

"I just want to see something. Smile." Enid parted her lips a little and Patrick beamed. "There! That little wrinkle on the enamel of your tooth. I've got one too. Look."

He pointed to one of his molars, and sure enough, Enid could see a slight indentation in the tooth, second from the center. "The dentist has a name for it; I can't remember what it is."

"Me either. I never even think about it any more," she said.

"Try having your face blown up to twenty times its size on the screen," Patrick said, gritting his teeth. "Believe me, you'd think about it. You wouldn't believe how tiresome it is, the constant scrutiny. Sometimes I feel like a product. And all anybody cares about is the packaging, not what's inside."

He was fishing for reassurance, and imagined his shrink, Ellen, shaking her finger at him.

"But people do care about you as a person. That's why they love your films," Enid spoke her lines as though on cue. "What comes through is a warm, fun, sensitive man. At least to me."

"You mean they don't love me for my devastating good looks and animal magnetism?"

She'd done it again. "I didn't mean . . ."

"I'm just teasing." He took her hand and squeezed it. "I know what you mean, and thank you. I'm glad you can see a person through the persona." *Good,* he thought, *things are finally moving in the right direction.*

The phone rang. *LeMar, shit,* he thought. His timing was impeccable. Patrick sighed theatrically, "Probably my agent . . ." He picked up the phone. "Hello? Yes, LeMar . . ." He turned ever so slightly away from Enid to let her know that this was a private conversation.

And apparently she got the hint. She stood and took her espresso cup to the kitchen counter. Patrick put his hand over the mouthpiece of the phone and whispered, "Take a look around, make yourself at home. I'll only be a minute."

Enid nodded and headed for the living room. The little brown dog trotted along behind her, keeping a wary distance, but not letting her out of his sight. She bent to talk to him.

"So you're the one who needs that silly old wall built. Come here." She held out her hand, but the dog was obviously not interested in being friends. He ignored Enid's overture and trotted past her into a room off the living room. Enid followed him.

It was Patrick's study. Interestingly, its decor was completely different from the more public rooms. Bookshelves lined every wall, and a faded Oriental carpet replaced the wall-to-wall shag that made it difficult to walk in the living room. The little dog ran behind a beautiful antique desk and jumped into a suede chair, growling softly at Enid as she approached.

But she was not looking at the dog. She was looking out the window, staring at her own window, not ten feet away.

She could see into her own house from here! How could it be? The windows of her house were glazed with a tinted glass, which was supposed to make it impossible to see in. But from this vantage point, Enid could clearly see right into her own den, and there was Wallase bent over the filing cabinet, leafing through her papers without her permission. She almost rapped on the window to let him know she'd caught him in the act.

"Nice view, isn't it?"

Enid wheeled around. Patrick was leaning against the doorjamb watching her. She blushed, "I can't believe it. You can see right into my house."

"Really? I never noticed," he said, with a twinkle of sarcasm. Visibly suppressing a smile, he came and stood next to her, looking out the window. "Why, if we can see into your house, I'll bet that means you can see into mine," he said, his tongue firmly wedged in his cheek.

Enid could feel her body deflate like a punctured balloon. There was no point in denying it. "You've seen me?"

Patrick nodded.

"I'm so embarrassed." She tried to laugh, but it came out in a choked gasp, and she was afraid she was going to cry instead. "You must think I'm horrid."

"Not at all, I'm flattered, really," he said softly. "I just wondered, all this time, what you could possibly be looking at."

It took Enid a moment to answer. "I don't really know. I just felt drawn to you. I've never known a movie star before. I guess I wanted to see what you were really like." She lowered her head. "I suppose that's why you're building the wall, to stop me from spying on you."

Patrick shrugged. "I didn't know what else to do. If I pull the curtains, I feel claustrophobic. And I could hardly call you up on the phone and tell you to quit looking at me.

"God, you must think I'm a pervert or something."

"No, I don't." Patrick knew an opening when he saw one, and this one was gaping wide and inviting. He put a hand on each of her shoulders and turned her slowly so that they were facing each other. Gently, very gently, he lifted her chin so that her lips were only inches from his own. "So, do you like what you see?"

She nodded, unable to breathe, not even wanting to.

"In that case, I would be most pleased to show you much, much more than you could ever see from your window."

His kiss was so sweet and soft and brief that Enid might even have imagined it. But when he kissed her a second time, behind the sweetness was a hint of passion. For some reason she thought of the Fish

Shanty Restaurant, where she and Sam frequently ate. How could she know it was because of the faint aroma of trout on Patrick's breath?

It wasn't until she was walking home minutes later, when the afterglow of this encounter began to dissipate, that she remembered Wallase standing near the window of her den. Had he seen them?

And why had he been going through her papers?

7

Sam and Carmen

There were five messages waiting for Sam when he arrived at his office. One was an invitation to an art opening at Photoluxe, where he'd bought the Mapplethorpe photo, and one was from his mechanic, saying that the European-style headlights for his Porsche had come in. Neither of these calls needed to be returned immediately.

But the other three were important. His contact at Sanwa had checked in for a report on the mayor's response to the proposed entertainment complex, and Sam was eager to relay his optimism that he thought he would be able to turn Carson around to their way of thinking.

Another call was from one of his clients, Art Lawson. Sam was not surprised. Art was a major shareholder in Dominion, which had been founded by his father, and he was no doubt frantic about the announcement in the paper. Art had had his own financial difficulties over the past year, and as his lawyer, Sam had done his best to keep him out of the bankruptcy courts and to help him quietly restructure his portfolio. The truth was, if the Dominion sale were to go through, it would give Art the financial boost he needed to get out of trouble. Sam had tried to convince Art to sell the stock countless times, but

Art refused to surrender control of the studio his father had built. He loved the glamour and status of being a player in Hollywood, and he swore he'd give up the ghost before he'd give up Dominion. Sam decided he'd better get more information before he returned Art's call.

The last call was from Carmen Leventhal. No message, just a number. He buzzed Margie and asked her to bring in his decaf, and to hold his calls. He shuffled the little pink slips of paper, trying to decide which call to make first.

Margie tapped on the door and entered without waiting for Sam's approval, setting the mug on a bronze coaster not far from the phone. "No Very Veggie this morning?"

Sam shook his head. "Maybe later." He took a sip. The coffee was, of course, just as he liked it, scalding hot with a squeeze of lemon juice. "Do you know if Leo's in yet?"

"I doubt it. Karen said something about after lunch. I can check."

"Tell her I need to chat with him. Anytime this afternoon. Make sure she understands it's important, but don't make too big a deal out of it, okay?"

"Sure. Anything else?"

"No, thanks, just close the door on your way out, if you will."

Sam waited until he heard the door click, then he picked up the phone to dial. "Yes, Carmen Leventhal please." He opened his desk drawer and took out a rubber hand grip, working it first in his right hand, then in his left, feeling the strength of his forearms responding to the exercise.

"Leventhal, here." Her voice was harsh, grating on him like a dull razor blade scraping the label off a piece of cheap glassware.

"Sam Carrouthers, Carmen."

"Sam, I was expecting your call." Her voice miraculously morphed into a soothing balm, which oozed through the receiver into Sam's ear. He didn't know whether to be pleased or annoyed by the change in tone. When he didn't say anything, she continued, "I was sure you'd see the piece in the paper, just as I told you."

"I saw it all right."

"And?"

"And what? I'm still a little in the dark, but Leo will fill me in when we get together later today."

"What time are you meeting with him?"

"Why?"

"I have some more information. You should hear it before you see him."

Sam hesitated. He sensed Carmen was trying to manipulate him again. But still, she might be able to shed some light on this murky situation. He decided to feel her out.

"What's the price of this information?"

Carmen laughed. "It's free, Sam."

"Then why — "

"I could give you a lot of reasons. But you're a busy man, let's settle for two. First of all, on a professional level, I'm not exactly best friends with the guy who's handling the WIT story. In fact, I'd be happier than hell to see him go down in flames on this one. And between the two of us, we just might be able to engineer that nosedive.

"Second," she paused, then continued in a husky voice, "I think I made it pretty clear at lunch yesterday where my interests lie *personally*, and that's an area I'd like to explore."

Sam heard a tap on his door and swung around. Jim stuck his head in. He was holding the business section of the *Times*. Sam waved him in, and motioned to him to sit. "I see. Well, how do you propose we proceed?"

"I suggest we get together at lunchtime today to discuss it."

"I told you, I don't eat lunch."

"Who said anything about eating? Meet me at my house at noon. Nobody will bother us there. I'll have my secretary fax you a map.

The directions are kind of complicated. Bye."

Sam sat staring at the receiver for a second before carefully setting it back into its cradle.

"Interesting call, I gather."

Sam had forgotten all about Jim, and he now turned around to face his partner. "Hey, Jimmy, what's up?"

Jim looked like he'd been wearing the same suit for a week. The tail of his shirt flapped out angrily behind him, and his tie looked as though he'd used it for a napkin at his last meal. The expression on his face was the perfect complement to this picture of dishevelment.

"I assume you saw the paper this morning," he said.

"Yep."

"Son of a bitch, Sam, we can't just sit back and let him do it to us again. Fuckin' Leo Choate. He acts like a one-man circus. It's as though the rest of us, his *partners*, don't even exist."

"I know, I know."

"You also know what this will do to your Sanwa deal, if it happens. To say nothing of my negotiation with the Taiwanese. My guys are very cautious as it is, and if word gets out Leo's racing around town doing his own deals, they're going to wonder what kind of an organization we're running here."

"It's a bitch, I agree."

"Well you don't sound very pissed about it. I'm about to explode."

"Yeah, you look it."

Jim had worked himself into a sweat. His blue eyes bulged out behind his rimless glasses, and a shock of blond hair fell forward across his brow. "Sam we've got to do something. We've taken this sitting down too many times."

"I agree, I'm just trying not to get too worked up about it until I know all of the facts, and I expect to know a lot more by this afternoon."

"What do you want me to do?"

"Take your blood pressure. When it gets back down to normal, call Karen and make sure she's set up a meeting for us with Leo. Then see if you can get a call through to Harry. I think he's on his boat in the Mediterranean. Roxie will find him. Try to feel him out on this, see if he knows anything. But be cool about it. I'll call you when I know more."

"Okay, buddy, I'm counting on you."

"You can."

On the drive to Carmen's, Sam tried to concentrate on the pleasure of putting the Porsche through its paces, taking the sharp canyon curves at forty miles an hour. How long had it been since he had driven on this road when it wasn't choked with rush-hour traffic? For that matter, how long had it been since he'd driven anywhere outside of the citadel of Century City in the middle of the day? He felt like a kid playing hooky — deliciously free, deliberately hedonistic, like it was breaking the law to be driving on a street where there were trees and birds and a woman watering her lawn in a bathrobe. He had almost forgotten that a daytime world existed outside the concrete and steel-girded boundaries of the business community.

He had no trouble following Carmen's faxed directions — driving up Beverly Glen, turning left at the first street past the Four Oaks Cafe and right on the road with no street sign, just past the Frank Gehry house, to the third house on the left, a California bungalow-style structure smothered in bougainvillea.

Where he ran into trouble was getting up the nerve to get out of the Porsche and knock on her door.

He stared at the house, trying to will himself to move. He had expected something a little more hard-edged and contemporary from her, a living space rather than a home. But this place had to be seventy or eighty years old, and in perfect repair, obviously restored with patient, loving hands. Carmen's? He found it hard to believe, but then, how well did he know her?

A flagstone pathway led to wooden stairs and a wide front porch with, of all things, an old swing covered in polished cotton off to the side. Sam hadn't seen one of these since he was a kid and the family had gone to his aunt's and uncle's cabin in Big Bear. He'd kissed his first girl on that swing. What was her name, Carey or Mary, something like that. Her family owned the cabin next door to his aunt, and over one delicious summer they'd locked sights on each other and fallen in love the way only fourteen-year-olds can, not by speaking or spending time together, but rather by exchanging meaningful looks across the boat docks and performing intricate dives that had more splash than style, hoping the other would notice.

The kiss itself had been an experiment. Knowing he probably would not see Carey or Mary again until the following summer, Sam had waited until the very last day of his vacation before approaching her, just in case he screwed it up. He had made sure to pick a time when his family would be down at the lake, and he chose the porch swing as the place, because it reminded him of something he'd seen in the movies.

Carey or Mary had been surprisingly eager to play her role in the scenario. In fact, she had been the one to make the first move, anointing him with a dry, chaste kiss that tasted like the lemonade they'd been drinking. The whole summer was wrapped up in that sweet-sour kiss, and when Sam's hormones finally kicked in and he kissed her back, he was rewarded with Carey or Mary's moist, parted lips, which seemed to suck his surprised tongue out of his mouth and into hers. He could still feel the nub of the scar that the sharp edge of her braces had made on his tongue.

Sam was still smiling and remembering this image of his innocence when the screen door swung open and Carmen stepped out.

"Hi," she said, "I got tired of waiting for you to knock."

How was it she always managed to catch him off guard? "Just getting my bearings," he replied, and got out of the car. "I can't remember when I was up in the Glen last, probably not since law school."

"It hasn't changed much, I'll bet."

"Hardly at all." He walked up the path toward the porch. "How long have you lived here?"

"About six, seven years." He followed her up the stairs. "I was going with a guy and we decided to share this place. No long-term commitments, right? We didn't buy, we leased. We didn't get married, we lived together. We planted annuals, not perennials." She shrugged. "I thought we were being terribly mature and up front with each other."

"So what happened to him?"

"He went back to his wife. He'd sworn she was out of the picture when we moved in together. Then she just showed up here one Saturday while we were having breakfast, and told him that when he was through playing house with me, she and *the family* would like him to come home. And he did." She looked at Sam. "Isn't that the oldest one in the book?"

Sam didn't reply. He was too busy taking in the decor of the bungalow, which was sparse and eclectic, yet comfortable and inviting. He recognized a Sam Maloof rocking chair on a small Tabriz carpet, and a Rookwood vase beneath an Ed Moses oil painting. The juxtaposition of fine art from four different periods was surprising, but it worked. She had good taste, he'd have to give her that. Good, and expensive — the Moses alone had to be worth twenty-five thousand, despite its small size.

Carmen waited until Sam had his fill of the room and returned his eyes to her. Then, when she had his full attention, she shrugged off the jacket to her business suit, and matter-of-factly hung it on the back of a chair as she continued, "So now I'm careful only to date men who know *I* know they're married. That way nobody gets surprised."

Sam, however, was surprised. Out of the strict business suit, Carmen was a different person. Her blouse was a soft, tawny silk that ached to be touched, and her full figure caused it to strain just enough at the buttons to rouse his attention.

She wasn't wearing a bra. He tried not to stare, but it was obvious she intended him to, had timed this maneuver so his eyes would be on her as she unveiled herself.

She smiled at him and kicked off her shoes. "Don't mind me. When I'm home I like to be comfortable. You're welcome to take off your jacket and tie." *And the rest of your clothes as well,* she thought, but didn't say.

Sam hesitated.

"We can sit out on the porch if you're afraid to be alone in here with me."

"Should I be?"

"That's kind of up to you. I probably won't jump on you, but then again, I can't promise I won't try."

They stood staring at each other for a moment. It was disorienting to Sam being the pursued rather than the pursuer. It was flattering, but unsettling, just the same. He slipped out of his jacket and set it on the couch where he could reach it quickly if he decided to make a hasty departure.

"Something to drink?" Carmen asked.

"Just some water, with plenty of ice."

"Coming up." She padded into the kitchen, her nylons making a swishing sound on the peg-and-groove floors as she walked.

Sam looked around the room, admiring the detailing on the windows and door molding. "Nice place," he called to her. "Did you restore it yourself?"

"Yep. After he left. Took me four years," she called from the kitchen. "I considered it a form a therapy, a lot cheaper than going to a shrink, plus you've got something tangible to show for it when you're through." This was, of course, a lie, but how would Sam ever find out she had made her ex-lover pay through the nose for the professional contractor and restoration team who had gotten the old house into shape?

She reappeared with two glasses of water and a bowl of green grapes, balanced on a beautiful inlaid wood tray.

"I'll be honest with you," said Sam. "I'd never have pictured you in a house like this. I see you as more of a Century Towers or Bunker Hill type."

She handed him his water and sat on the couch, curling her feet up under her. "You mean, sterile, devoid of style, one-dimensional? Well, Sam, we're not all what we seem to be on the surface, are we?"

"I didn't mean — " he tried to explain.

She waved her hand dismissively. "Like your friend and partner Leo Choate. He certainly doesn't look like the kind of guy who'd make an under-the-table deal with WIT and stiff his partners, does he?"

Sam was relieved that she had switched the subject to business. "Look. I don't mean this to sound the way it probably will, but Leo has been my partner for years. His wife and my wife have known each other since high school. I barely know you. Why should I believe anything you tell me?"

"Two reasons. One, because everything I've told you so far has been true, and two, because you know Leo well enough to know he's capable of screwing his mother, let alone his business partners."

Sam was silent. She'd nailed that one.

"Now, do you want to know what I know, or not?"

"Tell me."

Her story was brief and to the point. "Paul and Leo met through their wives. I guess they're both members of that Music Center group, the Blue Ribbon Whatever. Sounds like a dog show doesn't it? Anyway, the women were working together on some kind of fund-raising event, and they got to talking about their husbands' businesses. Alice Whitney-Smith told Lacy Choate that WIT had a mandate from its mother company in Japan to find a film studio to purchase, and that they had the money to pay for it."

Sam was amazed. Did wives really gossip about their husbands' multimillion dollar negotiations? Did Enid share such secrets? He doubted it. But he wouldn't put anything past Lacy once she got wind of an opportunity. Talk about the woman behind the man — Lacy's ambition was like a loaded gun at Leo's head. And the pathetic part was that in some sadomasochistic way, he seemed to thrive on it.

Carmen's phone rang. She ignored it. "Aren't you going to answer it?" Sam asked.

She shook her head. "Nobody knows I'm home. I'll let the machine get it." They both listened as a male voice said, "Carmen it's Ray Strauss. I'm going to be in town Friday and I'd like to see you. Give me a call."

Sam didn't know Ray Strauss personally, but he'd heard of him — he was a partner at Goldman Sachs in New York. Sam would have loved to know if the call was business or pleasure, but he would never ask, and Carmen, obviously, wasn't saying.

She gave Sam an enigmatic half smile and continued. "Lacy Choate practically pees in her pants in her eagerness to tell Alice Whitney-Smith that her husband Leo is in fact just the person to help WIT out and suggests that the four of them have dinner so the men can meet."

"Just one question. How on earth did you get this information?"

"Why Sam, are you asking me to reveal my sources?" Carmen feigned shock, then laughed. "Actually, I got it straight from the horse's mouth. Lacy Choate and I go to the same hairdresser. I happened to be getting a trim while Rodney was doing her color. She tells him everything, even personal things you wouldn't believe."

Sam reddened. Lacy was a master of discretion. He and Enid used to joke that she got her buckteeth from all of the bullshit that was continually forcing its way out of her mouth.

"Your name even came up once," Carmen added, smiling deliciously.

He could tell she loved dropping this little bomb. "I don't even want to know in what context," he replied. And he honestly didn't.

"Whatever Lacy said about me could hardly be germane to WIT, and that's what I'm here to talk about," he said firmly.

Carmen smiled and continued, "So the two couples go to dinner, at Morton's or some such place, and apparently they hit it off, lots of friends in common, similar backgrounds."

Similar backgrounds? Sam nearly gagged. Paul Whitney-Smith came from English lineage, his blood as blue as the Atlantic Ocean, going back to the Earl of something in Hertfordshire, who purportedly had had a dalliance with Queen Victoria. Leo Choate was born in a suburb of Melbourne, Australia, the third child of a steel worker who had bought the farm when his wife was pregnant with number four.

Of course, Leo didn't tell people the truth about his background. He had fabricated a wonderful old family for himself, a dynasty that at one time had owned not only the steel mill in Melbourne, but a number of railroads, and even a shipyard or two in Perth.

The only reason Sam knew the truth was that Leo had confessed it to him in a drunken moment of bachelor party intimacy on the eve of his marriage to Lacy. Suddenly, with good reason, he had panicked at the thought of entering into a permanent relationship with a woman who believed he was something he wasn't. Sam had urged him to tell Lacy the truth, but as far as he knew, he hadn't.

Carmen was still talking, and Sam realized he had daydreamed through a good portion of her story. But his attention snapped back when he heard her mention Art Lawson's name. "What about Art?" he interrupted.

Carmen was annoyed. "As I just said two seconds ago, the block of stock that gives WIT the controlling interest belongs to Art Lawson, who is the son of . . ."

"I know who Art Lawson is. He's my client!" Sam interrupted again. "But how in hell did Leo get him to agree to sell? Damn!" Sam's mind raced backward and forward in an attempt to organize the facts. Art's financial difficulties had been openly discussed within the firm, but the information was strictly confidential. Apparently

Leo had capitalized on his insider knowledge and had cannibalized Art's position at Dominion, serving him up to WIT on a silver platter.

Sam was pissed. If this was true, what Leo was doing wasn't strictly illegal, but it was certainly unethical. The whole structure of the firm would be compromised if word of this got out, and no doubt it would in a deal this large. Something was going to have to be done to stop the transaction. And Sam relished the thought of being the one to do it. He stood.

"There's more."

Carmen patted the seat beside her, but Sam remained standing, and picked up his water glass.

"Apparently they've hit a stumbling block, because Leo wanted it written in the deal that he would have sole discretion over the studio, and even though most of the studios are being run by legal or financial guys these days, WIT isn't so sure it trusts Leo, since he has zero experience — you know how much the Japanese hate to give up control. So he's flying to Tokyo next week to meet with Isoku Tonitshi himself. He must have an ace up his sleeve and I'm still trying to find out what it is." She paused a moment and looked at Sam. "I was hoping you could help me find out. Will you do it?"

"And here I thought you were only interested in my body." Sam couldn't resist the sarcasm, although his voice was dull with anger.

Carmen rose to her stockinged feet and faced Sam. Her body was so close to his that wisps of her hair brushed against his shoulder. Slowly and deliberately, she put her arms around his neck.

"That, too," she said, her voice as smooth and rich as hot fudge in a silver chalice. His lips were irresistibly drawn to taste hers, and before he could think about it, he had bent his head and his anger at Leo was pouring like lava into their kiss.

It was a kiss they would both remember later, filled with tension, passion, curiosity, and, oddly, relief that they'd survived this inevitable moment. So caught up was Sam in the surprising flood of feelings that he forgot he was holding his water glass, and, as he held her tightly, he accidentally dumped it down her back, ice cubes and all.

She stepped away, laughing. "Is that your way of telling me I need to take a cold shower?"

But both of them knew he was the one who needed to cool off.

8

Patrick

May I have your autograph, Mr. Drake?"

"My pleasure."

Patrick was on Cloud Nine. The Rolls was running like a dream, his favorite khaki cords felt practically loose around his waist, his se-duction of his next-door neighbor was progressing apace, and now the guard at the entrance to Dominion Studios was actually asking for his autograph.

Imagine the flood of stars who surged through the gate each day, Patrick preened, allowing himself to feel a little smug that he was singled out. It was probably a good thing he had already rounded the curve and did not see the next car roll up to the gate, or hear the guard repeat his request for an autograph to the driver, Sylvester Stallone's cousin Vince Cannolini.

All of the parking spaces in front of the executive building were taken, but as though on cue, a Jaguar backed out of a spot at the very end. Patrick eased the Rolls in, taking care to position it as far as pos-sible from the Cadillac in the next stall, since any Caddie parked here would have to be a company-leased car, and drivers of leased cars were notoriously careless about dinging other cars.

The doorman opened the enormous glass entrance to Dominion's executive suite, and Patrick entered, nearly tripping on the extra-thick pile of the wall-to-wall carpet. It was appropriately tinted mint green — the exact shade of money.

Posters from Dominion's biggest hits over the past five decades lined the walls. Since Patrick's last visit to these hallowed halls, which was before Kesselman's rise to glory, something new had been added to the display: beside each poster was a title card, telling the name of the movie and the year it was made, as well as how much it had cost to produce and market it and how much money it had grossed worldwide.

At first Patrick was astonished at the blatancy of Dominion's bottom-line philosophy, but by the time he walked the length of the hall he had reconciled himself to the fact that the movies weren't just about art anymore, they were about money. Kesselman had been an accountant before he took over as head of production, and he'd probably never even seen half of the movies whose posters graced his office walls. Well, it was his loss, thought Patrick, as he entered Kesselman's private enclave. Many of them had been great, great entertainment.

The receptionist seemed to be expecting him and buzzed Kesselman's assistant, Marion. She materialized instantly, a vision of pinstriped efficiency, her hennaed hair tied back with a Hermes scarf, her body adorned in the requisite Armani suit.

In contrast, Patrick's attire was shabby and cheap. But they both knew which of them was the movie star who could command $2 million a picture, and which was a glorified, albeit Harvard-educated, gofer.

"Mr. Drake, I'm so glad to see you."

They shook hands. Patrick had never shaken hands with a woman who had such a strong grip. He was about to make a crack about it, but the receptionist interrupted.

"Marion, excuse me. There's another reporter from NBC holding for Mr. K. What shall I tell — "

"What you've told the others, Laverne," snapped Marion. "We know nothing about this WIT business, and Mr. Kesselman has no comment to make to anyone about the rumors. It's business as usual at Dominion."

She recovered her calm and smiled at Patrick. "The press — wherever do they get their information?"

"From your publicity department?" Patrick joked, but Marion did not laugh.

"Mr. Kesselman has already gone over to the commissary for lunch. May I walk over with you?" she said instead.

"He's already gone? Does that mean I'm late?"

"Oh, no. He had an earlier lunch today as well." She motioned to the door, and Patrick stood aside to let her lead the way out and down the hall.

"You mean, he eats two lunches?" Patrick asked. She nodded. "Every day?"

"Two or three times a week." She bent closer to him as though sharing a confidence. "Some people take offense if they're not invited to a meal. So Jeff — Mr. Kesselman — frequently doubles up on breakfast or lunch meetings. That way nobody's feelings get hurt."

"Must be hell on his diet."

"He's on Nutri/System, so it really doesn't matter."

🕶

Marion held open the door to the commissary and let Patrick enter first. He used to dread eating here, wasting a perfectly good meal on cafeteria-style food. But since Kesselman had taken over Dominion's Studio commissary, the food had improved markedly. Patrick was particularly fond of the warm scallop salad with feta cheese and Kalamata olives, and he had already planned to have it today. He hoped that watching Kesselman sipping beige sludge through a straw wouldn't ruin his appetite.

The best part of eating in a studio commissary was seeing all of the working actors in full costume and makeup, eating their lunches like normally attired people. As long as he'd been in The Business, Patrick still got a kick out of seeing a cowboy and a futuristic alien sharing a chef's salad, and a soldier covered in blood eating meat loaf covered in catsup.

As Patrick followed Marion, weaving a serpentine path through the tables, he saw a few familiar faces and waved or half-smiled, letting them know by his manner that someone of greater importance was waiting for him and that he couldn't linger.

There was Kesselman up ahead. Poor guy, he reminded Patrick of a balding, sleazy version of PeeWee Herman. He wouldn't have been so bad if it weren't for his allergies. The guy was perpetually blowing his honker. Consequently, it looked like a swollen, red bulb with hairs prickling out of it. But still, he was always surrounded by beautiful women. The seductive power of money and position never ceased to amaze him.

Today Jeffrey Kesselman was flanked by two beautiful women, one of whom Patrick thought was Kesselman's wife. But damn, he couldn't remember her name. Fortunately, a benefit of being famous was that nobody expected you to remember them. Sure enough, Kesselman rose when he saw Patrick and extended his hand, saying, "Patrick, glad you could make it. You remember my wife Terry, and this is Violet Doone."

Patrick shook hands all around. "Any relation to Lorna?" he asked Violet, but the joke was apparently lost on her. She shook her head no and said, "I've really got to run. The toddler clinic is at 1:30."

"Violet works for Good Vibrations, a school for the hearing impaired," Kesselman snorted, lifting his handkerchief to blow his nose.

"What?" Patrick cupped his hand over his ear in an exaggerated fashion to be sure they understood he was making a joke about hearing, but again it fell, so to speak, on deaf ears.

"Good Vibrations," Terry Kesselman enunciated, as though she really thought Patrick was hard of hearing." You must have heard of it, Patrick." She sounded worried, and the last thing Patrick wanted was to worry Jeffrey Kesselman's wife.

"Of course, Good Vibrations. Wonderful organization. Great that people care so much."

"Terry and I are hosting a premiere for them next week. We were just going over the details." Kesselman seemed proud of his wife, and prouder still of himself for being proud of her.

"The Kesselmans are incredibly generous," Violet beamed. "It's so gratifying that a man as busy as Jeffrey will take time out of his schedule to do charitable work."

"When you've been successful, it's important to give back to the community, don't you think, Patrick?"

"Absolutely." Patrick thought he heard an edge in Kesselman's voice, insinuating that he was not aware of Patrick giving anything back to the community. So he felt compelled to add, "As a matter of fact, I'm working on a fund-raiser myself. For the Westside Women's Shelter."

"Oh, they're a wonderful group! They do that Art and Architecture Tour in the Palisades," said Terry. "Remember, Jeff, we went two years ago when we were looking for a painting for over the sofa in the screening room."

"Sure, sure," Kesselman replied. "What are you doing for them, Paddy?"

Patrick looked at the three faces eager to hear his response, and he had no choice but to answer, "We're doing a premiere of *A Month of Sundays*."

"That's Tristar, isn't it? Barry Levinson's film, with Allison McGrath costarring?"

Patrick nodded.

"I just love Allison McGrath," added Terry. "I'll bet you two are terrific together."

"It wasn't exactly a hardship working with someone as lovely and talented as Allie," Patrick said, thinking to himself what a first-class bitch she had been, usually coked out, constantly butchering her own lines and stepping on his, forcing him to spend weeks on a sound stage dubbing his dialogue.

"How much are you trying to raise?"

"As much as we can," stumbled Patrick. "How much are you all planning to raise?"

"Our goal is five hundred," said Terry in the manner of someone to whom five hundred thousand was not an outlandish sum.

"Jeffrey's arranged for Dominion to pay all of the expenses," added Violet, "which means every penny we raise will go to Good Vibrations."

Suddenly, Patrick was aware of a particular glow in Violet's eyes as she looked at Kesselman, and the whole situation became clear. Kesselman was sticking it to Violet, and dumping corporate money into his wife's favorite charity, thus salving his guilt *and* making his mistress happy at the same time, to say nothing of the tax write off he was getting for Dominion. Patrick relaxed a little. This knowledge would make dealing with Kesselman much easier — not that Patrick would ever mention it, but it was nice to know Kesselman had a vulnerable spot.

"You know it is my pleasure to support such a worthy cause," said Kesselman, looking into Violet's eyes. "To give and give."

I'll bet it is, thought Patrick. The crosscurrent between Kesselman and Violet was so strong now that Patrick sat back in his chair to get out of its trajectory. He couldn't believe Terry didn't feel it too, but she apparently was too self-absorbed, or else she was in serious denial.

"I've got to get going too," said Terry. "Theo's school lets out in fifteen minutes. Shall I drop you, Vi?"

All four of them rose, and Jeffrey gave Terry a husbandly peck on the cheek. "I'll see you tonight, sweetheart. We've got the screening at Warners. Violet, give me a call later and we'll arrange that meeting with the ad department."

He shook her hand, holding onto it just a fraction of a second longer than necessary. Patrick had heard Kesselman was a player, but he was still amazed that with a puss like that, the guy was such a stud. His dick had to be two feet long.

The ladies exited, and the men sat down again. Kesselman signaled for a menu and handed it to Patrick. "You go ahead, I've already had my Nutri/System."

"You must have a great deal of willpower," Patrick said admiringly. His own willpower was limited to promising to diet the day after consuming an enormous meal.

"Whatever it takes to get the job done." Kesselman's eyes worked the room over Patrick's shoulder. "So, you're here about . . . which project was it?" Patrick's heart sank. Why was Kesselman playing dumb? He was the one who had called the meeting. He tried not to panic. *For Love or Money*," he said.

"Yeah, right," said Kesselman absently.

The silence was deafening, so Patrick stumbled into the void. "LeMar said it was a go project. Maybe he exaggerated just a little . . ."

"No, no, it's got a green light. Soon as it's cast. You know Marvin Holmes is set to direct."

Patrick touched his fingertips to his lips and blew a kiss into the air. "I love Marvin. Always wanted to work with him."

Kesselman nodded. "You and everyone else in town. *Late Bloomers* grossed $94 million domestic last year, $158 million worldwide, so far. The video presale alone paid for prints and ads. You can do that with a guy like Holmes, who has a reputation."

Patrick sensed Kesselman's implication, that Patrick's own reputation wasn't so hot. He decided to try an outside run.

"Who do you want for the female lead?"

Kesselman shrugged. "We're thinking about a new face. Got any ideas?"

Patrick did indeed. Sara would kill for this part. He wasn't sure her acting ability was strong enough, but what she lacked in talent she made up for in enthusiasm. And wouldn't he love to tell her he could get her a reading for the female lead in a major motion picture? She would be his slave for life. But first he had to figure out where he stood.

Kesselman seemed to read his mind. "LeMar and I tossed around some numbers. Your usual fee is a bit steeper than we think we can go for this picture, but maybe we can work something out with points."

Patrick's spirits plummeted. Points? A net deal? What kind of an idiot did Kesselman think he was? He got his money up front or he passed, and LeMar would never tell anyone anything different. Clearly Kesselman wanted Patrick to pass on the picture. But why? God damn LeMar for putting him in this humiliating situation. God damn Kesselman for treating him like shit. Well, when cornered, play dirty.

Patrick shrugged as though he were considering the offer. Then he said, "Say Jeff, tell me more about that Violet. She was kinda giving me the eye, and I wouldn't mind pollinating her flower. Can you give me her number?"

Patrick had not misjudged the situation. Without thinking, Kesselman stabbed a piece of cheese from Patrick's salad and stuffed it into his mouth.

"She's involved with someone," he said flatly.

Patrick smiled to himself. Fucking Kesselman.

9

Sam

Uncharacteristically, Leo Choate removed his jacket and conducted the meeting in his shirtsleeves. Sam couldn't remember ever seeing Leo clad so casually at the office; he was normally fanatical about being properly attired at all times. Sam recalled flying home from Chicago with Leo in a company jet in August. They'd been at a white tie testimonial that had dragged on into the wee hours of the morning. Not only had Leo worn his jacket through the entire flight, but he had kept his tie tied as well, even though Sam, Leo, and their wives were the only passengers aboard.

Sam watched Leo strut around the office, like Patton reviewing his troops. All that was missing was the riding crop. His starched, white-cuffed shirt, monogrammed on the cuff rather than on the pocket, was immaculately pressed and tucked into his trousers, which were specially tailored so that the waistband peaked at the center of the back to meet the suspenders. Without the jacket, from the back, the pants looked like a businessman's version of Oshkosh coveralls.

He watched Jim listening intently to Leo's evasive patter about golfing at the L.A. Country Club, as they waited for the conference call to their fourth partner, Harry Ingersol, to come through. Sam had to smile at the difference in his partners' styles. Leo had gone a long way on his ability to look and talk a good game. But without Sam and Jim to actually *do the work*, to bring in the clients and structure the deals that had made them all wealthy men, Leo would probably still be a staff lawyer for a giant corporation. His one claim to fame was that at a young age he had befriended Harry Ingersol, and he had parlayed that relationship into a career.

Poor Harry. Since his retirement from the practice of law, he'd scored with a series of well-timed leveraged buyouts and annually made *Forbes'* list of the 400 richest Americans. But even his wealth could not protect him from personal tragedy.

In 1987, his two sons, both graduates of Harvard, had drowned when their father's 120-foot yacht sank off the Great Barrier Reef in Australia. Harry and his wife Louise had been ashore at the time, and it was never determined what had caused the accident. But the deaths of his two boys left Harry with no heirs to his vast financial empire.

Enter Leo Choate, a guy with a talent for being in the right place at the right time. He had been working for the Australian subsidiary of a company Harry was trying to buy, and he had attracted the big man's attention by alerting him to a movement within the company to upset Harry's hostile takeover through an employee buyout of the stock.

This buyout had never surfaced (whether the threat was real or manufactured by Leo had never been determined), and Harry's takeover had been successfully completed only weeks after the deaths of his sons. Leo had been the hero of the day, and he had readily accepted Harry's offer of employment. Before long he became a surrogate son to Harry, and when Harry returned to the United States, Leo went with him as his lieutenant.

Sam had met Leo around this time, when Leo started dating Lacy. The men had become friends out of necessity, since Enid's and Lacy's friendship threw them together socially, and because of their shared interests in the world of law and finance. Leo curried favor with Sam by introducing him to Harry, who by this time was a media star.

Harry had taken an instant liking to Sam, seeing in him a younger version of himself. But a close friendship had never blossomed. Sam knew why: it was because Leo insisted on running interference between Harry and the rest of the world, distancing his boss from reality and serving as his only conduit of information. Needless to say, the information was often tainted by Leo's own agenda.

Sam had never understood why Harry had allowed Leo to play this role. There was clearly some bond between the two men that was irrevocable. And not one to force his friendship on anyone else, Sam respectfully kept his distance from Harry.

Eight years before, when Leo approached Sam, and through him, Jim, suggesting that they form a new law firm, Sam had made it a condition of the partnership that Le would bring Harry into the deal. Although they knew Harry would not actually participate in the daily work of the firm, his name on the letterhead would give them entree to the highest echelon of clients and the most prestigious deals. Hence, the law firm of Ingersol, Choate, Carrouthers, and Meyers was born. (Naturally, Harry's name was first on the letterhead; the others drew straws to determine the rest of the order. Had Leo manipulated that too?) And even though Harry was rarely in the office, he faxed and phoned in his contributions on issues of importance, from exotic vacation spots all over the globe.

Today he answered the conference call from his new boat, a 175-foot sloop out of Portofino, Italy, which was sailing the coast of Sardinia.

"Hello, hello. Who the hell's there?" Harry's voice crackled harshly over the speaker phone.

"Harry, it's Leo. Sam and Jim are with me. How's the trip?"

"Fantastic. Just came up from a dive and we're about to have lunch. Wish you guys could see this water. It's so clear I swear you can see the fish shitting."

For all of his worldly success, Harry had retained his earthy sense of humor. Perhaps that was one reason he had taken Leo under his wing, myopically seeing Leo's unctuous veneer as a gloss of refinement that would make him appear more sophisticated.

"Well, we're sorry to interrupt your communion with nature, Harry, but Sam thought you should be in on this conversation."

Sam shot a dirty look at Leo. His tone of voice implied that he, Leo, thought the call was a waste of time, leaving Sam to prove it wasn't.

"It had better be good, Sambo. My hot dogs and baked beans are waiting." Harry's tastes in food were as common as his language. Although his staff always offered more elaborate meals to his on-board guests, his own diet never varied from the most basic all-American staples: hot dogs, hamburgers, pizza, and French fries.

"I think it is important, Harry. Something you'd want to know about."

"Yeah, go on."

Sam figured he'd better play all of his cards at once. It was hard enough keeping Harry's attention when he was in the room, but on a call spanning over 5,000 miles, it would be nearly impossible. "There's some talk on the street about a deal with World Investment Trust. Are you aware of it?"

"The Paul Whitney-Smith thing? Hell yes, I'm aware of it. In fact, it looks like I'm going to be jumping into the sack with the Japs, if Leo has anything to say about it."

Damn, thought Sam, *if they're in this together, Jim and I are screwed.* "I'm not sure I follow you, Harry."

"What's there to follow? Leo got a line on an opportunity to put our friends at Dominion in business with WIT, and he's bringing it to a head."

"Harry, are you aware that Sam and I knew nothing about this?" Jim's voice trembled with indignation.

"What? It's my problem you guys don't talk to each other?" Harry cleverly volleyed the ball back into their court.

"I think the point Jim's trying to make is that he and I are waist deep in other deals that conflict with this one, and we're concerned they'll tank if the right hand doesn't know what the left hand is doing."

"Leo, are you there?"

"I'm here, Harry."

"Well don't just sit there stroking yourself with the left hand. Tell 'em what's going on. I'm going to eat my lunch before this damn seagull carts it off. But I'm listening. Y'hear?"

Leo repositioned himself in the giant leather chair behind his desk before he spoke. "I was approached by WIT and asked to help them purchase a movie studio. I've been in discussions with them about buying a controlling interest in Dominion."

Sam chose his words carefully. "No papers have crossed my desk in regard to this, Leo. Don't we have an agreement that all four of us are privy to all client matters?"

Leo sighed. "Paul Whitney-Smith asked me not to spread it around."

"Spread it around. To your own partners? What kind of a partnership is that?" Jim was livid. Sam was afraid he was going to have a stroke right there in Leo's office.

"The fact is, this isn't a deal for the whole partnership, Jim. It only concerns me and Harry."

"What?"

"WIT has asked me to run the studio, and they want Harry on board as well, as vice chairman and consultant, with stock options, of course. But it doesn't appear that they need any other top management manpower."

"What happens to my deal with Sanwa and Jim's with the Taiwanese? To say nothing about the thirty-seven other people this firm employs."

"You know as well as I do that your deals are long shots. This is a sure thing, and it's happening now," Leo responded, neglecting to comment on the fate of ICCM's employees.

"If you make this deal, it will bury the firm, and you know it," Jim said.

"ICCM has had its day, Jim. We've all made some money, and now it's time to move on to bigger and better things." Leo calmly took a nail file from his desk drawer and started to work on the rough edge of his thumbnail.

Without a word, Sam walked to Leo's desk and took the file from Leo's hand.

"What about Lawson? This will destroy him." Sam's fury was barely contained.

"There are always going to be winners and losers," Leo answered calmly. "You've just got to know which side to be on."

The sheer arrogance of Leo's attitude was more than Sam could bear. "What makes you think Art Lawson is going to sit still and let you bury him?"

"He has no choice. He's tapped out. In fact, he's glad to get out from under that load of debt."

"Really?" said Sam, reaching for the phone. "Why don't we call him and ask him?"

Leo smiled, his capped teeth glinting in the afternoon sun. "He can't be reached."

"What do you mean?"

"He's at a drug rehab in Michigan. They don't allow phone calls. He'll be there drying out for two months. By then the deal will be completed."

"Really? He just called me this morning," Sam insisted.

"He can make one call out a week. I guess he wasted it leaving you a message." He pulled a folder from his desk drawer and slid it across the desk to Sam. "I told him he'd better let you know he'd signed his power of attorney over to me. It's all in the file."

Sam didn't bother to open the file. He looked Leo square in the eye, a look so fierce that involuntarily Leo sat back in his chair. "This is a declaration of war, Leo, and you know it."

Leo shrugged. "If you guys want to make an issue out of it, go ahead. But I warn you, it won't deter WIT from going ahead with the deal. All it will do is make you look like fools."

Sam looked at the phone, as though he could see Harry's face. "Harry, is that how you feel too?"

"I hate to say it, Sam, but if you'd been on the ball you'd've known about this weeks ago, and maybe we could have factored you into the deal. But it's too late now. Hey, I've got to run. We're just pulling into Porte Cervo. You guys keep me current on this." The line went dead, and there was silence.

Jim broke it. "What I want to know is how in hell did you get Harry to come in with you on this? He hates the Japanese almost as much as he hates Democrats."

"There are big bucks riding on this deal," Leo said nonchalantly. "And everybody wants to be in show biz."

"Harry could care less about show biz. And he's going to have to eat a shitload of crow after all of the dirt he's dished out publicly about our Asian friends."

Leo shrugged and buzzed his intercom. "Karen, Sam and Jim are just leaving. You can start my calls." He stood. "So boys, if you'll excuse me, I've got a lot to get done. Lacy and I are leaving for Japan in the morning. Oh, I'll see you at Lacy's birthday party next Saturday night at the Bel Air. Remember, it's a surprise. And you know how she loves surprises, so don't be late." He turned his back to them and buried his head in the papers on his desk. Sam and Jim had no alternative but to leave the office.

Jim followed Sam into his office and closed the door. "That's one for the anatomy books — an asshole with balls! Do you believe he's planning to trash the firm on Tuesday and still expects us to pay tribute to his wife on Saturday?" He shook his head. "I can't believe it's over just like that."

"It's not over," said Sam. "This is just round one. We've got some time until the deal closes, and I for one am going to use it."

10

Enid and Patrick and Sam

As Enid's Mercedes rounded the corner to her house, her mood seesawed between anticipation and dread. For two days, she had prolonged her daily rounds of meetings and errands, forestalling the moment when she would have to face Wallace and try to determine from his attitude whether or not he had seen her kissing Patrick.

Just thinking about the kiss made her heart race, the way it had back in high school when she had dived off the ten-meter board — a mixture of eagerness and anxiety beforehand, the almost surreal physical intensity of the actual moment, a weak-in-the-knees catharsis of relief when it was over.

The kiss had come as a surprise, but now that it had happened, it seemed so . . . so right. What would happen next?

Enid pushed the remote control for her garage door and stared at Patrick's house as she waited for it to open. How odd, she'd never noticed that the window boxes above his garage door were planted with Icelandic poppies, her favorite garden flower. There was something heroic and trusting about their long stems and wide, platelike faces. She wondered if they were Patrick's favorite flower too. *Oh Enid*, she chided herself, *he probably doesn't know a poppy from a petunia.* He hardly seemed the sort of man who would spend a morning working with his gardener, poring over seed catalogs and fertilizers.

Suddenly, Patrick's garage door began to rise. Enid was mesmerized by its slow, upward motion. She knew she should pull forward into her own garage, whose door yawned open and expectant in front of her, but her foot would not press down on the gas. As though she were having an out-of-body experience, she watched Patrick's car back out of his garage, picking up speed as it rolled down the short slope of the driveway and into the street, straight for her car.

BAM! The right rear taillight of Patrick's Rolls exploded into a million shards of red plastic as it collided with the fender of her Mercedes. Her car was jolted sideways by the impact, but Enid felt nothing. She was still sitting in stunned, staring silence when Patrick rushed to her door, his face contorted with concern.

"Ohmygod, Enid, are you all right? I didn't see you." He leaned down to look in her window. "Enid?"

Seeing the worry in his eyes, Enid's heart flooded with emotion. Her mouth formed a broad, goofy smile. "Hi," was all she could say.

Patrick sighed with relief. "Thank God! For a minute there I thought you were unconscious." He opened the door to help her out. "Can you move?"

Gradually, Enid was regaining control of herself. She took Patrick's offered hand and let him pull her to her feet. "I'm fine really. You just took me by surprise. I should have gotten out of the way."

"No, no, it's my fault. I have a terrible habit of just closing my eyes and racing forward — or backward, as the case may be."

"I understand. Once you get started, it's hard to stop." Why did Enid get the feeling they were talking about something other than their cars?

Patrick's chuckle was relieved. "I've been thinking about you, and I was hoping I'd run into you again — but not quite this literally."

"I'm glad," Enid crooned. She still felt light-headed, but it wasn't from the crash.

"What, that I dented your car?"

"No, silly," she replied, "that you were thinking about me." Then, more boldly, "I've been thinking about you too."

He grinned at her, the grin that turned her heart and the hearts of women across America to mush. Was he thinking about kissing her again? Enid was positively starved for the feel of his lips on hers, but right here, in the middle of the street?

"Missy, Missy, you are okay?"

Wallase rushed toward her from the garage, his face a mask of concern. "I hear the crash and I look! There is the Mercedes!"

Enid took a step away from Patrick. "I'm fine, Wallase. Mr. Drake's car just hit my fender." Wallase stopped dead in his tracks when he saw Patrick. He immediately lowered his eyes, either afraid of or unwilling to register the sight of Enid and Patrick together. Enid's heart sank. This reaction could only mean that Wallase had seen them together in the window.

"I don't think it's as bad as it sounded," said Patrick, unaware of the personal drama between Enid and her houseman. He turned to assess the damage. "It looks like your fender's stuck under my bumper. Maybe I should call the Auto Club."

"I fix, I fix," said Wallase, and without waiting for permission he stomped on the Mercedes' fender with his Reeboked right foot, until it bent free of the Rolls.

"Please, you give me keys, Missy, I put in garage." Wallase held out his hand to Enid. He seemed impatient to move the car out of the street, so she gave him her key ring. He got into the Mercedes, started it, and pulled it forward into the garage.

"Are you sure you're okay? I'd be happy to pay for you to see a doctor," Patrick persisted, seeing the worry wrinkle forming between Enid's eyebrows.

Enid shook her head. "It's not that." She turned to look Patrick in the eye. "I'm afraid Wallase saw us," she whispered. "In the window. You know, when we were . . ."

"Kissing?"

Enid blushed and nodded. She couldn't have said that word if someone had offered her a million dollars. But she loved the ease with which it rolled off Patrick's tongue, and the erotic way his look made her feel.

"Let me give you a small piece of advice," he said. "The best way to handle a situation like that is to ignore it. Obviously he isn't going to bring it up and risk losing his job. And if you bring it up, you're just asking for trouble. Am I right?"

"I guess so," Enid replied.

"So then," Patrick continued, "we'll have to be more careful in the future. Won't we?" His eyes bored into Enid's. "Won't we?"

She nodded. Their pact was sealed.

Friday evening was usually Sam's favorite time of the week. Unlike many of his peers, who had little life outside of the working world, Sam tried to put business aside and enjoy his weekends. Of course, he was the first to admit that this was only possible since the advent of email and the fax machine, which allowed him to keep current with the work the junior associates cranked out twenty-four hours a day, seven days a week, and the sophisticated four-line phone system complete with speaker and conferencing capabilities he had installed two years earlier.

But this evening Sam was preoccupied with the events of the day. Himself honest and forthright to a fault, he was always surprised and disappointed by the deceptive, underhanded tactics of others.

Leo.

Harry.

Carmen Leventhal.

There were some major pieces missing from this puzzle, and he was anxious to put them into place so he could assess the whole picture.

His mind was working overtime on these thoughts as he rounded the corner in second gear, squinting into the sun. Before his brain had time to send a message to his foot to step on the brake, the Porsche slammed into the rear of Patrick's Rolls, which was still blocking the road.

It took him a moment to realize what had happened. Why in God's name had somebody parked a car in the middle of the street just beyond a blind corner? Sam jumped out to check the damage, ready to lambaste the sorry idiot, and to his surprise, he saw Enid running toward him.

"Oh, Sam, what a mess. Are you all right?"

"Son of a bitch. Look at this. The fender and the hood will have to be replaced. What pea brain left his car blocking the road?"

"Sam— " Enid tried.

"I suppose I'm the pea brain you had in mind," Patrick offered from a safe vantage point, some distance behind Enid.

"This is your car?" asked Sam, and Patrick nodded. "Why in hell did you leave it here?"

"Trying to kill two birds with one stone?" Patrick attempted a joke.

"I don't get it," Sam said.

"Oh, Sam, it's all my fault. I was waiting for *our* garage door to open and Patrick pulled out of *his* garage and hit my car. Wallase just moved the Mercedes out of the way so he could move his car when you came around the corner. I'm so sorry!"

Sam's anger began to dissipate. "Do you mean to tell me *you* were blocking the road and *he* ran into you, and now *I've* run into him?"

Enid nodded, cringing. Sam stared at Enid, then at Patrick, then back at Enid. He could see that she was aghast at what had happened, and his heart melted. He didn't like to be the bad guy.

"Are you expecting company this evening, Patrick? Because if you are I'd better get my car moved before they even the score." He gave Enid an "all is forgiven" hug and shook Patrick's relieved hand.

$\mathcal{S}$am waited for Enid to come to bed. She had put on the blue silk nightshirt he loved, an indication that she had more on her mind than sleep. So he turned on the news to keep himself awake.

On channel 5, correspondent Stan Chambers was reporting from the scene of a fire in a decrepit downtown apartment building. *Poor chump*, thought Sam, *he gets all the thankless assignments, every night a different emergency.* Sam wondered how it felt to hover around the site of a catastrophe, not to offer help or comfort to the people involved, but simply to record their pain. To be a reporter, a person had to be blind to the human condition or numb to it. He wondered which phrase described Carmen Leventhal.

Carmen Leventhal! She was the last thing he wanted to think about just before sleep. So he switched the remote control to the satellite and began the process of checking all 200 channels. He could hear the pulsing of the Interplak as Enid brushed her teeth, so he knew she would still be in the bathroom a few more minutes — time enough for him to click through the porno stations.

Sam had never watched one of these films from start to finish; he wasn't all that interested in them, it was more the residue of adolescent curiosity than anything else. Anyway, from what he'd seen, they all seemed to be telling the same story in endless variation: boy meets girl, boy fucks girl, girl sucks boy, girl and boy fuck and suck anyone else they can find. The films were mildly erotic, on occasion a nice prelude to intimacy with his wife.

Sam flicked through the stations until something caught his eye, a variation on the basic porno theme. Two couples were making love on a bed, only instead of pairing up man-woman, man-woman, they were paired up man-man, woman-woman. As the four people writhed, completely interlocked, the door to the room opened and a fully-clothed woman entered, accompanied by an enormous Great Dane. All four people on the bed stopped what they were doing and began to fawn over her, caressing her feet, stroking her inner thighs, kneading her buttocks, her breasts.

My God, Sam thought, *it's Carmen!* He put on his glasses to get a clearer image of the screen, and he was surprisingly disappointed to see that the woman didn't really look like Carmen after all, only her assertive and aggressive demeanor was the same.

Fascinated, Sam watched as the four sycophants undressed the woman. They unbuttoned her jacket, and her breasts erupted from bondage, thrust toward the camera. Sam felt himself harden under the covers and moved his hand down to soothe the ache that was building in his groin. Is that what Carmen looked like?

When the woman was completely naked, except for her silver spike heels, she stood with her feet apart, beckoning to the camera. Cut to the Great Dane, who was whining, raptly attentive. The camera focused on the dog's enormous muzzle as he rose and trotted toward the woman.

"Sam, did you turn on the alarm?"

Sam's reflex was automatic. He flicked the remote control to the off position and turned his body sideways to hide the tent pole that had risen midway down the bed.

"Sam?" Enid got into her side of the bed, snuggling tightly against his back.

"I must have dozed off," Sam mumbled.

"You forgot to take off your glasses, honey, and it's only 10:15." Enid moved her body closer to his under the covers. "If you go to sleep now, you'll be awake at dawn."

Sam could smell the sweet scent of Enid's moisturizer as she brought her face up to kiss him. Her body was against his, the silken nightshirt sliding against the muscles of his chest. Stimulated by the video, the thought of Carmen Leventhal naked, and the warm welcoming body of his wife so close at hand, he was ready to come immediately.

Enid felt Sam's hands struggling with the buttons of her night-shirt. It always struck her as odd that his fingers, which were so deft and sure in their caresses of her body, always had so much trouble with the buttons and snaps and zippers that contained it.

As he worked on the second button, she began at the bottom, and by the time he finished number two, she had undone the rest. She allowed Sam the final unveiling honors, and he pushed the silk off of her shoulders.

While he was doing this, Enid's own hands stroked Sam's chest, moving down his body, which was coyly turned toward the bed, hiding the very spot her fingers were seeking. This was unlike Sam. One of the best parts of their lovemaking was the eagerness with which their bodies responded to each other's touch, the knowledge gained through years together, of what the other liked to feel. Patiently, Enid worked her hand between the bed and Sam's body until it hit home. At the same moment, his fingers found her center, and her body opened up to him.

Enid was grateful for the dark as she felt Sam begin the familiar rhythm, because that made it easier for her to imagine Patrick's face rising above hers, his body pressed eagerly against hers. She moaned softly, both in response to Sam's gentle but firm attentions, as well as to the fantasy her mind was projecting.

No doubt, Patrick was a wonderful lover. He was famous for it. And although she lacked the experience to imagine any greater plea-sure from lovemaking than she and Sam had together, the idea of a new man so close to her was highly erotic, and her body erupted in hot, undulating waves.

If Sam had not been imagining Carmen under him at that moment, he would have been surprised by his wife's swift, abandoned response. But as Enid imagined Patrick on top of her, Sam imagined Carmen under him, and his body also responded with a vigor that was lustful and new.

Later, lying back to back with their feet entwined, Enid and Sam were awake, thinking their separate thoughts, each feeling remotely unfaithful to the other. Enid's mind was still on Patrick, wondering who he was with at that moment and if he were thinking about her. Sam couldn't stop thinking about the dog in the porno film and wondering what on earth he had done to his mistress.

11

Carmen and Enid and Sam

S

weet Jesus, you look incredible! What on earth did I do to deserve this?"

Not enough, Carmen thought, but what she said was, "You just happened to be in the right place at the right time, lucky you."

Carmen was sorry she didn't feel anything deeper than friendship for Ray Strauss, because he was crazy about her. They had met years before, when Ray was coming up the ladder at Drexel Burnham, a steady, swift climb despite the competition in the fast track of the '80s junk bond market. Some people said Ray was successful because he was Milken's boy, acting as a buffer between The King and his restless subjects, willing to suppress his own career goals to serve the mighty Milken. But others said Ray had made it to the top echelon of Drexel power because he was smart enough and cagey enough to milk Milken, so to speak, learning at the master's knee and putting what he learned into action.

At least, thought Carmen, he was smart enough to spin out and sign on with Goldman at a propitious time, months before Milken's indictment. And now, years later, he had as respectable and honest a reputation as money could buy.

Ray held open the door of the limousine, and Carmen got in. She noticed that the car had been rented from a second-rate firm; the driver wasn't even wearing a uniform, and several days' worth of newspapers littered the floor. That was the problem: Despite his position and success, Ray didn't have enough style to hire the best, even when his company was footing the bill.

He handed Carmen's small Louis Vuitton travel case to the driver, who put it into the trunk. She didn't mind spending the night with him on his occasional trips to the Coast, but she refused to let him invade the tranquillity of her home. Anyway, she'd put a moratorium on all sleep-overs. This honor was now reserved and waiting for Sam Carrouthers alone.

"Where to, Sir?" the driver asked.

Ray turned to Carmen. "It's your call."

"I made us reservations at Michael's," she said. "I'm sure you know how to get there," she added to the driver.

"Yes, ma'am," he replied, and turned on the engine.

"Michael's? I thought we were going to try one of the newer places, Drai's or Le Colonial," whined Ray.

This whining was one of the other things Carmen didn't like about Ray, but she tried to hide her irritation. "I know, but the garden at Michael's is so romantic, and it's a perfect night to sit outside," she said, squeezing his hand. The real reason she had chosen this restaurant was that Sam and his wife were having dinner there. She knew because she had sneaked a look at his secretary's Daytimer when she had been waiting to see him.

"Whatever you want," Ray conceded, "just promise me you won't let him talk us into one of his 'special' bottles of wine again. That set me back $275. And it wasn't even French!"

"That was years ago. I can't believe you're still carrying a grudge against poor Michael," Carmen teased.

"I swore I'd never go back there," said Ray, "but one whiff of your perfume and I'm willing to do almost anything." He bent to kiss her neck. Carmen shuddered at the touch of his rubbery lips, but covered

her repulsion by putting her hand on Ray's thigh and rubbing it ever
so seductively.

"That's nice," Carmen said, sweetly. She gave Ray's thigh an extra
squeeze. "So tell me, how are Roxanne and the girls?"

Ray sighed and sat up straight. "You pick the damnedest times to
ask about my wife and kids. Can't we just forget about them for the
one or two nights I'm out here?"

"I like Roxanne, you know that," said Carmen.

Ray pulled away, not realizing that putting this distance between
them was Carmen's intent when she asked about his wife, and that
she would continue to use Roxanne's name like a cattle prod to keep
Ray at bay. It would never do to have him fawning all over her at dinner, in front of Sam Carrouthers.

"Well, I can tell you for a fact that she doesn't like you."

"What have I ever done to her?"

"It's not what you've done to *her*, sweetcakes, it's what you've done
to *me*."

Carmen detested pet names, and sweetcakes was one of the worst.
She could feel disgust for Ray spreading over her body like a rash.
"You don't mean to say you've told her you see me."

"She's my wife. It's nearly impossible to keep secrets from her."
Ray's tone was surprisingly matter-of-fact.

"You're rather cavalier about it. What if she decides to file for divorce and drags your ass into court?"

"She won't," Ray smiled confidently.

"Why not?"

"Because of an airtight prenuptial agreement that wouldn't keep
her in manicures, let alone in the manner to which she's become ac-
customed," Ray told her, his tone bursting with macho pride at his
cunning.

While Ray droned on about the tenets of his agreement with his
wife, Carmen made a mental note to call her lawyer in the morning
to tell him to begin researching prenuptials — sooner or later, if all

went according to plan, she'd be facing one of these, and she wanted to be armed with the best legal advice money could buy before she put her signature on any dotted line. And after all, Sam Carrouthers was a lawyer. He'd no doubt be impressed by her preparedness.

                                ⚭

Michael's was packed, and by the look on the face of the beleaguered hostess when Carmen and Ray entered, a number of people who generally did not have to wait for anything were waiting for their tables. Carmen felt the eyes of the other patrons on her as she moved with purpose to intercept Michael's wife Kim when she appeared on the staircase, descending from the upstairs bar. Carmen had bonded with Kim (or so she thought) years before when she had noticed the McCarty signature on the restaurant's menu covers and introduced herself to Kim to congratulate her on her work. She had even gone so far as to convince her date for the evening that he needed to buy one of Kim's paintings for his collection. If there was anything Carmen had learned, it was the value of friendships at the right restaurants.

"Kim, I didn't know you'd be here tonight!" Carmen gushed, knowing full well Kim would be there, as she always was on Saturday nights.

"Hello, Carmen, how nice to see you again."

Like all restaurateurs, Kim had a knack for remembering names and faces, and she was gracious enough to be polite to Carmen, even though she saw right through Carmen's false friendliness.

"You remember Ray Strauss, Kim McCarty," Carmen introduced, looking over Kim's head to survey the crowd in the restaurant. "Kim is the artist who did the paintings on the menus. You remember, Ray."

"Indeed I do," Ray supplied.

"Ray's in New York now, and he's only in town tonight. Michael's is his very favorite restaurant, and he insists on coming here when he's in town. So here we are."

"How nice," Kim responded, then added, "of course, you know we've got a Michael's on 55th Street in Manhattan now as well. Same menu and everything." She began to move away. "Let me see how they're doing on your table. We're a little backed up tonight."

"Thanks, Kim, we are absolutely starved. I think I'm going to order everything on the menu," effused Carmen, trying to look over Kim's shoulder at the reservation book to see if Sam and his party had been seated yet.

"I can give you a table inside right now, but if you want the corner table by the fountain as you requested, it'll be a few more minutes."

"Inside is fine, isn't it Carmen? I'm still on New York time, and it's past my bedtime."

Carmen resented Ray's unsubtle hint about bed and decided she would have to punish him by not spending the night with him at the Beverly Hills Hotel after all.

"Oh, Ray, you know how I love the garden," she said aloud, adding to herself, *especially when I know Sam Carrouthers is sitting in it.* "I'd rather wait, if Kim doesn't think it will be too long."

"I thought you were so hungry," Ray whined, starting to lose his good humor.

"But it's so much more romantic outside. We'll just have a glass of champagne while we wait." Kim nodded and went to greet another arriving party.

"Order us something wonderful, sweetcakes," she said. "I'll just go up and powder my nose. By the time I get back, I'm sure our table will be ready."

How dare he try to tell me where we're going to sit, she thought as she mounted the stairs to the powder room. After all, she was doing him a huge favor just by seeing him, tonight or any night. Her anger thrust ahead of her like a dagger, Carmen pushed open the ladies room door a bit too forcefully, almost knocking over a lady in a red dress who was exiting the tiny anteroom. The woman gave Carmen a surprised look as they passed, perhaps expecting an apology, but she didn't get one from Carmen.

Then Carmen recognized the woman from pictures she'd seen of her in the papers. It was Sam's wife, Enid Carrouthers.

🍳

$\mathcal{E}$nid slipped back into her chair in the garden. She hadn't missed anything. Their entrees had still not arrived, and Marcie and Jim were still elaborating on plans for their daughter's upcoming wedding.

As Marcie detailed the hors d'oeuvres —canapes made of tiny blinis topped with smoked salmon and a dollop of caviar and tied into a purse with a chive, miniature blue corn tortilla enchiladas filled with lobster, and on and on — Enid was struck by Marcie's and Jim's preoccupation with food. *Eat each meal as though it is your last,* Jim had been known to say. And he did.

For dinner, in addition to his entree, he had asked the waiter to bring two appetizers and an extra order of French fries. Sometimes instead of ordering one dessert, he would ask the waiter to bring samples of each item on the menu, a fun idea, but inevitably everyone at the table ate too much and was sorry later. And yet, neither Jim nor Marcie appeared overweight. She wondered what their secret was. She would have to ask Sam. He knew all of Jim's secrets.

The waiter appeared with their meals: grilled chicken with steamed vegetables for Enid, salmon in a Dijon mustard sauce for Sam, seafood pasta for Marcie, and an enormous platter of osso buco for Jim, with the order of French fries set in the middle of the table.

"Ah," sighed Jim, taking a few fries before the plate hit the tablecloth. "Almost as good as McDonald's." He turned to the waiter. "Could you bring some catsup?"

"I don't know if we have any in the kitchen, sir," the waiter sneered. "I'll check."

"I wonder if that attitude is part of their training," mused Sam, to let Jim know it was okay with him if Jim was not sophisticated in his eating habits.

"I'm sure it is," said Marcie, "Michael is so careful about all of the other details. Especially the flowers. Did you see the arrangement by the stairs?"

They all turned to look at the flowers at exactly the moment Carmen Leventhal and Ray Strauss started to descend the stairs.

Carmen could not have planned this better. Instinctively, she responded to the attention focused on her by playing the part to the hilt. Although there were only three steps to descend, Carmen paused and took Ray's arm, placing one foot directly in front of the other, in mincing steps, like a bride coming down the aisle or a model down the runway. Then, in a very unbridelike way, she shook her head so that her hair flailed her bare shoulders and laughed in orgasmic delight at some unspoken joke of Ray's. She had almost reached Sam's table before she let her eyes find his, which were, of course, staring at her. But they were disappointingly devoid of emotion. Could he have missed the pointed message of her dramatic entrance?

"Sam, how nice to run into you!" Carmen bent to give him what would look to the others like a peck on the cheek. What she really did was lick his earlobe with a swift flick of her tongue that shocked Sam so deeply he leapt to his feet, knocking over his chair.

A busboy jumped to rescue the chair and hovered close by, clearly expecting further repercussions from this encounter.

"Hello, Ca . . .Ca . . ." Sam stumbled over the word, as though he had forgotten Carmen's name. They both knew he had not.

"You know Ray Strauss, don't you?" she introduced. "This is Sam Carrouthers."

"Yes, of course." The men shook hands solemnly.

"And this must be your wife, Enid. I'm Carmen Leventhal." Carmen had been around enough married men to know that the best way to deflect a wife's jealousy was to call her by her name, and then to add, as she did, "Sam couldn't stop talking about you when we had lunch last week."

Enid took the hand that was so aggressively proffered by this un- known and already disliked woman and shook it, murmuring her hello, as Sam explained that she was a reporter from the *Times*. But she wondered why Sam hadn't told her that his lunch last week had been with a woman. What was he hiding?

She looked at Sam and was even more concerned when she saw the dazed expression on his face. It clearly indicated that he had not forgotten to mention the woman and the lunch, but that he had not wanted Enid to know about either.

She watched this Carmen person shake hands with both Marcie and Jim, solid, manly handshakes that belied the softness of the hands, the carefully manicured ovals of the fingernails.

Jim rose politely as he shook Carmen's hand and then Ray's. To Carmen he said, "Your series on the S & L crisis was most impressive. You remember it, don't you Marcie?"

"How could I forget? You read it to me while I was brushing my teeth every morning for a week."

"How in hell did you get Marvin Castroni to admit that when he was a member of the Federal Reserve, he kept his own savings in- vested in precious gems?" Jim asked. "Talk about not trusting the sys- tem."

"It was easy, if you know Marv. All you have to do is play to his ego and he's like putty in your hands . . . not unlike a lot of other busi- nessmen I know." Carmen looked at Ray when she said this, not ma- liciously, but so the others would assume she was affectionately teasing her date.

Ever willing to play his part in this drama, even though he had no idea what the plot was, Ray improvised, "I have no ego at all where you're concerned, Carmen dear."

"Oh come now, Ray, you know how much I love a man with a

huge ego," Carmen replied, licking her lips lightly. She gave Sam a knowing smile, and when he didn't smile back, Carmen boldly leaned over him and snatched a French fry off of the plate in the center of the table. "Mmm, delicious. We'd better get to our table, Ray, before I devour everything in sight."

Enid watched Sam watching Carmen Leventhal sashay away. Who was she, and why was she causing Sam to drool like a libidinous teenager? If Enid hadn't known her husband better, she would have been jealous.

But did she really know this man she'd been married to for twelve years? As she stared at him now, thinking about this secret he had withheld from her, wondering what other secrets lurked inside of his heart, she wasn't so sure. All of a sudden he seemed like a complete stranger.

🕶

So tell me about this Carmen Leventhal," said Enid later, as they drove home from the restaurant. She tried to make her voice sound blasé, but it was obvious to her that Sam and this woman were more than just business acquaintances. And while she was afraid of what her question might uncover, she could not stop herself from asking it.

"There's nothing to tell," Sam said dismissively, as she knew he would, his legal training automatically kicking in, forcing her to dig deeper.

"You could have fooled me," she said, hating the way he turned into F. Lee Bailey when all she wanted was a straight answer.

"Look, Enid, don't go looking for trouble where none exists. She's a reporter researching a story about Leo and the WIT deal I told you about. She came to talk to me last week. That's all there is to it."

"Why didn't you mention her to me before?"

Enid hated being forced into the role of the suspicious wife, but she knew that life was an emotional minefield through which you had to maneuver carefully to arrive at the goal of a happy marriage. She couldn't ignore the mines; she had to find each one and defuse it in order to proceed. "She doesn't look like the kind of woman you could forget to mention."

"Listen to yourself, Enid." Sam's voice admitted an edge of irritation. "If Carmen were overweight and ugly, you'd never have given her a second thought. Don't you think it's an insult both to her professionalism and to mine that you automatically imagine that something is going on between us other than business, just because she's a babe?"

A babe? Enid thought. She'd never heard her husband describe another woman this way. "I can't help what I feel, Sam, and something about the way you and that woman reacted to each other makes me uncomfortable. I'm sorry. I don't want to feel this way, but I do." Enid was wounded and wished she hadn't let Jim talk her into that last glass of champagne after dinner, which had loosened her tongue — and her imagination.

"How do I know what you do with yourself all day?" Enid asked. "You leave home at 6:30 in the morning and I don't hear from you or see you most days until dinnertime. For all I know, you're having a passionate affair and spend every afternoon in a motel room in Santa Monica."

"I could say the same about you, you know," Sam countered. *I* have responsibilities to the firm and my work. *You* are free all day. How do I know you aren't meeting somebody at the Seaside Lodge when you say you're at those Westside Women's Shelter meetings?"

"Because I'm not," said Enid.

"Well neither am I," said Sam.

Enid was silent for a moment, thinking about this. What good would it do to pursue this subject when she had no proof of any wrongdoing on Sam's part? Besides, he was right, even though he didn't know it: she wasn't altogether innocent herself.

So she squeezed his hand and said sweetly, "I'm glad. Let's keep it that way."

Sam relaxed visibly and squeezed Enid's hand back. "Deal," he said. But they both knew that this wasn't the end of the story. This was only chapter one.

12

Sam and Carmen

Sweat soaked and out of breath, Sam was glad to pause between sets to mop his face and take a long drink of water. If perspiration was any indication of energy expenditure, Sam should have been tapped out by now. But there was time for one more set, and since he and his partner Blair had each won two so far, they decided to go for it.

Sam watched Blair position himself at center court, bouncing on the balls of his feet, waiting for Sam to serve. The kid was fresh as a daisy, his shirt barely damp, while Sam's was wringing wet. This, thought Sam, was what was depressing about getting old. His body was as strong and fit and willing as ever, but it was simply unable to rebound the way Blair's twenty-five-year-old body did.

He gave the ball a quick bounce, then tossed it high into the air and slammed it over the net. Blair was on top of it in an instant, tapping it lightly so that Sam was forced to run for his shot. Calculating his remaining stamina in a split second, Sam decided to let it go. A lost shot early in the game could preserve the energy he would need at the end to win. This kind of mental volley was the only defense age had against youth, and Sam had been using it with increasing frequency in past years.

"Hey, old man, you're not dying on me, are you?" Blair's teasing was part of the game, and Sam took it with good grace. Then he got off his next serve so quickly that Blair could barely see it, let alone return it.

The kid shook his head. "Damn. Did you serve that sucker or was it some kind of trick photography?"

"They say the eyes are the first to go," Sam said, and lined up for his next serve.

In the twenty-some years Sam had been playing the game, he'd had a wide variety of partners, ranging from college chums to business associates. Even a girlfriend or two had had the guts and athletic ability to put up a good competitive struggle. Blair was one of the best players he'd met, young and strong and agile, deft with his strokes and a good sport on the few occasions he had lost. Something Sam hated more than anything else was a sore loser. It ruined the game and soured the relationships between the players. He believed that in tennis, as in business, patience, politeness, and persistence paid off.

As he lobbed the ball over the net, he wondered what kind of businessman Blair would be. He didn't have a son to bring into the business world, and it would be nice to show the ropes to a young kid, someone he could trust and who would respect him. He decided to talk this over with Blair later. Then he turned his attention back to the game.

Carmen pulled her 190 SL into the parking lot near the Palisades Public Courts and looked for Sam's black Porsche. "Damn it," she said aloud, seeing nothing but a sea of Toyotas, trucks, and vans. She'd suspected that her information was wrong about his daily workouts at the park — a man of Sam's caliber certainly would belong to a private club, most likely the Sports Club on Sepulveda, or he would have a tennis court of his own.

But she'd gotten up an extra hour early and made the trip down here, so she might as well be sure. She parked in the blue handicapped parking spot near the gate and hauled herself out of the car.

Actually the park was not so bad, verdant and well manicured and practically deserted at this early hour. She saw a twosome playing on a court near the bleachers, and sure enough, one of the men was Sam. Once again, she couldn't believe her luck. Fate seemed to be playing matchmaker in her budding relationship with Sam Carrouthers. At best, she had thought she would wait for him to finish playing and catch him as he left the park. But to be able to watch him play, to see his body respond to the physical challenge of the sport, was more than she had expected.

She settled herself in the corner of the highest tier of the bleachers, hoping the glare of the rising sun would blind Sam to her presence, and leaned forward to watch. Hidden behind sunglasses, her eyes were riveted on Sam, drinking in the knowledge of his body and how it moved.

He was not as graceful as she had expected him to be, but he moved with strength and purpose. She could see the muscles of his legs, solid as iron, glistening with sweat. His shirt, wet and dripping, clung to his torso. She was more than pleased with what she saw. To think this gorgeous man was as powerful in the world of business as he was here on the court! Just consider what he must be like in bed!

The thought was apparently so potent that it reached Sam, for he chose that instant to roll his eyes upward, and he saw Carmen sitting in the bleachers, watching him.

He stopped dead in his tracks, and the ball slammed into his hip, leaving a bright red bruise.

"Carmen?"

She took off her glasses and waved down at him, sorry to lose the chance to admire him in secret but glad to have his attention just the same.

"What the hell are you doing here?"

"I wanted to talk to you, so I thought I'd catch you before work. I hope it's okay."

Sam shrugged. "We still have to finish this game, and then I have to shower. It'll be at least twenty minutes."

"I don't mind," said Carmen, wishing there were bleachers over-looking the men's locker room.

"Suit yourself."

Sam turned back to the game and readied himself for Blair's serve.

"Who's the hot chick?" Blair called, grinning.

"A reporter. It's business. Let's play."

Sam couldn't believe how much his game improved now that he knew he was being observed by Carmen Leventhal. Whatever fatigue he had been feeling evaporated like sweat off his body. Blair, too, was surprised to see Sam leap for a high shot that would have gone out of bounds, and actually make the shot. The final score was three sets to one. Sam couldn't remember the last time he'd beaten Blair, but he felt good enough now that he could go another set, if there were time — and if Carmen weren't waiting for him.

"I'll be ten minutes. Meet me in the parking lot," he called to her as he walked off the court. She smiled and waved in acknowledgment.

W hy don't you belong to the Tennis Club?" Carmen asked min-utes later as they waited for their coffee at a small nondescript diner on Entrada.

"What for? I don't want to socialize, I go to play tennis, and the courts at Pali Park are as good as any in town," he answered. "Besides, I like knowing the money I pay for court fees goes to keeping up the park, rather than financing a Ferrari for the fat cat owner of a club."

Carmen nodded, impressed, seeing the error of her own thinking. He was right. It was far more classy to support a public facility than to do the obvious thing and strive for exclusivity like everyone else.

"I don't belong to a private club either," she said, not explaining that this was due to lack of money rather than lack of snobbery.

The waitress brought the coffee. "Do you have a slice of lemon?" Sam asked. She nodded and went to get one.

"Lemon? For your coffee?" asked Carmen.

Sam shrugged. "Enid got me started on it. She puts lemon on everything."

Carmen made a mental note to eliminate lemon from her shopping list for the rest of time.

They sipped their coffee in silence, Enid's aura now hovering between them. Then they both started to talk at once. They laughed and lapsed into silence again.

"You first," said Sam.

"I was going to say that your wife is very attractive."

"Yes, she is," Sam agreed. "She apparently thinks the same thing about you, because she acted very strangely after we saw you last Saturday night."

Carmen was pleased. "Strangely?"

"Jealously is probably a more accurate word."

"I see," said Carmen, glad that she had put a sour taste in the mouth of Sam's lemon-loving wife. "Certainly I'm not the first woman you've done business with."

"No, but you're the first one who's shaken my hand and licked my ear at the same time. Either privately or publicly."

"Good," said Carmen.

There didn't seem to be anything to say after this. But the table between them was small enough so that Carmen could reach over and touch that ear, finding it still damp from Sam's recent shower. He responded by turning his head ever so slightly into her touch, so she could run her fingers through his hair. Unconsciously, he closed his eyes as her fingers traced the delicate surface of his skull.

She decided it was time to put her cards on the table.

"Sam, I will stop this, if you want me to. But you'll have to tell me you want me to."

Sam looked at her for a long time. There was a touch of sadness in his eyes. "I don't want you to stop," he said simply.

13

Patrick and Enid

What Patrick loved most about his biweekly sessions with his therapist Ellen was not the actual therapy itself, but the delicious comfort of Ellen's office.

It floated above Santa Monica, on the top floor of a tall building near the San Diego Freeway, so it had an unobstructed view, west to the beach and east to the distant skyline of Century City. Just looking out gave him a feeling of superiority and omniscience, sensations that he missed living at sea level.

But it was more than just the view. Ellen's office was a haven from the contemporary world of hard-edged, high-tech design. Entering the room felt like reentering the womb: soft, chintz-covered furniture, made comfortable by years of use, was accented by low, indirect lighting. Thick carpet invited him to remove his shoes, and he often stretched out on the couch, cushioning his head on a floral, down-filled pillow scented with jasmine, or some such garden aroma.

The couch was just close enough to the window to allow him to enjoy the view of sky and sea without seeing any buildings. No noise from outside could penetrate the triple pane glass; nothing to distract him from the voices in his own head.

There was no desk in the room. Ellen preferred to see her patients in a homelike setting. And she always had cookies or freshly baked breads available to them, with mugs of cinnamon-scented coffee in the winter and iced tea flavored with apple juice in the summer. She routinely allowed a patient five minutes alone at the beginning of a session to let him or her relax and collect his or her feelings, and Patrick was now enjoying those few minutes, thinking about Ellen.

He had been her patient for fourteen years, which meant that their association had lasted longer than any love relationship he had ever had — in fact, longer than all of his marriages combined. For some years he had thought that their bond endured simply because they *weren't* lovers.

So, of course, he had had to test that theory.

Catching Ellen in a rare disarmed moment one summer, he persuaded her to reveal that she and her husband were in the process of a painful divorce. Years of therapy had trained Patrick to realize that Ellen had allowed him to extract this personal tidbit because she wanted to open a door to him, and Patrick had charged right through it, seducing Ellen for the first time that afternoon on the chintz couch.

As unprofessional as this liaison has been, it had cemented their bond and made it much easier for Patrick to confide in Ellen. And though their flame burned only briefly, they had remained fast friends.

Ellen entered the room through a side door, and he turned to greet her. She was not beautiful in a conventional way. Her forehead was creased by the troubles of dozens of patients, and her small, frail body hardly seemed strong enough to bear the burden of so much human distress. But her hands were large and calloused. Patrick thought the callouses were the most erotic thing about Ellen, physical testament to the vigorous way she dug into the psyches of her patients. If he'd known the truth, that they were the product of Ellen's own private fetish, the need to vacuum her house twice a day, once before work and once after, he may not have been so aroused by them.

"So where did we leave off last time?" She wasted no time in beginning the session.

"Most likely we were talking about sex. It does seem to be at the *root* of my problem, so to speak," replied Patrick.

Ellen smiled at his pun. "If I remember correctly, you told me that your next-door neighbor had," here she paused to find the right words, "made herself available to you. Is that accurate?"

"I think that would be a fair assessment of the situation," said Patrick, "although I should point out that I did give her some modicum of encouragement."

"Meaning?"

"Meaning I suggested to her that sex was her real motive for inviting me to lunch."

"Why did she say she invited you?"

"To ask me to help her with a charity event."

"And why do you think there was more than that on her mind?"

Patrick gave Ellen the benefit of one of his famous smiles. "Because there's always more on a woman's mind. Even if she doesn't know it."

Ellen smiled back. Although their relationship had returned to doctor-patient status, the undercurrents remained, and Ellen was not immune to Patrick's charm.

"Remember when we discussed your need to make every woman you meet fall in love with you, or should I say, want to make love to you?"

"Of course, it is a recurring theme in my life. I don't deny it, I thrive on it. It's what I live for."

Patrick was teasing now, but Ellen cut through his sarcasm. "Why do you think you don't seem to be able to sustain a friendship with a woman you haven't made love to? Is making love a prerequisite to friendship for you?"

"Well, you've got to admit it's a pretty good way to get to know another person."

"Not necessarily. It doesn't help you understand what they think or feel."

"No, but it helps you know what they feel like."

"Patrick, let's try to consider this without making jokes." Ellen had assumed her role as doctor again.

"All right, I'll try, I promise. Let's see, why would making love with a woman be a prerequisite to friendship?" He stroked his chin thoughtfully, feeling manly comfort in the roughness of the bristling hairs.

"I suppose sharing that sort of affection puts us on equal footing. A *baring* of the souls."

She gave him a dirty look.

"Sorry."

"You're saying it sort of balances the scales? Literally leaving nothing hidden?" Ellen prodded.

"I guess so."

"Predisposing her to like you?"

"Not necessarily. What if she doesn't like making love to me?"

Ellen smiled at him. "I doubt that is ever the case."

"Well, I've got to admit it's nothing I've ever worried about before."

"Describe this particular woman. Her name is Enid?"

Patrick nodded. "Are you asking me as my therapist, or as a jealous lover?"

"You know I'm not jealous of your relationships, Patrick. I only want to help you understand them better," Ellen replied, although she was not entirely sure jealousy wasn't at least a small factor in her curiosity.

"Does that mean you don't love me any more?" teased Patrick.

"No, it means I love you dearly and I want you to live a happy and healthy life. So please, tell me about Enid. What is it about her that draws you to her? Her appearance?"

Patrick thought for a moment, looking out the window for inspiration. "You know, it's odd. I can't really remember what she looks like. I mean she has light brown hair and brown eyes. She's slender. Clean, that's it. I would call everything about her *clean*. But I can't really explain how it all fits together."

"Close your eyes and visualize her. What do you see?"

Patrick closed his eyes and tried to dredge up an image of Enid. "You'll laugh, but what I see is myself reflected in her sunglasses. There was a shot like that in Polanski's last film, what was it called? *Revenge*, or *Renegade?*"

"Patrick's let's not lose our track," Ellen reminded. "So you see yourself in her eyes. Do you think that means you and she are alike?"

"No, it's more like she's a mirror. When I look at her what I see is that she's focused on me."

"Where do you see her? What is she doing?"

Patrick closed his eyes. He smiled, then he began to laugh. "She's standing at her window, peeking through it into the window of my study, which is about ten feet away. She thinks I can't see her, but I can."

"What is she looking at?"

"That's the interesting part. I don't know. If she'd been watching me in the bedroom or the bathroom it would have been understandable. Kinky, but understandable. But to watch me working at my desk, that was pretty odd."

"Was?"

"When she came over to talk about the charity thing, she happened to wander into the study and saw that I could see clearly into her house. So she realized I had seen her watching me. And, as far as I can tell, she's stopped."

"So let's recap this. In other words, what got you interested in this woman was the fact that she was watching you?"

Patrick considered this. "I suppose that's true. But that's not all."

"Well, what else then?"

"It's difficult to say."

Patrick wished he could tell Ellen the truth, that pursuing this woman was sport to him. Some men played golf, others jogged or played tennis. He seduced women. It was the one game he had found that required both intellectual and physical finesse. And, if you won, there was such a nice reward: scoring was more than just numbers on a board in center field.

But Ellen would never have understood this. It would only alienate her and would have taken the sexual tension, hence the fun, out of their sessions.

So all he said was, "I really do like her as a person."

"And therefore you plan to have an affair with her, possibly destroying her marriage in the process? Can't you just be friends?"

"What would be the point?"

Ellen sighed and shook her head.

Patrick smiled sympathetically and said, "Come on, we've only been at this fourteen years. I just need a little more time."

Patrick pulled his rented Ford into the driveway of Sara's Benedict Canyon bungalow, blocking a late-model BMW that was parked in *his* spot. He didn't know what made him angrier — finding his parking place taken, or realizing Sara was not alone, waiting eagerly for his unannounced arrival.

He used his key to unlock the front door and entered. He had been feeling guilty about neglecting Sara this past week, while she recovered from her bout of food poisoning. But he was not a good nurse, and he hated to see women puffy with fever, their hair matted and greasy from too many days in bed, breath fetid with indigestion.

But now, after talking about sex for an hour with Ellen, his libido was raging, and he needed to relieve it.

Sara was not in the living room, but he found two wineglasses on the coffee table with an ominously empty bottle of Sonoma Cuttrer Chardonnay, which had left a dark wet stain on the expensive burlwood. The room was a jumble of discarded magazines and clothes, the paraphernalia of a manicure and a newly begun needlepoint canvas. Sara loved to stitch these pillows, probably because it took no brains to do the work, and she could do it while she watched the soaps, her favorite pastime.

Patrick checked the kitchen. Messy, but still no Sara. His curiosity was piqued. He was just about to open the sliding glass doors to look outside when he heard Sara's unmistakable giggle coming from the bedroom. Patrick felt a thrill building in his groin. Could she actually be entertaining another man? The thought was titillating and alarming at the same time. He knew he hadn't been the most faithful lover in the world, but he had certainly expected Sara to be.

Stealthily, as though he were a character in one of his own movies, Patrick inched down the hall toward Sara's bedroom. The door was open a crack and through it he could see part of the bedroom and into the dressing room, where Sara was stepping into the bright red jumpsuit he had given her for her birthday. How could she wear it for another man?

He waited just outside the door, watching her as she dressed, talking to an unseen figure who was apparently lounging on the bed.

"Do you like how I look?" Sara asked, her question directed toward the person on the bed. "I know red is your favorite color. I wore it just for you." The words sounded vaguely familiar; she had probably used the same line on him.

He watched as Sara leaned forward to adjust her breasts so they bulged seductively from the scoop neck of the jumpsuit. She looked in the mirror to admire her work, then vamped into the bedroom, modeling her outfit for the unseen visitor. "Would you like to touch me?" she breathed, a bad imitation of Marilyn Monroe. "I want you to. To touch me all over my body."

Patrick could stand it no longer. He kicked open the door and burst into the room. "What the hell's going on here?" he barked in his Robert De Niro voice.

To his deep dismay, he did not see a naked lover sprawled on the bed as he'd expected. It was only Elaine, Sara's agent, sitting propped against the headboard, a screenplay open on her lap.

"Paddy! Good grief you scared me." Sara ran to hug him. Over her shoulder he could see Elaine's self-satisfied smirk.

"So, Patrick, what'd'you think was going on? A little matinee? Don't we have a suspicious mind!"

Patrick ignored Elaine and turned to Sara. "What are you all dressed up for? I thought you were sick."

"Oh, I was. I lost four pounds, see?" She twirled for him, smoothing her hands along the curve of her waist. "But I had to get better because Elaine's got a reading set up for me over at Dominion. Oh, Paddy, it's the most exciting script."

"Dominion," he said, suddenly seeing that the script open on Elaine's lap had a light blue cover. "What's the name of the project?"

"*For Love or Money*," said Elaine, giving Patrick a smile that told him she knew he was negotiating for the lead in this film. The question was, did Sara know?

"It's the most wonderful part, a retarded girl who falls in love with a really rich guy, and he falls in love with her. It's practically the lead, and Elaine got me a reading, can you believe it?"

Apparently Sara didn't know, thank God. But he expected that Elaine was only biding her time before she let the cat out of the bag.

"Amazing," said Patrick. "And how did you do that?" he asked Elaine, not even trying to mask the venom in his voice. Wouldn't it be the pits if Dominion passed on him and gave a lead role to Sara?

Elaine shrugged. "It's my job to know what's going on around town, and who's doing what. There's a marvelous part in this one for you, too, Patrick," she rubbed it in.

"Oh, sweetie, wouldn't it be too fantastic for words if we could work together?" Sara gave him a kiss, the breathy kind that usually melted him. But at that moment, he was immune to such tenderness, still focusing his attention on Elaine.

"I'll have to have LeMar check it out," he said evenly.

"Well, Sara we should be off. Don't want to be late for Jeffrey Kesselman. You know what they say, if you keep Kesselman waiting — "

"He finds another actor," Sara and Patrick finished for her.

🕶

Patrick backed the Ford out of Sara's driveway, allowing Elaine's BMW to escape. He saw Sara blow him a kiss as the car sped off down the canyon, but he did not return it. He had envisioned such a nice afternoon — Sara eagerly awaiting his arrival, wearing that gauzy leopard print robe she'd gotten from the Frederick's of Hollywood catalog, and nothing else.

In his fantasy, her house had been immaculate and smelling of jasmine — a carryover from his session with Ellen, no doubt. She'd greeted him with a passionate, probing kiss, and a glass of Chateau d'Yquem, which he'd proceeded to pour over her body, slowly licking off every sweet drop.

Soon he was in the heart of Beverly Hills, feeling anonymous in the tacky loaner Ford. He considered how he might empty his tank of energy on this yawningly free afternoon. It was too late for lunch and too early for a drink, so The Grill was out. Maybe a stroll down Rodeo Drive and a little shopping. But his credit cards were tapped out — maybe just the stroll. He was sure to be recognized, and the adoration of his fans always did wonders for his spirits.

He pulled over to let the valet at Polo take his car and was gratified to see the look of delight on the boy's face when he recognized Patrick.

"If you can lose this car, you'll be doing me a favor," said Patrick.

"Yessir, Mr. Drake, anything you say," worshipped the boy, and Patrick wondered if the kid realized he had been joking. He decided to step into Polo for a moment. Hadn't he gotten a notice about a sale? He could always use his house charge.

Enid thumbed through the cashmere and silk blend sweaters, looking for Sam's size. She had felt lousy since their argument, knowing she'd hurt Sam by implying that she didn't trust him. The more she thought about it, the more she realized that she doubted him because her own mind had been running rampant with erotic images of herself and Patrick. Not that she actually thought anything would come of it, but the fantasy was stunning and all consuming, like the pain of a broken arm. Only it felt good.

So here she was, in Sam's favorite store, looking for a gift to assuage her guilt. She found the size forty-eight and unfolded it. Sam liked to wear these lightweight sweaters next to his skin, so he usually bought them a bit small. She held it up in front of the mirror, wondering if it would fit him.

Her own reflection caught her attention. She had never looked better. But why? Her hair, makeup, clothes — everything was the same. Ah, but it was the expression in her eyes that was different, the way she felt. Since her lunch with Patrick, she had been energized. Everyone seemed to be staring at her — smiling, flirting, telegraphing erotic messages. As if to illustrate her point, the salesman in the shoe department was striding toward her, drawn by some kind of magnetic radiance she was emitting.

"May I do something for you, Mrs. Carrouthers?" he asked.

"What did you have in mind?" she teased, as shocked by her choice of words and her insinuating tone as he was.

"Er, well, another color, or a different style?" he fumbled. "We have more in the back."

"If that's for me, I must tell you, you are greatly underestimating my size," boomed a voice behind Enid, and she wheeled around to find Patrick beaming down on her.

"It is for me, isn't it?" he teased, and he took the sweater from her, holding it up to his chest. "Shall I slip it on?"

Other shoppers gathered to watch this exchange, and Patrick

played to them, glad for an audience. They smiled and nodded, peering curiously at Enid, wondering if she too were a famous person.

"Why not?" Enid replied, more pleased than she could say by this coincidence, and by Patrick's flattering and public attention. He took her hand. "Come with me. I'll give you a peep show."

"No! Patrick, I can't." But he was pulling her toward the dressing room.

"They don't mind, do you boys?" he asked the salesmen, who smiled and winked at Patrick. "The dressing rooms are coed aren't they?"

"Patrick, please," Enid pulled her hand away and stopped. "I can't go in there with you!"

"Well then, I'll just have to try it on right here, in front of all of these wonderful people. Shall I?" he asked the crowd.

"Yes," they responded, delighted to witness a famous person making a fool out of himself. A flashbulb snapped as someone with enough forethought to carry a camera took a picture.

Patrick faced Enid and coyly slipped off his jacket, tossing it onto a pile of trousers.

"Patrick, please don't. I'm not kidding. This isn't funny," Enid pleaded.

He ignored her, and began to unbutton his shirt, playing to the crowd, circling around Enid like a stripper. Someone shouted "take it off." Patrick batted his eyes in mock modesty, then slowly shrugged the shirt off one shoulder. Enid took one look at his bare skin, turned and headed for the door.

"Enid!" Patrick called, but she ducked her head and hurried out of the store. He quickly rebuttoned his shirt. "Sorry, everybody, I guess the lady wants to save me for herself." He followed her, ignoring the chorus of disappointed "ohs" from the crowd.

Enid was already at the corner when Patrick caught up with her. Her face was rigid and pale, eyes hidden behind dark glasses.

"Enid, I was only clowning." He was panting from the exertion of the run. "People expect it of me. It was only a joke."

"I'm sorry if it's a joke to you," she said, urgently pushing the walk button, "but I know the people in that store. The name on our charge account is *Mr. and Mrs. Sam Carrouthers.* What if it got back to Sam that you were doing a striptease for me in front of half of Beverly Hills?"

"You're right, I'm sorry. I just got carried away. Please, Enid. It's such a small thing. Why are you so upset?"

The light turned green, and Enid started to cross. Patrick didn't follow.

She walked a few more steps, stopped and looked back at Patrick. Then she slowly walked back to him, despite the flashing "Don't Walk."

Enid stood in front of him, studying her Gucci loafers as though their navy blue tassels held the answers to all of the burning questions of the universe. Finally she lowered her sunglasses and said, "Because, Patrick, when you started to unbutton your shirt, I realized how much I wanted . . . to . . . see your body," she finished in a rush.

She turned away again, this time almost running in her haste to escape her embarrassment at what she had revealed. But Patrick grabbed her arm.

"Wait a minute. You can't just say something like that and walk away. What's wrong with your wanting to see my body? That's a good thing. I want to see yours too."

Enid flushed scarlet and put her sunglasses back on. "Patrick, I don't know what kind of a relationship you have with Sara Benton, but I'm a married woman! And I can't . . . won't . . . I'm not going to do anything to jeopardize my marriage! All right?"

"No, it's not all right," said Patrick with a smile, slowly running his fingers up the inside of Enid's arm.

"What?"

"You didn't say *happily* married. There's a big difference."

🕶

$\mathcal{E}$nid's head was spinning. Five minutes ago she had been trying to purge herself of guilt for thinking about adultery. Now, following Patrick into the dimly lit bar of the Rangoon Racquet Club, she was a step closer to actually committing the act. What had happened to her resolve to be a good wife? How could she let this man, this stranger, so effortlessly sway her from twelve faithful years? Was she that weak?

Or was he that powerful?

The waiter came for their order. Patrick reached across the table and squeezed Enid's hand. "How does a Kir Royale sound?"

"Like something out of Noel Coward."

She loved the way he was tickling her palm with his fingertip. Her whole being was focused on that sensation. She and Patrick were at the center of the universe, and nothing else existed. Had she ever felt that way with Sam? Of course. But not recently, not for a long time.

"What are you feeling?" Patrick asked, when the waiter left them alone.

"That I shouldn't be here, in a bar in the middle of the afternoon, drinking Kir Royales with a man who isn't my husband." She pulled her hand away. "I don't do this."

"Are you're trying to tell me you're not that kind of a girl?" teased Patrick. Enid reddened. "Come on, it's not so terrible. Is it?" He slid around the booth so he could put his arm around her, and leaned close to whisper in her ear, "Doesn't this feel good?"

She didn't even hesitate. "Yes."

Then he kissed her, electricity sparking from his wet lips to her dry hair. "It feels good to me too," he said. "Enid," his voice became a tiger's purr, "we would be so good together. You make me crazy! I don't know, when I'm around you, all I can think about is making love to you. And you know it."

"Patrick, I can't."

Patrick sighed and slid away, pouting. "You're really a piece of work. This is supposed to be fun, enjoyment, playtime. You're acting like it's a job, like cleaning the toilet or something."

"No, no, I don't mean to, please don't think that," Enid pleaded. "I'm just so confused. Ever since we had lunch I can't stop thinking about . . ." She sighed. "I went to Neiman's earlier, to pick up some lipstick, and all of a sudden I found myself in the lingerie department, looking at skimpy silk negligees."

"I wish I'd been there. I know just what I'd buy for you."

"The weird thing is, I don't even wear that sort of thing. I never have."

"Tell me what you wear to bed." It was not a question, but an urgent command.

"Well, I get cold, so I can't wear anything too bare." Was she really telling him these intimate facts of her life?

"I'd keep you warm," Patrick said. "Body against body, my flesh against your flesh." He let his hand slip under her sweater, rubbing her spine in a circular motion, an advanced variation of "the stroke." "Mmmm. You feel very warm right now."

Enid said nothing. The moment his hand touched the bare skin of her back, her resolve and inhibitions disappeared. She allowed him to draw her closer, wanting, urging his hand to sweep around her rib cage and caress her breast. And when he kissed her, she responded with abandon, forgetting the waiter, who placed the drinks on the table and slipped away smiling, and the people in the next booth who were staring at them, shocked, but envious too, and the fact that this was the first man other than her husband whom she had kissed passionately in twelve years.

When she finally opened her eyes Patrick was smiling at her as though he had just won some kind of prize. "I knew that was in there," he beamed.

14

Carmen and Sam

From where Carmen sat in the newsroom, she had a clear view of Ralph's office. So it was a constant irritation to her that he had a window and a couch, while her cell was dark, and barely big enough for the old leather wing chair she'd bought at a flea market because it looked like it belonged in a senior editor's office.

Carmen hated everything about Ralph, from the way he tried to comb his few remaining strands of hair over his bald spot, which itself was disgustingly riddled with liver spots and moles, to his teeth, yellowed the color of bile. As physically revolting as Ralph was to her, his personality disgusted her even more. He was the kind of man who called women "honey" or "sweetheart" regardless of his relationship to them, and often she had overheard him in the hallway, telling a lewd joke to the other old boys, or braying like a camel in response to one of theirs.

She watched him now as he stared at the passage he had just written on his ancient Royal typewriter, then unconsciously thrust one of the all-important index fingers deeply into his nose, rooted out a revolting mass of matter, examined it, and wiped it on the bottom of his chair. Carmen felt her gorge rise as she considered the masses of fossilized globs on the underside of that chair, plucked from Ralph's hairy nostrils over the course of the last seven years.

Finally, Ralph wheeled his chair away from the desk, stood and stretched, immodestly scratching his ass, readjusting his balls, and hefting his belt up over his protruding stomach. He hooked his coat on his finger and left the office, dropping his sloppily typed pages onto his secretary's desk as he passed.

The secretary, Hilda, a no-nonsense Hispanic woman in her mid forties, was immersed in her work, earphones from a Dictaphone covering her ears. She didn't seem to see the papers Ralph deposited, and didn't even look up as he passed.

Carmen caught the eye of her own secretary, Rhoda, and nodded curtly. Thus cued, Rhoda picked up her purse and walked over to Hilda's desk. They chatted for a moment, then Hilda picked up her purse and the two women exited. Perfect, thought Carmen, well worth the twenty bucks she'd given to Rhoda so she could invite Hilda to lunch, her treat.

Once the coast was clear, Carmen sauntered by Hilda's desk and scooped up the papers on her way out the door. The irony of Ralph's stubborn refusal to use a computer was that there was no file record of what he had just typed on the Royal, and if these pages happened to disappear from Hilda's desk, he would have to start from scratch to write it again. Carmen knew she was putting Hilda in the hot seat, but it was no more than she deserved for compromising her principles by working for a misogynist like Ralph.

"Mr. Carrouthers, Miss Leventhal is here to see you."

Margie's voice brought Sam out of his stupor. He was surprised, and yet somehow he'd known Carmen would come. "Have her wait," he stalled.

"Yes, sir." Margie knew better than to question her boss, although she could see for herself that he was not occupied, had not made or accepted a phone call since he'd arrived, uncharacteristically late, that morning. She closed the door behind her.

Sam continued to sit in stunned silence, playing over in his mind his earlier conversation with Carmen at the diner. Was he really planning to have an affair with her? All indications pointed in that direction. Obviously she was willing, but she had nothing to lose from this liaison and everything to gain. He, on the other hand, would be risking his honor and his marriage, the two things he valued most, if he pursued this freak passion. It was completely wrong, and yet the thought of her was so alluring, his desire for her had become so insistent, it was really not something he could control any longer, let alone understand.

Carmen waited in the outer office of ICCM, Ralph's story folded neatly in her bag. At first she was afraid Sam's secretary was going to give her the runaround again, but instead the girl had said Mr. Carrouthers was on a long distance call, would she wait, and offered Carmen some coffee. So Carmen realized she had crossed some invisible line, and that she was now counted as one of the select few who rated special consideration from Sam's support staff.

Carmen didn't mind the wait. It gave her time to decide what she was going to say to Sam about Ralph's story, what line of action she would suggest they take. According to Ralph's sources, Leo Choate was in Japan to meet with Isoku Tonitshi, the Japanese head of WIT's parent company, to get approval to proceed with the Dominion buyout, pursuant, of course, to the due diligence and finalization of the contracts. The story as it stood still wasn't front-page news, but from what Ralph had written, he planned to inflate it by doing a companion piece on Leo himself, his background, his personal life, and his goals for the future. And there was the odd reference to Harry Ingersol. Where did he fit in?

Since Leo was in Tokyo, it would be impossible for Ralph to interview and photograph him until the coming week. Carmen hoped she and Sam could come up with some salient facts before then, which would, in effect, quash Ralph's story. Then she could replace it with one of her own.

Carmen tried to sit back in the uncomfortable faux Louis XIV chair. What inspired people to create these sterile waiting areas? Clearly the talentless designer who picked the somber colors and hard-backed furniture never considered for a moment how it would feel to sit here. If only she could have a cigarette —

Then a Korean girl in an immaculate Ellen Tracy suit glided out of the inner offices. Carmen marveled at how her feet didn't seem to touch the floor. She moved like a human hovercraft, floating on a cushion of air. Her complexion was flawless, her thick, black hair shockingly straight. And yet she masked her natural beauty in boring clothes, an uninteresting hairdo, and a blank facial expression. Some women just didn't get it, Carmen thought. Beauty was a trump card, why not play it?

"Jean, I'm going to run by Mr. Choate's house," the Korean girl said. "Mrs. Choate asked me to go through the mail every day to make sure she didn't miss anything important. Can you watch the phones while I'm out?" The Korean girl spoke as smoothly as she moved.

"Sure thing, Karen," replied the girl behind the reception desk. "Could you bring me a Diet Coke and a Milky Way from the sundry shop when you come back?"

"Doesn't the candy bar kind of cancel out the Diet Coke?" asked Karen with a smile, taking a dollar bill from Jean.

"You're right," Jean said, "just bring me the Milky Way." Both girls laughed.

Carmen, however, wasn't laughing. She was putting two and two together and coming up with a golden opportunity. As soon as Karen was safely in the elevator, Carmen approached Jean.

"I'm sorry to bother you," she said in a *just-between-us-girls* voice, "but is there a phone I can use?"

"There's one on the side table," Jean replied, pointing to an instrument on the table right next to Carmen's chair.

"What would be great would be if I could use one with a little privacy. I don't think Karen would mind if I used hers, just for a second, do you? As long as Leo is out of town."

Jean considered this. Carmen's clever introduction of Karen's and Leo's first names in such a friendly, offhand way threw her. She knew it was her job to guard the sanctity of the office, but she also knew people liked their friends to be treated well, and maybe this woman was a friend of Mr. Choate. From the way Margie had treated her, she certainly was a friend of Mr. Carrouthers.

"I suppose it would be all right. Do you know where it is?"

"Sure," Carmen lied. "Thanks." She hurried down the hall before Jean could change her mind.

Carmen assumed Karen's office would be a modest cubbyhole next to Leo Choate's palatial space, which she had noticed last time she came to visit Sam. And sure enough, there it was, a small, windowless room, not unlike her own office, with the name *Karen Koo* on the doorplate.

Carmen entered and dropped her bag on the chair, going around the desk to sit in Karen's chair. She considered closing the door but thought better of it and picked up the phone as a cover, in case anyone walked by the office. She let her eyes scan the papers neatly piled on the desk: some interoffice memos and legal briefs, an appointment register that showed Leo would be in Tokyo at the Hotel Okura through Thursday, returning to town on Friday. There was a notation that the following Saturday was Lacy Choate's birthday and a list of ten couples who had been invited to dinner at the Hotel Bel Air to celebrate.

Carmen skimmed the list. Sam and Enid Carrouthers' names were listed second from the bottom. She recognized several of the other names as movers and shakers in Los Angeles society, but she knew none personally. That, she thought, would soon change.

Judging that she had only a few more minutes of privacy before the receptionist got suspicious, Carmen flipped on Karen's computer screen, thanking God for the computer programming courses she'd forced herself to sit through. A main menu appeared on the screen, offering Carmen the choices of (a) Correspondence (b) Client Files — Active (c) Client Files — Inactive (d) Expenses (e) ICCM Management (f) LHC — Personal (g) New Business.

Carmen would have loved to explore "Personal" but decided, in the interest of time, on "New Business" and pushed the letter "g." The New Business directory contained at least fifty files. Carmen skimmed the list quickly, looking for, and finally finding, a configuration of letters in a file name which contained the letters "WIT." Quickly she called up the file, but to her frustration the computer refused to cooperate. Instead of the information she wanted, the screen flashed "*Password?*"

"Shit," she said aloud. She should have known it would be a locked file. She hunted around the desk for some kind of clue to the secret name Karen used — the name of a pet, the date of a birthday, a favorite flower. She opened a drawer and started to rummage through it.

"Miss Leventhal?"

Carmen caught her breath and had the presence of mind to pull a pencil from the open drawer before looking up to see Sam's secretary, Margie, standing in the doorway. She motioned to her to wait a moment, then spoke into the phone, which mercifully was still wedged against her ear. "Okay, Rhoda, I found a pencil. Give me the number again. Right, Right. Thanks. I'll call you later."

She hung up and stood. "Why is it you never have a pencil when you need one?" she said to Margie and scooted out from behind the desk, realizing as she did that the computer screen was still blinking "*Password?*" Had Margie noticed?

"Has Sam finished his call?"

"Yes. He can see you now."

"Great."

Carmen followed Margie out the door, but lagged back until Margie was far enough ahead for her to say, "Oh, my notebook!" Then she ran back into the office and turned off the computer. Mission accomplished.

❧

Waiting for Margie to bring Carmen to him, Sam was still uneasy. For some reason he did not want to greet her from behind his desk, but if he moved to his couch or to a comfortable chair, he was worried that his posture would look too contrived and obvious. He could sit at the conference table, but then he should be examining some papers or meeting with someone to make the scene look natural.

As he was milling around the room trying to decide where to position himself, Margie tapped on the open door and announced, "Miss Leventhal is here," and Carmen breezed in.

"Send her in," said Sam redundantly, thrown off guard as he always was by Carmen's presence. Without asking or apparently even considering how Sam felt about it, she closed the door behind her, right in Margie's surprised face.

Sam was unaware of Margie's startled expression because he had fallen into the depths of Carmen's eyes. In them he saw lust, laughter, and longing. He felt himself drowning in a pool that was her desire for him, and his whole body prickled with the sensation. When he opened his mouth to speak, his words came out in a breathless gasp.

"To what do I owe this unexpected pleasure?"

Carmen threw back her head and howled with laughter, approaching him with a loose-limbed stride that could only be called a saunter. "Sam, Sam, Sam," she said.

He started to back away, feeling like a mouse cornered by a cat.

When he backed into his desk, he let himself sit against it as though he had planned this maneuver, and with an air of feigned nonchalance, watched her continue to approach. He was suddenly detached, as though he were seeing this all in a movie. *The Seduction of Sam Carrouthers,* he thought, and his mind ricocheted with the possibilities.

As though she were reading his mind, Carmen put both arms around his neck and roughly pulled his mouth to hers, welcoming it with hot, wet lips and a tongue thrust so far down his throat it nearly gagged him. His reaction was spontaneous and sure. He gripped her hair in handfuls and pulled her head back so he could see her quivering, open mouth, the white teeth, the obscenely pink tongue. Then he kissed her back, matching her fervor with a passion that surprised him. He could feel her pleasure as though it were his own. Or was it his own?

"Yes, Mr. Carrouthers."

"Huh!"

Margie's disembodied voice might as well have been a bucket of ice water dousing Sam's arousal. He was instantly shocked back into the real world, but confused. Who had called his name, and why?

"You buzzed me, Mr. Carrouthers?"

He realized he was sitting on the intercom, and had inadvertently rung Margie. He was both relieved and amused, and saw that Carmen was too, thus bonding them with the first shared secret of their relationship.

"Yes, Margie," replied Sam, not taking his eyes off Carmen. "Will you hold my calls, please. Miss Leventhal and I have something to go over."

"Yes, sir," Margie's voice replied, but Sam had already flipped off the intercom's power switch and pulled Carmen to him, feeling at the same time deliciously out of control and entirely sure of what was going to happen next.

This kiss was different than their first, because they both knew it was coming, and each wanted to impress the other. Sam let his instincts guide him, and they told him that for all of her aggressiveness,

Carmen wanted him to overpower her. So different than Enid, who was at her best when he allowed her to be the instigator.

With gentle solemnity, Sam took Carmen's hand and led her to his leather couch, detouring slightly to reach the lock on the door and turn it shut. He felt as though he were in a dream. No, not a dream, but a reel of one of those porno movies on the Direct TV. He couldn't deny the allure of knowing that thirty-seven people were hard at work just beyond the thin barrier of rosewood, while he and Carmen . . .

Carmen pulled her hand away from his, and for an instant Sam thought he had read her wrong, mistaking the invitation in her kiss. But then he saw she wanted to put the hand to better use — she wanted to unbutton the mother of pearl buttons on her coffee-colored blouse.

Sam was mesmerized by the deftness of her fingers, as they showed him how to release the buttons from the buttonholes. He helped eagerly, but in his clumsiness only unbuttoned two to her five. She stepped back and slowly drew open the blouse to reveal a beautiful lace brassiere. His fingers longed to trace the delicate filigree of the flesh-colored fabric, held taut by the fullness of her breasts. But he dared not move. He barely breathed, urging her on by the sheer force of his will.

Carmen had never been more grateful for the vigilance of her daily morning ablutions. She had not dressed today knowing she would be undressing for a man, but because all of her lingerie had been purchased with that possibility in mind, despite the spontaneity of this moment, she was able to showcase herself to her best advantage. She also was glad that she had already met her competition. Because now that she had seen Enid, observed her attitude and her body type, she could play to Sam, certain of where his fantasies lay. Married to a flat-chested wimp of a woman, Sam obviously fantasized about more zaftig bodies. And if there was anything Carmen knew, it was how to play her body to an appreciative audience.

Carmen let her hands run across the lace cups of the brassiere, imagining them as Sam's hands. She knew her nipples were visible through the sheer fabric; that was why she'd purchased this particular garment. She let her fingers trace the ridges, soft now but growing firm, and she watched Sam's face to see what effect this was having on him. Just as she had expected, his gaze was riveted on her breasts, as though through some visual magic he could feel them with his eyes.

She was impressed by his restraint. Most men would have been on top of her by now, groping and heaving, balls out. But by holding back, Sam was getting the full effect of her performance, and by playing a more passive role, he was actually orchestrating hers. His restraint was forcing her to work harder to intuit what he wanted from her, and in the process she was becoming more aroused herself.

Suddenly the game they were playing seemed to become too much of what it was, simply an act, and Carmen's need for Sam's hands on her body became urgent. She hastily unfastened the brassiere and let her breasts slip out of it, a relief, both physically and emotionally, to feel the freedom. She stepped closer to Sam so her nipples were just level with his lips, barely two inches away. She could almost see his mouth water in anticipation.

Then, tentatively, as though in slow motion, he lifted his hand and touched her so gently that at first she wasn't sure whether it was his hand or the thought of it caressing her breast that she felt. But her body knew. A groan escaped her lips.

It was this sound that snapped Sam out of his trance and brought him back to reality. He withdrew his hand and stood, awkwardly looking away from Carmen's naked torso, as though the sight of it would turn him to stone.

"Carmen," he began, then stopped, not knowing how to proceed.

"What happened?" she asked.

"Too much," he said. "This isn't the time or the place."

He picked up the blouse and the brassiere from the floor and held them out to her. She stared at him, brazenly unashamed of her nakedness.

"You tell me where and when, and I'll be there," she said.

"Please," he said, pressing the clothes into her hand. "What I mean is, I can't do this, not here, not at all."

Carmen took the blouse from him and started to put it on. "Unfortunately, you didn't do anything, did you?" She ignored the brassiere hanging limply in his hand.

They were silent while Carmen buttoned her blouse. She saw with satisfaction that Sam was still watching her with the same intensity as he had when she was unbuttoning it. When the blouse was fully closed and tucked back into her skirt, Carmen took Sam's hand and drew him to the couch where they sat, facing each other.

"Sam, I'm only going to say this once, so listen well. I am perfectly aware that you are a married man. But it doesn't change the way I feel about you, or the fact that we belong together. I didn't plan this. Something in the way our bodies reacted to each other made it happen, and I think you know a feeling that strong comes from two people, not just one."

Sam didn't say anything because he knew what she said was true. And he didn't want it to be true.

She continued, "This isn't going to go away. If we ignore it, it's only going to get worse. What we need to do is play it out, see where we stand once we've gotten beyond the first blush." She smiled. "Of course, getting there will be half the fun."

She paused to let this sink in. "Think about it. But not for too long. I'm not the world's most patient person. Now, shall we get down to business?"

She pulled the draft of Ralph's column from her purse and handed it to Sam.

"What is this?" he asked, stunned by her ability to shift gears in mid emotion.

"A draft of the feature Ralph is working on for next week. It mentions Harry Ingersol."

"Yeah, Harry's in on the deal, which is a helluva shock considering how outspoken he is about his feelings for the Japanese."

"Why would he go into this deal with Leo then? Certainly not for the money. I mean we're talking ten figures on his financial statement, aren't we?"

"Right. But you never know with Harry. The guy still buys suits off the rack. Last time I saw him he was bragging about the slacks he'd had made in Hong Kong for three bucks. He was even wearing the damn things."

"Maybe the money's part of it, but it couldn't be everything. Do you think?"

"I agree. There must be more."

"How can we find out?"

Sam shrugged. "Harry's on his boat off the coast of Sardinia. I hardly think this is something we could get into over the phone."

"What if you were to fly over there and see him?"

"Well, it would certainly get the point across that I was concerned."

"Exactly. And he'd have to see you if you came that far."

"Oh, I know he'd see me. Harry's been more than open with me in the past. We are partners."

"You and Leo Choate are partners too."

"Don't remind me."

Sam paced the room, then went to sit behind his desk to think. He buzzed the intercom.

"Yes, Mr. Carrouthers."

"Margie, get Roxie on the phone for me."

"Yes, sir."

"Who's Roxie?" Carmen asked.

"Harry's secretary. She knows how to reach him twenty-four hours a day."

"Good."

They stared at each other in silence, waiting.

"Mr. Carrouthers, Roxie's away from her desk. I left word for her to call you ASAP."

"Thank you, Margie."

Carmen rose and approached Sam's desk. He could not help but notice the gentle undulation of her breasts under the silken fabric of her blouse. "I'd better be off," she said. "Let me know what happens. And Sam, remember what I said."

"How could I forget?"

She walked to the door, putting her hand on the knob. "On second thought, I've never been to Sardinia. And the sooner we get the facts in print, the better for us both. So I'll go with you. Let me know when."

Before he could protest, she opened the door and left without looking at him.

In the outer office, Jim Morris pressed himself to the wall to let her pass, then stormed into Sam's office.

"Wasn't that the reporter from the *Times?*"

Sam nodded, still stunned from the encounter.

"What'd she want?"

Sam sighed. "Everything."

Jim sighed too. "Don't they all?" He plopped down wearily in the chair in front of Sam's desk. "Hey, Sambo, what the hell've you got there?" He gestured to Sam's hand, perplexed.

Sam looked down. He was still holding Carmen's brassiere.

3

15

Enid

nid dropped a tomato into the pan of boiling water and waited while the heat loosened the skin from the pulp. Then, with a slotted spoon, she removed it and ran it under a stream of cold tap water. When it was cool, she used her fingers to peel off the skin and set the firm red orb on the granite counter while she worked on another.

Laborious though this might be, the mindlessness of the work was soothing to Enid. And she preferred to do the tomatoes, using this method taught to her years ago by Sam's mother, rather than chop the rest of the vegetables for the minestrone soup she was preparing for Sam's dinner. So Wallase was tackling that chore.

She watched his strokes with the knife, precise and true. He hummed as he worked, setting a serene tone in the kitchen. Wallase was the perfect amalgam of housekeeper, chauffeur, chef, maintenance man, secretary, and companion — quiet and efficient, always cheerful, always willing to help, whatever the task. As Enid worked on the third tomato, she ruminated on how lucky they had been to find Wallase to run their household.

She had already interviewed six applicants before his tentative knock had announced him at her door, ten minutes early. When she opened the door, he had apologized for being early, but not wanting to be late he had overcompensated. And after sitting in his car for a full fifteen minutes, he had decided it was close enough to the appointed hour to knock on the door.

Enid had known instantly that he was her man.

The interview had gone splendidly from that point. As Enid had shown Wallase around the house, she had watched his reaction carefully. He hadn't spoken, but in his eyes she had seen an appreciation of the finer things as she had pointed them out. His manners had been impeccable. When they sat down to talk, Wallase had waited politely for her to be seated before taking the chair she had shown him. And even then, he had sat poised on the edge of the cushion, as though ready to jump up if she required anything.

That had been ten years ago. Now Wallase was so much a part of Enid's and Sam's lives that she could not imagine getting through a week without him. She had come to love and respect him for the fine human being he was, and to be grateful for his dedication to their household.

And she had enjoyed the days they had spent together, working well as a team. That is, until . . . Now, assuming he had seen her with Patrick, he had a power over her that upset the balance of their relationship. And she had no idea what to do about it. Or about the fact that she had seen him going through her private papers.

She watched him chop cilantro for the soup. Did she see a hint of arrogant disdain? A disapproving frown? There was definitely something different about him, but she couldn't think what.

"Eiiyo!" Wallase dropped the knife and sucked his bleeding finger.

"Are you okay?" Enid asked.

"I cut. Again!" he said. "This is for I have my old glasses and I am not used to."

Ah, thought Enid, that's what it was. He was wearing steel-rimmed glasses rather than the tortoise shell pair she was used to seeing.

"What happened to your others?"

"Last Monday I am cleaning the shower and they slide! Off my nose! I am so clumsy I step on, crunch, and break. These have I for many years before, but the subscription is too old. I cannot see very good the far, even from my face to my hand. I try find name of eye doctor in Missy's file but can see not."

"You poor thing. Here, let me do the cutting, you do the tomatoes."

If he'd broken his other glasses Monday, she calculated, and could not see "the far'" without them, then surely he could not have seen her in Patrick's house ten feet away on Tuesday. Relief shot through her like a drug. "Do you need a Band-Aid?"

"No, Missy, now the bleed is stop."

With her mind blissfully relieved from worry about Wallase, Enid could turn her full attention to the all-consuming thought of Patrick. She knew they were headed for trouble, but she seemed unable to stop herself.

Dear Sam, she didn't want to hurt him. And she certainly didn't want to risk damaging their marriage. But the momentum had already built past the point where she could control it. She looked at the final tomato in the pan of boiling water. As she watched, its skin burst from the heat, curling back to expose the soft red flesh. She, too, felt about ready to burst. And the water she was in was just as hot.

The phone rang. "Wallase, can you —"

But he was already wiping his hands on the dish towel he characteristically stuffed into his belt when they were working in the kitchen, so he could answer the phone.

"Carrouthers residence. Oh, hi, Mister. Yes, she's right here. Just a minute. It's Mr. Carrouthers," he chirped, holding out the phone to Enid.

"Hi," she said, wiping the tomato mush from her fingers. "Wallase and I are making a delicious minestrone for dinner, and I picked up some fresh sourdough from the Bread Pan."

"Enid, I hate to do this, to you and to me," Sam's voice sounded distant and strained. "I've got to catch a plane tonight. Something critical has come up, and I need to fly to Sardinia to meet Harry on his boat."

"Tonight? You're going to Italy tonight?"

"I know it's sudden, but there's room on the United flight to Rome at eight o'clock, and if I don't catch this one I have to wait until Friday, which may be too late."

Enid was speechless, trying to catch up to Sam's train of thought. "How long will you be gone?" she managed.

"I don't know. Hopefully only a couple of days. Hell, it takes about sixteen hours to get there and I only have to talk to Harry for a few hours. So if I can see him right away, I'll jump on the next plane home."

Enid turned off the fire under the boiling water. She hated it when Sam traveled without her, and the suddenness of this trip was a shock. She fumbled for words, trying to get used to the idea. "But we've got that Good Vibrations benefit tomorrow night," she said lamely. "The premiere of the new Harrison Ford movie."

"I know. I'm sorry. But there's nothing I can do about it. I have to talk to Harry and it won't wait."

"What about?"

On the other end of the phone Enid heard Sam sigh. "I don't have time to go into it right now. I promise I'll explain everything when I get home. It's something that concerns the firm, and if I don't have it out with Harry, face to face, the whole thing could blow apart."

"You mean ICCM is in trouble?" Now Enid was really concerned, visions of Ivan Boesky and Michael Milken dancing before her eyes.

"Not how you think. Look, I feel terrible to do this to you. When I get back, we'll plan a weekend away, just the two of us, I promise. Now I need a favor. Can you pack a few things for me and have Wallase bring them to the Red Carpet Club at United?"

"You mean you aren't even going to come home first?"

"Enid, it's five o'clock already. I have to be at the airport early to get the tickets and I'll be lucky if I make it."

Enid heard the word tickets loud and clear. "Who's going with you?"

"No one."

"But you said tickets. Plural."

"You know what I meant."

"I can rearrange things if you want me to come."

Enid could hear the desperation in her voice, and she knew why it was there: the way her relationship with Patrick was fermenting, she was afraid of what might bubble to the surface if Sam left her alone.

"Honey," Sam said, and she knew he was desperate because he only used such endearments when he was flustered and at the end of his rope, "nobody wants to fly sixteen hours to be in Sardinia for half a day and then fly back. You'd be miserable and I'd feel terrible for dragging you along."

"You can't leave me alone right now," Enid whined, hating herself for playing on his sympathies, but desperate now.

"Why not? What do you mean? Is anything wrong?"

"It's not that . . ."

"Look, I hate it too. But it's only for a couple of days. I've really got to go now. Tell Wallase not to forget my passport. Oh, and can you try to find me another pair of sunglasses? My good ones are broken. I had to send them back to Germany. I think I've got another pair in my top drawer. Okay?"

Enid didn't reply.

"Okay, Enid?" he repeated.

She sighed, the battle lost. "Okay."

"I love you," Sam signed off, predictably.

"I love you too," she answered. But he had already hung up.

A few moments later, as she was selecting the clothes Sam would need, she decided she would deliver the suitcase to LAX herself and give him a proper good-bye. Why not? She had nothing better to do, and maybe seeing him face to face would give her the self-control to make it through the next few days without doing anything she would later regret.

While Wallase finished the packing, Enid allowed herself to succumb to the guilty pleasure of peeking out the window of her den into Patrick's study. Through the window, she could see Patrick at his desk, his head bent, reading something.

Ready or not, here I come, she thought.

"Missy, what airline Mr. Carrouthers take?" asked Wallase.

"United," she replied, with a pang of anxiety. Sam was clearly trying to avoid her. Why else would he not have taken the time to stop at home for a brief good-bye and to pick up his luggage? It would only have taken him an extra five or ten minutes.

Why would he be avoiding her? Was it something she had done, something he did not want to confront? Or was it something he was doing, something he did not want to admit?

Wallase pulled up in front of the terminal and ran around to Enid's side to help her set up the luggage cart. With ease she snapped the wheels into place and strapped on Sam's bag.

"The plane is due to leave at 8, so he'll probably board at 7:30," said Enid. "That's in fifteen minutes, so maybe you want to park until then."

"No, Missy, I circle, I circle, is easier for you."

"Whatever, Wallase. I'll come right back to this spot as soon as he leaves," she said. "Thanks."

Wheeling the cart into the terminal, Enid was immediately surrounded by the members of a foreign sports team of some sort, traveling en masse, all in identical red sweat suits. Although she could not understand their conversation, she felt their excitement, arriving in this foreign land, ready to compete for the greater glory of their homeland. Their enthusiasm was catching, and Enid felt her spirits lift as the escalator carried her up one floor to the departure gates.

She passed through the security check and hoisted the bag back onto the luggage cart, wheeling it the short distance to the Red Carpet Club, where Sam was due to rendezvous with Wallase. She buzzed the bell and in a moment the door clicked open.

The lounge was chaotic. Either several flights had been delayed, or this was a very busy departure time for United. If Sam were already there waiting, it would take her awhile to find him. She decided to see if he had checked in.

"May I help you, Miss?"

A Clarice Latimer looked at Enid over the top of her glasses, not returning Enid's smile. It obviously had been a long day for her, and from the look of the lounge, there was no relief in sight.

"Yes, I want to know if Mr. Carrouthers has checked in for your flight to Rome tonight, Mr. Sam Carrouthers."

"Checking." The woman turned her attention to the computer, her talonlike pink fingernails tapping out a staccato rhythm on its keys. She pushed up her glasses to study the screen more closely. "No, they haven't checked in yet."

"They?" Enid's heart sank. "What do you mean *they*?" she asked.

"It's a party of two. Next." The person behind Enid elbowed his way forward and handed his ticket book to Clarice Latimer.

Enid wheeled the cart to an empty chair and sat. Soon enough Sam would be there, and she would see for herself who had replaced her as his traveling companion.

Sam

Up there, there's a spot."

Sam knew the cabby did not appreciate his commands, but the suddenness of his trip, combined with his guilt for lying to Enid, and his anxiety about ICCM, were overriding his usual self-control.

"You can pull up behind the Marriott van," he directed.

"Mister, I got two eyes and a brain. I can figure it out, okay?" the cabby snapped, demonstrating his annoyance by cutting across two lanes of traffic without looking.

Sam thrust a twenty at him and got out, checking in both directions. He had suggested that they go to the airport in separate cabs, but Carmen had scoffed at the idea so he'd caved in, despite his apprehensions about getting caught.

But the coast looked clear. He extended his hand to Carmen.

"Mister Carrouthers, Mister Carrouthers!" Sam recognized Wallase's voice before he saw the Toyota FourRunner pull up behind the taxi, and instinctively he swung the cab door closed, nearly severing the toes of Carmen's Ferragamo loafers. Fortunately, her reflexes were swift and she retreated unharmed into the cab to wait while Sam dealt with the situation.

"Lady, are you getting out or do I keep the meter running?"

Carmen pulled out a five dollar bill from her pocket. She always kept small bills handy at airports and hotels; they smoothed over the rough spots inherent in travel. "I'll just be another minute or two," she told the cabby.

Wallase jumped out of the truck and ran over to pump Sam's hand with a warm, double-handed grip. "Mister Carrouthers, how you are?" he beamed, his affection and respect for his boss clear in his face and tone.

"I'm good, good, Wallase, but sorry I have to take this trip so suddenly. Have you been waiting long?" Sam peered into the window of the truck to look for his bags.

"No, Mister, maybe five, ten minutes I wait."

"Wallase, where are my bags?"

"Oh, Missy Carrouthers she take. She wait for you at the Club."

"Enid is here?"

"Yes. She want to come, say bye-bye. A surprise." Wallase realized he had ruined the surprise, and his face fell. "Oh, so sorry, I make mistake."

"She's inside?"

"Yes, yes, she wait for you."

"Thank you, Wallase, thank you." Sam couldn't believe his luck, to have averted disaster by this coincidental meeting. "You can go on home now, Wallase. Thank you for bringing Enid."

"But Mister, I must to wait, to take home."

"Oh yes. Of course." He made a gesture that implied he was over-worked and overly rushed, and waved Wallase off. "You'd better cir-cle around again. They'll give you a ticket if you wait here. I'll tell Enid I saw you."

"Okay, I go. Thank you, Mister Carrouthers. Safe journey."

"Thanks, Wallase, good-bye."

He waited until Wallase's Toyota truck merged with the traffic be-fore returning to the cab. "I knew we should have come in separate cabs," he said, extending his hand to Carmen for the second time.

"You seemed to handle that just fine," she replied

"It's not Wallase, it's Enid. She came to see me off. She's at the Red Carpet Club."

"No problem. I'll just check my bags and meet you on the plane," Carmen said calmly.

"You're going to check your bags?"

"Of course. Aren't you?"

"Hell, no. I always carry on. It saves time when you land, to say nothing of the wear and tear on the luggage and the possibility of bags getting lost or stolen."

Carmen let Sam complete his lecture, then said, "Why don't you concentrate on saying good-bye to your wife and I'll take care of my bags? See you on board."

"Right." Sam hurried into the terminal. It was 7:20. They'd prob-ably be boarding in ten minutes. By the time he checked in and got his bags from Enid, there would only be a minute or two for him to say good-bye. How much guilt could he possibly feel in one or two minutes?

As soon as he entered the Red Carpet Club, he spotted Enid. He waved cheerily, remembering to look surprised, and went to greet her. She did not look happy, but then what did he expect?

"Hi! This is a great surprise!" He hoped his voice sounded enthusiastic, and he hugged her so she wouldn't be able to look him in the eye.

"I couldn't bear the thought of your leaving without at least seeing you to say good-bye." She pulled out of the hug and looked at him.

Why was she looking at him so strangely? Did the guilt show? Was he that transparent? But he hadn't even done anything yet, and who knew if he would?

"I'm sorry to do this. I never would have made it if I'd tried to come home first. Look how late it is. I'd better check in."

"Yes, you'd better," she said, with a hint of mystery. Still, as they turned toward the reception desk, Sam let down his guard, sensing he was just moments away from a clean escape. And then she hit him with, "There seems to be some mix-up about your reservation."

"There is?" He could feel his adrenaline surge.

"They've got you listed as a party of two."

Damn Margie. He'd specifically told her to book the tickets on two separate records for just this reason. Why did she always do things the easy way? "But that's impossible. There's only one of me."

Sam's head was spinning. If he canceled Carmen's reservation, what was going to happen when she tried to check in at the gate? And if he didn't, what was Enid going to say? There seemed to be no way out of this conundrum, so he decided to leave it to fate, and handed Clarice Latimer his ticket.

"Mr. Carrouthers?" He nodded. Clarice did her fancy fingerwork on the keyboard and wrote his seat number and the gate number on the ticket cover. "There you are sir, seat 4B, leaving at Gate 74. They're boarding now, I believe. Next?"

"Excuse me," Enid reached around him to ask, "didn't you tell me before there were two in that party?"

"Miss, I can hardly remember everything I said to every passenger on every flight. Now there's a line behind you and we don't want to make these people miss their flights, do we?"

"I don't understand it. I'm sure she told me — "

"Forget it, you know how these people are." Sam pulled Enid to the side and took a moment to look at her. Exhilarated by his successful deception and warmed by Enid's obvious despondency at the thought of his leaving, he assured himself if anything did happen with Carmen, it would be merely a fling that would be over before they got back to L.A. He was already anticipating coming home to his comfortable and uncomplicated life with Enid. He kissed her, hoping to communicate this mouth to mouth.

She smiled and put her arms around him. "Oh, Sam, I hate it when you go away without me. And it sounds so romantic, flying off to Sardinia to meet Harry on his yacht."

"What do you think, this is a pleasure trip?" Sam scoffed. "You know Harry. He'll probably offer me a peanut butter sandwich and force me to go scuba diving with him, despite the fact that he knows I've got an inner ear problem."

"I know, but — "

"When I get back, we'll plan something really romantic for the two of us, okay?"

Enid nodded and rested her head on his shoulder.

Sam never loved her more than he did at this minute.

"I'd better board. It'd be a pain in the ass to miss the flight after all this hassle."

"Don't you want to change into your flying clothes?" She held up a small garment bag. "And I'll take that suit and shirt home."

"You take such good care of me."

"It's my job," she said, "and I like being good at it."

Sam took the bag and hurried off to the men's room to change. When he returned, Enid was waiting by the door. He put his arms around her again.

"Thank you for bringing my stuff and for coming to say good-bye. I do feel better now."

"So do I."

They walked out of the Red Carpet Club, and Sam gave Enid a final kiss. "See you in a couple of days."

"I'll walk you to the gate."

"No, no, you go on. Wallase is probably wondering what happened to you."

"But I've got nothing else to do tonight."

"Go, go, I need to run. Love you." He hurried away before she could insist.

At last he was home free. He hurried through the terminal, past the sundry shop and the bar, and down the jetway, his luggage cart bouncing over the joints in the long, narrow corridor. He showed his boarding pass to the flight attendant at the gate, a pretty girl in her early twenties who gave him a tempting smile and directed him toward the first class cabin. "You can hang that bag in the front compartment, sir."

"Thank you," said Sam. He walked up the aisle, checking the seats on both sides for the red hair and the long slender legs that would identify Carmen to him. But she was nowhere to be seen. Maybe she got bumped off the flight in the mix-up. He wondered if the tightness in his chest was concern or relief.

After hanging his garment bag, he found his way back to seat 4B and stuffed his luggage cart and briefcase into the overhead bin. He was just settling into his seat, next to an Englishman who was already snoring, when he spied Carmen, coming out of the lavatory.

Apparently she was enough of a traveler to know the flight would be easier in casual clothes, and she had changed into a mauve jersey jumpsuit that somehow managed to look clingy and comfortable at the same time. She came down the aisle toward Sam.

"You made it. For a minute there I was worried."

"It was a little tricky," Sam conceded. "I'll feel a lot better when they close the door."

As if she'd heard his words, the flight attendant intoned, "Will all passengers take their seats, and will all ground crew please exit the aircraft? Flight attendants prepare for departure."

"Where are you sitting?"

Carmen pointed to an empty chair, 2D. "When I checked my bag, I had them split our ticket into two separate seat assignments. I was afraid . . ."

"You did the right thing. We'll switch around after we're airborne. I don't think this fellow will mind where he sits," he said, motioning to his snoring seatmate.

Sam watched Carmen find her seat and strap herself in, her red hair visible over the top of the seat. *She is no dummy*, he thought.

Either that, or she's done this a few times before.

Carmen

The truth be told, Carmen was glad Sam was not with her on the walk to the gate, because he might have scoffed at her for stopping to buy $1,000,000 worth of flight insurance, which was something she always did before getting on a flight, no matter what. Because Carmen was terrified of flying. Actually, she hated to do anything that required her to relinquish all control to someone she'd never met, in this case, the flight crew of the 747, the air traffic controllers at the airports in Los Angeles, New York, and Rome, and the pilots of whatever other aircraft were in the vicinity. But once she had the insurance in hand, she was able to sublimate her fear and mask it in a serene demeanor.

As the plane taxied down the runway, the infant nestled on the lap of her seatmate started to howl. She had always detested children, especially in movie theaters, on airplanes, and in restaurants. They were like cigarettes, she thought, they ought to be banned in public places. The mere idea of sitting next to a child was irritating enough, but the infant's shrieks heightened Carmen's anxiety, and she couldn't afford to lose her cool right now.

"Can you keep it quiet?" she snapped.

The mother, a bedraggled post-teenager, still soft and lumpy from her pregnancy, gave Carmen a weary smile. "She will quiet down as soon we're airborne, it's just the change in cabin pressure." The baby howled louder and farted, smothering Carmen in a putrid odor.

"My God, that is revolting," she hissed.

"Lady, I'm sorry, but it's only natural. When you're scared, nature takes its course, right?"

"Stewardess!" Carmen pressed her call button, and the nearest flight attendant unsnapped her harness and stumbled down the aisle to her side.

"Is there a problem?"

"Yes, I cannot sit here. The noise and the odor are unbearable. Will you do something about it?"

The flight attendant gave the mother a "can you believe this" look and turned a somber eye to Carmen. "Well, ma'am, we're next in line for takeoff. If you like I can radio the pilot and tell him to abort, and we'll see if someone will switch seats with you. Other than that, I think you'll just have to live with the situation for a few minutes."

"Thank you so much," Carmen spit sarcastically, fanning herself with the in-flight magazine." There must be an empty seat some-where on this airplane."

"Yes, there are a few in coach, if you'd prefer to go to the back of the plane. Perhaps you'd be happier there."

"Why doesn't she go back there?" asked Carmen.

"I don't fly coach," the mother said over the baby's screams. "My mom's a travel agent."

Carmen gave her a scathing look and craned her neck to see if there was somewhere else she could sit. What she saw was Sam star-ing earnestly in her direction, obviously worried and wanting to help, but equally unwilling to embarrass himself by coming to her aid.

"Flight attendants prepare for takeoff," the pilot's voice commanded.

"I've got to take my seat now. Are you two going to be all right?" the flight attendant asked.

"For now," Carmen muttered angrily. She whipped on her headphones and turned the dial to the easy listening station, hoping to drown out the ambient noise.

Carmen closed her eyes against her fear and tried to focus on happy thoughts. She imagined herself with Sam, arriving at the Hotel Bel Air for a black tie party. They'd drive up in Sam's Porsche — no, she'd talk him into buying one of those elegant Bentley Turbos she'd seen around town. Anyone could drive a Porsche, but a Bentley implied so much more: the financial wherewithal to purchase a $200,000 automobile, the refinement to prefer the understated Bentley to the ostentatious Rolls Royce, the potency to desire a car that could go from 0 to 60 in under six seconds.

They would get out of the car and enter the hotel. Carmen would be wearing a Bob Mackie original, something slinky and sequined, quite bare on top to showcase her necklace, a tasteful trinket from Bvlgari, encrusted with sapphires, emeralds, and just enough diamonds to make it sparkle. She would check her watch, a Patek Phillipe, of course, to make sure they were timely, and in glancing at the watch, she also would take a moment to adjust the latest gift from her adoring mate, an antique bracelet bought at auction at Sotheby's from the estate collection of Elizabeth Taylor.

As they'd cross the bridge to the hotel, Sam would take her arm and whisper in her ear that she was the most beautiful woman he'd ever met, and then he'd proceed to tell her what he wanted to do to her when they got home after the party. Why not just take a suite at the hotel, Carmen would suggest, and her answer would be another kiss from Sam, this one on the secret spot at the nape of her neck, which he would know caused her to swoon.

Carmen was just relaxing into a pleasant sense of arousal when she felt the plane lift off. She opened her eyes to look out the window and saw to her horror that the mother was now nursing her baby off the breast closest to Carmen. Filled with a mixture of repulsion and fascination, Carmen could not tear her eyes away. Both mother's and child's eyes were closed, intensely absorbed in the miracle of their relationship.

Carmen had never wanted to be a mother, nor had she ever been pregnant. *In this day and age you have to be a fool to get knocked up*, she thought. Women who got pregnant on purpose were equally demented. Which was not to say that couples should not procreate. Some women were suited for nothing else. Carmen herself was not one of them.

She had heard that some women found nursing erotic, but this young mother was all business. Her breathing was deep and regular, as her body pumped out nourishment. Her breast was ample and well rounded, turgid with milk. With one hand she supported the hairless head of the child as it suckled; with the other, she began unharnessing her other breast. For a moment the baby lost her grip, and the nipple burst free of her mouth. Carmen could see the tiny rivulets of milk oozing out, and she felt a tug in her own bosom, as though the mere sight of this lactating mammary was causing her own glands to respond in sympathy.

"You've obviously never had a child."

The woman's voice startled Carmen. She tore her eyes away from the breast and found her seatmate smiling condescendingly at her. Quickly, and with efficient, practiced ease, the woman transferred the child to her other breast.

"Why do you say that? "

"Because if you had, you would be a little more understanding. And you wouldn't stare."

"I'm staring because I'm revolted," said Carmen with outrage. "That should be done in private."

"Why does the sight of a breast bother you so much?" the woman asked, still not bothering to cover hers. "Are you jealous because yours aren't real?" Outrageously, she let her fingers cup her breast, hefting it as if to feel the weight in her hand. Carmen was mesmerized, and speechless.

"Carmen, is everything okay?"

Carmen whipped her head around to see Sam leaning over her solicitously. Now he too noticed the nursing mother who smilingly stuffed her nipple into her baby's mouth. Sam smiled back, and averted his eyes in polite embarrassment as the child sucked loudly and contentedly.

"I'd like to move now. Have you asked your seatmate if he'll switch?"

"Not a problem," said the Englishman, now appearing behind Sam with his belongings gathered in his arms. "I love the wee tots and I can sleep through anything."

"Well bully for you." Carmen got up and slid out of the seat, allowing the man to settle into her place. Sam and Carmen had to wait for the flight attendant pushing the drink cart to pass before they could go to their seats.

"What would you like to drink?" the attendant asked the mother.

"Milk for me, please," responded the woman.

"And you sir?"

"The same," replied the Englishman, feasting on the spectacle of motherhood beside him. "But I'll have mine in a glass, please."

When Sam and Carmen were finally settled in their seats, she said, "You don't have children."

It was a statement, not a question, but Sam answered, "I know this sounds strange, but that was never really an issue for either of us. Enid and I are both only children. Neither of us was around kids much growing up. I guess we like our lives the way they are. How about you?"

"I have two younger brothers, and I probably spent more time taking care of them than our mother did. It wasn't her fault. She had a hard life." Carmen wished she could explain the whole story to Sam, but she didn't usually saddle men with personal details about her past this early in a relationship. Time enough for that later, when their bond was secure.

"So you essentially acted as a parent to your brothers?" Sam prodded. Carmen wasn't sure why he wanted to know, but she figured she should play for compassion. Sam seemed like the kind of man who wanted to be protective of a woman; she'd throw him a morsel and see if he picked it up.

"Let me tell you, you haven't lived until you've been stuck with two screaming brats who've got temperatures of 104 degrees and not enough money to buy them medicine. We didn't have a washing machine and couldn't afford to buy those disposable diapers, so I was the live-in laundry service. Maybe fifteen, twenty diapers a day. It was not a pretty picture."

"How old were you at the time?"

"Eight, nine, ten, something like that. I didn't have what you'd call an ideal childhood."

"I guess not."

Carmen saw the concern etched on Sam's face and hoped she hadn't said too much. The drink cart stopped by their seats. "I definitely need a drink," she said.

"What would you like?" the attendant asked.

"How does champagne sound?" asked Sam.

"Perfect," Carmen beamed. She was right, her confession had inspired Sam's eagerness to comfort her.

"And you sir?"

"The same. Can we get a bottle?"

Patrick

"Can I get you anything else before I go?" Jeremy asked, setting an ice bucket and a bottle of Pellegrino on Patrick's nightstand.

Patrick's eyes were riveted on the television, a commercial for body lotion that featured a lithe young girl wrapped in a towel, smoothing cream on her already smooth legs. "Get me her, and a lifetime supply of that cream," barked Patrick, without looking at Jeremy.

"I'll see you tomorrow then."

"If you're lucky."

Jeremy shook his head and started down the stairs. He was worried about his boss, and with good reason. The current issue of *People*, which had arrived in the mail, offered a nasty and mean-spirited blurb about *A Month of Sundays*, Patrick's latest movie. Although the film wouldn't be out for months, some enterprising reporter had managed to get his hands on a rough cut and was spreading the word that it was a bomb.

Knowing he was notoriously sensitive to criticism, Patrick's retinue of friends, family, and staff never discussed reviews with him, sheltering him from negative reactions to his work. But who would have imagined that *People* would print something about *A Month of Sundays* three months in advance of its release?

The issue in question was open on the bed next to Patrick. Also on the bed were three remote controls, one for the TV, one for the VCR, and one for the satellite dish, Patrick's Daytimer and address book, Extra Strength Excedrin, Alka Seltzer and a heating pad, the rest of the day's mail, the telephone, a tray of chocolate chip cookies, the remains of a meat loaf sandwich, some potato salad with a fly on it, and a turkey drumstick that YoYo was about to devour.

Why would they print a thing like this? Patrick flagellated himself with the magazine. *What good does it do to review a rough cut, without music or effects or even a final assembly of takes? Clearly, this Brad King is out to get me. But why?*

Patrick racked his brain to put a face on the name Brad King, but he couldn't come up with one. Had he done something to offend this stranger? Why else would the man write lines like "Patrick Drake drags himself through the part like a ghost, an aging, overweight, overacting ghost at that. Whatever charm and talent he displayed in his early films are invisible in this one, as are the plot line and the story."

The worst part of it was, in his heart of hearts, Patrick knew what the guy said was true. He was aging and overweight, and his dislike of his costar had been so intense that he had been forced to take a few drinks before their big love scenes just to get into bed with her.

But he hadn't realized all of that had come through on film. He wished now that he'd gone to dailies to see what the director had had to work with. At the time, it had seemed like such an effort to sit in a dark room each evening rehashing the previous day's work, after putting in twelve hours on the set. Plus, it put a crimp in the torrid if brief location romance he was having with the wardrobe mistress.

The phone rang. Normally Patrick didn't answer it when he was feeling like this, but he had picked up the receiver by reflex and was speaking into it before he could stop himself.

"Yeah?"

There was silence on the other end, then, "So you've seen it?"

LeMar's irritating voice. Patrick should have known. "How can you tell?"

"I know when you don't answer the phone with 'Whadda you want,' you're in trouble."

"Shit, who the hell is Brad King, and why is he writing these terrible things about me?"

"Paddy, Paddy, you know these guys. It's not news if it's good, it's only news if it crucifies someone, right?"

"Great choice of words, LeMar."

"Hey, nobody looks at this shit anyway, do they? I mean, page thirty-one, buried in the lower left corner. Who could find it?"

"I did. And you did."

"Okay, okay, well, we know to look for it."

"And so does everyone else who counts in this business."

That shut up LeMar because he knew Patrick was right. As full of bullshit as LeMar was, and all good agents were, he knew when to cut the crap.

"Paddy. I don't like to hear you sounding like this."

"So what do you want me to do? Crack a few jokes? Shit, Lee, it isn't very funny to me."

"I'll tell you what I want you to do. I want you to go out and drum up a little positive publicity to counteract this. You know, give the folks something else to talk about."

"Well, I could rob a convenience store. That would get me some press. Or maybe I could molest a few fourth graders. That always works."

"You know what I mean, get out amongst 'em and schmeuse a little. Tell Sara to get all dolled up and take her out on the town, somewhere where there'll be some paparazzi. Some charity thing."

"My favorite way to spend an evening."

"So it's not for fun, it's for your career for Chrissakes. I'll tell you what I'm going to do. Put a call in to Peter and see if he knows anything." LeMar's words were muffled, as though he were speaking to someone else in his office. Probably one of his ass-wiping agent aspirants who got their rocks off eavesdropping on LeMar's personal conversations with his clients. Had they no sense of a man's need for privacy?

"LeMar, the last thing I want to do tonight is get all dressed up and stand around some ballroom making nice with nerds I don't know."

"It doesn't have to be tonight." Patrick heard LeMar's muffled voice commanding, "Tell him to hold." And then he said into the phone, "Paddy, Peter's holding for me now. Do you want to conference or shall I get back to you."

"Later." Patrick slammed down the receiver, for once beating LeMar to the punch. He picked up *TV Guide*. What in the world did people do before television? The tube had become his best friend. His only friend, come to think of it. When he was alone, it kept him company. And when he was "entertaining," it frequently provided an appropriate ambiance. Tonight it would be an anesthetic.

At eight o'clock was Sara's all-time favorite show, *Married . . .with children*. He didn't know why she liked this program so much; she wasn't married and she didn't have children. But he loved hearing her laugh out loud at the caustic humor, most of which undoubtedly went over her head. He'd probably watch it out of habit.

Ah, but at nine o'clock on Channel 5 there was a rerun of *Wind Jammers*, the movie he had made ten years ago with Meg Ryan. Wasn't he just telling someone about — oh yes, Enid, when she came over the other morning. Patrick checked the clock. It was only 7:49, but he flicked the remote to channel 5 anyway. Might as well be ready. Even though he had a video of the film, there was nothing like watching it on TV, knowing millions of other viewers were watching it with him. He rifled through the stockpile on the bed for something appetizing, wondering if Enid knew it was on. He would love for her to watch *Wind Jammers*. It was one of his better outings, still reissued now and again in Europe, especially in France, where it had been filmed. Hell, he was almost as popular there as Jerry Lewis. This thought cheered him.

Since nothing on the bed sparked his appetite, Patrick decided to muster his energy and make a provisions run down to the kitchen. Perhaps there was still some barbecued lamb from dinner at Chinois on Monday, or did he finish it Tuesday at lunch?

Patrick padded through the darkened house, not bothering to turn on any lights. Behind him, YoYo waddled noiselessly, knowing from experience that Patrick was headed for the kitchen.

Patrick's spirits had lifted somewhat. Just thinking about *Wind Jammers* was a shot in the arm. He had been on top of his career then.

Even Meg had been ready and willing to go a few rounds with him. He sighed. Meg Ryan.

He remembered phoning his parents to tell them that he was going to be costarring in a movie with her. Muriel and Harold were both decrepit and houseridden then, and his calls were, he knew, the high points of their days. To them he was a living manifestation of the American dream: an unremarkable boy from a small Midwestern town who went to Hollywood and became a movie star. Well, by their standards, he was still on top of the heap. Nobody else from Kewasha, Indiana, had ever been on *The Johnny Carson Show*, or had gone to the Academy Awards, let alone been nominated for a Golden Globe. Besides Meg Ryan, he had kissed a dozen top female stars, everyone from Julia Roberts to Goldie Hawn, and he had had the privilege of acting alongside Meryl Streep, although, thankfully, there had been no romantic subplot in that picture.

As Patrick opened the refrigerator, he started to hum to himself. Yes, he was definitely feeling better. Who gave a shit what some self-righteous little turd wrote in *People*. He found the container of lamb and put it in the microwave to warm.

Maybe he'd just call Enid Carrouthers and leave a message on her machine, to tell her to watch *Wind Jammers*. He was certain she'd be glad to know it was on, if she hadn't already read about it in *TV Guide*.

He had dialed her number before he considered that her husband might answer, and that he might not be all that interested in watching *Wind Jammers*. Patrick was just about to set the phone in its cradle when he heard Enid's voice.

"Hello?" She sounded out of breath.

"Hello," Patrick answered, in the same breathless tone.

"Who's this?"

"Who'd'ya think it is?"

"Patrick?" Her voice rose an octave.

"The very same."

"Oh, hi. Gosh, I just came in this minute. I'm glad I didn't miss your call. How are you?"

"I've been better. But I've been worse too, I suppose. Only I can't remember when."

"Yeah, me too."

She sounded depressed. Perversely, the realization that he was not the only one who was down in the dumps perked him up.

"Really? We must be on the same wavelength."

There was a pause. Now that he had her on the phone, Patrick wasn't sure how to segue into *Wind Jammers* without sounding too obvious. He decided that the best approach would be a direct one.

"Listen, I called because I was remembering we talked the other morning about my movie *Wind Jammers*.

"With Meg Ryan?" Enid supplied.

"The very same." He was relieved she remembered.

"God, I'm so sorry I never saw that one. I tried to rent it on video, but you know how it is. They're always out of the good ones."

"Well, this must be your lucky night. It's playing on channel 5 at nine o'clock.

"Oh, that's great! I'm going to be home, and I'm alone tonight anyway."

"Me too," Patrick replied, and a deafening silence settled between them. They both knew the natural response to this situation would be for one to invite the other over to watch the movie. But, for very different reasons, neither wanted to broach the subject. Enid, still wounded from Sam's sudden, unexplained departure, was feeling fragile and vulnerable. Besides, her hair was filthy, and she had a terrible pimple on her cheek that no amount of foundation would cover.

Patrick had his own problems. All of this anxiety about *People* had brought on a pinch of pain in his groin, which could indicate an outbreak of herpes. While he was ready and willing emotionally, the last thing he wanted was to leave his next-door neighbor with a lasting physical memory of an evening with him.

The silence between them screamed to be broken, but neither knew what to say. Fortunately, Patrick's phone rang.

"Can I put you on hold, Enid?" he asked.

"Sure," she replied with relief.

He picked up the other line. "Hello?"

"Patrick?"

It was Sara. Either she was calling from her car, or she had a terrible cold. God, women were uncanny. How on earth could she have known to call right now? It must be some sixth sense they had, an instinct that warned them when a relationship was in imminent danger. "Yeah? What's your problem?"

"I'm depressed, and I'm coming over so you can make me feel better."

"But —" Patrick tried, but Sara continued right over him.

"I had my callback at Dominion today and that guy Jeffrey whatshisname, what a schmuck he is. He tells me I'm too pretty for the part. Pretty! What does he mean pretty? I can give him as ugly as he wants, I tell him, and so I start to mess up my hair and make a face. You know that face I make when I'm mad."

"I know, but— "

"So I give him my best shot at it, and he and these other guys, I think it was the director and the cameraman, they can hardly look at me without laughing. Well you know how pissed off I get when people laugh at me. AND I WASN'T EVEN DOING ANYTHING! So I said to the stupid . . ."

Patrick knew that Sara would drone on whether he was listening or not, so he put her on hold and went back to Enid.

"Enid, I'm sorry, I've got to take this other call."

"That's okay. I want to go get ready for bed so I can watch the movie. Thanks for calling to tell me about it."

"My pleasure. I hope you enjoy it."

"I know I will. Oh, Patrick, I wanted to ask you a favor, and as long as I've got you on the phone . . ."

"Give it your best shot," he said, eyes on Sara's blinking red light.

"There's a meeting at the Shelter tomorrow morning, to discuss the fund-raiser. It would be perfect if you could come with me, you know, see the facilities, meet some of the board and the residents. I promise it won't take more than an hour."

She'd done it again, surprised him by taking the initiative and leaving him with no alternative.

"I do have a lunch date," he lied lamely, "so I couldn't stay long."

"No, no, I promise I'll have you home by eleven. Thank you, that's great. They'll be so pleased."

"Then I'll see you in the morning," he said.

"I'll come by about 9:45, if that's okay."

"Fine. Look, I've got to take this call."

"Oh, sorry. Thanks so much. See you tomorrow."

"'Night." Patrick sighed and plugged himself back into Sara.

". . . by that time I was so mad I couldn't see straight. I kept looking around for Elaine and she . . ." Sara was still babbling.

Patrick turned on the portable TV in the kitchen to keep him company while Sara finished her spiel. At least he wouldn't have to spend tonight alone. And Sara would be so wrapped up in her anger she probably wouldn't want to make love anyway, so it was okay that he was out of commission. Or was he? The pain in his groin seemed to be moving into his intestines. Maybe it was just that meat loaf sandwich after all.

16

Sam and Carmen

Sam lifted his eye shade enough to peek at his watch and saw that it was eleven o'clock. They would be landing in Rome in less than an hour. That meant he had been asleep for more than eight hours, thanks to a little blue tablet called Halcion.

He tried to get up, but he could not move his arm to dislodge the blanket wrapped around him. In fact, he couldn't *find* his arm! He looked to his left and saw that a mass of red hair was covering it from elbow to hand. The hair was attached to a body, which was curled fetally into the chair beside him, a body he did not recognize at first, except to know that it definitely was not Enid's.

Then in a flash it all came back to him: Carmen, the bottle of Dom Perignon, and then the Halcion, a tablet for each of them to ensure a sound sleep.

Sam felt a surge of panic. Whatever had caused him to get on this plane with a strange woman was a reality of the past. What mattered now was wresting free his arm before the pressure of her head cut off the circulation to his hand. Frantically, he tried to wriggle it loose, and finally, by supporting her head with his other hand, he managed to pull it out from under the red weight.

"Are we landing?" Carmen's voice was thick with sleep. She didn't even try to remove her eye mask.

"Another hour," said Sam as he slid out of the seat and padded to the lavatory in his stockinged feet. He wanted to be out of sight before she opened her eyes. Talk about the embarrassment of waking up together for the first time — right now he couldn't cope with that much intimacy.

Safe behind the locked door, Sam looked at himself in the mirror and was shocked at his reflection. The angst he had been suppressing for the past twenty-four hours had emerged and settled into the cross-hatch of sleep wrinkles on his face. His eyes were bloodshot and puffy and his hair was a matted mess. What was he doing here?

A knock on the door reminded him that he did not have the luxury of unlimited time and privacy. He splashed water on his face and rubbed some of the complimentary toothpaste onto his teeth.

Hot towel?" The flight attendant held a terry cloth rag in front of Carmen's nose. Its cloying scent was an aromatic insult.

"No, thank you, but please bring me a glass of mineral water," Carmen replied, waving the cloth away and delving into her handbag for her own naturally scented fresheners. The knockoff Hermes handbag was a godsend. It had cost an arm and a leg even though it was a fake, but it was efficient and impressive, neatly organizing everything a woman needed for a long trip. Carmen always kept it stocked and ready to go, so last-minute trips were never a problem.

She found her moisturizer and dabbed it around her eyes, relishing the relief it brought to her taut, tired skin. The attendant returned with the water, and Carmen drank it down, saving some to pat onto her hair as she brushed it back into a strict ponytail.

By the time Sam stepped out of the lavatory, she looked as presentable and poised as he did disheveled and uneasy. Carmen was moved by the sight of stubble on Sam's proud chin and the puffy pockets under his eyes. She felt privileged to see him looking less than his best, because it clearly signaled that his guard was down.

"How long do we have in Rome before our flight to Sardinia?" she asked, to break the awkward silence.

"Not long." Sam pulled his ticket from his wallet to check. "An hour and ten minutes."

He stared at the ticket as though composing what he was going to say next. Carmen smiled to herself. She knew what was coming and would like to have saved Sam the agony of putting it into words. But there was no way around the subject. They might as well get it out of the way now. She waited for him to speak.

"You know, it's going to be kind of awkward, us showing up together," Sam began. "I don't want Harry to get the wrong idea."

"Oh, from what I've heard about Harry Ingersol, he'll get the right idea."

"What I mean is, he's crazy about Enid. Hell, I think that's one of the reasons he's so nice to me. Enid charms the pants off him."

"Literally?"

Sam gave her a pained look. "No, not literally."

"I'm sure Harry will like me just fine," said Carmen with a patient smile, unable to stop herself from adding, "Enid's not the only one who knows how to handle powerful men."

"But you're missing the point."

Carmen sighed. The "Fasten Seat Belt" sign flashed, and she fastened hers before replying, "No, I know exactly what you're trying to say. You don't want Harry to think you're fooling around on your wife because it will make you look bad. So you want to make sure I keep it very professional and above board."

"Which is the way it is," insisted Sam.

"So far," Carmen said. "Oh Sam," she sighed, seeing his distress, "as far as anyone knows we've come here to get some information from Harry, and we're going to get it and then go home. Whatever else happens or doesn't happen, it's nobody's business but our own. And you can be sure I don't want to mislead Harry Ingersol any more than you do."

"Fine," said Sam. But he was not at all sure that it was.

The landing formalities went as smoothly as was possible at Rome's Fiumicino Airport, until a wheel fell off of Sam's luggage cart and he was forced to ditch it and haul his bags around. No big deal, except Carmen seemed to be laughing at him, since she had nothing to carry but the small Hermes tote that hung neatly on her shoulder.

Her smile broadened when Sam nearly got into a fistfight with the flight attendant when he tried to board the tiny Alitalia prop engine plane to Sardinia. There was no way this Madonna of the Sky was going to allow him to board her crowded aircraft with so much luggage, and there was no way he was going to let her check it.

Finally, Carmen saved the day by offering that she was with Sam, and that together they were not over the luggage limit. The flight attendant backed down reluctantly, satisfying her need to have the upper hand by putting Sam and Carmen in seats at the very back of the one-class flight where the engine noise was the loudest.

They struggled on with the bags, and Sam crammed them into the overhead compartment.

"You actually think that's good for the clothes?" teased Carmen.

"At least they'll be in Sardinia when I get there. You'd better not talk until you see if yours are."

"Fine, I won't say a word," Carmen answered, and she put in earplugs to diminish the aggravating hum of the engines.

Thirty minutes later, the plane touched down on the Costa Smerelda. As Carmen and Sam deplaned, they were hit with a blast of warm air, as fragrant as a loaf of focaccia hot from the oven. Carmen was flooded with a sense of well-being. This was the life she was meant to lead.

While she waited for her bags, Sam went off to locate the driver from the Hotel Pitrizza, where they would shower and change and wait to be picked up to go to Harry's boat. Miraculously, Carmen's two Louis Vuitton bags were among the first lowered from the plane, and she was ready and waiting when Sam appeared with the hotel van. She read surprise and annoyance in his face. This was a man who did not like to be bested by a woman. She'd have to remember that.

The road to the hotel was narrow and winding and led through a landscape of craggy hills and low brush, which was dry and brown.

"Odd that they call this the Emerald Coast," Carmen said. "Green does not seem to be the operative color."

"The name refers to the water," Sam explained. "You can't really see it from here, but once we're out on the boat you'll be astonished at how clear it is, really the color of emeralds."

"You've come here with Enid, I suppose."

Sam nodded. "We came on our honeymoon, and oh, I guess two or three times since."

Then I'll have my work cut out for me, Carmen thought. "Has she been with you on Harry's boat?"

"No. He's invited us many times. But Enid isn't a great sailor. She gets seasick."

Good, thought Carmen, who had never been seasick in her life. *Score one for my side.*

"See there?" Sam was pointing to a quaint village with a magnificent harbor. "That's Porto Cervo. We'll meet the boat there this afternoon. The hotel's just a few minutes farther."

The road turned inland and wound into the hills, challenging the van to a steep incline. Then suddenly the pavement dipped into a gully and around a curve. Before them, Carmen saw a cluster of cottages built low to the ground, their roofs covered with sod so that they appeared to be growing out of the hillside. It was a fascinating natural form of camouflage; if she had not been looking for the hotel, she would have missed it.

"Ah, Meester Carrouthers, we are so happy to have you back."

A slight Italian man rushed up to shake Sam's hand as he got out of the van. The man bowed low to Carmen when she alit and touched her hand lightly to his lips. "Signora," he said respectfully, not looking her in the eye. "Come, come, please, your room he is prepared. We bring the bags later." He led them down a pathway that was overgrown with bougainvillea and coral.

"Excusa da flowers," the man said. "We no cut because is bella, no? But is bigga problemo someathetime."

"Beauty is never a problem," said Carmen, and the man nodded appreciatively.

"I giva you da best room I got," he said. "There he is."

He stopped at the door to bungalow number 14. It was set off some distance from the others, but it was similarly covered with sod and cascading vines, which he brushed aside to reveal a carved wooden door. The Italian ducked into the room and motioned to them to follow.

Inside the bungalow was dark and cool. He drew the curtains and threw open a window, which overlooked an extraordinary sapphire swimming pool surrounded on three sides by rocks and set out on a ledge over the ocean. At the far edge of the pool, water cascaded over the edge, dropping, it seemed, like a waterfall into the ocean. Although there were several comfortable lounge chairs by the pool and on the porch, there were no people around.

"Where is everybody?" Carmen asked.

The Italian shrugged. "They eat, then they sleep. For the sun, is better in the morning or the evening."

"Beautiful," said Carmen.

"I'm glad you like, Signora," he replied.

"You take this room, if you like," Sam told Carmen, picking up his bag.

"Where will you be?" she asked.

"Not far, I'm sure," he said, "they've only got twenty-some rooms." He turned to the Italian. "What is my room number?"

The Italian lowered his eyes. "Meester Carrouthers, I am so very sorry. But we have only the one room today."

"But I wired ahead," said Sam, feeling the panic rise in his gut.

"I've got the confirmation here somewhere."

Carmen had to turn away to hide her smile. How endearing that Sam was so flustered. And how perfect for her plans.

"No, no, is such short notice, you see. I can give only one room. Is problemo?"

"Yes, it is a problemo." Stress had lowered Sam's boiling point, and he was about to erupt.

"Sam, it's fine. Really. There's plenty of room, and we'll be staying on the boat tonight anyway, won't we?" Carmen turned to the Italian and shook his hand. "We'll be fine, thank you very much."

"Thank you, Signora," he said. "I am sorry, please. He bowed. "With your luggage come something from the cucina, for my apology. Ciao."

He left, and Carmen and Sam were alone. Sam felt the walls closing in on him. He moved to open a window but Carmen beat him to it. "Molto bene," she said, "Molto, molto bene."

17

Enid and Patrick

nid had mixed emotions about taking Patrick with her to the Westside Women's Shelter meeting. On the one hand, she was eager to show him off to the staff and board. She imagined herself strolling in on Patrick's arm, sharing a private joke, much to the awe and envy of her associates and co-volunteers. She also wanted Patrick to see the Shelter. It was one thing to write a check to a far-flung charitable organization and to hope that your dollars were being put to good use. But with the Shelter you could actually see money being translated into housing and care for the ever-growing number of abused women. Enid was proud of this. And she wanted Patrick to be proud too.

Yet she worried that the experience might be too overwhelming for him. There was something very vulnerable about Patrick, a quality that made her want to wrap her arms around him and protect him from the world. She hoped the neediness of the patients and the curiosity of the staff and volunteers would not be too much for him.

But really, she had no choice. They couldn't proceed with the planning of the event unless they took this all-important step. She'd already told her committee that she could deliver Patrick Drake and his movie, and everyone was waiting for her to come up with the goods.

Patrick had seemed surprisingly willing to come to the meeting. When she buzzed the intercom on his back wall, his disembodied voice had answered instantly with an "I'm on my way." And in a moment he had let himself out the side door.

"I hope I didn't keep you waiting," he said, instead of hello.

"Not at all," replied Enid. "I'm just delighted you're able to come on such short notice."

"You caught me at a good time — when I'm in production I don't have a minute to myself."

As they got into Enid's Mercedes, she noticed that he was looking a little tired and puffy around the eyes. She hoped he wasn't upset at her for dragging him out of bed and to this meeting.

"Your car's fixed already?" he asked.

"It wasn't too bad, actually. I had it serviced while it was in so I killed two birds with one stone."

"Mine's supposed to be ready tomorrow, thank God. I feel so anonymous in that damn loaner."

"I'll be happy to take you wherever you have to go," Enid offered, and immediately regretted it. Why was she always throwing herself at him? To cover, she changed the subject. "I really loved watching *Wind Jammers* last night."

"You did?" Patrick beamed.

She nodded. "It was funny and romantic. I laughed and I cried. Isn't that silly? Lying there in bed all alone laughing and crying."

"No, I don't think it's funny. I think it's a great waste."

"What?"

"You, lying there all alone." Patrick put his hand on her thigh and rubbed it lightly. In response, her foot jammed down the gas pedal and the car surged forward.

"Sorry," he said, withdrawing his hand.

"My fault," she said, hoping he couldn't hear how hard her heart was beating. To her own ears, the sound was deafening.

"I don't generally sleep well anyway, when Sam is out of town. But when I finally did go to sleep last night, I had a really weird dream," she told him. "You were in it."

"I was?" Patrick smiled at Enid, studying her profile as she drove. "I like it that I'm in your dreams," he said softly. "It makes me feel close to you."

Embarrassed, Enid turned on the radio. "What kind of music do you like?"

"Depends on my mood. I'll find something." He began to fiddle with the automatic search.

Enid was glad to have distracted him from questioning her about her dream, because just remembering it made her break into a cold sweat. It was one of those rare dreams that was so real she could recall every detail when she woke up — her actions and reactions, the way things looked, and oddly enough, even the smells.

In the dream she had short, black hair and a voluptuous body. She was on a boat, a large and luxurious yacht, sailing through the canals of Venice. The atmosphere was redolent with the stale odors of dead fish and decay, and some other musky smell that Enid couldn't identify.

Then, as can only happen in a dream, Enid was thrust backward in time. She was a ten-year-old piano student, in the middle of her Saturday afternoon lesson. In the dream, the teacher was not her real teacher, a frowzy, bleached blonde dowager named Miss Blanche, who tipped the scales at 220 pounds and reeked of garlic, but a somewhat distorted and idealized manifestation of the person of Patrick Drake. He had leaned over the piano, his breath warm on her neck, as he had corrected the placement of her fingers on the keys, admonishing her, *but you didn't play it happily. There's a big difference.* He had commanded her to play the piece another time.

The student Enid had been consternated, not understanding how to play the song *happily*, unable to remember the notes. And when she did touch her fingers to the keyboard, no amount of pressure would force music from the keys.

Play, play, he had commanded her.

But I can't remember the notes, she had cried. *I don't know what it's supposed to sound like.*

Then I will play it for you, he had said, and he sat down beside her on the piano bench, put his hand over hers, and began to play the piece.

Again the locale shifted and the "dream Enid" was a full-grown woman, lying on a bed she didn't recognize. She felt hands on her body, but they were not stroking it, they were playing it like a piano. And to her horror, music was coming out, different notes for different parts of her body. Enormously embarrassed, she had tried to stifle them, but couldn't. It was terrible, the sense of being so helpless and vulnerable.

She had awakened feeling fascinated that her body had been capable of this bizarre reaction and horrified that someone else had been controlling it. But mostly, she had been, and remained, afraid to analyze the meaning of the dream.

"Here. Do you like Oscar Peterson?" Patrick asked, breaking her reverie.

"Oh yes, very much," Enid replied evenly, then nearly rear-ended the bus in front of them when she realized that the melody Oscar Peterson was playing on the radio was the same one her body had "played" in the dream.

Patrick was not the first movie star to visit the Westside Women's Shelter, but his arrival was nevertheless a major event for residents, staff, and volunteers. As Enid led him down the narrow corridor to the conference room (actually the children's play room, which doubled for a meeting space), he was greeted with curious, smiling faces, laughter, and exclamations of excitement. His spirits lifted as they always did when the public received him in this fashion.

"Thank you so much for coming, Patrick," said Enid. "You can see how much it means to everybody."

If only she knew how much it meant to him. This kind of adulation was a much-needed massage to his psyche, a thousand healing hands gently caressing his pride, still inflamed from the *People* debacle. Fortunately the article was rapidly fading into history, and would be forgotten in a few days when next week's issue came out.

Patrick followed Enid into a room that looked like a Salvation Army thrift shop. The linoleum floor was littered with toys of all description, uniform only in their shabbiness. A couch that was more springs and foam than fabric had been shoved against a wall to make room for twelve scarred, ragged folding chairs, on which sat ten middle-aged ladies.

Suzanne was conspicuously trying to be inconspicuous, looking for something in her purse. But Enid could feel the heat of her neighbor's jealousy, and part of her reveled in this moment of triumph.

And there was Shelley, sitting somewhat apart from the group. She was smiling at Enid, but it was a peculiar smile that Enid couldn't interpret.

"Shelley, hi, shall we sit with you?" Enid half called, half gestured over the heads of the other ladies. Shelley shrugged unenthusiastically and got up to rearrange the chairs to accommodate Enid and Patrick.

"Patrick, I'd like you to meet Ivy Lanigan, our executive director."

Enid stepped aside so that a diminutive white-haired woman in polyester pants and crepe-soled shoes could approach.

"We are so very honored that you could come to the Westside Women's Shelter today, Mr. Drake," she enthused, pumping Patrick's hand between both of her own.

"It's my pleasure. What more could I ask than to be the only man in a room full of beautiful women?"

The ladies tittered politely.

"You must forgive our mess," Ivy continued. "Unfortunately, we don't have enough space in this building to have a separate room for meetings, so we have to use the children's playroom. I hope you don't mind."

"Mind? I'm in my element. Put me in a room with a computer and a fax machine. Then I'll get uncomfortable."

The ladies laughed again.

"Enid, shall we start? We don't want to take any more of Mr. Drake's valuable time than necessary."

At first, Patrick seemed almost to be enjoying the interplay between the board members, as they discussed the finer points of invitation design, caterers, and ticket pricing. The entire session was going exceedingly well, in fact, until Suzanne raised her hand.

"I hate to say this, but . . . are we sure the subject matter of this movie is appropriate for the Shelter's image?"

Enid felt rage building inside of her as Suzanne continued, "I mean, what if there's too much sex or violence in it? There was an article in *People* this week. . . ."

"I'm sure we all feel that any movie Patrick Drake stars in will be good, clean family entertainment," Ivy said, deftly cutting Suzanne off. "And we are more than lucky to have an opportunity to host its premiere."

Murmurs of assent from around the room supported Ivy's pronouncement, but Enid had seen a wave of distress wash over Patrick's face. She, too, had read the terrible notice in *People*, and she suspected that every woman in the room was harboring the same fear — what if the movie turned out to be a bomb. The fund-raiser would be a disaster, the Shelter would lose money, and worst of all, they would be the laughingstock of the Westside.

Enid looked at Patrick. The distress on his face turned out to be a passing cloud. He rose to speak, as confident and relaxed as he had been when he entered the Shelter.

"Ladies, I certainly cannot promise *A Month of Sundays* will be a blockbuster. I wish I could, because I've got a percentage of the profits coming to me." He waited for laughter, but the women were silent. "But the truth is, nobody can forecast these things. That's part of the mystery of the film business.

"The way it works is this: the studio has promised to put a lot of money into promoting the film, so by the time it opens, by the time of this premiere, everyone will be talking about it. And if even one hundredth of all the people who know about the film go see it, it will be a huge success. That's called marketing, and the big studios are good at hedging their bets that way."

The ladies nodded their agreement and their eagerness to believe anything Patrick Drake told them.

"As far as *People* goes, wasn't it *People* that did the article about Elvis being alive and well and living in Newark, and the interview with the family who swore they were abducted by alien cockroaches? What I mean is, I think *People* is a little like the Bible." He paused for effect, then continued, "You've got to take what you read with a grain of salt." He turned to look at Suzanne. "Or else you might turn into a pillar of salt."

Enid took her cue and jumped to her feet, sweeping Patrick out of the room on the excuse that she had promised to get him home in time for a lunch meeting. Patrick let her lead him away, following her silently to the car.

Stopped at a red light, Enid looked over at him. He turned to her and smiled a sad smile. Although his eyes were hidden behind sunglasses, she saw the hurt he had not wanted to reveal in front of the others.

"I'm sorry about Suzanne. She has a big mouth, and a bad attitude," she said.

"She didn't mean anything by it I'm sure," he said sweetly, then added in a gruff voice, "the conniving cunt."

He smiled at Enid's delighted look. "Sorry, I'm not a very good sport when people bring up my bad reviews."

"No, it's true. She is conniving. And she's a gossip and a trouble-maker. The way she gets the upper hand is by putting other people down."

"She might not be wrong," Patrick admitted. A *Month of Sundays* could turn into a disaster. But believe me, there's no way anyone can tell this early on. I hate it when people say terrible things about my films. It's like telling you you have an ugly child, you know? And however bad a film may turn out to be, nobody sets out to make a rotten one. It just happens. You still work just as many fourteen-hour days and seven-day weeks. But sometimes the end result isn't what you planned. Life is like that too, don't you think?"

"Yes, I do," said Enid. She pulled the car up behind Patrick's garage. "You were wonderful to come today, and I'm sorry if what Suzanne said upset you."

He got out of the car. "Oh, I'm fine now. But if you hear a scream in a few minutes, it's just me setting fire to my body."

He walked a few steps away from the car, then turned back and leaned in her window. "You wouldn't by any chance be free for dinner tonight? Maybe life wouldn't look so bleak if I could look forward to a little company."

"I can't tonight. I have this charity thing. I'm sorry," said Enid, and she truly was.

"Another time."

"I'd love it. Really I would. Any day," she said.

Moments later Enid stood at the window of her den, staring past the half-built wall into Patrick's study. She held a note Wallase left for her, saying he was at the market, and that Sam had called to tell her he had arrived safely and would call her later to tell her what his return plans were.

Damn him, she fumed. Why had Sam flown halfway around the

world to meet with Harry? Was the firm in trouble? Or was the whole trip just a cover for some clandestine tryst? How dare he not tell her the truth. Or was it the truth? Frustration raged inside of her, all out of proportion to the situation.

She picked up the phone and dialed.

"You have reached the machine of Patrick Drake," the voice said. "I'm not taking this call because I may not want to talk to you, so please leave your name and number after the beep and either I will get back to you or I won't, depending on how I feel."

Enid waited for the tone. "Patrick, it's Enid. I just had a thought about tonight. I'm supposed to go to a charity benefit, it's a premiere of Harrison Ford's new movie, I forgot the name. Well, since Sam is out of town I was going to go alone. But if you're still free, I was thinking, maybe you would come with me. I'm sure you go to a lot of these things, but maybe it would be better than spending the evening all alone . . ."

Lying on his bed, semicomatose, Patrick listened as Enid concluded her message, "and I can't tell you how much it would mean to me if you would be my date."

Patrick stared into space contemplating the possibilities. LeMar had told him to get out and be seen, and surely there would be a lot of press at this event. But to mobilize the forces at this late date for a public appearance would be such a pain in the ass. He decided to call Peter and see what it would take.

18

Sam and Carmen

The winding road to the Hotel Pitrizza was steeper than Sam remembered. He was only a half mile from the hotel and already out of breath. Maybe it had something to do with jet lag, or maybe his heart just wasn't in this afternoon jog.

A car sped by, throwing up a spray of loose gravel, and Sam ground to a halt, rubbing dust from his eyes. Bent over, hands on his thighs, head hung low, he waited for the throbbing in his abdomen to subside. He'd felt this way before on a difficult journey, but he knew exercise was the best antidote to travel fatigue. And if he were going to make it through the afternoon and be sharp for the evening's discussions with Harry, he had to muster his energy.

On the other hand, the bed back at the hotel had looked damn inviting. He imagined Carmen in it, and straightened up, starting to walk slowly at first, then picking up speed as he recalled their first few minutes in the room.

It had been as awkward as a first date. He hadn't known how to act, where to stand, what to do with his hands. Carmen, on the other hand, had seemed completely at ease being in a hotel room with a strange man. She had simply opened her suitcase and removed everything she would need for a shower, and had excused herself into the bathroom. Well, maybe this was nothing new for her.

Sam had sat for a long time at the foot of the bed listening through the closed door. And damn it all if the simple sounds of whatever the hell it was she was doing in there hadn't started to turn him on.

Sam tried to break into a jog, to erase this memory, but his legs wouldn't cooperate. Since when had his body become his enemy? With a mixture of reluctance and anticipation, he turned around and headed back to the hotel. He hadn't been gone long. Maybe she'd still be in the shower.

But when he unlocked the door, the bungalow was empty. Carmen's things were neatly stowed on one side and her heady scent hung in the air. Sam went into the bathroom and took the damp towel from the hook behind the door. He rubbed the moist terry cloth along his body, savoring the cool, musky scent that clung to it. He saw a little round container on the counter, similar to the one Enid used to carry her diaphragm when they traveled. He stared at it for a moment, then slowly reached for it, to see if indeed that was what it contained.

Suddenly, he heard a key in the lock. He froze as Carmen entered, carrying two tall tropical drinks and a straw hat.

"Oh, Sam, you're back already."

"It was too hot to run. I gave up."

"Really? That doesn't sound like you. Here, the manager insisted we try these drinks. He promises me they're just fruit juice, but I suspect there's alcohol lurking beneath the surface." She held out a tall, frosty glass and Sam took it. Normally, he wouldn't drink in the afternoon, but then what was normal about his life at this moment?

He took a long swallow and let the icy liquid slide down his throat, a sensuous and sybaritic feeling.

"Are you okay?" Carmen asked. "You don't look all that well."

"I'm fine, just a little whacked out from the Halcion, I guess."

"Well I never felt better in my life. This is the most beautiful place I've ever been, and I can hardly wait to see Harry Ingersol's boat. Oh,

I checked to see if there were any messages and there was one from Harry. He says his man will pick us up at Dock 72 in Port Cervo at six o'clock and take us out to the boat for dinner."

Sam nodded and sat on the bed. The drink was making him sleepy. It was only 2:30, plenty of time for a nap. But what about Carmen? How could he relax with her in the room?

Before he could figure out what to say, she said, "You look like you could use a little rest. Don't mind me. I'm just going to sit out on the porch for a little while. Maybe I'll take a walk. What time do you want me to wake you up?"

"Five o'clock would be great. That'll give us plenty of time to get to Porto Cervo." He stretched out on the bed and closed his eyes.

"Sam, wouldn't you be more comfortable if you showered first?"

"I'm too wiped out."

"You'll rest so much better if you're clean instead of all sweaty."

He ignored her and closed his eyes. She was probably right, but he wasn't going to set a precedent by letting her tell him what to do. He'd shower when he damn well pleased.

Sam was awakened by a bug tickling his neck. He tried to ignore it, but the damn thing persisted. Reluctantly he opened his eyes and yawned. God, he felt wrecked, like he'd just run the Boston Marathon. What the hell time was it?

He found his watch on the nightstand and squinted in the dim light to read the dial: 6:42. He sat bolt upright and shook the watch. How could it be that late? Carmen was supposed to wake him at 5. If he'd missed Harry's man with the launch, Harry would be pissed and the entire evening would be wasted. Damn!

Sam threw off the covers and stumbled into the bathroom. He turned on the shower full blast and got in, still wearing his running clothes. The rush of the water was a balm on his hot, sticky body. Relax, he told himself, you can call Harry ship to shore and explain what happened.

He stroked his body with the soap, planning what he would say to Harry, when a thought occurred to him — where the hell was Carmen? He stepped out of the shower covered with soap, and tracked water through the bathroom to the bedroom, to see if there was any evidence of her in the room. Her purse, hat, and jacket were missing.

She wouldn't have gone without him, would she?

He got back in the shower and hurriedly rinsed off, then toweled himself dry in ten seconds flat. Son of a bitch. She'd probably planned the whole thing. Even that drink — there must have been something in it to knock him out so she could go alone to Harry's boat, making up some story about what had happened to Sam.

It was all his fault for letting her talk him into this trip. What the hell was he doing here anyway, chasing after some rumor? She was just using him as a pawn for the story she was trying to scoop. And he had fallen for the whole thing, hook, line, and sinker.

Sam stepped into his pants and was just pulling on his shirt when the door opened. To his shock and surprise, Carmen peeked in, then smiled brightly. "Sam, you're awake! I was just going to get you."

Sam was speechless. He had convinced himself that Carmen was trying to pull something over on him, so her arrival didn't compute. "Yeah," he managed. "I woke up and it was nearly seven. We were supposed to meet the launch at six, weren't we?"

"Oh, that was before. Harry called back a few hours ago, while you were asleep. He's apparently got some other people coming out to the boat tonight and decided it would be a lot easier for the launch to just make one trip. So it's coming at eight. I guess they eat late in this part of the world."

"Other people? What other people?"

Carmen shrugged. "He didn't say, but he seemed glad that you had brought a 'chick,' as he called me, because apparently all of the others are couples."

Things were not going at all as he had planned. Indeed, it seemed that some alien force was masterminding this convoluted scenario. Sam slumped into the nearest chair and tried to rally his exhausted brain to sort things out.

"What's the matter, Sam, you look so perplexed," Carmen moved behind him and expertly massaged the tension out of his shoulders. In spite of everything, Sam relaxed into her touch.

"I wanted to get the business over with tonight and get on a plane home tomorrow. But if Harry's making a party out of it, there's no way."

"He probably had this planned before he knew you were coming, Sam. Remember, we didn't give him much notice. Besides, we can talk with him in the morning. I'm sure we'll all do better after we've had a good night's sleep. Don't you think?"

"I don't know what the hell to think," growled Sam.

"Well, I'm going to take a quick shower. Shall I meet you out by the pool at 7:15?"

Carmen stepped into the shower for the second time in half a day. Tonight might be the most important night of her life and she wanted everything to be perfect, starting, as always, with her appearance. She felt the confidence that came from being in control. Everything was falling into place so easily. Sam was playing right into her hand; he had become so malleable she was almost disappointed in him. But then, she had been fiendishly clever. And after all, this had been orchestrated for Sam's own good.

As Carmen applied her makeup, she thought back on the afternoon. While Sam had slept, courtesy of the little blue pills she'd slipped into his cocktail, she had made her preparations. First off was a telephone call to Harry Ingersol's boat.

The captain had told her that Mr. Ingersol was just coming up from a dive, would she hold on for a moment.

Harry had come to the phone, breathless and brusque. "Y'allo?"

"Hello, Harry."

A long pause, then he'd answered, "Who is this?"

"I know you know who it is, Harry. Are you afraid to say my name?"

"Carmen?" He spoke her name in a whisper, accented with trepidation.

"That's right. How are you, Harry?"

"I was fine until just a second ago. Right now I'm hyperventilating. How'd you get this number?"

"From your secretary, of course."

"She's knows better than to give it out arbitrarily, without checking with me first."

"She didn't give it to me," Carmen said, feeling a surge of resentment that he considered her "arbitrary." "She gave it to Sam Carrouthers," she finished evenly.

Another long pause. "How do you know Sam?"

"Harry, how does anybody know anybody? We met, we got friendly. You remember how it works, don't you?"

"Yes, I remember how it works. I remember it all rather vividly in fact." His voice had lost the edge of surprise and softened into a lower, intimate tone. "Even though it's been a long time."

"Seven years," Carmen said.

"A lotta water under the bridge," Harry replied.

"I can imagine," said Carmen.

"One hell of a lot of water," Harry said. "Things have changed a lot for me. Louise and I are doing great now. Really great. Since my operation — I had a brain tumor two years ago, did you know about it?"

"I heard. Of course I heard. I wanted to call you, but I didn't want to upset Louise, and I knew she'd be with you."

"Yep. She was in the hospital every minute. A regular Florence Nightingale. It was a hell of an ordeal for us both, even though the damn thing turned out to be nonmalignant. Hell, it was the size of a grapefruit. But y'know, it brought me and Louise back together."

"Life-and-death situations tend to do that."

"You said it. Damn, I really thought I was history. And you know, it made me appreciate a lot of things I'd taken for granted before. Little things. Like how fantastic it feels to drink a glass of cold water, or eat a hot dog, or take a good piss. I thought about you a lot then."

Carmen laughed. "I was fourth in line, right after a good piss?"

"You know."

"Yeah, I know, Harry. Is Louise with you on the boat now?"

"Na. She's back in Connecticut. One of her sister's kids is getting hitched and you know Louise, she had to be there. Why?"

"Well, I don't want to upset her when things are going so well for the two of you."

"What do you mean upset her?"

"When I come out to the boat this evening with Sam."

"Wait, what? I musta missed something. You're here, in Sardinia right now?"

"At the Hotel Pitrizza. It's a gorgeous place. I wish I could stay here forever. But then I wouldn't miss seeing your boat for the world."

"Carmen, I'm not getting this. You're at the Hotel Pitrizza with Sam Carrouthers?"

"Yep."

"What happened to his wife?"

"Oh, Harry, you know how it is with men and their wives. You're not jealous are you?"

"What right have I to be jealous?"

"Exactly."

"Well, I am jealous. And I'm pissed off that you'd just appear here out of the blue without giving me any warning."

"That's why I'm calling now, Harry. I didn't want to throw you off tonight."

"Why the hell are you here? Sam's just coming to talk to me. I thought he was only staying overnight."

"He is."

"You've come six thousand miles to be with him for one night? Hell, it must be true love."

"I came because I'm interested in talking with you too."

"About?"

"About what Sam wants to discuss. The WIT deal."

"Jesus, you always did stick your nose in everybody's business."

"Harry, I'm a business journalist. It's my job to know." She let this sink in, then added, "And it's obvious you and Leo are giving Sam the shaft. I want you to rethink your game plan."

Harry was silent for a moment. "Does Sam know, about us?"

"Sam doesn't know shit. And I want to keep it that way. I think it's in the best interests of all parties involved if he thinks you're meeting me for the first time tonight. Don't you agree?"

"You, me, and Sam together on the boat. I don't know if I can pull it off."

"So invite some other people. Make it a party."

"When do *we* talk then? Carmen, I can't see you without seeing you, y'know?"

"I thought things were going so well with Louise."

"She's in Connecticut and you're here."

"Well Sam's asleep right now and I've got a couple of extra hours. How about meeting me in the little village, what's it called?"

"Porto Cervo?"

"Yeah. I can be there in fifteen minutes."

"Okay, okay. I'll get the launch and meet you. There's a little cafe called Pomodoro, right on the wharf. Everyone knows it. I'll be there in fifteen minutes, twenty at the most."

"See you."

And seeing Harry was the real point of the trip. Seven years earlier, she had really believed that he would leave his wife for her, and she was sure he'd thought so too. But the problem with men and their mistresses was that they couldn't be together every minute, and sometimes when they were apart, outside influences conspired to destroy the fragile relationship without giving either party a chance to protect what was theirs.

The story Carmen had told Sam about how she came to live in her house was only partially true. She was indeed having a relationship with a married man at the time. The man was Harry Ingersol. After the tragic deaths of his sons, Harry's marriage to Louise had gone sour, a sad, but not uncommon situation. Carmen had been in her mid twenties, Harry close to sixty when they'd met, and even though she was infinitely more savvy than he, at least in the realm of male-female relationships, naturally he had felt somewhat fatherly toward her. He had purchased the house in Laurel Canyon in her name, to give them a place to rendezvous and to give her a creative outlet for the times he could not be with her.

The arrangement had worked for nearly a year, until Louise had come to her senses and realized that if she didn't reclaim Harry she would probably spend the rest of her life living alone. This fear had eventually driven her to confront Harry and Carmen at breakfast, just as Carmen had told Sam. And with the weight of forty-some years of marriage behind her, Louise had managed to tip the scales of Harry's conscience and extricate him from his relationship with Carmen.

A year later, when Carmen had heard that Harry was having brain surgery, she had felt certain that the psychological reason for the operation was, quite simply, that Harry had lost his mind over losing her. She knew he still wanted her, even though his calls had become increasingly less frequent and more impersonal, until they finally stopped altogether. And at the same time, she knew he would never leave his wife. It was something they both had learned to live with: Harry, remembering their time together as a treasured romantic interlude, Carmen, considering it a lesson in reality. Never again would she make herself vulnerable to the Harry Ingersols of the world. From that time on, she had invested her efforts only where she could be sure of the dividends.

Such as in a man like Sam Carrouthers. And Harry would help her get him.

🕶️

Carmen had found her way to the Pomodoro Ristorante with no trouble. It was not a clandestine romantic hideaway with two or three checkered-clothed tables in an old piazza, as she had hoped, but a loud and lively pizza parlor in the center of a shopping mall. She had had a private laugh at herself for forgetting that Harry's tastes were so basic, and remembered the gift he had given her to commemorate their first night together. The box was Tiffany blue and she had been thrilled to untie the silken white ribbon, anticipating a jeweled bauble inside. What she had found instead was a tiny sewing kit with a solid gold needle.

I don't get it, she had told him. Get what, he had asked. I thought it would remind you of me whenever you have to sew on a button. And oddly enough it had; whenever she used the gold needle she remembered what a prick he could be.

At least today he had been waiting for her, and that was unlike the Harry Ingersol she remembered, who never waited for anyone because waiting was a waste of time.

Harry Ingersol had been a handsome man in his day, but at age seventy-two his still-boyish face seemed surprised to be capped by a thatch of sparse, silver hair, which did nothing to hide the hearing aid he wore in his right ear. His sideburns were unfashionably long, a failed attempt to look hip, since the cognoscenti were not wearing sideburns at all these days.

Harry had aged considerably since they had been together, seven years earlier. But Carmen was prepared for this, having seen his picture in countless newspapers and magazines over the years, the chronicling of a public man's progress through private life. At least his manner of dress had not changed — Hawaiian-style jams with a polo shirt over them, tennis shoes, and sweat socks. As a matter of fact, the jams and shirt were possibly the same ones he'd worn all those years ago on their outings to the beach, because Harry had a habit of wearing the same clothes for decades.

When he'd caught sight of her across the crowded restaurant, Harry had leapt to his feet and waved, and Carmen had returned the greeting, feeling what little bitterness remained in her heart evaporate on the spot.

Dear Harry, what she had loved most about him had been his vitality, and apparently this had been undiminished by time, ill health, or the aging process. He exuded such energy and intensity that when he entered a room people were sometimes repelled by the force of his personality. This could be a good thing or a bad thing. When Harry walked into an office to negotiate a business deal, it was a good thing. When he entered a small restaurant with his mistress in tow, it was a bad thing. Because nobody who dealt with Harry ever forgot him, and that went for gossipy receptionists and waiters as well as businessmen and reporters.

Harry had greeted Carmen with a hug that nearly suffocated her. This was more of the old Harry, unconcerned about what anyone would think, focusing only on what was foremost on his mind, whether it was greeting an old friend and lover, or ordering a drink, which he proceeded to do the minute Carmen sat down.

"What would you like, Carmen?" he had said, and without waiting for her to answer he had told the waiter, who was hovering in readiness, obviously already under Harry's thrall, "I'll have a gin fizz, extra heavy on the gin, in a highball glass with three pieces of ice. That's three, not two, not four, three. And make sure the glass is clean. Last time I was in here I got a glass with lipstick on it. And it woulda been okay, except it didn't match my outfit." He had guffawed loudly, allowing Carmen time to tell the waiter, "Beefeater's martini straight up, no olives, no onions, no Vermouth."

"I can see your taste in liquor hasn't changed," Harry had said.

"Neither has yours. I would have thought you'd've slowed down a little after the surgery."

"Hell, I was sipping a fizz ten minutes after they took me off the respirator. And I'll tell you, it was the best thing I coulda done. Brought me right back to reality. What with the drugs and the pain I was in outerspace-ville. But one cocktail, and I remembered how good it is to be alive."

"I'm glad, Harry. I can't tell you how dreadful I felt when I heard about the surgery."

"Not half as bad as I did. But that's ancient history. God it's good to see you. You look fantastic. Better than ever. How old are you now, twenty-eight, twenty-nine?"

"I'm thirty-four and you know it, damn you," Carmen had smiled. This was a running game between them. Harry, loving the idea that Carmen was so much younger than he, had taken to exaggerating the difference in their ages. They both thought this hilarious since the nearly forty years that separated them was more than enough to raise eyebrows among even the most liberal of their acquaintances.

"Remember the time we went to Abu Dhabi, and I went jogging in the street outside of the hotel?" she had asked.

"How could I forget? There was a knock on the door, I open it, and there you are, flanked by two armed policemen."

"They wanted to put handcuffs on me, but they were afraid to touch me," Carmen had laughed.

"Hell, I was afraid they were going to throw me in jail. Until you convinced them I was your father."

"Grandfather," Carmen had said.

"Just one big happy family," Harry had guffawed again, then he had looked deeply into Carmen's eyes. "We had some pretty nifty times together, didn't we?"

"The best."

"So why don't we just pick up where we left off?"

"What about Louise? I thought you said things were good between you?"

"How good can things be between two people who have been together for forty-seven years? Hell, we don't even sleep in the same room any more. She says my snoring keeps her awake."

"I don't remember you snoring."

"I only do it when I'm not getting any nookie. That wasn't a problem with us."

"That's ridiculous," Carmen had laughed.

"I'm serious. You know how they say the size of a man's schnozz relates to the size of his ding dong. Well, when the one gets clogged, the other one does too. They're related, I swear."

"Ding dong, Harry?" Carmen had teased.

"Yeah, ding dong. I call it that because you really ring my chimes."

"Harry, you are as corny as a Coney Island corndog."

"And just as yummy. Wanna bite?"

"You're impossible," she had smiled.

"So make me possible," he had replied, the longing in his tone touching her heart.

Carmen had been as aware of the intensity of Harry's desire at that moment as if he had pinned her to the table. She had decided to play her cards while he was at his most attentive.

"Harry, you know I love you and I always will. But I want more than you can give me."

"Nobody, but nobody can give you more than me," he had answered, as she had known he would.

"Okay, then give me what I need."

Patrick sucked in his stomach to button the waist of his tuxedo trousers. Why was he so bloated? There must have been MSG in the leftovers from Chinois, despite Wolfgang's claim that he didn't use any. Whatever, Patrick was in a foul mood, and the punishing waistband didn't help.

19

Patrick and Enid

The phone rang, and Jeremy answered it.

"Who's that?" Patrick yelled.

"Just the driver. He's waiting outside whenever you're ready."

"Tell him to go next door and get Mrs. Carrouthers. I'll be out in a few minutes."

"Will do."

Patrick turned his attention to the magnifying mirror that Sara had installed against his wishes. He hated this contraption. Its enlarged reality was a shock and an insult. *They shouldn't allow people over thirty to own these things*, he thought. *It'd probably cut the suicide rate in half.*

But as much as he detested the mirror, he was drawn to it, certain he would one day see the Patrick Drake he was looking for, a star of Academy Award proportions, a man with Cary Grant's bearing, Arnold Schwartzenegger's physique and Brad Pitt's good looks.

What had happened to his eyes? They used to sparkle and speak a language of their own. Now they were two dull orbs, punctuated by pupils that expanded and contracted like his waistline. Most likely it was the result of too much of the good life, and too little of the life that was good for you.

Patrick put his canceled gold American Express card and some loose bills for tips into his trouser pocket. He remembered to slip the obligatory sunglasses and a pen into his jacket pocket as well. There were bound to be hordes of autograph seekers out there. Dominion's marketing machine often spent millions more than the negative cost of the film to ensure that they would draw big crowds on opening weekend. And their premiere parties were legendary for their flamboyance and spectacle. At least he wouldn't have to suffer through rubbery chicken and watered-down drinks at the party following the screening.

Enid was not happy with her hair. She had planned to wear it down, letting it fall simply to her shoulders as usual, but seeing that the weather had turned foggy she worried that it would frizz. So she decided to wear it pinned up, a more elegant style anyway, something special on this special night with Patrick.

But as she looked at herself in the mirror when she was fully dressed, she realized the hairstyle was too traditional for the gown. Besides, the foundation of bobby pins that held it in place showed and threatened to slip at the least wisp of a breeze. She sighed and started pulling out the pins.

The front door intercom buzzed and Enid answered it, ripping out the pins as she spoke.

"Yes?"

"Mrs. Carrouthers. I'm from Celebrity Limo. Mr. Drake told me to pick you up first."

"I'll be right down."

"Yes ma'am."

Enid quickly brushed her hair into a ponytail, opting for simple elegance over elaborate style, in the interest of time. She hurried into the closet to put on her shoes.

The dress she had chosen was an iridescent Richard Tyler from three years ago. She'd worn it only once before because it wasn't very comfortable, and she had never been able to find the right shoes to complement it. Tonight she wasn't sure whether to wear the bronze Maud Frizon stack-heel sandals, which were a bit too casual, or the blue Charles Jourdan pumps, which were just a shade off color. She put on one of each shoe and raised the hem of her dress to contemplate.

The phone rang. She wanted to ignore it, but what if it was Patrick with some message about their date?

"Hello?"

"Enid?" The line crackled with long-distance static.

Damn, just what I need, she thought. And instantly she felt bad for not wanting to speak to her husband. "Sam?" She tried to make her voice sound relaxed and happy.

"It's me. Did you get the message that I called earlier?"

"Wallase told me. I was at the Shelter. So how was your flight?"

"Long, exhausting, boring. Hell, I was so wiped out I couldn't even run when we got here. I slept for six hours this afternoon."

Enid stopped listening after the word *we*. Normally she would consider this a slip of the tongue. Sam frequently lapsed into the royal use of the first-person plural, an annoying, self-aggrandizing habit that important men fell into. But after the confusion at the airport, his use of this word reinforced her suspicions that he was not traveling alone.

A thrill of fear shot through her body. Was Sam with another woman? Who in the world would it be? And if it were an innocent business associate, why was he hiding it from her?

"Sam, I would love to hear more about your trip, but I'm late."

"Where are you going?"

"That Good Vibrations premiere. You remember," she said, and then with carefully enunciated words added, *"We've* got a car waiting, so I've got to run. Call me when you know what your plans are," she finished, and hung up before he could respond. Flying on the righteous wings of revenge, she grabbed her sable coat and her Judith Leber bag and hurried down the stairs to the waiting car.

Her timing was perfect. Patrick was just walking out of his house when Enid emerged from hers, a shimmering vision backlit by the glow of the street lamp.

"Sorry to keep you waiting, the phone . . ."

Patrick silenced her by taking her hand and drawing it to his lips Cary Grant style. "You look absolutely stunning," he said. "And to think I was going to stay home and watch a rerun of *Roseanne*." Silenced by the kiss and the compliment, Enid lowered her eyes and swept by him into the car. Patrick followed, and they were off.

They drove in silence for a moment. Enid felt Patrick's eyes on her. "What? Is something wrong?"

"No, not at all. You look so beautiful, that's all."

"Thank you. You look beautiful yourself."

"Really? Do you think so?" said Patrick. "I had a haircut yesterday, and I think she butchered me." He turned on the little light by the vanity mirror and brushed a few strands of hair off his forehead. "My usual girl's on vacation, and I think this one's fresh out of beauty school. She tried to use a razor to trim the back, and I had to tell her that razor cuts went out with Richard Nixon. What I needed was a body wave. You don't think it's too curly, do you?"

Enid smiled to herself. She had never known a man to be so vain about his looks and so open about his complex efforts to achieve them. *But,* she thought, *he is a movie star, and millions of people sit in darkened theaters judging every follicle of hair and noticing each new wrinkle on his famous face. And tonight he is my date!*

Patrick leaned his famous face forward to the driver. "Do you know where we're going?"

"Yes sir, Mr. Drake. To the Chinese. Mr. Paltrain gave me the number of his portable phone to call him when we get close."

"Good," said Patrick, as he sat back in his seat.

"Who's Mr. Paltrain?" asked Enid.

"Peter Paltrain, from Reagan and Coward." Enid's face still registered a question mark, so he added, "My public relations manager." He smiled at her. "You thought it was just the two of us tonight, didn't you?" Enid nodded. "Oh no," he sighed, "it's much more complicated than that."

🕶

The traffic started to slow before they reached Hollywood Boulevard. Overhead, searchlights swept the starry sky. The limousine pulled out of the line of cars waiting to make the turn onto Hollywood and drove straight onto Franklin, stopping at the curb in front of a shabby apartment complex where a man was waiting. The passenger door opened, and the man climbed in next to the driver. He was heavyset and balding, and despite the warm evening he was wearing a yellow and purple striped sweater. One of the smallest cellular telephones Enid had ever seen was plastered to his ear.

"Stay on Franklin until Palm," he ordered the driver. "Then hang a right and that'll put us at the front of the lineup." The limousine sped off and the man turned in his seat to face Patrick and Enid. "How are'ya?" he asked.

"This is Peter," Patrick told Enid. "The man doesn't own a suit, let alone a tuxedo. Only sweaters, hundreds of them. Either he's got an interest in a sheep farm in Australia, or his wife is one hell of a knitter. Peter, this is Enid Carrouthers."

"Glad to meetcha," said Peter. He winked at Patrick, "Now I get it."

"Get what?" asked Patrick.

"What you meant when you said you were bringing your *next-door neighbor*."

"Enid *is* my next-door neighbor."

"Yeah, sure."

"Seriously, she is. Aren't you?" Patrick asked Enid.

Enid nodded. "One door to the south."

Peter made a face like he didn't believe either of them. "Well, we're going to have a tough time convincing the press, because she sure doesn't look like the girl next door."

"You can take that as a compliment, Enid," said Patrick. "For a PR guy, Peter isn't exactly Mr. Tactful. But he gets the job done. Who's on tonight?"

"Jack and DeWain are working the entrance. Lowell is inside. Oh, and LeMar and Betsy will be sitting with you. Lucky for you, I got markers out all over town." He handed Patrick the tickets. "Four together right behind Harrison and Melissa."

"But I already have tickets, row 27, seats E and F," said Enid, opening her purse.

Patrick sighed. "They like all of the celebrities to sit together, makes it easier for the press."

"But — " Enid tried.

Patrick patted her hand condescendingly. "You don't have any idea what an organizational nightmare it is for me to come to one of these things. I can't just appear. It takes a lot of planning, an entire support staff."

"But why?"

"Well, because I'm famous."

The car rounded the corner onto Hollywood Boulevard and butted its way into line in front of a Bentley and behind a white stretch limo. Through the tinted glass, Enid saw the street lined with people. Up in front of the theater, a small grandstand had been erected. Cheering, jeering fans leaned over its rails, reaching out to touch the entering luminaries.

A policeman signaled the driver to stop and looked inside the car. Peter leaned over the driver and said simply "Patrick Drake." The policeman waved them on to the waiting red carpet.

"Ever meet Army Archerd?" Patrick asked Enid.

"No."

"Well you're going to in about ten seconds. Just be natural, and whatever you do, don't let him know you're madly in love with me or it'll be all over the tabloids in the morning."

"Army Archerd?" Enid stammered, as the car screeched to a stop. Peter jumped out and opened her door, extending his hand to help her out.

She hesitated. "What about my coat?"

"Leave it," Patrick barked. "The driver will stay with the car. It'll be safe." He gave her a nudge toward the open door. "Don't be afraid. It'll all be over in a couple of minutes."

Enid took Peter's proffered hand and stepped from the car.

As she extended her foot to the curb, to her horror she saw that she was still wearing one bronze sandal and one blue pump. *Oh, God, what a klutz!* What was she going to do now? Around her cameras flashed and hands reached out from behind police barriers. She was dazzled by the brilliance and the noise, which swelled to a fevered pitch when Patrick emerged from the car.

"Patrick Drake! It's Patrick Drake."

"Paddy, over here."

"Paddy!"

Patrick smiled and waved at the crowd and gently pushed Enid in the direction that Peter was leading, toward the makeshift stage covered with crepe paper and streamers. Enid stumbled on the stairs, her mismatched shoes as obvious to her as club feet.

Fortunately, Patrick seemed oblivious to everything but himself and the impression he was making on his public. He tightened his grip around her waist to help her up, herding her to the microphone where a man was waiting.

"And here is America's favorite funny man, Patrick Drake. Hello, Patrick." Patrick shook hands with Army and slipped off his sunglasses. The crowd roared. "And who is this lovely lady?

Army thrust the microphone into Enid's face, but she was unable to speak, so Patrick leaned across her to say, "This is my dear friend Enid Carrouthers."

"So Patrick, we understand you're going to be doing a movie for Dominion."

"Well then, you know more than I do, Army," Patrick said with a twinkle in his eye, so very glad that he had mentioned to Peter to mention to Army that this was a good topic for him to bring up.

"Last I heard the contracts hadn't been signed. But it is a distinct possibility," Patrick winked.

"Can you give us a hint about the story?" Army probed.

"It's a love story, I can tell you that."

"And is there a part in it for the beautiful Miss Carrouthers?" Army asked, thrusting the microphone into Enid's face again.

"Oh, I'm not an actress," Enid blushed.

"Well then, perhaps you can tell us, is there a love story brewing in real life?"

"We're just friends," said Patrick, pushing Enid from the stage. "Just friends."

Amidst a cacophony of flashbulbs, Enid and Patrick made their way down the stairs to where Peter was waiting, slipping past a short man with a tall blonde woman who were going up to Army Archerd. "And here come Dudley Moore and Daryl Hannah," Army called to the crowd.

Peter led the way up a red carpet to the theater, the phone against his ear. "LeMar's in the lobby with Jeffrey Kesselman and his wife. Her name's Terry, and the charity is Good Vibrations. It's a — "

"School for deaf children."

"Very good, Paddy, you've been doing your homework," said Peter.

Patrick hooked his hand under Enid's elbow and whispered in her ear, "Get ready to run the gauntlet. If we get separated, wait for me just inside the door."

Enid nodded, and they moved forward together past the journalists and photographers lining each side of the carpet and calling out, "Patrick, over here, Patrick," and "Paddy, can we get a picture of the two of you?"

Patrick stopped to talk to someone named Katrina, who had a microphone that had a large "*E.T.*" on it, and Enid walked on, a dazed smile plastered to her face.

"Sweetheart, here, here," someone motioned to her from the side.

"A little old for him, isn't she?" said another.

"Spell your name for us, darling."

Enid started to comply, but Peter took her arm and ushered her forward, saying to the journalist, "I'll get that to you later. They want her inside."

Peter stashed Enid next to the drinking fountain with instructions to stay put until he returned with Patrick, which he did within seconds.

"We've just got time to say hello to the Kesselmans," Peter said to Enid. "He's the head of production for Dominion."

"I know," said Enid, but nobody was paying any attention to her. The next thing she knew Peter was introducing her to Terry Kesselman.

"Enid, I'm so glad you could make it!" Terry effused, her hostessy charm reflecting off of her like the light refracting off of the million sequins on her dress. "Where's Sam?"

"Out of the country on business, unfortunately," said Enid, aware that Patrick and Peter were eyeing her with surprise.

"They always call it business, don't they?" Terry muttered, looking at her husband who was deeply engrossed in the cleavage of a nameless starlet. Patrick stepped forward, into Terry's line of vision. "Good evening, Terry, you're looking lovely as always."

"Paddy!" Terry looked from Patrick to Enid and back again. "Are you two together?" And before either of them could answer, she called a bit too shrilly, "Jeff, darling, look who's here, it's Paddy Drake." She wrenched her husband away from the starlet and fairly dragged him over to Patrick and Enid. "And he's here with Enid Carrouthers," she continued, keeping a grip on his arm.

Kesselman planted a dry kiss on Enid's cheek and shook Paddy's hand. "Great of you to make it tonight, Paddy."

"Wouldn't have missed it for the world, Jeff. Say, I'm . . ."

Kesselman blew his nose so loudly that it silenced Patrick.

"Maybe we can get a chance to chat later," Kesselman said, and turned to Enid, effectively blocking Patrick out.

"Enid, darling! I expect we'll see you and Sam at Leo's surprise party for Lacy Saturday night?" asked Kesselman brightly.

Patrick was stunned. He'd never seen Kesselman act so gracious and respectful. What did it mean?

"I'll be there," Enid said, "and I hope Sam will be back by then."

"Back from where?" Suddenly Kesselman looked worried. He riveted his full attention on Enid.

"Sardinia. He's with Harry Ingersol."

"Why? What are they meeting about?" Kesselman probed.

"I don't know, really," Enid admitted.

"Can you find out?"

"I . . . " Enid stammered, taken aback at Kesselman's intensity.

"Darling, Violet wants us inside," Terry pulled her husband away. "Come on you two, we don't want to miss the opening credits."

Patrick saw that Kesselman was completely undone by his conversation with Enid. What was the mysterious power she wielded over him? Patrick didn't know yet, but he was going to find out. And when he did, he was going to use it to bury Kesselman.

"I didn't know you knew the Kesselmans," said Patrick, nudging Enid in the direction of Peter, who was waving them over from one of the entrances to the auditorium.

"Sam knows Jeff from business. One of his clients owns stock in Dominion."

"Hmmm," Patrick ruminated, wondering who and how much and what it meant, but knowing this was not the time to ask. The lights dimmed as Enid and Patrick stepped over John Travolta and Kelly Preston to find their seats. Patrick leaned across Enid to shake hands with the man on her other side, and whispered, "This is LeMar, my agent, and his wife Betsy. Enid Carrouthers."

The woman gave Enid a warm smile and the man sneered, an expression that looked like it was as close as he got to a smile. Then they all turned their attention to the screen.

☜

A phalanx of security guards formed a human barrier between the celebrities and the fans as the premiere festivities shifted from the theater to the upper level of the parking lot of the Holiday Inn, just a block away.

"How did you like the movie?" Patrick asked Enid, knowing she would say she loved it. Dominion's production team had an uncanny knack for making films that keyed into a certain emotional mainstream, miraculously eliciting a positive audience response to even the most inane dialogue and plotlines. Probably it had something to do with certain images or colors releasing endorphins or some other chemical reaction, because it certainly had nothing to do with good drama.

Patrick didn't mind being manipulated by films, but he wished his films would strike a chord with audiences this way, which was one of the reasons he was so eager to get the contract signed with Dominion.

"Oh, I did," Enid enthused. "Harrison Ford was wonderful. I didn't realize he was such a sensual man. In that scene when the English girl comes to his room at night . . . " And she described what Patrick considered a hackneyed and dull love scene.

Patrick hated to hear women gush over other men. And he knew Harrison well enough to know he was about as sensual as one of the oak planks he used to carve before his career took off, in the days when he supported himself as a furniture maker.

"But of course, Harrison and Michelle are nothing compared to you and Meg in *Wind Jammers*," Enid was saying. "It was so romantic the way you made love to her, even though you knew she had that deadly contagious virus."

Patrick was flooded with a sense of well-being. "You know, you have a very astute sense of cinema," he said, kissing her right ear, neither of them noticing in the confusion of the crowd the flash of light from a distant camera's flashbulb.

But twenty yards away the photographer adjusted his telephoto lens and shot again, then nodded to the reporter standing at his side. "Got 'em, Brad," he said.

Brad King smiled. More fodder for the gristmill that was *People*. Or better yet, *The Inquirer*. He could probably get a grand off a shot like this, if he could find out who the woman was, which, with his considerable talents, should be no problem at all.

Patrick and Enid finally arrived at the top tier of the parking structure, where a typically glamorous post-premiere extravaganza had been staged.

Enid had been to many charity events, but never one that had the full financial backing of a major motion picture studio. The film had been set in Aspen at Christmas, so Dominion had turned the parking lot of the Hollywood Holiday Inn into a gigantic winter wonderland. Fake snowdrifts, literally hundreds of twenty-foot tall Aspen trees, live reindeer, and twinkling lights were only part of the magic that had been assembled.

In the center of the lot, an entire Alpine village had been built. Under a sign that read "Santa's Edible Village," dwarf waiters and waitresses dressed like elves rushed from one structure to another, bringing out platter after platter of food. As Enid and Patrick wove their way through the display, the elves urged them to eat pieces of the structures themselves.

"It's all edible, even the toys," they were told.

And sure enough, other guests were eating the foliage off of the trees and breaking the shingles off of the houses. A conveyor belt producing what looked like toys was really churning out multilayered sandwiches, which the guests were gobbling down as quickly as they were produced.

"A bit overwhelming, isn't it?" Patrick said, reading the expression on Enid's face.

"This must have cost a fortune!" gasped Enid, her mind numbed by the prospect of having to create something equally elaborate for the Westside Women's Shelter premiere of Patrick's movie.

"Sure, but it's not real money."

"What do you mean?"

"Well, it doesn't come out of anybody's pocket. Probably it's part of the studio's overhead or their marketing budget. The only people who actually lose are the people who have a net participation deal on the film."

Just saying the words *net participation* made Patrick hot under the collar.

"I don't understand."

"Well, it works like this." Patrick took two glasses of champagne off a passing tray and handed one to Enid. "A picture costs, say ten million to make. But to market it, the studio spends another twenty million, pulling a couple of thousand prints so they can open it big all over the country. They buy ads on television, put lots of money into events like this, all to entice the press to write about the film, and to publicize the studio itself. So when the movie starts to make money, the first dollars go to pay for this stuff. And if the movie seems to be catching on, they'll spend even more money, to keep the momentum going."

"So a guy who's supposed to get paid his salary out of the profits never sees a penny, because the film never actually makes it to profit, since the studio supposedly has spent all that money publicizing itself."

Speaking of the inanity of net profits, Patrick saw LeMar talking to some nondescript junior executive and steered Enid in that direction. "Would you excuse me for a minute, I've got to have a word with LeMar." He ditched Enid near the reindeer, and approached

LeMar alone.

LeMar was stuffing his face with what looked to be shingles off of the side of a cottage.

"Be careful with that woman," LeMar said with his mouth full, as Patrick pulled off a shingle and examined it. It was a tortilla chip.

"Who, Enid? She's my next-door neighbor, for Chrissakes. You told me to be visible and here I am."

"If you want to screw some guy's wife, it's fine with me, but your fans aren't going to like it if they read in the paper that you were with a married woman."

Patrick sighed. There was no pleasing LeMar, the perpetual worrying machine. "Who's going to know who she is?"

LeMar gave him a sarcastic look. "In the first place, her husband Sam Carrouthers is not exactly the invisible man. Don't you ever read the business section?"

"You know I hate getting newspaper ink all over my hands," said Patrick.

LeMar shook his head. "He is a powerful person in this town. It would not be smart to get on his bad side."

"The guy's in Italy." Patrick insisted. "How's he going to find out?"

"Do I have to tell you that this place is crawling with reporters? And we know of at least one who seems to have a personal vendetta against you, don't we?"

How could he have forgotten about that asshole from *People*, Brad King? Patrick paled at the thought and looked furtively for his nemesis.

"LeMar, I think it's time Enid and I excused ourselves."

"Good. I'll talk to you tomorrow," said LeMar. "Lunch at Le Dome," he called as Patrick hurried off. "Be there!"

Clearly, Enid had had too much champagne. Patrick watched her list to the right with the movement of the car as it rounded the curve onto the freeway, and he considered his next line of action.

Contrary to what LeMar had said, he thought he could derive a great deal from consummating his relationship with Mrs. Sam Carrouthers, especially now that he knew her husband did business with Jeffrey Kesselman. Surely if they become bosom buddies he could convince her to put in a good word for him with her husband, who would then use his influence on Kesselman. Then, at the right moment, he could admit to Kesselman just what kind of "good friend" Enid Carrouthers was, knowing Kesselman would appreciate the gambit, being a player himself.

The movement of the car caused Enid's body to shift so she was leaning against him. He adjusted his right arm and put it around her shoulders. She was so delicate. He could probably crush her with one well-directed squeeze, so different from Sara, who, thanks to daily Pilates sessions with a private trainer, was stronger than he was.

He rested his chin on the top of Enid's head, allowing the scent of her perfume to envelope him, and he felt the first pang of anticipatory arousal. But it wasn't sexual. The idea that he would have Jeffrey Kesselman eating out of his hand filled him with a kind of excitement that transcended sexuality. Maybe he would bump his fee up to $3 million. If Stallone could get $9 million and Tom Cruise $10 million, then surely Dominion could afford $3 or $4 million for Patrick Drake. The key was clearly to get Enid on his side. And he knew of only one way to do that.

Fortunately, making women fall in love with him was one of his strongest suits. It was like asking Van Cliburn to play Bach, or Joe Montana to throw a pass. It was just a matter of doing what he did best.

His body was so stirred by this thought that he was inspired to try a little subliminal conditioning on Enid. If he could start the process now, while she was asleep, perhaps the follow-through would seem more natural to her when they got home, in about ten minutes.

Carefully, Patrick began "the stroke" on Enid's arm, and she responded by snuggling closer. With the deftness of experience, he gently picked up her hand and placed it on his crotch. At first she didn't respond. Her fingers just lay there, limply ignorant of the excitement they was generating in his body.

Although Patrick was intent on the hand, willing it to move, even encouraging it a bit by shifting his weight, out of the corner of his eye he noticed the driver was watching in the rearview mirror, even going so far as to adjust it so he could get a better view. Rather than deter Patrick, this aroused him even more, and he put his own hand on Enid's, guiding it to move in a stroking motion.

Apparently the telepathy of his body to her hand worked, because she picked up the rhythm and started to flex her fingers, closing them around the growing bulge.

So intent was the driver on the scene in the rearview mirror that he almost mowed down a pedestrian who had stepped out of the darkness into the crosswalk. When the car swerved to the right to avoid impact, the motion jarred Enid awake.

If she was shocked to find her hand nesting in Patrick's lap, she said nothing to betray her feelings. Rather, in a natural motion, she merely shifted her arm so it closed around Patrick's waist and snuggled into his chest.

"Are we home?" she asked in a sleepy voice.

"Almost," said Patrick. Gently, he lifted her chin, pressing his lips to hers with a tender promise of things to come.

20

Sam

Sam watched in astonishment that bordered on anger as Carmen flirted with Harry. He was shocked at her, jealous of Harry, and furious with himself all at the same time. How dare she stroke Harry's arm in that familiar way in front of this group of people who were well aware that he was a very married man? How could she make this play for him, when just hours before she had seemed fixated on Sam?

But most important, why did he care so much what she did?

Sam was in a fog of fatigue and jet-lagged confusion. He shook his head to clear it, then excused himself from the table and walked to the bow of the ship to get some air. Somewhere along the line, he had lost control of this trip, and he had no idea how to get it back.

Instead of having a one-on-one meeting with Harry, he found himself a guest at a dinner party for eight, five of whom were strangers he hoped never to see again. There had been no chance for a business discussion, only Harry's promise that he would make some time for Sam the following day. Sam heard Carmen's laughter in the background and felt like the joke was on him.

The night was clear and surprisingly cool. In the distance, the lights of Porto Cervo flickered, a reminder that they were not all that far from civilization. And yet Sam felt as though he were in another world, one in which the rules were different, and no one had told him what they were.

He realized he was out of his emotional league with Carmen Leventhal. As clever and perceptive as he was in his business dealings, he had never been very sophisticated in matters of the heart. So characteristically, he had always played to his strength, burying this emotional vulnerability in the solid, faithful relationship he had with Enid, who loved him enough not to manipulate him.

True, there had been times when he had been attracted to other women. But they were never real women like Carmen, or real attractions, for that matter. For the most part, they were flights of fancy with young women who reminded him of the unattainable dream girls of his youth.

He remembered the day last spring when he'd seen a girl hitchhiking on Sunset. He'd been on his way to work after tennis, invigorated by the exercise and especially virile because he had beaten Blair a rare three sets to zero. Normally, he did not pick up hitchers, feeling it was dangerous to encourage them. But this girl had been wearing a UCLA cheerleading sweater and a very short skirt. In a flash he was an undergraduate again, at a point in his life when a desirable girl like this had been out of reach.

But driving his $80,000 Porsche, his hand-tailored suit enhancing his physique, which was more muscular than when he had been in school, on his way to negotiate a multimillion dollar deal, he had felt the kind of confidence and power he had only dreamed of as a kid, the kind necessary to win a girl like this. He had pulled to the side of the road.

Christi was her name. She was not so much beautiful as she was bursting with freshness and vigor. Her hair was long and blonde; unruly waves of it massed about her shoulders and blew in the morning breeze. She wore a little too much makeup, but even that could not diminish the potency of youth, which oozed out of every pore. Sam felt that if he touched her, ten years would drop away. But he dared not, for fear she would evaporate, a figment of his imagination.

Her car had broken down, Christi explained, and she had to get to campus for a pep rally. Sam was more than happy to drive her there; at this point he would have driven her all the way to the University of Timbuctu. As he drove, he asked her the usual questions — where was she from (Portland), what was her major (theater arts), what kind of a career did she want to pursue (acting, of course)? But before he knew it, she was questioning him. Where did he work, where did he live, what restaurants did he like, had he ever had lunch at the Polo Lounge?

Pretty soon, Sam began to get the drift. As innocent as Christi seemed to be, it was all a routine. She was trying to entice him into a tryst, and clearly, money would be involved.

As her hand found its way to his thigh, her conversation became a monologue on how expensive it was to be a student and how difficult it was for her parents to pay for her education. Plus, she had added, moving her hand up his leg, just a bit closer to his wallet, she had recently broken up with her boyfriend, and had to find a new apartment.

By the time they had arrived at campus Sam was so depressed he couldn't have reacted if Christi had ripped off her clothes right there in the car. She had written her name and phone number on a piece of notebook paper and handed it to Sam, saying she would love to see him some time. With sadness, he had taken a hundred dollar bill from his wallet and pressed it into her hand, saying he didn't think so, but he hoped the money would help her get by.

As he had driven away, he had realized the hundred was all she had really been after, and sucker that he was, he had paid up without even asking for the goods he had bought. How did an eighteen-year-old become so calculating, he had wondered. A hundred bucks for a ten-minute ride, and he hadn't even laid a finger on her. It's just as well, he thought. If he'd touched her, he probably would have given her a guilty thousand.

A pair of arms encircled Sam's waist from behind, and a warm, shapely body snuggled against his back. "What are you doing out here all by yourself?" whispered Carmen. She was tall enough so that her lips were right next to his ear, and he could feel her hot breath flirting with the tiny hairs on his earlobe.

"Thinking," he said, trying not to respond to her touch.

"Wouldn't you rather feel instead of think?" she asked, moving around so that she was facing him, leaning against the rail. The breeze whipped her hair across both of their faces like punishment, and he raised his hand to smooth it back.

"What is it you want me to feel?" he asked, trying to be bold but sounding weak, he knew.

"Me." Carmen took his free hand and put it around her waist.

"Where's Harry?" Sam spit out sourly.

"He went to bed."

"I'm surprised you didn't go with him," Sam accused, instantly sorry to have given himself away.

Carmen smiled innocently. "Sam, you're not jealous, are you?"

"Should I be?"

"Only if it turns you on," said Carmen, putting her arms low around his waist. His buttocks tightened automatically as her fingers gripped them. "Because that is the point of all this."

"All what?"

"A romantic night on a beautiful yacht off the coast of Sardinia. Dinner with wine and cognac and the gentle rocking of the sea. A beautiful woman trying to get you into bed. Hey, if that doesn't turn you on, I don't know what will. But I'll try most anything," she added.

Suddenly, something inside of Sam erupted. It felt like anger, but it expressed itself as lust. He pinned Carmen to the rail and like a savage, gripped a handful of her hair, pulling backward so that the top of her head was bent to the sea.

"Sam —" she tried to speak, but he covered her mouth with his own and thrust his tongue so far down her throat that she almost gagged. But she didn't pull away. Instead, her body became limp and pliable, totally acquiescent.

Sam felt his physical dominance. She may have maneuvered him into this position, but from this moment on he was taking control. "I am going to make you scream for mercy," he said, shocked to hear himself talking like an X-rated video.

"I can't wait," Carmen whispered, and allowed Sam to pull her toward the stateroom, which Harry had indicated earlier would be Sam's should they decide not to go back to the hotel that night.

Enid

The engine of the Lionel train chugged into sight around the foot of the bed, pulling a dozen brightly colored cars behind it. Enid was amazed and delighted. Patrick's bedroom was exactly the way *Life* magazine had described it, an environment designed to appear child-like on the surface, but devoted to more adult tastes, if one looked closer.

Take the train, for example. At the outset, Enid had thought it was just your standard issue little boy's toy. But as it circled to her side of the bed, she realized that the bright plastic shapes loaded in each car were X-rated toys — dildos, ticklers, condoms, things she'd not even imagined, let alone seen. In one of the rear cars, there was a stash of pills, capsules, and condoms. She didn't know whether to be shocked or delighted.

But then what could be more shocking — or more delightful — than the fact that she was lying on Patrick Drake's bed in a silk robe, sipping champagne straight from the bottle?

Enid couldn't remember exactly how she had gotten there, although she would wrack her brain later to dredge up every detail of this night. But there she was, feeling only remotely ill at ease, similar to the way she felt when she knowingly parked her car in the red or made an illegal U-turn.

She didn't feel like she was committing a deadly sin, or doing anything so terribly out of the ordinary. In fact, her greatest worry at the moment was that she not say or do anything to look foolish.

She had surprised herself by having no trouble following Patrick into his house and up the stairs to his bedroom. Of course, he had been very encouraging, his firm but gentle hand on the small of her back, urging her onward, the straightforward way he had shown her the bathroom and a silk robe that he said she could put on, so as not to muss her dress.

Left alone in his bathroom, Enid had stifled the desire to look in the medicine cabinet and drawers. No, she had embarrassed herself before by peeking into Patrick's private space. Now that he had invited her into his life, she would not ruin it by being nosy. When she had drummed up the courage to come out of the bathroom, she had seen that he had modestly slipped into a robe as well. Endearingly, it was the ragged blue terry cloth relic he had worn when he had first kissed her. Had it been only a week ago? It seemed like an eternity.

Patrick had lowered the lights and put on some music while she had made herself comfortable on the bed. Then he had flipped on the switch activating the train.

"See anything that strikes your fancy?" Patrick asked, as the engine pulled up alongside the bed.

"I don't know, it's not as though, usually we . . . " Enid couldn't seem to make her mouth form a sentence. Was she drunk from the champagne or from the heady sensation of being alone with Patrick Drake in his famous bedroom? The problem was, who in the world could she tell that she'd been there? It somehow diminished the experience to realize that she would never be able to mention it to anyone.

"Usually? I hope this isn't 'the usual' to you," Patrick teased.

"Hardly," she replied. "The truth is, I don't even know what some of those things are."

"You never use any toys?" Patrick said. He was stretched out on the bed, his head propped up on his hand.

"No," she admitted. How annoying to be thirty-six years old and still feel like a virgin.

"Never?"

"Never. Well . . ." Enid took a sip of her champagne, "no, you wouldn't count that."

"Aha, there was a time then?"

"Yes, but it was so long ago." She smiled, then started to giggle.

"C'mon, tell me."

"Oh, I couldn't."

"Why not?"

"Because it's embarrassing."

Patrick turned onto his side to face her. "Here we are, two grown people, lying almost naked in front of each other for the first time. What could be more embarrassing than that?"

She smiled and ducked her head. He reached out and turned her face toward his. "You've got to tell me now. I'm dying of curiosity."

"I've never told this to another living soul. Not even Sam."

"Good," he smiled. "I think there should be something between us that doesn't include Sam." He took her hand and turned it over, gently kissing her palm. "Please?"

Her heart melted. So much tenderness. Who would have expected it?

"When I was about eleven or twelve my Girl Scout troop went on a camp out."

"You were a Girl Scout?" She nodded. "God, I love thinking about you in one of those little green outfits. Do you still have it?"

"Come on, do you want me to tell you this or not?"

"By all means."

"Anyway, they had us three to a tent and I ended up with two of the senior scouts. They must have been about sixteen, but they seemed so much older, so world-wise."

"Three Girl Scouts in a tent. This is getting good."

"So we had a cookout — hot dogs, beans, roasted marshmallows, the usual. And then we all went to our tents. Of course, nobody slept at those things, it was all whispers and stories about boys and who's done what and who's seen what. So these two older girls start talking about boys' things, you know."

Patrick knew. His own was getting hard at the thought. "What exactly?" Patrick asked, wondering if he would be able to hold out until the end of the story.

"Oh, sizes, shapes, stuff like that. Of course I'd never seen one, so it was all news to me. And then they started talking about this really popular guy in school, a football player named Jack Hunt who was kind of the local stud. I mean, they were getting very specific, arguing about the length and color and all of that, until one of them, Alice Sartoyan, I think it was, said she could show us exactly how big Jack's thing was. She crawled out of the tent and came back with a brown bag. What do you think was in it?"

"Jack's thing?"

"No! The leftover weenies from the cookout."

"Poor Jack. I hope they were bratwurst."

"Anyway, they started fooling around with the weenies, teasing each other and poking at me and pretty soon the conversation switched to masturbation. And the next think I knew the girls were, you know, pretending to use the hot dogs like they were . . . you know."

"You mean you sat there and watched them?"

"Of course not. I pretended I was asleep. Only I couldn't sleep. So when they finally conked out and I was just lying there awake, thinking about Jack Hunt and his you-know-what, I took one of the hot dogs and I . . ." Enid covered her face with her hands. "I can't believe I'm telling you this."

"So, how did it feel?"

"I don't know. Interesting. Sexy. Sad."

"Why sad?"

"Well, to this day I can't look a hot dog in the eye, let alone eat one, which, I suppose, isn't such a bad thing."

"I can give you something a lot better than Oscar Mayer if you promise not to take a bite out of it." He reached over and pulled on the sash of her robe. The smooth silk slid away from her body as though at his command. Now it was Patrick's turn to be the storyteller.

21

Sam and Carmen

The instant he closed the door behind them, Sam locked Carmen in an embrace. For the first time, the passion was unrestrained. And the sensation was dizzying to both of them. Like an Olympic athlete who had spent her life training for an event, Carmen was ready to surrender herself to this moment. For once she did not let her mind calculate and dictate her actions. She allowed her body to respond instinctively, trusting Sam's lead. And as before, he surprised her.

Usually Carmen found that a man's need to consume and consummate was far greater than his desire to savor. But Sam was not like most men. Instead of throwing her on the bed and ravaging her, he led her to a chair with a gentle hand and bade her to sit while he dimmed the lights to just the right intensity, opened the porthole cover to allow the moonlight to pour onto the bed, and carefully turned down the midnight blue coverlet.

Only then did he turn to face her. He pulled her up out of the chair and they swayed together, trancelike, to the gentle rocking motion of the ship. When Sam's fingers reached out to touch her, Carmen closed her eyes. Enough time later to revel in his body. For now, she allowed herself to be a tool of his imagination.

She felt his fingers unbutton her blouse with the excruciating care they would have used to dismantle a time bomb. If she turned her body just so, his fingers would brush against her breast. But she stood as still as she could and savored the light rush of air she felt against her belly as Sam slid the unbuttoned blouse off of her shoulders.

Then for a moment she felt nothing. She opened her eyes and saw that Sam was staring with rapt attention at her breasts, which were still harnessed in her brassiere, sheer, silken, expensive gauze that it was. She moved to unhook it, but Sam's hand caught hers, and she retreated.

At first it seemed that he only wanted to look, and she was afraid she was losing him. But she waited, allowing that Sam knew his own needs better than she did, and she wanted to let him fulfill his fantasies of her.

Finally, he raised his hands to her breasts, cupping them so gently that she felt only the silken lingerie against her skin and not the pressure of his fingers. She reached out to touch him, but he wouldn't allow it. And when she again acquiesced to his unspoken wishes, he rewarded her by lowering his hands to her waist and undoing her trousers. They dropped to the floor.

Then Sam knelt in front of her, and she could feel his hot breath through her delicate panties. She rolled her hips toward him, tucking her buttocks under so his tongue could find her center. But no, he did not kiss her there. Instead, he stood and stepped back until he was so far away from her she could hardly see him in the semidarkness. Ghostlike, his body lowered itself into the chair.

"What?" She was beginning to feel slightly queasy from the movement of the ship and the anxiety of relinquishing the control of this situation to Sam.

"I just want to enjoy this moment. I've thought about it so damn much, I don't want to waste it."

Good, thought Carmen, *neither do I.* She stood before him for a moment longer, then said, "I want to take these off now."

When Sam didn't reply, she unhooked her bra and let her breasts relax against her rib cage. Then she stooped to step out of her panties. They were already moist with anticipation.

Slowly Carmen walked across the room to where Sam was sitting and allowed him to stare at her body. "Do you want me?" she asked, surprised at the tremolo in her voice.

"Yes," Sam's response was immediate and definite. He stood, and in a few swift motions, disposed of his clothes. Carmen felt almost giddy with pleasure. Sam was more beautiful than she had imagined, and a little shy. He held himself proudly erect, taut as a bodybuilder striking a pose.

"May I touch you?"

She didn't know why she felt she must ask for permission, but apparently it was the right thing to do, for he answered simply, "Yes."

She dropped to the floor and let her hands play over his ankles and calves. They were bristled with hair and surprisingly delicate for a man as muscular as Sam. She ran her hands slowly upward, over his strong thighs to his firm buttocks. She dug her fingers in, letting her nails score the flesh. He responded by tensing his muscles, bracing himself so she could feel the power beneath the rounded surface.

Rock hard, his penis pressed toward her mouth, but she knew it was too soon. So she got to her feet, letting her breasts graze the delicate head in passing. And when she was standing, she pressed her whole body against his.

At last he wrapped his arms around her, and their bodies tasted the sweetness of skin against skin. The hairs on Sam's chest issued an electrical charge, causing her breasts to swell in response. Finally, body to body, mouth to mouth, they moved to the bed and Sam gently laid her against the cool Porthault sheets. Instinctively, his hands found her core, and she felt the pressure building. Then she was out of control. And before she could stop, her body reverberated with concentric waves of orgasm.

Although she squeezed her legs together to hide this embarrassing slip, he immediately pulled back to look into her eyes, clearly aware of what had happened.

"Don't worry. I'm just warming up," she assured him, and rolled over on top of him to prove she was nowhere near played out. "There's plenty more where that came from.

∾∾

Sam was no prude, and certainly he had had his share of lovers. But Carmen's facile response came as a surprise to him. Despite what he had read in books and heard other men brag about, he had been reluctant to believe in the myth of multiple orgasm, thinking it the product of men's egos and women's wishful thinking.

But when he finally entered Carmen some minutes later, he had already registered four separate tremors rippling through her body. And yet, she responded to his thrusts in an almost virginal way, moaning with enthusiasm and clutching his hair in her hands as though she would tear it out by the roots if he were not careful.

He was definitely gratified and aroused by Carmen's intense reaction, but also disappointed. There seemed to be little challenge to a woman who responded so easily. And so little satisfaction.

Sam moved his hand under the small of Carmen's back and pressed upward, locking her pelvis into his own. There was a rightness to their bodies together, his muscle mass against her soft curves, her ivory skin against his tanned and hairy hide, the unspoken certainty between them that there was nothing either one could desire that the other would not try to fulfill.

The rocking of the boat was a metronome to their passion, creating a rhythm that was at once monotonous and mesmerizing. Sam timed his thrusts, playing against the motion so that as the ship fell he withdrew, and when it rose he plunged deeper. The last time he'd felt this much erotic control was when he and his college sweetheart Patsy had visited her brother in Soho and slept on a waterbed. They had really made whitecaps that night, he remembered, and only the realization that her brother and his wife were in the next room had curbed their passion.

But tonight there was no brother-in-law to be concerned about, no one to stop them from exploring the depths of their arousal. Sam was getting close to his own climax now. He reveled in the knowledge that it was coming, yet strived to keep it in check for a few minutes longer, the pressure building, building. . . .

Carmen felt as though her body had become part of Sam's, a throbbing, clutching organ wrapped around his penis, at the mercy of his sexuality. But still, there was a disquieting sense of unease residing in the hollow of her stomach. Could it be he was thrusting so deeply that his tip was prodding at the lining of her stomach? She wasn't a whiz at anatomy, but she was almost certain this was impossible.

Why then was she feeling a wave of nausea beginning to tickle the base of her throat? The sensation was so disturbing that she tried to pull away from Sam. But he was caught in the throes of passion, too absorbed in his own body's machinations to understand. The more she struggled, the harder he held her to him. She tried to cry out, but opening her mouth only caused her gorge to rise. And, as Sam at last let go, shooting his passion into her, his final thrust pushed her over the edge too.

She vomited, spewing half-digested bits of grilled branzino and boiled potatoes all over Sam, the bed, and herself.

At first they just lay in the mess. Sam was so surprised and spent that he could not compute what had happened. Trapped under him, Carmen was so appalled by her body's traitorous reaction that for once in her life she had no idea what to do. Then she felt her gut begin to heave again.

Apparently Sam felt it too. Wordlessly, he rose and pulled Carmen up. She ran into the head, and this time reached the toilet before another wave of vomit erupted from her body.

❦

It was not until they were both showered and dressed, the soiled sheets stripped from the bed and balled into a corner, that Carmen dared to speak. "I'm so sorry. I can't believe I did that. I've never been seasick before." And then, to her horror, she started to cry.

Sam gave her a winning smile and put his arms around her, letting her bury her head in his shoulder. His arms wrapped around her gave her a sense of comfort that she had never felt before. Unconditional, not judgmental or angry, expectant or resentful. Just full of simple warmth and caring.

"Think of it this way," he said. "It's an experience neither one of us will ever forget."

Enid and Patrick

Now that they were finally naked, they stopped kissing and lay still for a moment. Enid wondered, *should I touch him, or should I let him take the initiative?* Waiting was agony, but making the wrong move at this sensitive moment could ruin the whole experience. She could almost hear the blood throbbing in her veins; so swift was its rush, everything else seemed to be happening in slow motion.

She tried to put thoughts about her own body out of her mind, but it was impossible. What did he think of her? Was he disappointed by her small breasts? Did he notice the slight protrusion of her belly, the one area of her body she could never seem to tone to her satisfaction? Maybe now that he'd seen her, he would no longer be interested in making love to her. Perhaps she should relieve the suspense by slipping back into her clothes and beating a hasty retreat, telling him this whole episode had been a mistake, a silly, drunken mistake. But was that really what she wanted?

Finally Patrick raised his hand and carefully lowered it to her breast. A low moan slipped from Enid's lips as his fingers deliberately traced the outline of her aureole with the tip of his fingernail. The sensation would not have been any more intense to her if he had been using a razor blade.

Then, with a suddenness that was almost cruel, he withdrew his finger and pressed it to her lips. As she kissed the tip, he parted her lips and thrust his finger deep into her mouth, running it over her tongue and teeth.

Enid's body seemed detached from her brain. She and Patrick both watched as he pulled his finger from her mouth and ran it in circles around her plastic-soft nipple, hardening it into a taut erection. Patrick squeezed it between his thumb and forefinger until Enid's whole body began to pulse with the pressure.

He lowered his lips to hers, then slid them down her neck to take the nipple between his teeth. His hand found her other breast, which seemed to force itself into his palm, and the game began again. But this time, instead of letting her kiss the wetness onto his finger, he thrust it between her legs and rubbed that warmth onto her breast. Enid looked at Patrick's face, amazed to see it so near. His eyes were closed, and beads of perspiration had formed at his hairline. She pressed her cheek to his head to wipe them away, feeling aroused but detached. How many times must he have enacted this scene to have refined his technique to such perfection?

Stop thinking, Enid, just go with it.

Easier said than done.

Patrick was on automatic pilot. If he was comfortable and confident in front of a camera, he was even more at ease in bed. He didn't have to think, he merely let his body follow the clues his partner's body projected. And while every woman responded to different stimuli, what they all seemed to love was slow, deliberate arousal, appreciation and adoration of their bodies, a resolute but respectful probing of their most secret places.

Patrick opened his eyes. Enid's breasts bobbed above his face, the nipples grazing his nose as she gently swayed, her own eyes clamped shut. They weren't particularly beautiful, as breasts went, and certainly nowhere near as ample as he liked. But at least there were no alarming pimples or wild hairs to contend with. He'd put up with worse for the sake of an easy conquest. He could handle this.

He dared a peek at the clock. It was 2:30. He'd better get a move on if he wanted to get any sleep tonight.

Oops. She'd seen him look at the clock.

He felt her body withdraw even before he turned to face her. Damn, he hoped she wasn't one of the sensitive ones who needed to have the whole event orchestrated like a Ken Russell movie, and pouted if one scene were played wrong.

She rolled off of him and lay on her side, running her hand up and down his belly. *This is good,* he thought. If she were mad, she wouldn't be stroking me. He grimaced inwardly as he felt her hand discover the bulges at his waist and the odd scar tissue on his rib cage where he'd had the birthmark removed. He chanced a look at her. She was smiling, almost laughing. Not at his body, he prayed.

"C'mon, it's not that bad, is it?"

"What?"

"My body."

"I'm not laughing at your body," she said to his relief. "It's a beautiful body. A real body. Not a suit of plastic armor like some men's."

"Then what's so funny?"

"Just being here. I thought I'd imagined it in every possible way, shape, and form. But this is nothing like I thought it would be."

"Do me a favor."

"What?"

"Stop thinking."

Enid smiled. "I'll try."

"Good. Now do me another favor . . ."

It wasn't until long after they had finished, after Enid had gone to the bathroom to sponge herself clean and come back to find Patrick slipping into his pants, that she realized what she had done. She had committed Adultery. God, what an awful word.

But the funny part was, it didn't feel awful. She didn't feel much of anything. In her fantasies, she had always wondered what it would be like to cross that line, to be Alice, falling into the rabbit hole. She had imagined it as a door to be stepped through, a one-way passage into a darker, guilty world where she would be forever marked with the knowledge of what she had done.

But there she was, calmly slipping on her coat, musing over whether she would take a shower when she got home, or if she would let the experience linger on her body. No feelings of remorse, none of the expected guilt. Only a quiet, spreading warmth, like the liquid love still sticky on her inner thighs. She supposed the remorse and guilt would come later.

It was as though Patrick had read her mind.

"Enid." He took both of her hands in his. "I had a wonderful time tonight. And I hope you did too." She nodded, grateful for the intimacy they had achieved without speaking. He knew how she felt, and he felt it too. It was enough.

"But I hope you won't be compelled to talk to anyone about this." Enid snapped back to reality, the mood broken. "Who would I talk to about it?" she asked.

"You know, girlfriends, your mother, your houseman, a slip of the tongue to Sam."

"Patrick, you can't think I would ever, ever tell Sam!"

"In a moment of anger maybe, you know, to hurt him or punish him. All I'm saying is it would be the worst thing that could happen. I mean, whatever else we are, we're neighbors. And I doubt it would be too terribly pleasant for any of us living this close together if Sam found out."

"I can't say it would thrill me if Sara found out either."

"I'm certainly not going to tell Sara, not because I'm afraid of her knowing, but because I don't want to hurt her needlessly. Sara's kind of fragile, believe it or not."

And I'm not? Enid thought, getting up to leave. Apparently the act of love had made them not lovers but coconspirators, who would now have to lie and pretend and conceal this act from the people they loved most. Was it worth it? Enid wasn't sure, and she was too tired, and now too annoyed, to think about it.

"You don't have to worry about me. I can keep my mouth shut. And I hope you can too." She kissed him lightly on the top of his head. "Now it's late, and I want to get home before the joggers start. Okay?

"Okay," Patrick answered.

He walked outside with her, checking in both directions to make sure the coast was clear.

"Looks good," he said, and stepped aside to let her pass through the gate.

Enid hurried to her own gate, so exhausted she barely remembered to be relieved when she was inside, the door locked behind her.

Unfortunately for Enid, the neighborhood was not as quiet as it should have been at that early hour. Across the street and down two doors, Suzanne's twins had had a bad night. So Suzanne was awake, alternately mothering her babies and drowning her annoyance in a bottle of Stoli.

She happened to be staring out of the window in a stupor when she saw Patrick's gate open and Enid come through it. The shock and delicious surprise of witnessing this clandestine rendezvous sobered her instantly. As she watched Enid scurry into her own house like a frightened mouse, the wheels in Suzanne's mind started to turn. She could hardly wait until morning.

*O*nce Enid was in her own bed, sleep did not come. Her mind raced with images of the past few hours, a montage of impressions and sensations, making her as dizzy as a drunk. Her mouth was dry, and her breath fetid. She needed a glass of water.

While she drank it, standing in the dark of the bathroom, she looked over to Sam's sink. His hairbrush and Waterpik sat on the counter as usual, next to the picture taken of them when they had visited Prague. She had always treasured this picture, because Sam had proposed to her on that trip. And although they didn't get married until the following summer, she had always associated this photo with the exact moment of their commitment to be man and wife.

Enid stared at the picture, trying hard to remember the girl she had been then. She remembered feeling exhausted and somewhat queasy, excited and afraid, completely full of emotion, and yet empty, as though she were just at the beginning of something.

How odd, she thought, *that is exactly how I feel now.*

4

22

Carmen

It was odd, but as Carmen felt her control over Sam dissipating, his power over her seemed to be growing. She looked at him across the deck, pulling on the scuba gear Harry had loaned him, his body backlit by the sun shimmering off of the green water. He was so sure of himself, so capable of anything on this dazzling morning.

And she felt sicker than a dog.

Harry muttered something to Sam that Carmen couldn't hear. But in Sam's responding laughter, she guessed that the two men were discussing her. Would Sam actually tell Harry about last night's fiasco? Her stomach flip-flopped with humiliation at the thought.

She watched them clamber over the side of the yacht in their wet suits and down the rope ladder to the water. They waved to her as they splashed backward into the limpid sea, bobbing like two black grapes in a bowl of green jello. At least they couldn't talk about her under water — or with Harry's state-of-the-art equipment maybe they could. Well, she wouldn't be able to hear them, and that was something.

She decided not to waste her energy thinking about it, but to use what little strength she had to get another cup of tea and prepare mentally for the meeting, scheduled to take place as soon as the men returned from their dive.

But the sun made her drowsy, its tranquilizing warmth finally deadening her mind to the thoughts that had been torturing her for the past eight hours, the first inkling of doubt about her future with Sam and her ability to make it happen.

She had never before felt betrayed by her body, but last night's mutiny was clearly an indication that something was amiss at the most basic level. Should she advance or retreat? Her mind was too muddled to function clearly. Maybe a little nap would help, even though she had just gotten up an hour earlier.

She found her way to a lounge chair and collapsed into it. As was her habit, she fit earplugs into her ears to block the ambient noise and put on her sunglasses, then she let the rocking of the boat lull her to sleep. Just before she drifted off, it occurred to her that she had forgotten to take out her diaphragm. *Later*, she thought, *I'll just have to remember to take it out when I wake up*.

Normally Carmen did not dream. She considered dreams figments of weak imaginations, fodder for dull minds. And because she felt that way, she rarely experienced one. But lack of sleep, stress, and the rocking of the boat conspired to change that.

In her dream, she was dozing in a lounge chair on Harry's boat, just as she was in real life, only in the dream she was awakened by the realization that she could hear the men talking underwater. Through their wet laughter, they seemed to be sharing some nasty private joke.

Without questioning why she could suddenly hear a discussion taking place between two men in separate scuba gear sixty feet below the surface of the ocean, Carmen listened to their conversation.

"But somebody will come looking," said Sam. His voice was worried.

"They'll never find the body," Harry chortled. "Not out here. Anyway, it won't last more than an hour. Sharks."

Carmen tried to figure out whose body they were talking about. Leo's perhaps, or, God forbid, Harry's wife Louise?

"What about the hotel? They saw me check in with her."

"Don't worry about it. We just have to get our stories straight — we were all out here together, and she decided to go home, so we took her to the airport and left her to wait for her plane."

Carmen shivered in her sleep, realizing that they were talking about her, about killing her! But why? What had she done to them?

Plenty.

She couldn't bear to continue listening, but she was unable to stop the conversation from echoing in her ears.

"How are we going to knock her out?"

"I've got some powder to sprinkle on her food. Arsenic. She'll never know, she'll just go to sleep. And then we toss her overboard. Fish food." This was Harry talking.

"It seems so underhanded," Sam said, sounding worried.

At least one of them had some compassion, thought Carmen.

"After what she's done to us? Come on, Sam, you're letting the broad buffalo you. Don't you think she'd do it to you?"

Carmen saw the men emerge from the water, returning from their dive. She was shocked to also see her body, still prone on the deck chair asleep, unaware of their return. Somehow her spirit and her body had become separated!

When the men went below to shower, her spirit self tried to awaken her body, to warn it of the danger. But the body was inert, unresponsive. In desperation, the spirit looked for a way to reenter the body.

The body's mouth was closed, and the ears were plugged. That left the nose, so the spirit willed itself to enter this aperture. It was a tight fit, but the need was so strong that the spirit forced its way in, blocking the air passage. The body began to fight back, unable to breathe. The spirit was shaken loose once, but again dove into the nostril pushing deeper, deeper, deeper.

➷

Carmen jerked awake, gasping for air. She couldn't see or hear or breathe. Flailing her arms wildly around her head, she managed at last to free herself from the beach towel, which the wind had blown across her face and into her mouth.

Finally she caught her breath, but her heart still raced. Never before had she stopped to consider how others must perceive her actions. "Don't you think she'd do it to you if she were in your shoes?" Harry's words echoed in her head.

It's true, I would do whatever it takes to get what I want, she admitted to herself. *But is that so wrong?*

What if it means hurting someone else? her newly chastened alter ego challenged.

Someone is always going to get hurt, Carmen decided. *I just want to make sure it isn't me.*

Sam

Foreign as scuba diving was to Sam, he had no problem keeping up with Harry under the water, but he maintained enough distance between them to allow Harry the sensation of leading, knowing how important it was to Harry to always be the boss. The last time they'd gone diving together, also off of Harry's yacht, had been in the Caribbean, two years ago. Leo and Lacy had been with them then, and naturally Lacy had insisted on joining the men on the dive. This meant another wet suit and tank had to be borrowed from a neighboring yacht, and one of the men had had to stay in the more shallow waters with her, because she was afraid to go too deep.

Not surprisingly, Sam had ended up as Lacy's partner, for there was no way Leo would let Harry dive one foot deeper than he did, or see one more tropical fish. The competitiveness between the two men was so intense that it was exhausting to be around. Later on deck, they'd hassled over a game of cards and fought over whose turn it was to reel in the fishing line when it suddenly pulled taut with the heft of a very large fish.

Harry had won out — it was, after all, his boat — but the fish had gotten away. Nobody had ever accused Harry of having the patience it took to be a great fisherman. His talents lay elsewhere.

As he paddled behind Harry now, Sam wondered why he felt so good. He hated to think it had anything to do with last night's episode with Carmen. Was he still so primal that sexual satisfaction was the key to his mental well-being? Whatever, he couldn't deny that he was filled with a sense of exuberance, a feeling that had eluded him for months. He was even looking forward to his confrontation with Harry later, and the thought surprised him.

Harry motioned to Sam to swim closer, and Sam did, not seeing five feet ahead the rotting carcass of a hammerhead shark. Even though the body was half eaten away, Sam recoiled reflexively in fear and disgust. But Harry grabbed his arm to reassure him, and together they watched as a school of smaller fish darted in and out of the shredded folds of flesh, ripping off mouthfuls in greedy glee, devouring the huge, soggy body as Sam and Harry watched. Harry mouthed some words, and even through the distorting glass of his mask, Sam got the message: Revenge is sweet.

The chef had offered to grill some freshly caught dorade for Sam and Carmen, but both demurred, albeit for different reasons. Carmen's dream was still too real in her mind; she wasn't going to eat anything that hadn't come out of a package. Sam couldn't get the picture of the rotted shark out of his head and doubted that he would be able to eat the flesh of any living creature for some time. He opted to join Harry in a peanut butter and jelly sandwich. Carmen had tea.

The three talked of trivia while they ate, prolonging the inevitable moment when the topic of business would be broached, each aware that the confrontation would have a profound impact on the rest of their lives.

Sam watched Carmen sip her tea. He found with surprise and relief that he could look at her body, now neatly contained in a one-piece fuchsia bathing suit with a white gauzy jacket thrown over it, without lusting after it. It was a magnificent body, to be sure, but he realized that at a point in the act of making love, the size, shape, and form of the person ceased to matter. Passion was not physical but emotional; the visuals only served to start the juices flowing. Of course, he had known this all along, he'd just forgotten it for a time.

"So let's talk."

Harry had finished his sandwich, and now he drummed his fingers against the table, impatient to get this out of the way. "I know you didn't come six thousand miles just to look at my ugly puss, so you'd better tell me what the hell you want, so I can go and take my nap."

Carmen cleared her throat and sat up straighter in her chair. Yesterday Harry had promised to act surprised when Sam laid out the story to him, but you never knew about Harry. Sometimes he put on a good act; other times, out of pure orneriness, he refused to play along. Since he'd just had a pleasant dive and eaten his favorite lunch, chances were he'd cooperate. Nevertheless, she held her breath.

"There are some things going on at the firm that I want to make you aware of, and I thought it best that we speak about them face to face," said Sam.

"I'm all ears," Harry replied.

"It's about the WIT/Dominion matter," Sam began.

"No shit," said Harry, rolling his eyes impatiently. Carmen shot him a warning look and Harry reacted to it. "Go on," he said politely.

The subtle interplay between Carmen and Harry was not lost on Sam, but he didn't know how to read it. And right now he had to concentrate on speaking his piece.

"Let me just lay the facts on the table. My friend and client — *our* client, Art Lawson, is in deep shit with his resort development in Phoenix. It came up at the partners' meeting last month. He needs cash in a big way, or the banks are going to bring the whole thing down around his head.

"We talked about Art's options. One was to sell his position at Dominion, but he refused. Adamantly. He begged us to find another solution, because that stock was a legacy from his father. Plus it's the Hollywood glamour thing. He likes to think of himself as being in The Business.

"I don't mean to put him down. We've all got some investment we don't want to trade on, and this one is Art's. And even though he's desperately strapped for cash, selling his Dominion stock would be a fate worse than death. He made that clear to us. So I've been working with Sanwa, hoping they'd refinance his Phoenix deal with some sort of equity kicker as an incentive. Anyway, that's another story.

"Now Art's problem was confidential information. Privileged conversation between client and counsel. Leo was aware of it, because he sat in on the meetings. And he knew as well as I did that it would kill Art to lose his stake in Dominion. But when he learned WIT was looking to buy into a studio, he stepped right up and offered them Art's stock on a silver platter."

Harry shifted uneasily in his chair. He knew what was coming, and he didn't want to hear it.

"Apparently, Art flipped out when they told him. He's in a drug rehab now, suspected intentional overdose. He'll recover eventually, I guess." Sam let this thought hang in the air.

"The guy got in too deep and the riptide grabbed him," Harry tried.

"No," Sam insisted. "Leo sold Art out to WIT. And in doing that, he also sold out ICCM."

"That's not necessarily true," Harry demurred.

"Harry, it's a damn fact, and you know it. Now, I'm not surprised that Leo went behind our backs, cutting himself a sweet deal, and cutting Jim and me out in the process. No one's ever accused him of being a team player. He's got his own agenda, and he's not going to let a little thing like ethics get in his way."

Sam stood and walked to the rail, his back to Harry and Carmen. Suddenly he was a litigator, cross-examining a star witness. He felt their eyes on him, sensed them waiting for what he was going to say next, and he milked the moment for dramatic effect. Finally, he wheeled and looked straight into Harry's eyes.

"But you Harry, I would never have believed you would go along with such an underhanded deal. In all the years I've known you, I've never seen you make a move that wasn't by the books, honest and aboveboard. Then two days ago, you tell me you not only support Leo, but you're going into the deal yourself, and to hell with the rest of us. Now something's behind this, and I want some answers."

Sam walked closer to Harry and said in a calm, confident voice, "What I need to know is, why are you letting Leo get away with murder, Harry?"

"Who the hell are you to question what I do?" Harry bellowed.

"Harry — "

Sam heard the warning in Carmen's voice and saw the stern look in her eyes. There was some unspoken pact between them, something utterly out of context. But rather than stop to ponder this issue, Sam quietly replied to Harry, "I'm your partner, Harry. Don't you think you owe your partner the truth?"

The two men stared at each other. *They might as well be ten-year-olds,* Carmen thought, *neither one wants to be the first to blink or look away.* Finally Harry exhaled, a sigh that seemed to deflate his whole body, and he said, "Yeah Sam, I suppose I do." He raised his eyes to Sam, who was still standing over him. "So park it and let me speak my piece."

Sam sat. "What I'm about to say can never leave this ship. I swear I'll have your head if it does, Carrouthers," said Harry.

"You know me better than that, Harry," Sam replied, "and I'm sure Carmen will understand if you want her to take a swim."

Harry and Carmen looked at each other and Harry shook his head. "She's part of it, Sam," he said. "She's in it up to her tits." Sam looked from Carmen to Harry and back to Carmen. There was a Mona Lisa dreaminess in her eyes that he hadn't seen before, like she knew something he didn't.

She turned her attention to Harry.

"I have some dirt on Leo that would put him away. Years ago, he sold some information. Insider stuff," Harry told Sam.

"Why haven't you told anyone about this before?"

"Because I'm the one he sold it to. I was the buyer."

"It wasn't like that," Carmen interrupted.

Sam looked at her in surprise. "How do you know?"

"Because she was there too. Let's cut the charade, okay? Carmen and I were together for a couple of years, what '90? '91? She knows everything about me there is to know. Okay?" said Harry gruffly.

"Okay," said Sam, because there was no other possible answer, although a million questions came to mind.

"So, during that time Leo came to me with a deal. The Cartwright Consolidated deal, remember it?"

"Sure," said Sam, "it was an LBO. You put in $2 or $3 million cash against a $50 million purchase price and sold it eleven months later for a tidy profit of $200 mil. A lucky hit."

"Well it wasn't luck. Leo had a source. Don't ask me who, because I won't tell you. He came to me saying he had a hunch about Cartwright, and that I should buy in. So I did. I found out later he'd hired a corporate mole to infiltrate their management and find out their strategy. But by then the deal had closed. I had too much to lose."

Sam let this sink in. He suspected Leo had something on Harry, but would never have believed it was something this virulent. He chose his words carefully. "If this comes out now, there'll be trouble."

"No shit." Harry sighed. "But I'm willing to risk it to finally get that bastard off my back. Besides, there's another debt I need to pay." He looked at Carmen.

"I already know how to write the story, Sam. I've got a draft of it here." She showed him a sheaf of papers. "It blows the whistle on Leo without mentioning Harry at all."

"But, if you already had all of the information, why . . ." Sam looked again from Carmen to Harry and back to Carmen.

"Because I would never let this out without Harry's permission. And he's given it to me." She gave Harry a brilliant smile.

"What if Leo retaliates? He'll obviously try to get back at Harry."

"I don't think so. He'll be completely discredited by this disclosure. Nobody's going to believe anything he says."

"But there must be records — "

"It's been taken care of," said Carmen. Sam looked at her questioningly. "Don't ask," she said. "Don't ask, don't tell."

Enid

The phone rang, and through the black fog that was Enid's conscience, she heard Wallase answer it and whisper to the caller that his mistress was ill in bed, could he take a message and have her call back later.

Enid hadn't realized guilt could have such physical manifestations. She had awoken after less than four hours of sleep, feeling such a heaviness in her limbs it was all she could do to get up to go to the bathroom. Then it was back to bed and back to sleep, until she heard the sound of Wallase's key in the lock and his habitually cheerful "good morning" as he entered the house.

Since it was such a rare event for Enid to be sick in bed, Wallase treated her like an invalid, monitoring calls in a hushed voice, tiptoeing upstairs to check on her hourly, bringing her mugs of fresh broth and tea, and generally pampering her with a protective blanket of pity. Thus buffered from contact with the outer world, Enid could lie in bed and dwell on her predicament. Not surprisingly, the distress symptoms began around her pelvis, an internal pressure building into what felt painfully like a bladder infection.

When the itchy sensation finally forced her to examine herself, she was horrified to find her pelvic area shrouded by tiny red corpuscles, clearly an allergy of sorts. An allergy to adultery?

These aches, coupled with an upset stomach and a hangover from too much alcohol, added up to pure misery. But the physical pain was nothing compared to the psychological agony. The onslaught of guilt and remorse was relentless, pummeling her brain into a fevered mush. *Why did I do it*, she kept asking herself. The sex wasn't even that great. After all, sex was just a bodily function; what elevated it was the emotions behind it. And the night before, without an emotional content, it was a question of performance rather than passion. So, like a musician after a concert, she felt relieved it was over and anxious about the reviews. Would Patrick call her? What did he think of her now?

Wallase tapped on the door and peered in to see if she was awake.

"Come on in," she said, not so much wanting his company as needing the comfort of a sympathetic soul.

"How you feel?" he asked, setting a tray of tea and toast next to her bed.

"Not so hot, Wallase," she answered.

"You get sick at party?" he asked with concern.

"No, not until after," she said, wondering if he could see the scarlet A branded on her forehead.

"Who called?" she asked, less out of interest than to change the subject.

"Missy Ivy from the Westside Women's Shelter. I tell her you sick. She very sorry, say she call you Monday. And your Mommy call too. When I tell her you sick she say she don't feel very good too, but you call her when you better. And Mister Patrick Drake call also."

At the mention of Patrick's name, her heart leapt to her throat, then dropped to the pit of her stomach. She was gratified that he had called, surely a signal that last night had not been insignificant to him. But her mind raced with worry. Now that she had allowed him access to the most sacrosanct part of her being, she was completely vulnerable to him.

He had counseled her against telling anyone about their night together, and most certainly she would not. But what about him? Would he tell his agent or his publicist, or his shrink, or his doctor if this infection flaring up between her legs were contagious? And would the story eventually find its way back to Sam, who would certainly be devastated by the knowledge that the sanctity of his marriage had been violated?

The intercom buzzed, and Wallase leapt to his feet to silence it. "Hello, yes? I go, I go."

Enid knew she should get up. Clearly there was nothing to be gained from lying here at the mercy of her imagination. But she was weighted to the bed by gloom. No wonder chronic depression was considered a physical malady. She had never felt so ill in her life.

"Missy, I can come?" Wallase asked, as he entered her room again, holding out a small shopping bag with a note attached. "Jeremy bring, from Mr. Patrick." He put the bag on Enid's nightstand and waited for her to roll over to open it.

But this was something she wanted to do in private. "I'll look at it later, Wallase, thanks." She snuggled into her pillow, waiting until Wallase got the hint and withdrew, shutting the door behind him.

Once she was alone, Enid sat up in bed and pulled the note off the bag. It read, "I was hoping we could have lunch, but since you're sick I thought I'd send over something for you to enjoy alone. Love, P."

Love, P., she thought, brightening a bit. How sweet of him. She picked up the bag and peered into it.

Wallase heard strange sounds coming room his mistress's room, so he tapped on the door and peeked in, worried that she had taken a turn for the worse. But she looked perfectly all right to him now, lying back against her pillows laughing so hard that tears rolled down her cheeks.

She was holding a package of Oscar Mayer hot dogs. Was that the gift from next door? *Strange*, he thought, knowing his mistress was a vegetarian. *Why for is she so happy?*

Patrick

It was just as well that Enid couldn't join him for lunch today, although he knew seeing a woman "the day after" was crucial to cement the bond. But Patrick was eager to let LeMar know that he had the Dominion situation well in hand. Besides, sending the weenies was a stroke of genius. If she were having recriminations — and no doubt she was — the hot dogs would make her laugh and take the onus off of him. He congratulated himself on his brilliant imagination.

Patrick pulled the Rolls into the parking lot at Le Dome and gave the keys to the valet. Thank God it was finally out of the shop. It was downright shocking the way people treated you in a rented Ford, no matter who you were.

But everything was back to normal now. The valet gave him a respectful, "Thank you, Mr. Drake," and Patrick entered the restaurant, thinking ahead to the French onion soup and the steak tartare, his two favorite items on the extensive menu.

The hostess, a beautiful girl with extravagant brunette curls, looked past the three or four society matrons who were hovering nearby trying to make eye contact with Patrick, and she motioned him forward. He had to squeeze by the others, and they telegraphed their resentment that he got special treatment, even if he was a movie star.

"Patrick, how are you?" the hostess asked, motioning to him to follow her beyond the circular bar to the room at the rear of the restaurant that overlooked the city.

"Great, great," he replied. "How are Georgio and the baby?"

"Super. In fact, we're getting married next month." She proudly held out her left hand and showed him a ring that featured at least a couple of carats of diamonds, in a modern setting. Not bad for a restaurant hostess, even in L.A. But Patrick knew this girl, in the biblical sense, and he wasn't surprised to see she'd gotten what she wanted.

"But what about me? I've been waiting around for the Italian Stallion to dump you, and here he goes and makes you an honest woman," Patrick teased. "I guess patience is its own reward."

The girl smiled and directed him to the table where LeMar sat, his head buried in the menu. "I didn't know it made a difference to you, married or not married," she said, giving him a smile that told him married or not married, she was, and would always be, available to him.

He dropped into the chair across from LeMar, who still hadn't raised his eyes from the menu. Finally, Patrick said, "I don't know why you spend so much time reading menus when all you're going to order is the house salad with the dressing on the side."

"I just want to see what I'm missing," said LeMar, finally lowering the menu. He glowered at Patrick. "It's kind of like sleeping with other men's wives — one doesn't really *want* them, one just wants to see what someone else has. You can relate to that, can't you?"

"LeMar, you aren't going to give me a hard time about Enid Carrouthers are you? Because if you are, I can easily find someone else to have lunch with." He half rose from his chair.

"Sit," LeMar roared, and Patrick did. "Have you slept with her yet?" he asked in a lower voice.

"LeMar, I'm shocked! That is privileged information."

"Well, give me the privilege of knowing, so I can tell you what a dumb schmuck you are."

"Why do I put up with this abuse?"

"You love it, and you know it."

"Yeah, you're right. It's no fun when people tell you how wonderful you are."

"Well you certainly don't need to hear that from me, when you've got ladies all over you, creaming compliments in your ear."

"I know what's wrong with you, you're jealous." Patrick beamed with the knowledge. "What'sa matter? You getting a little tired of Betsy?"

"I'll never get tired of Betsy," said LeMar with a haughty look. "She won't let me."

"Oh, sorry, for a moment there I mistook you for a guy who ran his own life. Let's see how the guilt chain works — Betsy runs your life, you run mine."

"And you're running Enid Carrouthers around in circles."

Sometimes this banter with LeMar was fun, but today Patrick was too weary to defend himself. Besides, he had an ace up his sleeve, and he was eager to pull it on LeMar. He called the waiter over and ordered his soup and steak tartare and, motioning to LeMar, said, "He doesn't need anything. He'll be making a meal out of his own words."

"What's that supposed to mean?" asked LeMar when the waiter left.

"For your information, I have no intention of ruining Enid Carrouthers life. I only wanted to get her on my side so I could score some points with her husband."

"You really are deranged," said LeMar. "Since when do you score points with a husband by boffing his wife?"

"LeMar, do I have to spell it all out to you? Enid likes me, she's crazy about me, and when I ask her, she'll put in a good word for me, not only with her husband, but she can also get the message across to Jeffrey Kesselman."

"Why? Is she sleeping with him too?"

"Of course not. At least I don't think so. He and her husband do business. She's definitely got his ear."

LeMar shook his head. "You've been in too many bad movies. Your reasoning is solid gold, except for two things. One, what happens if Kesselman or this guy Carrouthers ever find out why the wife is singing your praises? Don't you think somebody's balls are going to be in a sling?'"

Patrick shrugged. "Enid's not stupid. She won't tell."

"Of course she will, if she gets angry at you somewhere down the line, and you know she will, considering your track record."

"Are you finished, because I'd like to enjoy my soup in peace."

"No, I'm not finished. Point number two is even more interesting than point number one."

"And it is? . . ."

"The relationship between Kesselman and Carrouthers."

"Do tell," said Patrick.

"Carrouthers' firm is representing some Oriental group that's buying a controlling interest in Dominion." Patrick put down his spoon, afraid he didn't want to hear what was coming, but knowing LeMar was going to tell him anyway.

"And until the papers are signed on this negotiation, Kesselman's been told not to green light any more projects. In other words, he's as helpless as a eunuch in a whorehouse."

Patrick could feel his own testicles withering as he waited for LeMar to drop the other shoe.

"Word is, if the sale goes through, and it looks as though it will, Kesselman's out and *For Love or Money* will go into turnaround. In other words, it's dead."

Suddenly Patrick felt very, very tired. What happened to the old Hollywood, the one that ran on personalities and power rather than politics and profits? Here he'd done everything possible to get himself factored into this project on his own terms, and now it turned out that the whole package was on a conveyor belt straight to the garbage dump.

"Why didn't you tell me this last night?" he said softly.

"You didn't give me a chance. That's why I wanted to have lunch, to tell you Kesselman hasn't been dragging his feet on account of he doesn't like you or your fee, but because if what I hear is true, they've slipped the rug out from under him, and he's deadlier than a fart in an elevator."

Patrick sighed. He knew just how Kesselman felt.

23

Enid and Patrick

Although she still had thirty minutes before the car would pick her up to take her to Lacy Choate's surprise birthday dinner, Enid was completely dressed and waiting. Like a zombie, she was drawn to the window to stare through the darkness at Patrick's house. She had successfully avoided seeing or talking to him since "their night," and she was relieved to see his house was completely dark now. Still, it seemed to throb with his presence, and her own heart picked up the beat.

Stepping away from the window, she went over the events of the past forty-eight hours. It seemed as though her entire life had changed. Dear Sam, who in twelve years of marriage had never given her a jealous moment, was possibly off romancing an unknown woman in an idyllic setting. If that possibility did not signal the end of their union, her own unfaithfulness had certainly sounded the death knell.

And while she might be able to avoid confronting Patrick for another day or two, even longer, she would have to face Sam tonight. His plane was due within the hour, and according to the message she'd received from Harry Ingersol's secretary Roxie, Sam planned to go right from the plane to the dinner party at the Hotel Bel Air.

Roxie had told Enid she had reserved a room at the hotel for Sam to shower and change in. And while Roxie's efficiency didn't surprise Enid, she was not at all sure if this had been her idea, or if Sam had some other ominous motive for reserving the room. Maybe he wasn't planning to come home with her afterward. Maybe the room was for the woman he had been traveling with. The thought sickened her.

Mercifully, the intercom rang. The driver at last. Enid rounded up Sam's tuxedo, which she had already slipped into a garment bag, and her own coat and purse, and let herself out the front door.

The driver stood by the passenger door, an odd, leering expression on his face. She panicked — why was this man looking at her so strangely? Did he know what she'd done? Did it show? *How pathetic,* she chided herself, ducking her head and pulling her coat around her so it didn't catch in the door, *I've turned into a paranoid mental case.* She entered the car backward to avoid ripping the long Armani skirt, and blindly groping behind her for the seat, she plunked down into it. The driver slammed the door shut.

Then she saw him, a figure theatrically shrouded in darkness, sitting in the jumpseat facing her. "Oh," was all she could get out, the surge of adrenaline silencing her.

"How are you feeling?" asked Patrick. He leaned forward so Enid could see the frown of concern handsomely etched on his face.

"Better," breathed Enid, "or at least I was. You scared me to death. What are you doing here?"

"I was in the neighborhood, and I thought I'd stop by," he said. Enid smiled in spite of herself, her heart beating in her throat.

"Shall we go, Ma'am?" asked the driver.

"Just a minute," she answered, and then said to Patrick, "I'm sorry, I'm going to a surprise party. I can't be late."

"No problem," Patrick replied. "I'll just go along for the ride, if it's not too much trouble."

"But why?"

Patrick slid onto the seat next to Enid and took her hand. "Because

I need to talk to you, and I've got a hunch you've been avoiding me."

"I'm not, I really was sick. I was in bed. You can ask Wallase."

Patrick didn't say anything, just raised his eyebrows and cocked his head. Enid had seen him do this in his movies and knew the gesture meant, "You and I both know there's something you're not telling me."

"Also, I need a ride into town. My car is back in the shop. The damn valet at Le Dome forgot to put on the parking brake yesterday and it rolled into a Geo, damn near crushed it." From the expression on his face, he might as well have been talking about a critically ill friend. "I'm supposed to meet Sara at The Bistro later, so when I saw the limo I thought maybe I could hitch a ride. I can get to the restaurant from the Bel Air, easy."

Enid sighed and let her body sink back into the seat. She might as well get this confrontation over with. "Okay, driver, we can go. To the Hotel Bel Air, please."

"Yes Ma'am," he said, and turned the key in the ignition.

Patrick and Enid rode in silence for a moment, each waiting for the other to speak. Then they both opened their mouths at the same instant, a comedy routine.

"You go ahead," said Enid.

"No, please, ladies first," said Patrick.

"I was only going to say thank you for the hot dogs," she said.

"It was the least I could do. Did you put them to good use?"

Enid reddened. "I knew I shouldn't have told you that story."

"Why not? It was endearing, really, to think of you there in that tent, teaching yourself the facts of life."

"Oh, God, you're never going to let me hear the end of this, are you?"

"Who, me?"

"Patrick, I swear, I will absolutely die if you tell that story to another living soul. It has been my deepest, darkest secret for twenty years."

Patrick leaned toward her with a shit-eating grin. "Well, now you've got another one."

"Don't remind me," Enid replied icily.

"Oh, come on, it wasn't that awful, was it? You're going to bruise my fragile ego," Patrick teased. "And you did seem to be enjoying yourself at the time."

"It's like drinking too much," Enid replied. "While you're doing it, it feels fine. But afterward when you're puking into the toilet at three in the morning, you start to wonder why you ever did it."

"It isn't that bad."

"Yes it is."

"Enid, I hate to be the one to break it to you, but *everybody does it.*"

"Not me. Not until yesterday."

"What you need is a little hair of the dog." He put his arm around her and whispered in her ear, "I'm madly in love with you, you know that don't you?"

"You are not," Enid said, hating the part of her that was wishing it were true.

"You're right. I'm in lust with you. We could take a room at the hotel and — "

Enid pulled away. "Don't, I told you. I've got a party to go to. And besides, Sam is meeting me there later."

"Aha! The husband returns. And what are you not going to tell him?"

"Is that what you wanted to talk about? To make me promise again not to tell?"

"No, no, no. The truth is, I wanted to warn you about this." Patrick reached across the seat and picked up a newspaper. Even in the dim light, Enid could see it was one of those supermarket tabloids, *The Inquirer.*

Patrick flipped on the light, and Enid raised the paper. To her horror, her own face stared back in living color. She was clinging to Patrick, an idiotic grin on her face. On the other side of Patrick, the visage of an irate Sara Benton had been spliced in, so Patrick was sandwiched between the two of them. The caption read, *New Love For Patrick Drake Or Is He Just Being Neighborly? Sara Benton Bent Out Of Shape — Vows To Find Out.*

"Oh, my God," was all Enid could say.

"I warned you it could happen."

"But I didn't think it really would."

He let her stare at the page for a moment. "Enid." He spoke her name in a voice low and thick with emotion. He never ceased to amaze himself with this ability to dredge up the semblance of passion where none existed. But then, that's what acting was all about.

Slowly he initiated "the stroke," starting at the inner crevice of her elbow and moving upward. He noted with satisfaction that her concentration on *The Inquirer* was wavering, and she was beginning to focus on the sensations emanating from her right arm.

"I wish we could have a little more time together," he breathed.

"I have to meet Sam," said Enid, not looking at him.

"I know," he said, snaking his fingers high enough up her arm to feel the stubble of hair in her armpit. "But maybe Monday. He'll go to work in the morning, won't he?" Patrick put his mouth against her ear to whisper, "I'll be home all day. Alone."

Enid hated herself for the feeling of longing that was taunting her body. Patrick's touch was hypnotic, and she felt stripped of her earlier resolve to end this flirtation. For a split second she imagined leaving Sam and running away with Patrick, just like people did in the movies. A ridiculous thought, but so romantic. She had her platinum American Express Card. What if she just told the driver to take them to LAX. They could catch the first plane out. . . .

Patrick tried to assess Enid's dreamy expression. She looked dazzled and vulnerable, totally under his spell, just where he wanted her. He had to make this last-ditch effort; his career hung in the balance.

"Enid, I have a teensy weensy little favor to ask of you. I wouldn't even bring it up, except that I feel so close to you."

"Hmmm?" she said, still floating free in her fantasy. Patrick took both of Enid's hands in his. Oddly, they were cold and clammy. The limousine was turning onto Stone Canyon Drive. They'd be at the hotel in two minutes. He had no choice but to forge ahead while the door was open.

"Dominion Studios is making a movie called *For Love or Money*. They want me to star in it, but now that the studio is being sold, everything is up for grabs. All it would take is one little push. You know, if you could put in a good word for me with Sam, tell him how much it would mean to you if they went ahead and made the movie and if I got the part."

Enid crashed back to earth at Patrick's invocation of Sam's name. "What does Sam have to do with the movies Dominion Studios makes?"

"Well your husband's company is buying the studio, isn't it? Or no, some Japanese company he works with. That's what my agent told me."

"I don't have the slightest idea." *Maybe that's the big deal he went to talk to Harry about*, she thought. *But why wouldn't he have told me about it? News like that is too big to keep secret. Unless it's just a symptom of how far apart we've grown.*

"It would really mean a great, great deal to me to have that part." Patrick nuzzled close to Enid and wrapped her into a hug. "If you could help me, I'd be putty in your hands." He gave her his famous sexy smile, the one that had melted her before. But this time it didn't work.

Because, at that moment, Enid felt the bubble of her vulnerability burst and she was drenched in the realization that Patrick felt nothing for her, that this was all an act because he wanted something from her. She stared at him, awed that he could manufacture emotion and wear it like an article of clothing. She wondered if he stood in front of the mirror each morning, deciding what feelings to put on, much as she stood in her closet to choose a dress.

"So that's what all this is about," she said in a surprisingly calm voice.

"All what?" he asked innocently.

"The big come-on, "our night," this — " she said, jerking her arm out from under his stroke, "groping. You've just been using me to get that part."

"Enid, listen — "

"No, *you* listen. I have . . . had . . . real feelings for you! Do you think I would have just jumped into bed with you if I hadn't felt . . ." She stopped, searching for the right word to describe her feelings. It couldn't be love, because she didn't know Patrick well enough to *love* him, but *like* was definitely not a strong enough word. The only word that fit was infatuation, and nobody over the age of fourteen would admit to that.

"Hey, let's not get into a pissing contest about whose motive was the purest. You played up to me from the very beginning, because you wanted to use my fame for that damn charity thing. Am I wrong?"

Enid didn't answer, because he wasn't wrong. She'd conveniently forgotten that this whole mess started because she would have done anything to get him involved in her benefit for the Westside Women's Shelter.

"That may have been what started it, but when I got to know you better — " she tried.

"Face it, Enid, you aren't interested in me as a person. You wanted Patrick Drake, the movie star. That's what turned you on. Am I right or am I right?" It hurt him to say this, but he knew it was true. Being a movie star was his biggest asset . . . and his greatest curse.

"You certainly don't give yourself very much credit," Enid replied, looking out the window. The hotel was in sight just ahead.

If Patrick knew one thing about women, it was that they always wanted to believe you were in love with them. Whether you acted on the feeling or not, they wanted to be told you were out there, silently adoring them, even when they knew in their hearts it was a lie.

"Enid, I do care about you," he said. "I'd hate to admit how much, because even if I said the words I could never do anything about it without disrupting your whole life. And God forbid I would be responsible for breaking up your marriage."

Enid had to admit he was clever. Even now, with all pretense of true feelings destroyed, he'd cast himself in the role of Sir Gallahad, who would sit outside her moat and love her from afar, rather than despoil the sanctity of her ivory tower. But instead of wearing a suit of chain mail, he was using the slightest suggestion of blackmail, implying he could indeed strike a fatal blow to her marriage if she didn't cooperate with him. How could she have been taken in by this man? He was nothing but a manipulative, self-serving shit. She was beginning to hate him.

But what was the point of hating him? She knew she'd brought this whole thing on herself. She should have been thankful that her schoolgirl crush had died a natural death before she made herself any more ridiculous. And it would do no good to make an enemy of Patrick. After all, they were neighbors. And then there was the matter of the Shelter's benefit.

The car pulled into the parking lot in front of the hotel. Enid was late, and if she didn't hurry, she was going to ruin Lacy's surprise. She looked at Patrick, who for once was at a loss to know how to act, waiting to see which side of the fence she was going to land on.

"No more ulterior motives, nothing up my sleeve, I promise," Patrick swore.

"I can't promise anything, but I'll try to talk to Sam," Enid told him. "And let's forget this week ever happened."

"Have a nice time tonight," Patrick called, as Enid walked away.

As soon as she was out of hearing range, Patrick leaned toward the driver, "Hey buddy, could you drop me at The Bistro?"

"Sorry, sir," the driver said. "I've got another pickup."

"Yeah, right. I'll get a cab or something." He stepped back and the car pulled away, leaving him alone on the curb of the hotel in a rush of swirling, dead leaves.

24

Sam and Carmen

Of all things, Sam's and Carmen's flight from Rome was early. And since neither of them had anything to declare, they were through Customs and into the waiting limo forty-five minutes before they had been scheduled to arrive.

Sam told the driver to take him to the Bel Air, then to drop Carmen at her house in Laurel Canyon, as they had planned on the plane. They rode in silence, both wearing sunglasses, despite the tinted windows of the limousine and the falling darkness of evening.

Carmen was spent, both physically and emotionally. And while she considered the meeting a success, she was pessimistic about the future of her relationship with Sam. In winning the battle, she may have lost the war.

Sam was entrenched in his thoughts as the limo sped north on the 405 freeway. Harry's revelations had caught him off guard. Sure, he had suspected that Leo was blackmailing Harry in some way, but never in a million years would he have guessed that Carmen Leventhal would be the key that unlocked the mystery. Harry and Carmen? Sam was speechless with amazement.

He couldn't look at her, so he pointedly kept his eyes glued on the passing scenery. Sam could hardly believe that barely twenty-four hours ago he and Carmen had been writhing around in the throes of passion, each so caught up in the other's body that the rest of the world had ceased to exist.

Now when he looked at her, all he felt was a mild flutter of revulsion. No passion, no longing, no recollection of what she felt like or smelled like or tasted like, and no desire to remember. Was this just his mind's way of blocking out the guilt of adultery, or could he chalk it all up to jet lag and those damn Halcion pills, causing a kind of moral amnesia?

Whatever. He was more than eager to see Enid, to kiss her and to feel the comfort of her love cleansing him of the emotional residue of the past two and a half days.

But first he had to get through this evening and the face-to-face confrontation with Leo. Sam, Harry, and Carmen had agreed that nothing should be said to Leo by any of them until Carmen's story appeared in the *Times*, which could be as early as Tuesday morning. Sam was more than happy to postpone the real confrontation until then, but he would be interested to see Leo tonight, now that he knew he had the upper hand.

"Sam," Carmen began, "for what it's worth, I'm sorry."

Sam was careful not to let his face register the surprise he felt. Although he had not known Carmen long or well, he could tell that apologies rarely passed her lips. She looked so fragile and ill at ease, he started to reach out to comfort her. But discretion arrested his hand in mid motion, and he let it drop to the seat between them.

"I guess I should have told you about Harry, but I didn't know how. And anyway, it's completely over now. It has been for years. I'm just sorry it upset you."

"You don't need to apologize," Sam said, and he meant it. "It's none of my business who you've spent your time with. The truth is, I'm relieved to finally get a clear picture of what's been going on between Leo and Harry. And I guess I'm grateful to you for bringing it all to a head."

He sighed and looked out the window again, hoping he could find the right words for what he wanted to say next. "But we need to talk about . . . what happened on the boat between us."

Carmen's smile was encouraging. Her heart pounded, as though she were a diver who had just executed a triple back flip and was now waiting for the scores of the judges.

"You are a beautiful and very desirable woman," Sam said.

Flattery was a bad sign. Carmen wondered where he was going with it. Absently she began to play with the zipper of her faux Hermes bag. Open shut, open shut. *Time to get off the fence, Sam, say what you think,* she thought.

"This is very awkward for me to say," Sam tried again. "I've never been in this position."

"What position is that?" Carmen snapped, unable to keep the edge from her voice.

"I've never been unfaithful to Enid before," Sam said in a rush. "It would be devastating to her and to our marriage if she found out what happened."

Oh, here we go, thought Carmen. Guilt was the obvious response, she knew, but she had expected more from Sam. No, not *expected,* hoped for, was more accurate. Clearly he was a moral man, not the type of person to hurt another purposely. But Carmen knew from her experience with married men that this verbal expression of guilt was mostly self-serving. It gave the man a prefab escape route; if he wanted out later, he had already established the excuse that he was merely protecting the feelings of his poor wife.

"If you're worried that I was the role model for Glenn Close in *Fatal Attraction* you can forget it." Carmen tried to inject some levity into their conversation, but a deadly serious look remained etched in the fatigue lines on Sam's face. Worry churned in her gut. "Sam, we could be a great team. I know what you want, and I can help you get it. When my article comes out, Leo Choate will be dog meat. Somebody's got to step into the void and pick up the pieces. I'm giving you that opportunity. I created that opportunity for you, and I want to be there to help you — "

"Stop right there," Sam cut her off. "Let's get one thing straight. You didn't orchestrate this whole scenario for me, you did it for yourself. I'm just one of the pawns you're trying to manipulate to get what you want."

"What are you talking about?" Carmen started.

"I don't know whether to be flattered or insulted that you thought you could maneuver me so easily," said Sam. "But don't think for a second that I don't see what your motives really are."

Carmen felt a surge of rage that she tried to control, knowing all would be lost if she didn't. "What exactly are you saying?"

"You're looking for an "E" ticket, a free ride on the first-class train. All of these people you write about, careers you've trashed." He shook his head. "You think the public sees you as an impartial observer, a Robin Hood, revealing the bad guys and handing their heads to the people on a silver platter. Well, let me tell you, we see right through you. Your motives aren't in the least altruistic. You hate these guys. Hate their guts. Not for what they've done that may or may not be wrong, but because you're jealous of what they have achieved."

"Wait a God damn minute," Carmen seethed. "Are you implying that I manufacture what I write?"

"No, but I know enough about journalism to know you can manipulate the facts by the words you choose to tell a story."

"If that's really what you think, I'm surprised that you're not afraid of the shit I might stir up about you."

"Sure I'm afraid of it. It's what led me into this in the first place."

Carmen was speechless, not so much because of what Sam was saying, but because of the way he was saying it. His voice was not angry or shrill, but sad, resigned, and honestly scared.

"Then, I admit it, I got hooked. Like I said, you're a very beautiful and desirable woman. And I am a man, only that. There are things inside of me that I can't completely control, and the closer you came, the more I wanted you. It was an obsession, an irrational obsession. I had to play it out to its inevitable end, which was Thursday night."

Despite her anger, Carmen felt her female core melt at his flattery. And she hated herself for it. She had always used her sexuality as her secret weapon against the enemy. Now this enemy (*when had she started thinking of Sam as her enemy?* the voice in the back of her mind asked) was turning his back on her, trying to soften her fall by appealing to her female ego. She was furious with Sam for doing this, and with herself for responding.

"What makes you so lily white?" she countered. "You wanted to bury Leo Choate, and you knew I could do the dirty work for you. So don't try to hide behind this 'I am only a man' crap. My article is going to get you exactly what you wanted."

Sam took a minute to compose himself before answering. She was not entirely wrong, but the attorney in him wouldn't let her distort his motives with semantics. "I never wanted you to bury Leo. I just wanted you to write the facts, so people could make their own assessments. If you attack Leo directly, he's not going to roll over and die, I assure you. He'll come after us with the biggest guns money can buy, and the issue will be lost in the muck and mire of legal entanglements."

"This is incredible, it really is." Carmen couldn't help but let a little awe creep into her voice. "You're telling me to be fair to that asshole? I can't believe you aren't pleading with me to hand you his head. Aren't you just a little bit pissed off that he tried to walk all over you? Doesn't a part of you want to eat him for breakfast?"

"Of course I'm angry, but I've been through this kind of thing enough times to know that nobody wins if you end up in an out-and-out war. I want to stop Leo from doing what he's doing, but I think the best way to accomplish that is to give him enough rope to hang himself and wait for the results." Sam took a sheaf of papers from his briefcase. "I made a few notes on your story while you were asleep on the plane, some changes you might want to consider."

He handed her the papers, and she skimmed them quickly. "You've castrated it! This sounds like something in *Woman's Day*."

"If you just lay the facts out there, the revenge will take care of itself, you'll see," said Sam confidently.

Carmen felt the car come to a halt. She had been so focused on Sam and what he was saying that she didn't even realize they had turned off Sunset. Now, as she looked through the darkened window of the limousine, she could see the lush overhanging trees at the entrance to the Hotel Bel Air. A doorman dressed in a pink oxford cloth shirt and khakis opened her door, and money-scented air wafted into the car.

Despite herself, Carmen could sense tears welling up in her eyes. It was unlike her to show emotion like this, in fact, it was unlike her to *feel* emotion like this. But everything she had wanted so desperately and had worked so hard to get seemed close at hand, yet remained just outside of her grasp. And because she knew Sam was about to walk out of her life forever, for the second time in as many days, Carmen allowed the tears to come.

25

Sam and Carmen and Patrick and Enid

Sam opened the door of the limo and got out. If he had known Enid was entering the hotel at this moment, he could have looked up and seen her. But as it was, he was facing away from the building, looking back into the car at Carmen.

"I'll give you a call tomorrow to tell you how it went," he said to her.

"Fine," she answered. And Sam closed the door and hurried out of her life.

Carmen watched him go. She felt an emptiness that was strange to her — defeat. She hoped it was true what they said about failure building character, because she couldn't think of another compensation for this bleakness.

As she watched Sam walk over the bridge, past the stream and into the hotel, she saw a man who could only be the actor Patrick Drake, talking to the doorman. *Patrick Drake*, she mused. The steel trap that was her mind instantly snapped shut against feelings of gloom and doom, and reopened to contemplate this celebrity whom she had admired from afar but had never met. He looked even better in person, she thought, wondering why both he and the doorman were looking her way.

As if in response, the doorman approached her driver and leaned to the window. "Hey Buddy, Mr. Drake is looking for a lift to Beverly Hills. I told him it'd take about thirty minutes for a cab to get here, and he suggested I check with you to see if you've got time to make an extra twenty bucks."

"Sorry," the driver replied, "I've still got a passenger in the back to drop off."

"No problem, I'll just tell him you're booked."

Carmen rolled down her window. "Young man," she said to the doorman, "it would be all right with me if Mr. Drake would like us to drop him off somewhere."

"Thank you, Ma'am, I'll tell him."

Carmen watched as the doorman delivered this message to Patrick. He looked over at Carmen and gave her a Hollywood smile, which glinted with gratitude and also, she was certain, delight over seeing that his savior was an attractive young woman. As Patrick walked toward her, Carmen could feel her strength and self-esteem return in a rush.

What juicy tidbits had she read about him? The only one that flashed to mind was something she'd found last year while doing research for a story on an illegal importing ring operating out of LAX. The article had told how Patrick Drake had been stopped going through customs with a suitcase full of dildos and vibrators, or some such nonsense. Good, a man who wasn't afraid of his sexuality!

Carmen smiled. *I could use a double dose of that right now*, she thought. And when Patrick leaned to her window to greet her and thank her for the offered ride, she was able to flash a dazzling smile, which she knew spoke volumes about her interest in him, and her availability.

"Can I give you a lift?" she asked.

As Patrick stuffed himself into Carmen's limo, he considered his options. He could keep his date with Sara at Vincenti, but he was already fifteen minutes late, and undoubtedly she would rake him over the coals when he arrived. Or, he could see what this gorgeous girl had to offer.

No contest.

"Do you always hang around the Bel Air in a limo waiting for available men who need a lift?" he joked.

"Nope," she smiled back, "it's a once-in-a-lifetime offer."

"Then it must be my lucky night. I'm Patrick Drake, by the way," he said, even though he knew she knew who he was. It was the fastest way to find out who she was and where she'd been all of his life.

"I wouldn't have picked you up if you weren't," she said.

"I guess that means you like my movies," he fished.

"I don't go to movies much," Carmen admitted, "but I do like what I've read about you."

"I hope you're not talking about that silly story in today's *Inquirer*."

"No," she smiled, "I was referring to an article in the *Times*."

"Recently?"

"No, this was a while ago — 1994, I think."

"My, you must have an exceptional memory," he said.

"No, I saw it recently, in the microfilm file. I work for the *Times*. I was researching a story on illegal imports coming through LAX, and I pulled up this little tidbit. I don't remember seeing it then. . . ."

"Yes, I think I know the article you're talking about." *Damn, another reporter.* He hated the way she was smiling at him, relishing his unease. Maybe he should just ask the driver to let him out.

"Just out of curiosity, did they confiscate all of the . . . toys, or do you still have them?"

Was this a trick question? "They kept them," he said.

"What a shame. I bet that musical dildo was hard to replace."

Patrick couldn't tell if she were joking or not. She seemed to be sincere, but you never knew. Maybe she was an undercover cop. Vice squad. Just what he needed tonight.

"Excuse me, Ma'am," the driver called. "Where shall I take you?"

Carmen looked at Patrick. "If you're not in a hurry, my house isn't too far from here. I've got a beautiful bottle of Armagnac and nobody to drink it with." As a further enticement, Carmen put her hand on Patrick's knee. It was as light as a feather, but heavy with promise, as it slowly stroked his thigh. "I hope you don't think I'm being too direct, but it's been a rough couple of days. I could use the comfort of another body. And yours looks very appealing."

Patrick couldn't believe it. Not only was this woman coming on to him, she was using his own personal technique! For a split second, he wondered if he should be wary. She did look a little strung out. A cokehead perhaps, or a loony? But at the Hotel Bel Air?

He flashed on Sara, her beautiful body and the groveling he would have to do before she allowed him access to it. It was exhausting just to think about it, whereas this woman looked equally voluptuous, and she seemed entirely willing to produce and direct a love scene. All he would have to do would be to sit back and see where she took it. What a luxury. How could he refuse?

🕶

Sam had to hand it to Leo. He was a lying, cheating, two-faced son of a bitch, but he did know how to throw a great party. Rather than use one of the hotel's private dining rooms, which, though elegant, still reeked of "rented room," Leo had arranged to use the hotel's best suite for Lacy's surprise party. Sam knew this suite rented for thirty-two hundred dollars a day, because one of his Sanwa clients had insisted on renting it for the retiring chairman of the board the one time he had visited Los Angeles. No doubt, Leo would write it off to ICCM as a business expense, which meant one-fourth of the cost was coming out of Sam's pocket. Typical.

For tonight's gathering, much of the furniture had been removed, and the room had been outfitted with five round tables of four, each swathed in silk and graced by arching sprays of orchids. A dozen violinists lined the foyer, playing refined and romantic music. Sam felt conspicuous in his flying fatigues, his chin stubbled, his eyes blood-shot, and apparently he looked as out of place as he felt, because before he had stepped two feet into the room, a man in a tuxedo hurried over to intercept him.

"May I help you, sir?"

"Yes, I'm a guest at this party, even if I don't look like it. My wife was going to bring my tuxedo from home since I've come straight from the — "

"Mr. Carrouthers?" The man seemed relieved when Sam nodded. "Yes, certainly. You are early, sir, I think."

"The plane was, for a change."

"Excellent, excellent. Your wife has brought your things. They're waiting in Room 28-F. May I direct you now, or did you want to speak to your wife first? I believe she's out on the patio."

"I'll find her first, thank you."

Sam knew everybody in the room, but for some reason they looked like strangers, and they were all staring at him like he was an alien. All he could think about was holding Enid in his arms and picking up the threads of his life.

$\mathbf{E}$nid felt almost invisible. Was it being in a group of friends without Sam, or was it the fact that the whole world looked different to her after the events and revelations of the past few days which had made the old Enid disappear?

She watched Lacy's and Leo's dramatic entrance. Never one to disappoint a crowd, when everyone shouted "surprise," Lacy shrieked and hugged Leo, tears, presumably of joy, running prettily down her cheeks. How clever of her to wear waterproof mascara, thought Enid, observing her from an outpost on the patio.

Enid had to admit that Lacy looked stunning in her brazen Issey Miyaki bustier and pleated rayon pants, but it was the kind of "beautiful" achieved by experts spending hours of expensive time. Enid did not begrudge Lacy her retinue of beauty purveyors; indeed, she wished she had the patience and the desire to spend the time and money necessary to achieve such a look.

But it was ridiculous for Lacy to pretend as she always did, that she had just stepped out of the shower minutes before and had thrown together this outfit in less time than it took most women to apply their lipstick. Lacy had always been good at pretending, and Enid was weary of the act.

"Enid, darling," Lacy screeched, her nervousness betrayed by the shrill tone of her voice. "You meanie! You should have told me." She kissed the air next to Enid's ear, her eyes scouring the room.

"Oh, for God sakes Lacy," said Enid, sure Lacy had known about this party longer than anyone, and probably planned most of it herself.

"Isn't Leo a sweetheart to have done all of this for me?" Lacy purred, ignoring Enid's comment and throwing a kiss and a look of adoration at Leo, who was basking in the reflected glow of her staged enthusiasm. "And especially when he's been so — "

Abruptly, Lacy stopped babbling, as though her air supply had been cut off. She was looking past Enid to something behind her, with a queer expression on her face.

Enid turned to see what Lacy was looking at, and there was Sam, across the room, staring at her.

"What happened to Sam? He looks like hell," Lacy scolded. "I told Leo I wanted everyone in black tie," she said, not realizing she had completely given herself away.

"He just got off of a plane," said Enid, returning Sam's gaze. "He's been in Italy with Harry," she continued, trying to get a rise out of Lacy, who hated it if anyone but Leo talked to Harry. But Lacy had already moved past her to the next set of friends, and Enid was left with only the lingering scent of her perfume. Poison.

❧

$\mathcal{S}$am stared at Enid, frozen in place by the power of his feelings for her. Out of the corner of his eye, he saw Leo approaching, and he knew he was going to have to confront either Leo or Enid. He chose Enid.

❧

$\mathcal{E}$nid saw Sam moving toward her. He was in focus, but the rest of the room became a blur. It was like a scene in a bad television movie, strangers locking eyes across a crowded room, seeing nothing except each other as they moved toward each other in slow motion.

Only Enid and Sam were not strangers. Far from it.

Enid could see the exhaustion and sadness in Sam's face. And in some deep part of her, she knew something had happened, that he was sorry for it, and that he loved her. Her heart melted, and she moved toward him.

To Sam, Enid too looked changed, and at the same time she appeared just as desirable as ever. His emotions were so raw and close to the surface that his skin tingled.

They walked toward each other, meeting in the center of the room, each with so much to tell the other, a history of emotions that could never be explained in words. All they needed to do to put the past behind them was to kiss. And they did.

Epilogue

Sam and Enid and Patrick and Carmen

Two little girls, twins, put the finishing touches on their sand castle just inches from the water's edge. Sam had been watching them for some time, impressed by their concentration on their work. For the past several weeks, he had found it impossible to focus his attention on anything related to work, as evidenced by *The Wall Street Journal* in his canvas tote bag, purchased hours ago, but still unread.

Rather than reading, he had been thinking about things that did not relate to business, such as these two six-year-olds. They had started him wondering why he and Enid had never had children, and if it was too late to start a family now.

They had been in Hawaii for five days. Five perfect days of balmy trade winds, rustling through exuberantly healthy palm trees, so unlike their smog-choked L.A. cousins. The sun burned all serious thoughts from his brain, leaving only a gossamer sensation of well-being. He was glad he had proposed this trip to Enid, gladder still that they had been able to put the events of the past weeks behind them. Luckily, in this spectacular setting, no one could stay angry or anxious for long. Those emotions simply did not fit.

The mother of the twin castle builders called her daughters to lunch, and Sam shut his eyes, allowing the lapping of the waves on the pristine beach to lull him into a reverie. Later, when he finally decided to read *The Journal*, he saw an article chronicling the collapse of the WIT/Dominion deal, blaming its demise on WIT's parent company, who cited a recent downward trend on the Nikkei-Dow as the reason for their withdrawal from the negotiations.

Sam knew better, although he was content to have the world believe what it read in *The Journal*. He knew that the deal died the moment he showed Leo Carmen's story. She had toned it down to his specifications, so it was not accusatory but rather offered bulleted points about Leo and Harry and the foundation of their business relationship.

Sam marveled that Carmen's hold over Harry was so strong that she could convince him to risk opening this can of worms. And it relieved him to know that he was not the only man who had been taken in by her charms.

Still, it stunned him to realize that she had been able to manipulate him within an inch of his life. Enid knew nothing about this, although he was certain she suspected. Thank goodness she was too smart to bring it up, because he didn't ever want to lie to her again, and the truth would be painful for both of them. As it was, he had to live with the fact that Carmen had used him to get what she wanted, a fact he knew she would always hold over his head.

At least he'd gotten what he'd wanted out of the ordeal, a new law firm, Ingersol, Carrouthers & Morris, which was launched with a client roster that could rival that of any firm in town.

The last he'd heard, Leo had retreated back home to Australia, where nobody cared if you broke a few laws making a buck, just as long as you didn't get caught. Supposedly, Lacy was planning to join him there, but Sam wouldn't be surprised if she sent divorce papers instead.

❦

From the window of their room, Enid could see Sam out on the beach. She had gone upstairs to call Wallase, to check on things at home. Now, satisfied that all was well in L.A. she took a moment to reapply her sunscreen and to gather her thoughts about the past two weeks.

While Sam had been occupied sorting out the problems at his office, Enid had been immersed in her own troubles. The Monday after Lacy Choate's birthday party, Ivy had called from the Westside Women's Shelter to tell her that they had been notified by Tristar that due to negative preview reactions to *A Month of Sundays*, the director had decided to shoot a new ending and reedit the film. Therefore, they had apologized, the film would not be completed in time for the planned fund-raising benefit.

Enid would have been disappointed had Ivy's call come a few days earlier. But as it was, she had felt nothing but relief. She told Ivy that in light of this development, and due to some personal complications, she felt it would be wise for her to step down as chairman of the fund-raiser, and she suggested Suzanne Marshall as her replacement.

Ivy had balked at first, but after Enid promised to convince the other board members to go along with the nomination, she reluctantly agreed to accept Suzanne. Why had Enid been so eager to give her neighbor this coveted position? All it had taken was a one-line note scribbled in Suzanne's unmistakable handwriting and left in Enid's mailbox the day after Sam's return. The note read, *"Does Sam know you visit your neighbors in the middle of the night?"*

Fortunately, Enid had retrieved the mail that day and had seen the note before Sam had. And she was wise enough to confront Suzanne directly, not admitting to anything, but allowing Suzanne to suggest a way that her memory might be erased of anything it could have witnessed that early Friday morning.

Now, two weeks later, everybody seemed happy. Suzanne had gotten approval from the board to stage the fund-raiser on the set of

Friends, and she had been able to arrange to raffle off a small role in one episode. The Shelter was thrilled, Suzanne was the toast of the neighborhood, and Enid was off the hook.

She also had been surprised and relieved to hear from Jo Beth that Patrick had not renewed his lease on the house next door. Not that she had meant to force him out of the neighborhood, but it would be much easier for her to go on with her life if she didn't have to worry about running into him every time she walked out of her front door.

Of course, she had not told Sam about her indiscretion, nor had she questioned him about his trip to Sardinia. Maybe they would talk about it all in twenty years or so, when they could look back at this period of their lives and laugh.

Patrick had thought he'd miss living in the Palisades with the view of the beach and the clean sea breezes. But now that he'd settled in at Carmen's house, he was feeling quite at home. When she'd invited him to stay after their night together, he'd immediately called Jeremy and told him to gather up the few things — his Biedimeier, his 52-inch Sony television, his train set, YoYo, some of his "special" toys — and send them over.

Surrounded by his favorite things, he found that he enjoyed waking up in leafy-green Laurel Canyon. Thinking back, living in suburbia had always annoyed him; there was no privacy. And everyone seemed to have big dogs, small children, or both.

The only thing he missed were the sunsets, which, here in the canyon, were obscured by the hillside and trees. No matter, most nights by the time evening fell, he was already curled up with Carmen in the four-poster bed that had become home.

Patrick thanked the lucky star that had led him to Carmen that night at the Hotel Bel Air. He had been at the nadir of his life and his career. Then, stepping into Carmen's limousine, and looking into her eyes, his world had turned around. She was everything he had ever wanted in a woman, but he never dreamt that he could get it all in one package: an incredible body, hot, eager, and able to teach him a few new tricks, a sharp mind, which could catch him at his own game and force him to be honest with himself and with her, and best of all, an ambitious nature and the savvy to use it on his behalf. He was in heaven.

And he hadn't blinked an eye when he'd run into Elaine at Morton's and learned that Sara was having an affair with Jeffrey Kesselman. Old Jeff had indeed been booted out of Dominion's executive ranks into a puny two-picture indy prod deal. More power to both Jeff and Sara. Patrick was so wrapped up in Carmen, he couldn't even think about revenge or other women.

Mercifully, that included Enid Carrouthers, for if he thought about her at all, it would be with remorse and embarrassment. How could he have debased himself to such an extent that he would plead with her to help him get work? He hoped that she would forget their brief interlude. As far as he was concerned, it had never even happened, and if he ran into her by chance at some social gathering, he'd greet her as somebody whose face looked familiar but whose name he couldn't remember. It never failed to work.

Besides, he was going to be too busy in the coming months to do much socializing. Carmen had him back on the fast track again. And he loved the action. Especially because she was right there with him every second, backing him up, urging him on, forcing open the right doors. Like he said, he was in heaven.

He heard her car in the drive and flicked off the television, picking up one of the scripts she'd left him to read. Who would have imagined at this stage in his life that his old heart would get all fluttery and nervous about a woman? But she wasn't just any woman. This would be the one he mated with for life. He was sure of it. And even if he weren't sure, she was, and they both knew that she was the one calling the shots.

Carmen was at the top of her game. She could barely remember why she'd thought Sam Carrouthers was the man for her. Clearly he didn't have the killer instinct she knew was necessary to rise to the top of the heap. But all the same, she was glad she had pursued him, because that pursuit had led her to Patrick, which was right where she belonged.

Fortunately, the transition had been swift. One minute she was bawling her eyes out about Sam, the next she was balling Patrick Drake. And it was a good thing. Because when the rest of the world had come crashing down around her, she had been so insulated by her new love, she had barely felt a shudder.

When she'd gotten the call from her editor, telling her she'd been canned, she'd thought it was a joke. No joke, Thompson told her, Ralph had gone on a rampage to find out who had stolen his copy, and all roads led to Carmen. Hilda, his secretary, had given Carmen the finger; he'd even gotten Marty Wollinsky to fess up.

Fortunately, the tape she'd made of Ralph and the bimbos at the Pacific Club had saved her from a lawsuit. The paper had simply fired her, effective immediately, and that had been that. They hadn't even wanted to see her story about Leo Choate and Harry, so she'd handed over the draft to Sam, who had shown the rough copy to Leo and scared the shit out of him.

Although she was pissed that Ralph had gotten the better of her, she hadn't cared all that much that she'd been fired. Because now she had Patrick, and with him a ticket into *The Industry*. It hadn't taken her long to marshal her forces: Patrick had told her about the script of *For Love or Money*, which was going into turnaround at Dominion, and Carmen had not hesitated to slap a mortgage on her house and buy the option. In three days, she had set up meetings with Fox, Miramax, and Avenue Pictures, thanks to Harry — though his confession to Sam had evened up the score between them, Carmen knew she'd always be able to count on Harry for a favor. Call it guilt, call it gratitude, most men never stopped being vulnerable to the women they'd slept with.

And as far as Hollywood went, it was obvious when Carmen took her first meeting that she was born to be a film producer. She had the guts, she had the imagination, and she had Patrick Drake. Their new production company would make *For Love or Money* as its first venture. She'd even come up with what she considered a perfect new title for it, and she could hardly wait to try it on Patrick.

She planned to call their first collaborative effort *Indiscretions*.

🕶

ACKNOWLEDGMENTS

I am grateful to the people who contributed
to this book:

Earlier readers
Angela Dyborn, Carol Ellis, Anne Kresl,
Connie Linn, Linda Stewart

Editorial eyes
John Barber, Michele Lansing

Aesthetic Experts
John Deep, Danny Ducovny, John Clark

Emotional support
my family, Heine Prato, Jasper and Zazu

Inspiration
you know who you are

The text of this book was set in Goudy,
a typeface designed by Frederic W. Goudy in 1915
for the American Type Founders Company.
One of the most popular and prolific
American type designers,
Goudy drew inspiration for this design
from classical old style faces.
Round characters have a strong diagonal stress,
ascenders are fairly long
but descenders are very short.
Its graceful letterforms make it visually appealing,
well balanced, and elegant.

FIC
DOUMANI

Doumani, Carol.

Indiscretions.

4/99

DATE			

14 DAY BOOK-10¢ A DAY
OVERDUE CHARGE

HICKSVILLE PUBLIC LIBRARY
169 JERUSALEM AVE.
HICKSVILLE, N Y

BAKER & TAYLOR